QUIETUS
COPYRIGHT © 2017 MADELAINE SHAW-WONG

THIS IS A WORK OF FICTION.
SIMILARITIES TO REAL PEOPLE,
PLACES, OR EVENTS ARE ENTIRELY COINCIDENTAL.

FIRST EDITION. NOVEMBER 2017.
ISBN: 978-09811099-2-3

WRITTEN BY MADELAINE SHAW-WONG
EDITED BY T. MORGAN EDITING SERVICES
COVER PHOTOGRAPH BY KOPITINPHOTO
WONG, MADELAINE, 1959-
NOSE HILL PUBLISHING
CALGARY, ALBERTA
WWW.NOSEHILLPUBLISHING.COM

Quietus

QUIETUS

kwī-ˈē-təs

For who would bear the whips
and scorns of time, ...
When he himself might his quietus make
With a bare bodkin?
Hamlet

By Madelaine Shaw-Wong

DEDICATION

For Elizabeth and Christopher Shaw,

whose challenges taught me

that happiness is found in little things

and fitting in is overrated.

CHAPTER ONE

Summer War

Piter Dram stepped out of the basement and into a nightmare. A gaping hole had been blasted through the front wall of his parents' house. Every window was shattered. The back door hung crookedly on its hinges. The kitchen table, where last night they shared a meal, was in splinters. The sun shone on Piter's face through a gap in the ceiling where his bedroom used to be. He felt like he was looking at the scene through a mist. His parents and brother emerged after him and stood frozen in their spots; their bulging eyes scanned the destruction.

His father was the first to speak. "Let's see what we can salvage."

Piter's brother, Hadar, kicked aside what used to be the door of the pantry and picked up some cans, putting them into a backpack.

Pages of Piter's notebook lay scattered. His chest tightened. He stooped, gathered some, glancing at what he had been studying last night, *Polymers of monosaccharides that are connected by dehydration reaction...* His

Biochemistry final was supposed to be today, his last exam before completing medical school. He had attained one of few medical residency spots at Covona University Hospital. Many years and much effort had been expended to make his dreams come true. Last week, Solime declared war on his country.

Like ants from an underground nest, his neighbours across the street climbed out of the basement of their destroyed home. Two carried a limp body between them. Piter dropped the pages, letting them flutter away, crawled across the wreckage and ran across the street to help.

By late afternoon, eighteen corpses lay on the street. The air was thick with the smell of concrete dust and blood. Piter listened for sirens, for the whirr of helicopter blades, but no help came. The uninjured toiled for hours, working with shovels and picks or their bare hands in a desperate attempt to find survivors.

Having had nothing to eat since last night, Piter thought he would collapse from exhaustion. His bruised, scraped hands throbbed with pain. He paused to remove a splinter from his palm, digging at it with a fingernail. A woman stepped from one body to the next, lifting the coverings, a notebook in her hand, recording the names of the dead. She fell to her knees beside a bloody body and wailed. Piter stood behind her with a hand on her shoulder. "I'm so sorry for your loss."

Evening came and help arrived in the form of a bulldozer to clear the roads, an army truck to load the deceased and buses for the survivors. Piter, his family, and others climbed aboard and collapsed into seats. He leaned against the window taking in the chaotic scene as the bus bumped down the roads. Every street was the same—flattened houses, cratered apartment buildings, impassible streets. He closed his sleepy eyes.

Piter awoke the next morning five hundred kilometres away from his home on the coast. He rubbed his cramped neck and nudged Hadar awake. Through the front window of the bus, the Keque Mountains towered like sentries over the city.

"Welcome to Ackim," the driver said.

The bus pulled into the parking lot of a church and a man boarded. "I'm sure you're all hungry. We have a hot meal waiting for you inside and you'll have a place to stay until more suitable arrangements can be made. Follow me."

§

Days later, Piter was startled awake by loud explosions. A woman screamed. A baby yowled. The church's fluorescent lights flickered on. He sat up and swung his legs over the edge of his cot.

"Turn off the lights!" Piter's father, Hyron, shouted. "Do you want to make us a target? Everyone stay right where you are. This is the safest place for us."

The lights went out and the thirty-six newly-homeless people in the basement of St. Anthony's Church sat in darkness.

His father was a "take charge" kind of man. Piter was just glad for the darkness, that no one saw the tears form from his eyes. A woman across the room wept without shame. Piter sat as if glued in his place, struggling to control his breathing. On the cot beside him, his mother, Odilia, prayed the Rosary.

§

The only good thing that came out of the war was he met Yun. She and her family had also been exiled from Covona City and occupied a group of cots at the other side of the church basement. She had just graduated from Covona University when the war started.

The war against Solime ended ten days after it began, with Covona trounced and humiliated. Thousands of people were killed and tens of thousands injured. Medical facilities could not handle the number of casualties. Buildings, roads, bridges and railway lines across the country were destroyed. Covona did not have the resources to repair them. For the first time in its history, the number of unemployed exceeded those with jobs. The Covonan economy collapsed under the pressure.

Piter and Yun married three months after they met, and though he was thousands of frezens in debt, he was confident that the economy would improve. In a few years, he hoped to open his own medical practice. He would then be able to afford all the things he wanted. Doctors were well-paid in Covona—at least, they were before the war.

No amount of medical training could have prepared Dr. Dram for what he was about to face when he began his practice.

CHAPTER TWO

Ackim Free Clinic

Dr. Piter Dram wrapped a scarf around his face, leaving only his eyes exposed. He leaned into the wintery blast, hands buried deep in his pockets. A recent storm had left a thick glaze of ice on the sidewalk, making the short walk to the Ackim Free Clinic slippery and slow.

Across the street, a growing line of people wrapped in coats or blankets huddled on the sidewalk outside the clinic, waiting to be seen by one of the overworked doctors. The queue extended down the block.

Piter stopped at the corner, blinked away ice crystals on his lashes, looked left and right, and stepped onto the street. A car horn blasted. A vehicle came to a sliding stop, narrowly missing him.

He thumped the hood of the car with his fist. "Watch where you're going!"

Piter avoided eye contact with those shivering in line. This was not his dream assignment—long hours, low pay. His wife, Yun, said it was the same for teachers and they should be grateful to have jobs in this economy.

Piter's breath steamed through his scarf. He picked up his pace. Above his head, balconies protruded from the sides of decaying sandstone buildings with lines of laundry strung between them. Frozen shirts, trousers and underwear hung unbending in the winter wind. A few stark trees with blackened bark, survivors of the war, stood in sidewalk depressions.

He squeezed past a woman blocking the doorway of the free clinic and stepped inside, inhaling the stench of unwashed bodies. Patients sprawled on plastic chairs or sat on the floor of the waiting room. An old man coughed, phlegmy and wet. Red-cheeked children whimpered in their mothers' arms. An infant coughed in staccato rhythm followed by a gasping inhale. "Pertussis," he whispered. The end of free vaccines for the poor was another government cutback.

A man lay on the floor. Piter rested his fingers on the young man's neck to feel for a pulse. The man opened his eyes halfway and wheezed. Piter wished he could call an ambulance and send this man and the baby to emergency, but none of the patients in this room could afford the cost of a hospital visit. The Ackim Free was one of few clinics in the city that offered medical care and medicine to the poor. Chronic underfunding meant doctors could offer only cursory treatment and only to those in dire circumstances.

A student nurse sat taking information from a man leaning on her desk. She spoke from behind a surgical mask. "Good morning, Dr. Dram. Your first patient is in exam room one. Dr. Bant called in sick."

Piter frowned. "But I'm just the resident. How can I do it on my own?"

Her large, blue eyes were full of pity. "Sorry about that."

He was glad she didn't burst into tears anymore at the sight of all the misery. "Any space in the short-stay wing?"

"Nope. Completely full."

Piter gritted his teeth. "Let's make room for the baby with whooping cough." He pointed with his thumb. "Put her in the pediatric crib. I'll be in to check on her shortly." Piter changed into his white lab coat and entered the exam room to see his first patient.

§

Hours later, his growling stomach reminded Piter he had not taken a lunch break. He gobbled half a sandwich and at one o'clock went to see his forty-first patient of the day.

After a brief examination Piter said, "I'm sorry. I can't help you." The disappointed man left the clinic with no prescription for painkillers despite frequent migraines. Piter unclenched his jaw and rolled his neck. He took a moment to complete his notes before seeing his next patient.

The young woman's thin face was covered in sores and her bloodshot eyes were like slits. Under her eyes were deep bags, like half-moons. She wore a mini skirt, ripped tights and knee-high black boots. Her body trembled. Sweat beaded on her forehead.

"What can I do for you?" He didn't recognize her until she spoke.

"It hurts." She put her hand on her lower back.

She was his neighbour. He had seen her selling herself on the street in front of their apartment building. Piter stretched out her arm, revealing needle marks and bruising. "What are you taking? Heroin? Methadone? Crack?"

She nodded. "Whatever."

"You're pale and thin. You're not getting enough to eat."

"I'm not hungry. So, my back, how about some morphine or oxy?"

"We've a limited supply of painkillers. I'm not about to give them out to junkies."

"You gotta help me. I'm sick." Her body shook. "It's hard making enough money to live."

Piter felt a twinge of compassion for the pathetic woman, but the waiting room full of sick people and the ones standing on the sidewalk took precedence in his mind. "Get yourself clean. Find an honest job. There's nothing I can do for you."

"Dr. Dram, please. I need some painkillers. I'll give you a free B.J." She got off the table and put her hands on his belt buckle.

"Out!" She was so thin Piter could put his hand all the way around her upper arm. He led her to the entrance of the clinic and pushed her out the door. He threw her coat at her and turned to the student nurse. "Send in the next patient." In the hallway he stopped, leaned against the wall and squeezed his temples.

"Number forty-three," the student nurse called.

"You're going to let a moogie see the doctor first?" a woman yelled. She held a little girl against her chest. The child's face was flushed with fever.

Another woman, carrying a disabled child, pushed her way through the crowded reception area and hurried to the exam room before anyone could stop her. Her mouth was set in a thin line. She gave Piter a curt nod as she passed. He followed. She lay her son on the exam table. The child's hands were curled in tight fists, arms and legs bent towards his torso. The boy's eyes were red and runny from what appeared to be conjunctivitis. He coughed and gagged. His mother lifted him to a sitting position and thumped his back to help him breathe.

Piter held a stethoscope to the child's chest and heard deep rattling. "Could be pneumonia."

"Some antibiotics then?"

Piter shook his head. He couldn't justify to the Expense Department why he would deplete the limited supply of oral antibiotics by giving them to a child with cerebral palsy. If Piter gave medicine to everyone who came through the doors, the clinic's supply would be drained by ten in the morning. In a flat monotone he said, "I'll give you some antibiotic eye drops. Make him as comfortable as you can and hope for his recovery."

"It's because he's a moogie, isn't it? Please, Doctor, he's all I have left in the world." Tears ran down her cheeks.

"I prefer not to use the word moogie." The word was derived from mosquito, an irritating pest that served no purpose except to suck blood and spread diseases. Piter put some drops in the child's eyes and, wishing the woman well, sent her on her way. He doubted the boy would last a week.

Patient number forty-four entered, carrying a three-year-old girl. The little girl's enflamed, swollen tonsils and lymph nodes suggested tonsillitis. Piter gave her a prescription for an antibiotic and sent her to the pharmacy next door.

The student nurse interrupted him before he could see his next patient. "Dr. Dram? The paramedics need you to sign off on this one."

"Why are they here?"

"Sorry, you were so busy and he looked like he wasn't breathing."

Two paramedics stood beside a stretcher in the waiting room. On it lay the man Piter had seen on the floor a few hours earlier. The other patients in the waiting room quietly watched Piter put his stethoscope to the man's chest, confirm death and sign the paper on the clipboard.

"See if you can locate his next of kin," he said to the student nurse.

§

Piter had begun his residency five months ago, only a month after his arrival in Ackim. He took the position at the Free Clinic, not out of benevolence, or wanting to serve the poorest of the poor, but because he had reached an agreement with government-owned banks. If he worked at the clinic for five years his debt would be forgiven.

He pictured a medical practice where he could help people; a job where he would be respected. He wanted the good things in life—a beautiful house, nice vehicle, delicious food and fine wine. His wife would greet him at the door and one or two children would fly into his arms…but unless something changed drastically in the country, that was not to be.

§

"Dr. Dram, a spot opened up at the hospital. The paramedics say they can bring one patient. Who should we send?" the student nurse said.

Patients too sick to be sent home waited in the short-stay wing, hoping for a "charity spot" to open in the hospital. Piter thought for a moment. In the clinic's short-stay wing was a middle-aged woman experiencing chest pain, one with gall bladder issues and another woman in labour. One patient had been hit by a car and was suffering head trauma. Two men suffered from the flu and a boy likely needed his appendix out. The other three patients were in less life-threatening conditions. "Take the boy with appendicitis. He's the most critical."

§

A half hour and five patients later, the student nurse poked her head into the exam room. "Sorry to interrupt you, but I thought I should let you know. The boy's appendix burst in the ambulance. He died. So, a spot is still open at the hospital. Who should we send?"

"Damn it!" Piter sucked in his breath and pounded on the exam table with his fist, startling the woman sitting there. He stormed to his office, picked up his tea cup and flung it at the wall where it shattered, and then leaned on his desk.

The nurse stood at the door, her hands folded in front of her, waiting for an answer.

"Send the head trauma."

She nodded and in a quiet voice said, "I'm so sorry, Dr. Dram. I'll give you a few minutes."

He sat. Struggling for self-control, he focused on a spot on the wall where the dull green paint peeled. His eyes travelled around the room to an anatomical poster on the wall showing the body's internal organs and another that showed the circulatory system. He noticed dirt imbedded in the baseboards, a spider web in the corner and the crack in the window. Taking a deep breath, he rose and called for the next patient.

At five o'clock, the student nurse hustled the people who had not been seen out of the waiting room and pulled the door closed. Some pressed their faces on the glass, pleading to be let in. Piter turned his back on them. He was exhausted.

Someone pounded on the window.

"Ignore them," Piter said.

"It's your wife. She looks upset."

CHAPTER THREE

The Shop and Save

Yun's cheeks were red from the cold.

Piter opened the door and she pushed her way in. A man followed her, put his foot in the doorway, followed by his shoulder as he tried to force the door open. "Help me, please! I've been waiting for hours."

"Come back tomorrow." Piter shoved the man, forcing him to step back.

The man kicked the door and stomped off, hands in his pockets.

Yun spoke quickly. "My salary was cut again and they gave me five more students. I don't even have enough textbooks for all of them." She wiped her dripping nose with the back of her mitten.

Piter was in no mood to hear bad news. "Do the best you can, I suppose. Let's go home."

She followed him back to his office. "Will things ever get better?"

Piter took off his lab coat and put on his winter coat. His finger brushed a strand of long, black hair away from her face as he bent and kissed her forehead and then hugged her to his chest. He loved the way the top of her head nestled just under his chin.

Yun removed a mitten and wiped her eyes. "I cashed my cheque on the way here. They have groceries at the Shop and Save today. Let's go before they're sold out or raise the prices again."

His feet ached and he was not in the mood to stand in line for groceries. "We can go to the convenience store."

"But they're so expensive. I hate buying black market."

They exited by the back door so as not to be spotted by hopeful patients who may be hovering still by the front door. The wind had died down, making the cold tolerable. Piles of garbage lined the alleyway. Scrounging through the piles of trash were rats and children.

Six children surrounded Piter and Yun, holding out dirty hands. "Do you have money?" they asked. They tugged on Piter's coat. He

[15]

pulled away. Yun reached into her pocket of her red wool coat and gave each child a one frozen coin. They scampered away with their treasure.

"You shouldn't have done that. It only encourages them," Piter said.

"They're hungry."

"So are we."

The children disappeared into a crumbling building.

"At least we don't have to live in a place like that," she said.

"No one should have to. This country is in trouble." Piter was tired of the rhetoric and empty promises from government officials, who talked and talked, but did nothing to ease peoples' suffering. Some sections of Covona looked no better than the day Solime's bombs fell. Great holes still dotted the sides and roofs of some buildings and concrete chunks littered the streets.

This was a beautiful city when Piter came here on a holiday at age twenty-one. He had a drink in a pub around the corner and watched a stage show in a theatre down the street. Those two establishments no longer existed, destroyed in the short but devastating war.

Piter and Yun joined a queue outside the Shop and Save, the largest grocery store chain in the country. Before the war, Piter used to push a grocery cart up and down aisles to choose items from fully stocked shelves. Now, a long counter barred customers' access to thinly stocked shelves. After an hour, Piter and Yun made their way to the counter.

Yun said, "Two loaves of bread, six rolls of toilet paper, a box of tea, potatoes, three cans of baked beans, a bag of oranges…"

"No oranges," said the clerk.

"What fruit do you have?"

"Apples." The clerk glanced at the long line of people behind Yun and tapped on the counter. "Well? Make up your mind."

"Apples."

The clerk placed the items on the table. "That'll be one hundred and fifty-seven frezens."

Yun's mouth dropped open. "That's at least ten percent higher than yesterday."

"Then you should have shopped yesterday." He sneered at Yun.

She looked at Piter as if she was going to cry.

"Take back the apples," Piter said to the clerk. "They're all bruised anyway."

"No, they're better than nothing." Yun reached for the bag, taking it from the clerk's hand.

"We'll find a way, Yun." Piter doubted the words even as they came out of his mouth. He put his hand on her back and they stepped outside. The temperature had decreased with the setting sun. Snow swirled around them. A chilly breeze blew up Piter's pant leg. He shivered and put his arm around his wife.

Piter spotted his former biochemistry professor standing in queue. To complete his medical degree, Piter had to re-do biochemistry at night school at Ackim University. He had missed his final exam due to the war.

"Isn't the price of groceries atrocious?" asked Tresha. "On the positive side, I'm eating less, losing some weight."

"And they have hardly anything in there," said Yun.

Fillip pulled his scarf over his mouth and nose. "Chronic shortages, higher inflation, more misery is the pattern we see in this country. I wonder why people don't rise up and object."

Tresha said, "It wouldn't do any good. No one listens." She removed a glove for a moment to push a stray strand of hair under her hat. She readjusted her glasses. "That's a nice coat, Yun." She ran her hand down Yun's sleeve. "Wool. Must be warm."

"I've had it for years. It's one of the few things that survived the destruction of my parents' house."

"Must be nice," Tresha said. "I'm freezing."

Their conversation was interrupted by a loud commotion from inside the Shop and Save. Two security guards pushed a man outside the door. He slipped and fell on the ice.

"Stay away from here if you know what's good for you!" the store manager shouted.

"I just want to feed my family." The man got up and swiped the snow from his clothes.

The manager waved his arm in an upward motion. "Everyone go home. Store's empty. Go on. Get out of here!"

A collective moan rose from the people as they dispersed.

"We're too late. We'll have to go to a convenience store," Tresha said. "Anyone know where they're located today?"

"Patient of mine said there's one down by the riverbank on Centre Avenue. Unless the police chased them off. It's on our way home. We can walk together." He and Yun led the way. They passed by an alleyway and Piter saw his patient, the junkie prostitute, squatting beside a garbage bin with a tourniquet tied around her upper arm. She held a needle in the other hand. Piter turned away. He doubted she would live another six months.

"Do you remember when we never had to worry about stores running out of food?" Yun asked.

Piter said, "President Jomb and the National Labour Party got us into this mess. All of us are employed and we still have trouble making ends meet. Imagine what it's like for the unemployed, like the families of these kids." He pointed to four teenage boys leaning against a wall. Their clothes were unkempt, and in the case of one boy, far too small. Bare wrists poked out the ends of his sleeves, bare ankles from his trousers. He elbowed another, pointing to the bags of groceries Piter and Yun carried. They appeared too young to shave, but their eyes were hard, as if they'd seen too much tragedy. Piter put his hand in his pocket and grasped the handle of his knife, just in case. He maintained eye contact with the group until they passed.

"I'm looking forward to the next election. Something drastic has to happen to make this country a better place to live." Piter missed his life before the war—his friends, the ocean and the well-stocked shops of his youth. Everything was in short supply now, from toothpaste to automobiles. He saw desperation in the sad eyes of his patients, in the slumped shoulders of people standing in line for necessities, and in the angry faces of youth who wandered the streets in gangs. They all looked for someone to blame and someone else who could lead them out of the chaos.

Fillip sniffled. "The NLP aren't responsible for the closed factories. The Zarling Corporation laid off their workers."

"Yesterday's newspaper said everyone was tightening their belts," Yun said.

"The rich aren't suffering," Fillip said. "Tresha was just researching a story about how big corporations, like Zarling Communications, control the media—"

Tresha flashed Fillip an exasperated look. "Do you really need to bring that up?"

"What did you find out?" asked Yun.

"I can't say. I could lose my job." She sidestepped around a small crater in the sidewalk.

Fillip raised his voice. "Then I'll tell them. Big businesses contribute to politicians' campaigns."

"Everyone knows that," Yun said.

"They then negotiate sweet deals if their candidate is elected. She wasn't allowed to print the story."

Yun's eyes widened. "Why not?" White crystals from her steamy breath clung to sprigs of her black hair peeking out from under her hat.

"The news media is complacent." Fillip huffed. Air steamed through his scarf like a chimney.

"The news needs to be inspiring in these hard times. I was told to leave out some facts. What could I do?"

"Couldn't you have insisted the story go forward as is?" Piter asked. He could see the newspaper's point. People don't need to read about hardship. They see it every day.

"Why bother? I would only be told there was no room for it."

"Instead they fill the paper with re-hashed, feel-good stories," Fillip said.

"Anyway, what good does it do to print controversial stories? If I do what I'm told, I get my bonuses. I'd like to replace some of my old wardrobe, maybe buy a new coat." She looked at Yun.

They stopped and faced each other. Despite his gloves, Piter's fingers were getting cold. "This is where we live." He pointed to an apartment building. He wanted to get inside before Fillip started sermonizing. The man used to spend valuable class time talking about human rights instead of biochemistry—a habit that annoyed Piter. A sudden gust of wind lifted snow from the ground and blew it into the faces of the small group.

Yun shivered and zipped her coat to her chin. "I wish we could do something. When I think of the food I used to waste…"

Fillip said, "Tresha and I joined Human Rights for All. We fight for the rights of the poor and vulnerable. You two should join."

"HRFA. I've heard of them. When's the next meeting?" Yun asked.

Piter turned his back to the wind. He was tired, cold and hungry and only wanted to go home, not join some radical human rights group. "Let's go, Yun." He put his hand on her back and directed her home.

§

Back in their one-room apartment, Yun unpacked the measly bags of groceries. Piter lay on the couch to soak in the last rays of sunlight trickling through the window and turned on the television. Faded wallpaper printed with a gaudy sunflower design peeled from the wall behind the T.V. Piter was tempted to tear the paper off, but was afraid the room would look even more depressing if he did. Four and a half years of servitude at the Free Clinic remained, then he could open his own medical practice and live the good life he'd always dreamed about.

He chewed his nails while watching the news: The disputed land, over which the war had been fought, was declared a no man's land, belonging to neither country, though both claimed ownership. Each erected razor-wire fences on their side of the border, leaving the disputed land free of human inhabitants. Solimese troops patrolled on their side of the border.

The news anchor said, "In response, our Covonan troops were sent to patrol our side of the fence. In a statement today, the president announced, 'We will not give up another centimetre of land, but rest assured, we are doing everything we can to rectify the situation. Covona's troubles will soon be over.'"

Piter knew his anger was shared by other Covonans. Attempts by the government to bolster the economy were ineffective so far, leading to greater deficit, unemployment, scarcity of goods and out-of-control inflation. The neighbouring countries of Sura, to the north-west, and Dule, beyond the Keque Mountains to the north, sided with Solime and refused economic aid to Covona.

Next door, a child coughed. Piter hoped his neighbour would not come over again, asking for free medical advice. Not that he didn't want to help, but if word got out that a doctor lived in the building, he'd never get any peace.

Piter had confidence that those in government would do what was right for the people. These were hard times, but things would surely improve.

CHAPTER FOUR

Human Rights for All

On a spring morning, Tresha Farwell stepped onto the street to avoid a puddle of melted snow. Without warning, a chunk of concrete as large as her head crashed onto the ground beside her, exploding into pieces. She jumped and held her hand over her heart. "Oh, my God!" From the top of the eroded building several smaller bits of concrete followed the first, clattering onto the pavement. Tresha shook her head in disbelief.

Little progress had been done to return Ackim to its former glory. A year after the war, damaged buildings were stark reminders of the country's failure to recover, unrepaired and unusable, scorched and lifeless skeletons, reminders of a happier time. Winter's cold had caused the concrete to crack, and the spring thaw allowed melting snow to creep into the cracks, weakening structures.

A young man leaned against the Ackim City News Building, holding a cigarette. "Close call." He inhaled the smoke and exhaled through his nose, tapping ashes onto the ground and holding her in a steady gaze.

She clutched her designer handbag a little tighter. Months ago, Fillip had suggested she sell the bag. They could use the money, but she wouldn't part with it, liking the way it felt on her shoulder. Tresha increased her pace.

§

Twenty years ago, when she and Fillip married, their worries were few. Covona's economy prospered. Fillip had a secure position teaching at Ackim University. She had received a promotion at the newspaper. The couple bought a house and looked forward to raising a family. They had difficulty conceiving a child and had almost given up hope when Jakon came along.

Tresha was fifty-two years old when Ackim came under attack. She and Fillip had bolted upright in bed when fighter jets screamed over the house. Loud explosions shook the walls. Their home wasn't hit, but other buildings, including Jakon's school and sections of the downtown business district, were demolished. After the bombing, the streets ran with oily goo, reeking of raw sewage. Even a whiff of decay reminded her of the terror she felt that night.

§

Tresha continued to tremble after her almost fatal experience. She breathed deeply. The spring air smelled of loam thawing in the warmth of the morning sun. Birds twittered and chirped in a budding tree. Icy streams of melted snow trickled down the gutters. The wind was picking up and the sky was clouding over. A spring snowfall was on the way.

She entered her workplace and draped her jacket over the back of her chair. Notes and memos were tacked on the walls of her cubicle. The trash cans overflowed. She wondered if this was another cost-cutting measure of the newspaper, that they'd have to empty their own trash from now on. Next, they'd have to take turns cleaning the toilet.

"Tresha!" her editor called, waving her to his office.

"What's up, Raimond?" she asked.

"Have a seat." He stared at his computer screen, his face grim. "People are upset by the editorial you wrote yesterday." Raimond opened his email and turned the screen to show Tresha the hundreds of responses to her article: "People Scramble as Homes for the Elderly Close."

"Mr. Teador Zarling called my office. He's livid." Raimond looked at her over the top of his glasses and chewed on the end of his moustache.

Tresha was dizzy for a moment. "Why is he angry?"

"It makes him look bad. Who do you think owns most of the care centres? What the hell were you thinking?"

"You okayed it," she answered in a small voice, feeling like a disobedient child called into the principal's office.

"Who is this person you interviewed?"

"I don't have to tell you." She crossed her arms.

"Very well. Your mysterious woman complains about having to take her elderly father home when she already has a moogie to care for."

"I never said moogie." Tresha felt her heart pound in her chest. She hated that dehumanizing word.

His lips were tight as he tapped the mouse. "Let me read a couple of the responses. 'You would trade my daughter's education for your eighty-four-year-old father's care.' And then there's this one: 'Do you expect the people of this country to care for your retarded son when we can't afford groceries? You should have aborted him.'"

Tresha eyes teared up. She removed her glasses and wiped them on her blouse.

"It's you. Isn't it?"

Tresha hung her head. "I'm not the only one in this situation. Weren't there any letters of support?"

"No one is as foolish as you, to say it out loud." Raimond got up and started to pace the room. "I can't allow you to cause any more controversy. Mr. Zarling could shut down this paper."

She crossed her arms. "My only mistake was pissing off the wrong person. You put more effort into keeping stories out of the news than reporting the truth."

His eyes protruded and his cheeks flushed. "In this country, we pull our own weight and don't depend on the government for handouts." Spittle flew from his mouth.

Tresha had never seen her editor like this. "I can't understand why you of all people would say that. I thought you believed in human rights. Your son…"

Raimond slammed his hand on the desk, making Tresha flinch. "You're not to mention my son. Ever!"

Tresha tried to control her voice. She gripped the arms of her chair. "You're ashamed of your own child? It's not his fault he has autism."

He pointed his finger at her. "You're playing with fire. Write another editorial, an apology. It will go in tomorrow's paper."

"What happened to freedom of speech?"

"Have it on my desk tomorrow morning." He sat in his chair and turned his face to his computer screen.

"You write the editorial and grow a pair while you're at it!"

"Tresha! Write it or don't bother coming to work."

"Fine! I'll write it." Tresha was barely able to control her rage as she walked back to her desk. She plunked in front of her black computer screen, her hands in tight fists. She sat for several minutes, fuming, before booting her computer and pulling up the editorial that had been printed the day before. She re-read the last paragraph:

> *Old-age centres are being shut down. Group homes for the disabled are losing funding. People wait for years for some surgeries. Our leaders used to have the best interests of the people at heart, but no more. Those in dire financial situations are forced to care for their loved ones at home with no government support. This is a travesty. Average people are like helpless fish, caught in nets of greed and deceit. If society is judged on how it treats its most vulnerable, then the world will judge Covona harshly.*

The press was not always so skittish. Before the war, the media actively sought controversial stories. Now, it was as if Covonans lost both their heart and their ability to see the truth. Tresha watched fat flakes of snow fall past her office window. She rubbed her hands on her face and tried to think of a way to soften the truth.

§

Tresha worried about leaving her father alone all day. How she wished she could afford to pay someone to stay with him. She always left water and snacks by his bed, but he was immobile and so helpless.

She turned the key in the lock, opened her front door and was greeted by the strong smell of excrement.

Her father looked up from his bed in the living room, a mortified expression on his face. "Sorry. I made a mess."

"It's okay, Dad. Let's get you cleaned up." Tresha hurried to the kitchen to fetch some soapy cloths to wash her father. She returned to see him struggling to control his trembling lips.

"I'm a useless old man."

"It's the stroke. You can't help it." She pulled away the stinking diaper from his bottom and deposited it in a pail. After rolling him on his side, she saw bed sores on his back and diaper rash on his behind.

"I'm ashamed. A daughter shouldn't have to see her father this way."

"I don't mind, Dad." She dared not look him in the eye as she washed him and wrapped a large homemade diaper around his privates.

Tresha feared she'd have to quit her job to look after him, but she couldn't afford to stay home. The bed where he lay was supported on one corner by a pile of bricks. The sheets she stuffed into the washing machine were faded and worn. She hoped Fillip would bring something home for supper. There was little food left in the house.

CHAPTER FIVE

Freedom of Speech

Tresha added a dash of chili powder to the steaming pot—anything to give the plain meal a hint of flavour. She scooped the concoction of rice and baked beans into four bowls. "Wouldn't it be nice to eat meat more than once a week? I can't believe you had to pay fifty-two frezens for a bag of rice. If average people have such trouble getting by, what about the poor?"

Fillip said, "At least the weather is warming up and we won't have to spend so much on heating."

Tresha's father slumped in his wheelchair, leaning to the left. A belt tied around his chest kept him upright. His left arm, the fingers curled into a crooked fist, dangled on his lap. His eyes shifted from his daughter to son-in-law as they spoke. He placed his shaky right hand on the table, reaching for his spoon. "Sorry for putting you out."

She placed a bowl of food in front of him. "Dad, no. It's not your fault."

He fisted the spoon, scooped the rice and bean mixture, dropped some on his lap, and eventually brought the spoon to his mouth.

"Dad? Remember when I was a little girl? You used to lift me into the air and spin me in a circle. I loved that. It felt like flying."

He smiled and some food leaked from the corner of his mouth. She used a napkin to wipe the dribbles from his chin.

Fillip turned the newspaper towards Tresha. "You wrote this? Do you really believe President Jomb destroyed the economy?"

Tresha held up her hands, palms forward. "I feel like a fake, but if I don't do what I'm told, I'm fired."

"So, quit. We'll get by."

Tresha folded her arms across her chest. "Our next-door neighbours got thrown out of their home because they couldn't make mortgage payments. Their house will never sell and will sit empty like all the others. We thought our house would be part of our retirement package. Remember? Now, we couldn't sell if we tried. We need the money."

Jakon reached over and pulled his grandfather's hair. The old man let out a yelp.

"Jakon, no! Don't hurt Grandpa!" Fillip said. He got up and moved the boy's chair away.

"We need to keep our voices down," said Tresha. "Jakon senses the tension. That's why he's acting out."

§

The family went skating after supper, but before the sun went down. It was early spring, but cold enough for ice to remain on Lake Rania. Fillip pushed his father-in-law's wheelchair through the soft snow.

Jakon's cheeks were pink with excitement as he ran. "Going skating! Going skating!" He pulled so hard on Tresha's hand she had trouble keeping up.

She laughed. "Wait for us, Jakon."

The boy found a bench by the partially frozen pond. Tresha knelt and tied his skates. The crisp, pine-scented air reminded her of Christmas, though that season had already passed. A cold breeze slipped down Tresha's collar, making her shiver. She thought about Yun's warm coat. Tresha had hoped to save enough money for a new coat, but every paycheque was eaten up just buying essentials.

Jakon held his mother's hand and stepped onto the ice. He slipped, fell on his bottom and laughed.

"Up you get." Tresha helped the boy to his feet and swiped the snow from his bottom. He took a step and fell again. As he lay flat on his back, his contagious laughter had them all in fits of giggles.

That evening, Tresha finished writing a new editorial for the Ackim Times:

> *In response to the feedback I received about*
> *the editorial I wrote yesterday, I realize I was wrong to*
> *criticize our government's decision to close care homes*
> *for the elderly. We must consider the hard realities of*

the economic depression. When nursing homes were still in operation, listless old people did nothing but sit in their chairs, stare into space and wait to die.

It doesn't matter that those old folks are still loved, that small children climb onto their laps for a hug, and for a moment ancient eyes clear and smiles spread across wrinkled faces. What matters is we have more money to spend on ourselves.

It doesn't matter that old people spent their lives building this country only to be told they are useless and unwanted. Old people must get out of the way. Food should go to us rather than those dried-up sacks of people. We should send them home to die.

The money saved by closing the nursing homes will be used to improve medical care for the rest of us and improve our quality of life. Jobs will be created; social programs will be put back into place and suffering will be reduced. Society can no longer be expected to support those who can't support themselves. It's time to think of the future. We all must be willing to do our part to towards economic recovery.

Fillip stood over her shoulder and read from the computer screen. "Not exactly an apology." He smiled. "He won't let you get away with that."

"I know." She clicked send, emailing the new editorial to Raimond before she could change her mind.

§

Raimond came by Tresha's desk the next day. Deep frown lines surrounded his mouth. "You think you're pretty clever, don't you?"

"What do you mean?" She gave him a wide-eyed expression.

He stared hard at her and threw the edited version on her cluttered desk. "This is how it will appear."

Tresha looked at Raimond's edited version—the same, but the second and third paragraphs were deleted.

"If you want to keep your job, you damn well better do as you're told," Raimond said.

Tresha clenched her teeth to prevent herself from telling him where he could stuff his job.

CHAPTER SIX

Expedited End-of-Life Care

The usual line-up formed outside the Ackim Free Clinic. Those walking alone in this part of the city had to be vigilant of gangs of unemployed, disenchanted young men. Piter took long strides, walking straight and tall, letting would-be thieves know he was not an easy target. He had been robbed before, the five-centimetre scar on his arm proof of defending himself against a knife-wielding attacker. Piter felt hopeful today. Spring was here. The sun rose now before 6:00 a.m. and set after 10:00 p.m. The ice was gone from Lake Rania and the trees were budding. Perhaps now the country would get busy and repair buildings and roads.

He felt a tug on his coat sleeve. In one quick motion, Piter wrenched his arm away, drew a switchblade from his pocket and held it in front of the man's face.

"Dr. Dram!" The startled man stepped back and held up his hands. "I waited all day yesterday to see you. The pain in my stomach. I can't take it." The man had trouble standing up straight. He looked at Piter with pleading eyes and winced, pressing his hands on his belly, his face contorted with pain.

Piter folded the knife and put it away. "Sorry. Reflex. You have to wait to see me." He turned his back on the man and took a few steps towards the door of the clinic.

Someone else stepped out of the queue and blocked his path. "My wife had a baby at home yesterday. Both are sick. Please come and see them."

"I can't. No time."

Piter dodged, but was stopped again by a woman who placed the palm of her hand on his chest. "Please stop. My father is having trouble breathing!" She rested her other hand on an old man drooped in a wheelchair.

Piter pressed his fingers on the man's cold neck, but felt no pulse. With his fingertips, Piter opened one of the old man's glassy eyes. "Too late. He's dead. Sorry for your loss." He jogged to the clinic's front door before anyone else could stop him. He stepped inside, scrunched up his face and relaxed it, trying to regain composure, and wondered again how he was going to get through the next four years.

§

Midway through the morning, a couple brought an elderly man to see Piter. After checking vital signs, Piter saw no urgent medical care was required. "What seems to be the problem?"

The woman pushed her father's wheelchair into the hall, came back into the room and shut the door. She blushed and hung her head, picked at the sleeve of her coat and in a small voice asked, "Can you help us to let him go?"

"What do you mean?"

She took her husband's arm. One word tumbled into the other as she spoke. "We can't take care of him. He can't walk, no control of his bladder. I can't leave him alone, can't go to work. My children are hungry."

"What do you want me to do?"

"Give us something to mix in his food," the man whispered. His breath smelled of tooth decay.

Piter took a step back. "You're not serious."

The man took a quick glance at the closed door and spoke quietly. "Then help us in another way. My uncle was…put down, at another clinic a few weeks back. No food, no water until he died."

The room felt small, suddenly. Piter looked the couple straight in the eyes to make sure they understood. "Only when administering fluids and nutrition is excessively burdensome to the patient are they discontinued. Your father is not dying. He could have years to live."

"Exactly. He's totally dependent on us. What about our children?" the woman asked. "He used to live in a care centre, but they told us to take him home."

"There's really nothing I can…"

"We don't know what else to do," said the man. "Do you think this is easy for us?"

"What you're asking for is cruel and unwarranted. It's murder." The fluorescent ceiling lights flickered. Piter felt a headache coming on.

"Should my whole family go hungry? Look, I love my father. We're just trying to survive." The woman's voice shook. Her eyes blinked rapidly.

"I understand the strain you're under, but I can't help you," Piter said.

"Wait," the man said. He took out his wallet and offered Piter a handful of bills.

Piter turned his face so as not to smell the man's putrefying breath. "I can't accept a bribe. I would lose my licence."

The woman's face was full of pain. She turned her back to the men, took out a tissue and blew her nose. "Do you know how hard it was for us to come to you?"

Piter's mouth was dry. This couple had three children. The man had recently lost his job. Piter watched a fly bash its body repeatedly against the window. For a moment, his eyes were drawn to the fly carcasses that already littered the window sill.

The man, not getting an answer, put the cash back in his wallet and turned to his wife. "What are we going to do?"

Piter looked at their pale, pinched faces, the man's arm around his wife's thin shoulders. "I'm just a resident. Let me talk to the doctor in charge." He thought perhaps Jeniver could talk some sense into them.

Moments later, he returned with Dr. Jeniver Bant.

Dr. Bant said, "So, you're saying your father is in a great deal of pain? Perhaps we can keep him here for observation. You could donate to the clinic."

Piter's mouth dropped open. The man opened his wallet again.

She reassured the couple everything would be taken care of and wheeled the old man into the short-stay wing where all but one of the ten beds were occupied.

"What's this about?" the old man asked. "Do I need an operation?"

"Lie down, please," Jeniver said. She gave the old man a shot of morphine. The man soon fell asleep.

[33]

She posted a sign above the patient's bed. "No food. No water." She took Piter aside and whispered in his ear, "The old man won't suffer if he's heavily drugged. The government doesn't care enough about Free Clinics to look closely at the records."

Piter knew death could take many days.

Another patient called out to Piter. "When will you send me to the hospital to get this hernia taken care of, Doctor? I've been here two days."

"I've been here longer," called a woman. "You said I needed to be seen by a cardiologist. When will that happen?"

Piter kept his tone even and nodded with sympathy. "We need to wait for spots to open up at the hospital."

A man across the room was lying on his back, his eyes unblinking. Piter approached, shook his shoulder and then held a stethoscope to his chest. No heartbeat. Now, there was another spot open in the short-stay wing.

Jeniver approached Piter as he drew the sheet over the man's face. She whispered in his ear again, "I know you're not comfortable with putting the old man down. Help me and I'll split the money."

The man will die whether I'm involved or not. I could buy a few groceries with the cash. "Okay," he said.

§

Days passed. The old man, condemned to die, continued to sleep on and off. His daughter sat on a chair beside her father. His condition deteriorated. When his lips cracked and dried, his daughter wet them with a sponge. He looked around the room, sometimes focusing on a person. He moved his tongue in and out of his mouth and made breathy sounds.

"Is he trying to talk to us?" the daughter asked.

Even though Piter believed her father was trying to communicate, he told her otherwise. He looked gravely at the patient, then at her, and assured her what she was seeing was all part of the process. "It's just reflex. There's no pain. Just in case, I'll up his dose of morphine."

Over the next five days, the old man had occasional moments of lucidity. Fear and confusion showed in his eyes. He looked at Piter and mouthed the word, "Why?"

Piter was tempted to put a stop to the procedure. Instead, he turned his back.

More days passed and the old man withered, curled into a fetal position. Piter knew kidney failure was imminent.

The woman continued to sit at her father's side. "I don't want him to be alone," she said.

Piter would have preferred if she weren't present. When he saw the agony on her face, he had to work hard to remain detached.

The next day, the old man slipped into a coma, and Piter knew it would soon be over.

Days later came the bawling, the lost look in the woman's eyes as if she couldn't believe her dad was dead. Piter was relieved she didn't fling her body on the corpse.

It wasn't long before another family entered the clinic with an elderly relative, and a few days later, another. Word had gotten out. The clinic would, for a donation, take a burden away. Piter didn't like to say, "allowing people to die of thirst," but preferred the euphemism, "euthanasia by omission or EBO." Somehow, softening the words made the procedure more acceptable to his ears.

§

The clinic took in thirteen EBO patients over the next three weeks. Despite Piter's increased income and his cupboards full of food, he became more irritable. He had wanted to surprise Yun by bringing home roast beef, a luxury they hadn't seen in months.

Instead of being happy, all she said was, "How can we afford beef?"

He snapped at her, "Why are you so suspicious of me? I bought it especially for you, but if you don't want it—"

Yun touched his arm. "I'm sorry, dear. You've had a long, hard day. Go and relax. I'll make supper."

[35]

He opened his mouth, about to say, "Don't bother," but then thought better of it.

"You mustn't allow the darkness in, Piter."

The sound of her voice had a calming effect on him. "I'm happy to be with you." He ran his finger down the length of her spine.

"Remember Psalm 119? 'Happy are those whose way is blameless, who walk in the law of the Lord—'"

Piter drew back as if he'd been slapped and held up his hand. He didn't like Yun quoting the *Bible* to him. "I don't want to hear it, Yun."

"Why not?"

He hesitated. "I don't believe in God."

"That can't be true." The colour drained from her face.

He gazed at her, not smiling.

Her lower lip quivered. She crossed her arms over her stomach. "But I thought… When did you…?"

"A few years ago. Sorry."

§

Piter thought they were in trouble the day a government agent entered the clinic and asked to see the doctors privately. "We know what you're up to. Did you think you could get away with it?"

Piter denied nothing and fully expected to go to jail.

"We'd like you to convert all ten beds in your short-stay wing for 'Expedited End-of-Life Care.' The government is prepared to compensate you and the clinic for your trouble."

Piter took a step back and leaned against a desk. "Why?"

The government agent spoke in a whisper. "If you tell anyone I said this, I'll deny it. Do you know how much this government spends on old age pension and health care for the elderly?"

"You need a way to save public funds?" Jeniver said.

"Exactly."

Piter knew they couldn't stop the train now that it was in motion.

§

At supper that evening, Piter felt Yun's eyes on him. He stared at his plate and chewed his food.

"You're so brooding lately. What's wrong?" asked Yun.

He lifted his head and met her gaze. "I'm just tired. The job gets to me sometimes." He sighed. "This isn't exactly the life we envisioned, is it?"

"Take life as it comes. Focus on doing what is right."

Piter decided there was no right or wrong. Everyone had to do what they could to survive in this crazy world.

§

A special graduation ceremony was held at Ackim University for former students of Covona University who had been denied a celebration due to the war. Piter would not have bothered, but Yun and Hadar were eager to attend.

Afterwards, Piter stood in cap and gown, his Doctor of Medicine Degree in hand. He scanned the faces of the people as they swarmed out of the university auditorium following the Convocation speeches. The spring air was fragrant with the scent of the lilac bushes that separated the university lawns from the boulevard.

Hadar, also in cap and gown, ran up and threw his arm around Piter's shoulder, nearly knocking him over. "Congrats, brother."

"Same to you." Piter forced a smile. "I can't believe you're leaving in a few days." What he wanted to say was, "Don't go."

Hadar looked genuinely happy. "Yep. Summer classes at the seminary start next week."

Their mother, Odilia, approached, camera in hand. "There you are, you two." She trudged across the lawn, her high heels sticking in the soft grass. "Look this way." She aimed the camera at them. "Back up. I want to get the lilac bushes in the background. I'm so proud of my boys."

Hyron said, "Piter, this is your graduation day. Smile, for goodness sake." A newspaper was folded under his arm.

Piter put his arm around Hadar's shoulder and smiled. Odilia snapped a photo.

They were interrupted by Yun, who wrapped her arms around Piter's neck. "You look so handsome." She kissed him on the lips.

Piter wasn't comfortable with public displays of affection. He longed to control his blushing.

"Look. It's official. Masters of Education." Yun grinned, displaying her degree for all to see.

"Glad those speeches are done?" Hadar asked.

"President Jomb does go on and on, doesn't he?" Piter pointed his finger at Hadar and said in a mocking tone, "It's up to you. The young men and women of this country must fight to keep us strong, free and democratic." He emphasized the last word by pointing at the sky.

Hadar laughed. "Good imitation, Piter. Dad, were you reading the newspaper when you should have been listening to the speeches?" He snatched the paper away and used it to give his father a playful slap on the arm.

"Let me see that." Piter took the newspaper from Hadar. On the front page was a photo of Aura Zarling, the step-daughter of billionaire Teador Zarling. He turned the front page towards the others. "She's the new leader of the Freedom Party. Do you think she has a chance?"

"She seems like a smart woman. Maybe now the country can go forward," said Hyron.

"I don't trust her," Hadar said.

§

A week passed. The phone rang as they washed the after-supper dishes. Yun answered, talked for a while, then waved Piter over. "It's your brother." She returned to the sink of dirty dishes.

Hadar now lived in Citron, on the east coast of Covona at the mouth of the Alain Inlet, a four-hour drive from Ackim. The brothers promised to speak on the telephone once a week. Piter took the phone, hoping to talk some sense into Hadar before it was too late. After several minutes of small talk, Piter got to the point. "You're throwing away your life by becoming a priest."

Yun turned to Piter. Her mouth hung open. "What?"

"You know that's not true," Hadar said. "We're the same. You heal bodies. I heal souls."

Piter tightened his grip on the phone. "You're so happy to give your life to that unfeeling God."

Yun shook the water from her hands and dried them on a towel. "That's a terrible thing to say!"

"God loves us. He's not unfeeling," Hadar said.

Yun said, "Hadar is smart, loves people and is so devout. He'll make a great priest. Besides, he can do what he wants with his life."

Piter held his tongue. "Sorry, Hadar. It's been a hell of a day."

Hadar laughed. "It's all right. Tell Yun thanks."

"I will." Piter turned his back to Yun and squeezed the bridge of his nose.

"Yun says you two are lobbying for human rights. Too few people are concerned about those in need," Hadar said.

Piter ran his hand over his chin. "Well, I haven't much time with my medical practice. Yun is involved though."

"Well, you've dedicated your practice to helping the neediest and saving lives. Did you hear there's a court decision coming soon? Physician-assisted suicide could be legalized."

Piter hesitated. He put one hand in his pocket and carried the phone to the window to look outside. "I know. They're coming up with strict guidelines. We don't need to worry."

On the sidewalk below, an elderly woman was bent over, untangling a branch from the wheels of her walker. She succeeded and continued to make slow progress towards her destination. Children, dressed in shorts, ran past her down the street chasing a slightly deflated soccer ball.

"Did you see the Minister of Health on television?" asked Hadar. "She says two doctors must be of the opinion the person requesting PAS meets all the criteria and the person's natural death must be reasonably foreseeable."

"You see? PAS will be restricted to the terminally ill."

"That's how you interpret it? 'Reasonably foreseeable? Be of the opinion?' That could mean anything. So much for strict guidelines."

"We need to be compassionate to those facing death."

"Noble sounding words, Piter, but they're redefining a form of homicide to make it sound acceptable. It will soon spiral out of control."

"Government regulations will ensure that doesn't happen."

"You have more faith in the system than I do," Hadar said. "What about regulations to protect freedom of conscience for doctors? Can you imagine if you were told to kill someone?"

Piter cleared his throat. "That would be awful. Can we talk about something else?"

"I'm a deacon now at a beautiful parish here in Citron. You and Yun should come visit."

"We'll try." Piter hadn't set foot inside a church since his wedding day and had no desire to see the seminary or Hadar's parish.

"How is your research coming along?" Hadar asked. "Did you know Mom still has that medical journal where your article on ALS was published?"

"What is she hanging on to that for? She wouldn't even understand it."

"She brought it here when she came to visit, showed it to everyone. You should have heard her brag, 'My son has a theory on how to cure Lou Gehrig's disease…'"

"Maybe once I get more established I can find a position with a research company."

"Too bad. After you won an award—"

"It's the economy. Anyway, I don't want your phone bill to get too high. We'll talk again soon." As he hung up the phone, the words "I miss you" stuck in Piter's throat.

CHAPTER SEVEN

New Covona

The sky was grey. Thunder rumbled in the distance. The air smelled muggy and thick. Piter's shirt was damp with sweat by the time he and Yun arrived at City Hall for the speech. Most of the people gathered were dressed casually, jeans and t-shirts. Several young men had bandanas tied around their heads.

A line of policemen dressed in riot gear—helmets and bullet-proof vests, held semiautomatic weapons. They stood shoulder to shoulder, their backs to the stage, facing the crowd. More police patrolled the periphery. Piter took Yun's hand and they maneuvered closer to the stage where Fillip and Tresha were waiting. He guessed about four hundred were in attendance.

He and Yun stood beside a woman pushing a baby stroller. The baby was completely covered by a blanket. "The child could overheat," he told her.

"None of your business, mister." She moved away from him.

Aura Zarling took the stage. There was a smattering of applause.

She raised both fists in the air and shouted, "Are you ready for a new Covona?"

A few people clapped. Others milled about or talked among themselves.

Piter leaned over and said to Fillip, "She's attractive, for a middle-aged woman. Nice figure."

Fillip nodded in agreement. "Never married or had children."

Tresha wore her "Ackim City News" badge and was busy scribbling notes. Her recording device was in a bag slung over her shoulder.

Yun asked her, "Why aren't you up there with them?" She pointed to the group of reporters who had microphones set up on the stage to capture Aura's words.

"I wasn't given the privilege," Tresha said. "My editor is punishing me." She pointed at Aura with her pen. "We were friends in high school. You never saw anyone so spoiled and mean."

Aura shouted, "What we need in this country is stability, harmony and peace." She raised two fists in the air again.

The crowd applauded and the speech continued.

The police stood, staring stone-faced at the gathering crowd. Beads of sweat rolled down their foreheads. Piter almost felt sorry for them in their black uniforms.

"Why were you friends if she was so terrible?" Yun asked.

"She could be lots of fun, bought me stuff, gave me her hand-me-downs. My parents couldn't afford to keep me clothed like that," Tresha said.

Ms. Zarling shouted, "We will not have peace or justice until Jomb's government is overthrown. The removal of governmental restraint is the only way to freedom."

Piter was uncertain what Aura was getting at but assumed she would clarify herself later. He counted cameras from four T.V. stations, all owned by Zarling Communications. "She's not making a lot of sense."

Tresha said, "Don't let her good looks or ditzy behaviour fool you. She's smart. Look at all the monopolies she's created—Zarling Communications, Zarling Hotels and Casinos, Zarling Oil and Gas. She's known as a ruthless negotiator. Doesn't hurt she comes from a wealthy family."

"Hated and admired," Fillip said.

Aura yelled from the podium, "This government ignores the rights of the workers. Social justice will come when all have equality! I know what you're thinking. How can Aura talk about social justice? The Zarling Empire is large. True, I have been blessed in my life, but I am just like you. I care about my fellow Covonans." She placed her hand over her heart. "I pledge to use my good fortune to offer health care, housing and education. I promise to increase employment. The people of this country want to go back to work."

Loud cheering followed. The clouds had dissipated and the sun was high in the sky. Piter squinted at the stage and wiped the sweat from the back of his neck.

"The National Labour Party's policies led to out-of-control inflation. The Conservatives would use your tax money to fight wars."

Someone in the crowd shouted, "We want a new Covona!"

Aura shouted into the microphone, "We need to do away with the old system and become free thinkers!"

A man standing close to the stage held up a sign and pumped it up and down. "We want jobs, not Jomb!"

Tresha wrote madly in her notebook.

A man in a bandana reached into the baby carriage, took out a rock, and hurled it towards the line of police officers. It bounced off a policeman's shield. In unison, the police raised their shields and clubs and took a few steps towards the crowd. The group of men took the bandanas from their heads and tied them around their faces. Aura was whisked off the stage.

Excitement grew. People raised their fists in the air and chanted, "We want change! We want a new Covona!"

The masked men reached one after the other into the baby carriage and more rocks followed the first, crashing into the shields of the heavily-armed men. Riot police thumped their clubs against their shields, making a terrible racket. They closed in on the crowd from three sides.

Piter grabbed Yun's hand and backed away. "Let's get out of here."

A choking, misty cloud drifted over the heads of the people. A woman screamed, "Tear gas!"

The crowd degenerated into a heaving, squirming mass of humanity. The noise was terrible. Shouts of terror filled the air. People, wide-eyed like panicked cattle, stampeded. They pushed and shoved. Piter yelped as his toes were crushed. Yun received an elbow to the head. A woman fell in front of Piter, almost tripping him. He helped her to her feet. A policeman raised his club and brought it down on a young man. Blood poured from the young man's head.

Sirens blared. Police shouted through bullhorns, "Clear the area!

Piter's heart raced. He was filled with a terror he hadn't felt since bombs fell on his house. His toe throbbed inside his shoe, but they couldn't stop. Holding Yun's sweaty hand, they ran with the crowd towards the city park. Piter pulled his shirt over his mouth and nose as tear gas threatened to choke him.

The four friends reached a city park and sat down on a bench to catch their breath.

"That was horrifying," Fillip said.

Tresha struggled to breathe. "I wouldn't put it past Aura to have planted those troublemakers in the crowd."

"Why? It doesn't make sense." Fillip used the sleeve of his jacket to wipe tears from his eyes. "Damn. That stuff stings." He rinsed his eyes in the outdoor fountain.

Yun asked, "Do you really think she arranged the whole riot and tear gas thing?" She placed the palms of her hands over her eyes.

Tresha said, "Maybe my article will make the national news. I can see the headlines, 'Aura Zarling appeals to the marginalized.'"

They all remarked at what a terrible leader she would be, except Piter. Despite what he had just experienced, he liked the idea of change. He bent over the fountain and took a long, refreshing drink.

CHAPTER EIGHT

The Freedom Party

Tresha savoured a glass of wine, a full-bodied red with a hint of blueberry. She could almost forget her troubles on a warm summer night like this. She crossed her legs and leaned back on the lawn chair. Once this bottle was gone, there was no more. She swirled the liquid in her glass and sniffed, enjoying the fruity aroma. "We should have picked up more when we toured Karia." Now, wine was too expensive for the average person. "It was a lovely drive. Beautiful scenery."

"I love wine country. That's where I'd like to live, if we had a choice," he said.

"Too dry there."

"Good for growing fruit."

Tresha's mouth watered at the thought of all the delicious fresh fruit that was once available—crunchy apples, sweet peaches, pears, plums, blueberries and blackberries. "Wouldn't you love to sink your teeth into a blueberry pie?"

Fillip leaned his head on the back of his soft chair and closed his eyes. "Or a big, juicy steak. Remember the prime rib at that hotel in Citron? Mmm. Was it part of the Zarling chain back then?"

"I think so. Nice place, but poor Jakon was afraid of the ocean waves. He clung to my leg and we were only ankle-deep." Her eyes prickled. "Everything was simpler then."

"Don't complain. We have more than most people." Fillip opened the newspaper.

"I'm not talking about having things. Everything changed so fast—"

"Look." He held up the newspaper. "The disturbance at the rally made the front page, but this doesn't sound like your writing. 'Aura Zarling promises to restore the economy and bring pride and dignity back to the people of this great land. It's criminal what President Jomb did...' Didn't Raimond like your piece?"

Tresha shook her head. "He said mine was too negative. He wants articles that are uplifting."

Fillip pointed to Aura's picture in the paper. "She's our age. Facelift, I assume."

Tresha stood, put on her glasses and leaned over Fillip's shoulder. "Back when we were friends, I had to warn my mom if Aura was coming over, give her time to hide all the cookies and everything sweet. Her mother was a former model and never allowed fattening things so Aura always went nuts at my house. It was the only thing I had that she didn't. One day, she found a jar of icing in our pantry. She dipped her finger into the chocolate, stuck it in her mouth and slowly sucked it off." Tresha demonstrated. "Mmm."

"That looks sexual."

"She dipped her finger into the jar and into her mouth again and again, and made all these slurping, sucking sounds. She flicked her tongue in and out of her mouth, licking her lips. Her eyes rolled back in her head."

Fillip laughed. "Did you try to stop her?"

"Yeah. She wouldn't listen. She gripped the jar against her chest. My mom yelled, 'What are you doing?' Aura had this maniacal look on her face and ate faster and faster. Chocolate was smeared all over her lips and teeth. It was revolting. Then she ran to the bathroom and spewed chocolate all over the toilet. My mom handed Aura the toilet brush and told her to clean it up. Aura stood there looking at the brush like she had never cleaned anything in her life. She probably hadn't. You should have seen her pathetic attempt. She swirled the brush around, holding it between her thumb and index finger. My mom snatched the brush and finished the job."

"And yet here she is, set to be our leader." Fillip tapped the newspaper. "She's so successful in business. I wonder why she's leaving that to go into politics."

"Apparently, she's going to fix everything."

"Why the Freedom Party? They didn't do well in previous elections."

"Five percent of the popular vote, but with Aura in charge, they're doing much better."

Fillip drained the last of the wine from his glass and smacked his lips. "The National Labour Party is still favoured to win. Fighting for the rights of the common person and all that. They'll be hard to topple."

"True, but after twenty-one years, people want change."

"I would think, with the economic crisis, that the Conservatives would do better," Fillip said.

"They're losing ground to the Freedom Party, too. And then there's the Liberal Democrats. You know their spiel—free, open society, liberty, equality. They had twenty percent of the votes in the last election, but they lost their leader—"

"In a car crash. Have they nominated a replacement yet?" asked Fillip.

"Not yet." Tresha sipped her wine. She sighed, looking at her empty glass. "And then there's the Green Party."

Fillip sniffed. "Right. Who cares about the environment when you can't feed your family?"

"No one takes them seriously, but it's getting harder to predict a winner in this election."

§

Later that evening, Tresha sat down to watch her favourite television host, the only one who still delivered hard news. So many television stations seemed to show nothing but celebrity cook-offs and dance contests. Her heart sank when she learned today's guest was Aura Zarling.

The talk show host said, "Here at last is hope, a heroine who can lead us out of the mess the NLP have gotten us into. Let's welcome Aura Zarling." He extended his arm and Aura walked across the stage with two fists in the air, took a seat and gracefully crossed her legs.

"We want a new Covona!" the studio audience chanted.

Aura smiled. "And you'll get one!"

The talk show host leaned in close, his expression serious. "Ms. Zarling, the countdown to the election is on. Your party is gaining in popularity, as we can see from our studio audience. How confident do you feel?"

"Oh, I know I'll win. My people will make sure."

The talk show host laughed. "But, of course, it's the public who will decide, in the upcoming election."

Aura smiled. "That's what I mean by 'my people.'"

Fillip interrupted. "A meeting's been called. I have the address. We need to leave right away."

Tresha turned off the television. "That's okay. I can't stand looking at her smug face anyway. You must admit, her enthusiasm to create a new country is infectious."

Tonight's Human Rights for All meeting was held in an abandoned building. Pillars held up what was left of the roof. The floor was littered with chunks of concrete, metal and glass. The walls were blackened and pockmarked. Tresha was surprised to see a painting on the wall, a path running through a forest. Tresha failed to make out the signature scrawled in the bottom righthand corner. She wiped the face of the painting with her sleeve. "Such a peaceful scene. I don't think anyone would mind if I took this home." She tried to lift it down, but it was bolted securely to the wall.

Fillip and Piter unfolded the legs of a table, set it in the middle of the room and went in search of chairs.

A rusted filing cabinet stood in the corner. Tresha opened it and inside were alphabetized file folders, their papers undamaged. She fingered through them while waiting for other members of the group to arrive. "Financial statements. Just imagine. All these people carefully put aside money for the future. Meaningless now." She closed the drawer.

When the final member arrived, they took their places around the table. Piter plunked down on a chair. He had a sour expression on his face. "We're all wasting our time. Do you think a little group of people can do anything to change the future?"

Yun whispered, "Give it a chance. You need to hear a different point of view."

Tresha didn't know the names of most of the people in the room. This was intentional to protect everyone's identity.

"This election is important," said one of the members. "If Zarling is elected our freedoms are in danger. But how do we convince people that she's dangerous?"

"Don't be ridiculous. How is she dangerous?" Piter asked.

Fillip said, "She feeds on this country's sense of victimhood. The people find a champion in Aura, but she's a sham, not only blaming the president, but also capitalism for the country's problems. And she's against freedom of religion."

"We need to set up safe houses," Tresha said.

Piter leaned back in his chair and crossed his arms. "Look, I'm not against what you're doing. Human rights are important, but Zarling never said anything against your religion."

Tresha said, "She and I got together a couple of times in university. She called me a deluded fanatic for attending church. That was the last time I talked to her."

"We won't lose freedom of religion in this country," Piter said.

Fillip said, "Not all at once. Piter, you know how rights have been diluted over the years. The government decides what's taught, even in private religious schools. We don't hear Christmas carols. When was the last time you saw a manger scene? Printed calendars don't show religious holidays."

"So? Those sorts of things cause derisiveness in society," Piter said.

"If Aura becomes president, I'm afraid she'll make it worse," Fillip said.

Piter leaned forward. "You're worrying about nothing. This is a free country. We need a strong leader to bring us back on track. Open your eyes and look around." He waved his arm indicating the decrepit building where they were meeting. "We can't even afford to tear down old buildings and you're worried about manger scenes."

Yun placed her hand on Piter's. "This is about having freedoms taken away. The people want change so badly, I'm afraid she'll get elected in a protest vote."

Fillip pointed his finger at Piter. "She's too powerful. Aura Zarling bailed out Covo Motors when they were facing bankruptcy. You

[49]

think she won't want something in return? She's without conscious, cares nothing about the poor."

"You're being paranoid, fear mongering." Piter sneered.

"Zarling Oil and Gas illegally dumped waste. My colleague had videos and interviews," Tresha said.

"Why didn't he submit the evidence to the courts?"

"They were stolen out of his car." Tresha hung her head. From the corner of her eye she saw two small eyes glowing in the dim light. She jumped a bit in her seat as a cat burst from behind a shelf and scurried across the floor.

"His word against theirs," Piter said.

"The election is only two weeks away. I pray she's not elected president. She's a magnet of deception into the hellish horror of despotism," Fillip said.

Piter rolled his eyes. "Don't be so dramatic. The people of this country are too shrewd to allow just anybody to be president."

"We must attend to the main issue of this meeting," Fillip said. "Who has suggestions for locations of safe houses? Many people may soon need protection."

CHAPTER NINE

President Aura Zarling

"The final results are in. The Freedom Party won with thirty-eight percent of the popular vote." Fillip sat on the bed and read the news aloud. "The rest of the votes were split between the other parties."

"No! I can't believe it." Tresha covered her head with a pillow. It felt safer in bed, warm and dark, like a cocoon.

He nudged her shoulder. "I'm going to meet with some of our members to make some signs. I'll be back tonight and we'll go to the victory rally."

"I'm not going anywhere. What's the point? They were warning people with 'rebellious attitudes' to stay away. Why look for trouble?"

Fillip's voice was muffled and far away. "This is still a democratic country. We have the right to protest."

She peeked out from under the pillow. "You really think we should?"

He took the pillow away and kissed her cheek. "It'll be fine." He smiled, climbed out of bed and scratched his potbelly.

"What about Jakon? I can't leave him alone."

"Stop making excuses." Fillip went into the washroom and yelped when the shower came on. "No hot water this morning!" He began to sing in a high-pitched voice.

Tresha smiled, admiring Fillip's ability to be cheerful even in difficult circumstances. She looked up at the ceiling, trying to gather the courage to enter enemy territory.

§

The rally was about to begin. Tresha and Fillip spotted Piter and handed him a sign that read, "Protect Human Dignity. Support HRFA."

He stepped back, as if they were trying to hand him something filthy. "I don't want to carry that."

"It's for Yun," Fillip said.

Piter took the sign, but looked ashamed. He held it upside-down.

"Stay here, Tresha. I'll be back." Fillip walked away with a few more signs on his shoulder, seeking more members of HRFA who had promised to be at the rally.

A crowd continued to gather. The former Zarling mansion stood atop a small hill looking down upon the city of Ackim. Built over two hundred years ago, the three-storey building was an imposing structure. Marble columns stood on either side of the tall front doors. Rows of arched windows looked down on a grassy lawn and a long, curved driveway. The former capitol buildings in Covona City were bombed by Solime during the war. The Zarling family donated the mansion on the agreement the centre of government be moved to Ackim, their hometown.

Tresha realized she was one of few people in this crowd who had been inside. She remembered running up and down the long halls with Aura, pretending they were sisters, imagining she was also an heiress. Today, most of the house was blocked by a stage and a massive screen. Police officers in full riot gear with automatic weapons at the ready stood shoulder to shoulder in front of the mansion.

Tresha held Jakon's hand, even though he was a teenager and they were now the same height. He muttered to himself and bounced up and down on his toes, agitated by the noise, large number of people, and growing excitement. She pulled him by the hand. "Let's go where there are fewer people." In Tresha's other hand she carried a "Protect Human Dignity" sign.

Soon, the grounds swarmed with people. Tresha lost sight of Fillip and Piter in the writhing crowd. She hooked her arm through Jakon's.

"Mom. Go home." He pulled to get away.

"Okay, Jakon. Be calm, dear. Let's find Daddy first." She dropped her sign on the ground to hold Jakon's arm with both hands. Standing on tiptoe, she stretched her neck, but couldn't see Fillip or any familiar faces among the thousands.

A man stepped up to the microphone. "Ladies and gentlemen, put your hands together for our new president, Aura Zarling!" He swung his arm wide towards a smiling woman dressed in a white suit jacket and knee-length skirt. Her image was projected on the screen. She strutted to the microphone. A tremendous shout went up from the crowd. President Aura Zarling, radiant in her white suit, flashed her toothy smile. She raised both fists in the air. People jostled each other to get closer to the stage; some had tears running down their faces. Tresha and Jakon were pressed ever closer into the mass of exuberant supporters.

Aura said, "Thank you, my people. Thank you for the trust you placed in me."

People cheered and raised their arms in the air, copying Aura's two-fisted salute.

Aura held her hand over her heart. "You're not just citizens. You're my people, my family. So, let's dispense with awful formal titles. From now on, you, my brothers and sisters, may call me Aura." She flipped her long, brown hair and smiled. "You asked for a government that will stand up for autonomy. In the coming years, all of you will be called upon to defend the rights we fought so hard to gain. We must not be fearful or timid. The NLPs impoverished you. I'm here to help. Solime and the other union nations will never give us our fair share. We need to stand on our own two feet. We need a redistribution of wealth, but some groups, like Human Rights for All, oppose this."

Security police pushed into the crowd. From her vantage point, Tresha couldn't see what happened, only heard the angry shouts and loud booing.

After a short pause, the new president said, "I guess someone's not happy about yesterday's results." She waited for the laughter to die down.

The sun was setting in the western sky; its last burning rays brought drops of sweat to Tresha's forehead. Her glasses slipped down her nose. Sticky heat radiated from the bodies around her and she wished she had remembered to bring some water. Jakon leaned his head on her shoulder, looking fearful.

"It's okay, my darling." She rubbed his back.

Aura continued. "Our country is in crisis. The past administration, the National Labour Party, failed us. First, they pushed us into a costly conflict with Solime. Then, Jomb negotiated peace with the people who stole our land. He led us straight into economic crisis. When we were most in need, the former president bowed to pressure from lobby groups."

The audience booed.

"These are tough economic times. We work hard and get little in return. You deserve to live in a rich nation, but inflation and taxes are too high. Why should working people be so burdened?"

"That's right, Aura!" someone shouted.

"We can't continue to support the elderly and the handicapped to the end of their natural lives. Society must not be on the hook to care for impaired people."

Aura gave the crowd two-fists-up. Several minutes passed before people were quiet enough for her to continue. "The reactionary faction, groups like Human Rights for All, want us to pay for the maintenance of people who make no contribution to society. We will fight for a better standard of living for Covona's citizens. Impaired people are their families' responsibility. If they chose to give birth to an impaired baby, they must care for that child without government handouts. You should not be called upon to fix other people's mistakes. Steps must be taken now!"

"Now! Now! Now!" chanted the crowd.

Tresha imagined pushing Aura off the stage. She was shocked her former friend said such a terrible thing, but was more horrified this large crowd agreed with her.

Jakon covered his ears to block the loud chanting. Tresha put her hand on the back of his head, pressing him against her. She worried he might have a tantrum as he sometimes did when he was stressed. "I should not have brought you with me," she told him, but he didn't seem to hear, or understand.

A smiling, teary-eyed woman turned to Tresha and said, "I can't believe I'm actually here, seeing her in person."

Tresha didn't respond, but kept her eyes focused at the stage.

"She's a leader for the people, isn't she?" teary-eyed woman said. She looked at Jakon and her smile disappeared. "Your boy has Down's syndrome. Too bad for you."

Tresha resisted the urge to kick the woman in the shins. She clenched her teeth. This was not the time or place to argue. She stroked her son's sweaty blond hair and looked for a way out of the sweltering crowd to find some shade.

Aura's face was projected onto a three-metre-high screen. She peered down; her immense eyes bored into the audience. Teary-eyed woman screamed and clasped her hands together. The sky grew darker as the image grew brighter.

"I'm tired." Jakon leaned against his mother.

Tresha put her arm around Jakon and held him close.

"Your taxes keep the dysfunctional population clothed and fed. Why? They have no quality of life." Aura's mouth opened wide as if to devour the audience. "They consume valuable resources, costing us millions every year."

A video was projected onto the screen. Photos of people with Down's syndrome, cerebral palsy and other disabilities were followed by flashes of swarming insects and rats scuttling in heaps of garbage. The crowd watched, entranced.

Aura's radiant face appeared again on a background of rolling ocean surf and trees swaying in a gentle breeze. She spoke softly. "We know objections will be raised by the reactionary faction. Those fanatics stand in our way. We will defeat them and accomplish great things." She went on to speak about corrupt church leaders, heaven and hell.

Tresha spoke soothing words to Jakon. "Be calm, darling. Mommy will take you home."

"It will be a hard struggle, but we will emerge, like a chick from an egg, and grow into a strong, fierce hawk. I have seen a bright new future and promise to lead you to the land of prosperity. United we are strong. The people will triumph!" With that, her face disappeared in an explosion of colour. Rays of light streamed from the screen and glowed with the setting sun.

The crowd roared. Jakon started to cry. She held Jakon's hand and forced their way out of the crowd. That night, Fillip told her his sign was torn from his hand. Tresha wondered at the stupidity of her countrymen. She found out the next day that what happened to Piter was worse.

CHAPTER TEN

Protecting Human Dignity

Piter was tired of the National Labour Party's empty promises. That's why he voted for Aura Zarling's Freedom Party. He exchanged smiles with others at the rally, eager to show support for the woman he helped elect. The noisy mass of humanity continued to gather outside the government building. The sun hung low, blazing with intensity. Sweat dripped into Piter's eyes, making them sting. The crowd pressed closer together.

Fillip handed him a protest sign, "Protect Human Dignity. Support HRFA."

"I'm not carrying that," Piter said.

"It's for Yun."

Piter didn't want Yun to carry the sign either, but she was a grown woman and he wouldn't tell her what to do. He took the sign, but held it upside-down and looked at the people standing nearby to see if anyone noticed. Fillip walked away with three more signs resting on his shoulder.

Piter's cell phone buzzed in his pocket, a text from Yun. "Won't be coming to the rally. Terrible headache. TTYL." He decided to give the sign back to Fillip, except he had lost sight of him. He put his cell phone back in his pocket, leaned on the stick and scanned the crowd.

He wondered if she was still angry with him over an argument they had the day before: "HRFA ideals are horribly old-fashioned," Piter had said as he removed a loaf of bread from a paper bag and sliced it.

Yun stirred a pot of soup. "Protecting human dignity is old-fashioned?" She lifted the ladle to taste and added salt.

"No, of course not. I'm talking about their objections to PAS."

"So, then we're talking about ethics. Wouldn't it be better to offer pain medication and love, instead of death?"

"If a person's quality of life is poor, why go on living?"

She raised her voice. "You're a doctor. Surely you see people don't lose their humanity because they're old or disabled. Besides, it's God's will."

"Okay, you just lost me." She opened her mouth to speak, but he interrupted her. "Forget it. We've had this same discussion before and we'll never agree. You're too hard-headed to see my point of view." He placed the knife on the counter and the bread on the table.

She placed her hands on her hips. "I'm hard-headed? You—"

"I don't want to argue." He held up his hand. "And you're not going to any more damn HRFA meetings."

"Dear God, give me patience," she whispered, and raised her eyes to the ceiling. "I'll go if I want. I'm a grown woman." She set her lips together.

He raised both hands in the air. "How can you believe in God in this modern era? It's not reasonable."

She put her hand on his chest. "You must believe in something larger than yourself."

"I believe in the human mind and imagination." He pointed to his head.

She returned to stirring the soup and took a deep breath. "You're not beyond redemption. I'm not giving up on you."

"Yun, you are my knight in shining armour, but what if I don't want to be saved?"

"That's it!" She threw the wet ladle at him, splattering soup on his clean shirt, stomped away and slammed the bedroom door.

"Over-sensitive," he muttered under his breath.

§

One bus after another pulled into the parking lot and emptied passengers onto the grounds. The mansion, now government building, was in a beautiful part of the city overlooking the river valley. The expansive grounds were dotted with trees. Piter stood near a fountain in the centre near a marble statue of Mars, the Roman god of war, riding a charging horse. Water shot from Mars' helmet. Security personal surrounded the fountain, preventing anyone from touching the clear water.

Thousands of feet trampled the lush grass. A stage had been erected in front of the mansion, complete with an enormous sound system, a giant screen and what seemed like a battalion of security personnel. It reminded Piter of rock concerts he had attended when he was a young man. Without thinking, Piter put the sign on his shoulder and maneuvered his way through the crowd, looking everywhere for Fillip.

A man stepped up to the microphone. "Ladies and gentlemen, put your hands together for our new president, Aura Zarling!" Her image was projected on the screen.

A roar of applause went up from the audience.

The new leader's voice boomed over the loudspeaker, "Thank you, my people. Thank you for the trust you placed in me." She went on to speak about autonomy and defending people's rights.

"The NLPs impoverished you. I'm here to change that. Solime and the other union nations will never give us our fair share. We need to stand on our own two feet. We need a redistribution of wealth, but some groups, like Human Rights for All, oppose this," Aura said.

The crowd cheered. Behind Piter, someone shouted, "Get that asshole!"

Before he had time to react, a punch to the back of the head sent Piter sprawling into the people in front. He fell to the ground. Someone stepped on his hand and his leg. He was kicked in the ribs. "Argh!" Things moved too quickly to process. Afraid the raging mob would kill him, he struggled to stand. Piter regained his footing just in time to see the sign he was carrying used as a weapon against him. He raised his hands, but too late. The end of the wooden handle caught him in the forehead. Dazed, he staggered, but managed to stay on his feet and push his way into the throng.

Two security officers shoved their way through the crowd towards him. "Stop!" they shouted.

Piter held his hand to his bleeding head. He wondered if the cops were yelling at him or the people beating him up.

"Grab that guy. Don't let him escape!" yelled a security officer.

Someone grabbed onto his shirt, but Piter pulled out of his grasp. He was strong and pushed his way through the multitude. He ducked behind a noisy group of people and hid. Knowing he could be easily spotted because of his height, he ducked and took furtive glances around the many writhing bodies, watching for the police.

The police gave up their search, so Piter squeezed through the press of people, off the government grounds and across the road. Behind him, Aura's voice grew fainter. He glanced around to be sure he wasn't being followed and pressed his hand to his head to stop the bleeding. *Didn't lose consciousness. Not a concussion.*

Aura Zarling looked at him from an election sign that had been erected on a front lawn, her arms reaching out as if she wanted a hug. "Aura Zarling for a bright and prosperous future." He continued walking along the almost deserted sidewalk and read another sign. "Believe in Aura," and then another sign, where she was pictured standing behind an old man with her hand on his shoulder, "Aura will alleviate suffering."

Piter climbed onto a bus, dropped some coins into the fare box and ignored the stares from fellow passengers. He took his bloodied hand from his head and wiped it on his shirt. Warm drops of blood rolled down his face. A ten-minute ride brought him to the Ackim Free Clinic. Piter bypassed the people standing in line and entered the crammed waiting room.

A television hung in the corner of the room, broadcasting President Zarling's live speech. All eyes in the room were focused on the screen. A wounded man coming into the clinic with his shirt covered in blood was not enough to raise anyone's eyebrows.

From the television, the president shouted, "Corrupt church leaders talk to you about sin. They are hypocrites! What about their extra-marital affairs? The squandering of church money? Their abuse of children? Who are they to tell you how to behave? They use guilt, making you cling to the belief there is a reward waiting for you in heaven, or punishment in hell. I think God would be glad we're trying to make a better world."

A man grabbed Piter's arm. "Hey, mister! You can't just budge in line!"

Piter pulled away from him.

Aura Zarling continued to speak from the television. "It will be a hard struggle, but we will emerge, like a chick from an egg, and grow into a strong, fierce hawk. I have seen a bright new future and promise to lead you to the land of prosperity. United we are strong. The people will triumph!"

The people in the waiting room clapped; their faces were smiling and hopeful.

A student nurse sitting at the reception desk looked up when Piter entered. "Dr. Dram, what happened?"

He waved at her to follow him and pushed open the door of an exam room and sat on the bed. "It looks worse than it is. Tell Dr. Jeniver I need stitches."

"She's at the speech. How did this happen?"

"I hit my head. Not here? She left the office with no doctor in charge? You're going to have to stitch me."

"I've only done it once before. Besides, we're out of Lidocaine. It will hurt. Wait until Dr. Jeniver gets back."

He sat on the exam table, closed his eyes and took a deep breath. "No time. Hurry." He flinched as she poked the needle into his forehead and drew the suture through.

"Were you at the speech?" she asked.

"No, missed it." He clenched his teeth as the needle poked his skin again. "Ouch," said Piter as the needle stabbed him.

"Sorry, Dr. Dram. Last one." She pulled the last suture through his skin and tied it off.

He stood in the mirror for a closer look. "Not bad. Thanks." He went to the washroom, removed his shirt and attempted to wash off the blood. He tensed when he heard voices from the waiting room. Peeking around the corner he didn't see anyone other than patients. Piter put his white lab coat over his bare skin. He fidgeted with the buttons, all his senses alert, and sneaked out the back door.

CHAPTER ELEVEN

A Civilized Society

Piter opened the window and took a deep breath, happy to live now in a safe neighbourhood and in an undamaged building. The autumn air had a frosty smell. The "extra" work he had taken on meant no more struggling to pay for essentials.

Aura Zarling was in office four months when it was announced on the evening news that physician-assisted suicide would be legalized. He sat down on the couch beside Yun and put his arm around her shoulder. "More good than bad will come of this if people are relieved of unnecessary suffering."

Yun clutched at her sweater, closing it at her throat. "I'm afraid, Piter. Trying to regulate euthanasia won't work. You can't stop a boulder once it's already crashing down a hill. I think you should call it what it really is: a ticket to kill the helpless."

"Don't worry. They're not going to just go around killing people. Don't listen to the fearmongers." He patted her on the top of the head. "It's going to be okay."

She batted his hand away. "Don't patronize me!"

He shook his head at her and tried not to raise his voice. "There you go again, getting all emotional and irrational."

"Argh!" She hit him with a seat cushion, went to the bedroom and slammed the door behind her.

Piter turned his eyes towards the television but didn't pay attention to any further news stories. He chewed his nails. *Let her be angry. She doesn't appreciate all the things I do.* Piter was filled with nervous energy and decided a brisk walk would make him feel better.

He stopped at a street corner, waiting for the light to change. A car pulled up beside him. Music streamed from its radio. Piter recognized it as Mozart Violin Concerto No. 3 in G Major. His father had tried to teach him to play violin, but Piter had given up after several years of lessons. The car drove off, taking the music with it.

Piter thought he must remind Yun to give his parents a phone call. They were getting older and he was concerned about them. Yun was better at small talk than him. He never knew what to say. His conversations with his parents usually ended with an argument. He was almost thirty and a married man, but they still tried to give him advice.

A breeze swirled brown fallen leaves into the air and deposited them in piles against fences and across roadways. His father, Hyron, used to send Piter and Hadar out to rake leaves in the fall. Together they filled black plastic bags and left them at the curb for the garbage collectors. Now, nobody bothered to pick up leaves. They crunched under Piter's shoes and blew into the gutter. They would soon clog the sewers and likely lead to street flooding issues, but he didn't care.

Piter walked by doorways covered in metal grills, the occupants' attempts to keep out thieves. A woman on the second floor of her apartment building harvested potatoes from a tiny balcony garden. Overwatering had left slimy drools of mud on the side of the building beneath her garden. From another balcony, a little boy's face peeked through the bars and watched Piter walk past. Piter noticed a bolt securing the balcony to the side of the concrete was loose. He hoped the child wouldn't fall.

In a small alleyway between the buildings, three garbage pickers, two men and one woman, were collecting paper, cardboard and wood. The woman opened a paper bag from a restaurant, put it towards her face, sniffed and put the bag in a shopping cart.

Piter wasn't paying attention to his surroundings and found himself in the slums. Everywhere, ragged clothes hung from lines between balconies and dripped to the sidewalk. Bare-bottomed toddlers wandered the streets. A little girl dragged a doll by its scraggly yellow hair. A boy carried an empty soda bottle.

Graffiti covered walls. Piter couldn't make sense of most the spray-painted symbols, but on the outside of one door were words he understood, "Will do anything for crank." A woman sat on a chair beside the door. She wore short shorts over her skinny bum and a black bikini top over her small breasts, shivering in the cool breeze. Her skin was covered in scabs and ulcers. Beside her stood a little girl, three or four years old, in oversized shoes. The child looked up at Piter with large, accusing eyes.

Piter wished he had never left the house. This decrepit neighbourhood did nothing to improve his mood. He quickened his pace, feeling worse than before.

Two men came forward and blocked Piter's path in the middle of the sidewalk. A man with a pockmarked face blew smoke through pursed lips. Squinting, he flicked the butt away. "Want something, mister? Looking to buy?"

Pockmark's companion looked at Piter from beneath a peaked cap.

"No." Piter noticed the knife.

"Give me your wallet," said Pockmark.

Piter took a step back, ready to defend himself.

"Let him be," said his companion. "This guy's a doctor down at the clinic."

Pockmark put his knife away. "You'd better go home, Doc. It's not safe in this neighbourhood."

Piter quick-walked all the way home.

§

At work the next day, Piter opened the newspaper. "Courts to decide on PAS and Euthanasia Guidelines."

He sat down at his desk and read the morning paper:

> *Laws that once banned assisted dying have led Covonans with terminal illnesses to suicide, sometimes violently. These terrible tragedies devastate families and scar first responders. It's time to stop the needless trauma. Government has no place in the death rooms of the nation.*
>
> *We are a compassionate society. We allow our citizens choice. It is cruel to deny a suffering person an easy death when they are already dying. Suffering serves no purpose.*

> *Competent adults may consent to termination*
> *of life if they suffer from a grievous and irremediable*
> *medical condition that causes enduring suffering that is*
> *intolerable to the person.*
>
> *New Quietus/Recycling/Research Centres*
> *will be opened, one in each major city in the country:*
> *Ackim, Covona City, Ducor, Citron and Okenfreim.*

The guideline went on to recommend doctors stop using negative terminology, like euthanasia, suicide and death. Instead they were to say, "assisted dying" and instead of death, call the moment when someone ceased to be alive: "Quietus—a time of happy release, to be discharged and freed from the stresses and pain of existence."

§

In the morning, a woman hobbled into Piter's office, leaning on a cane. "My arthritis is so bad I can hardly walk," she said.

He wrote on a prescription pad for some pain medication.

She waved the paper away. "You know I can't afford that stuff."

"Try taking warm baths, to ease the pain."

"Can't. My gas bills are already through the roof. Not much a pensioner can do." She rubbed her swollen knee.

"What would you like me to do for you?"

"I think it's about time I went to one of those QRR Centres."

"This is your only option?"

Her eyes filled with tears. "I'd like to see my grandchildren grow up, but the pain is intolerable. I can barely manage to make myself a cup of tea in the morning. What good am I?"

Piter put down his prescription pad and picked up a referral form. He cleared his throat. "Are you sure this is what you want?"

The woman nodded and looked out the window. A gust of wind blew brown leaves off a tree and they fluttered through the air. "Fall is a beautiful season, which only means winter is coming, with its bone-chilling cold."

Piter's hand shook as his signed his name.

[65]

Piter's next patient said, "Dad had a stroke. He can no longer feed himself or control his bowels. We just can't take care of him."

The old man sat in a wheelchair, his left arm limp, his head tilted to one side. Piter squatted down and put his hand on the man's arm, looking him in the eye. "What do you want me to do?"

"We want you to send him to a QRR Centre," the son interjected.

"Is that what you want?" Piter asked the old man.

The old man grunted, raised his right arm and waved it in front of his face.

"No use talking to him. He doesn't understand."

Piter stood, never taking his eyes off the old man. "That would probably be best." He signed the requisition form.

The old man grunted again and his eyes filled with tears.

Before the morning was done, Piter had signed eight requisition forms. Later, over his sandwich and coffee, he reread the guidelines for referring patients to Quietus. "Grievous and irremediable medical condition" could mean stage-four terminal cancer, but it could also mean blindness or even depression. He scratched his head. He knew why the government was working so hard to promote Quietus—to save money. Piter felt like that cartoon drawing of a distressed man with an angel on one shoulder and a devil on the other. He pressed his palms on his eyes.

That afternoon, Piter diagnosed a patient as having Parkinson's disease. The daughter asked, "What sort of treatments are available? Can I put Mom on a list for extended care?"

Piter shook his head. "The few extended care spots are expensive, beyond your means." Though the disease was not yet advanced, he handed the woman a requisition for admittance to a Quietus Centre, "To be used at a time when you see fit," and hustled her out of the door.

§

Five months had passed since the election. Piter sat in his new armchair and picked up the newspaper, eager to see who Aura Zarling appointed as her ministers. "All the government appointments seem to be connected to the president in some way, Yun."

Yun was sitting at the kitchen table marking students' assignments. She came and leaned on the back of his chair to read over his shoulder. "Aura picked General Bont as Vice-President. That's a little scary. He'll assume control if Aura Zarling is ever incapacitated," she said.

He smelled cheap soap on her skin and wondered if he should buy her some perfume, though she'd probably complain about the expense, just as she had about the chair. "Burna Oret is now Minister of Education. Here's what she says: 'Private educational facilities and homeschooling are contrary to the ideals of this country. The federal Minister of Education will oversee all educational decisions.'

"The owner of the largest hotel chain in the country was named the Minister of Foreign Affairs. Wait, this is something new. All churches will come under the control of the Minister of Spiritual Welfare, Kriston Boals. 'Churches today are divided. That is not the Covonan way. We will join as one people, one state, in the Light of Aura Church.' You should join."

Yun's mouth dropped open. "Like hell I will."

He tapped the article. "But, Yun, they're willing to work in conjunction with established churches. Their only demand is that all the churches fall under the direction of the Minister of Spiritual Welfare."

"Don't be so naïve. Then there would be no freedom of religion." Yun returned to the kitchen table, scraped the wooden chair across the linoleum and sat down.

CHAPTER TWELVE

A New Air of Optimism

Tresha quick-walked with a newspaper under her arm. She was eager to show Fillip her front-page article, her first in a long time. The headline screamed: "Covona Embraces New Air of Optimism." The article praised Aura's initiative to make unemployment a thing of the past in Covona.

A woman approached. Dead leaves clung to her trousers from the pile where she had been sitting. Her outstretched hand was red with cold, the nails dirty. A line of mucus ran from her nose to lip. Matted hair hung in her eyes. "Can you spare a few frezens?"

Tresha gave her a few coins and a tissue.

The woman wiped her nose and discarded the tissue on the sidewalk.

A man slept cross-legged on the sidewalk, his back against the wall and bare hands tucked into his armpits. His stubbly chin rested on his chest. An upturned empty hat, its rim coated with a crust of frost, sat on the sidewalk in front of him. He was taking a chance by falling asleep with police patrolling the street. Tresha averted her eyes and took a wide berth around the beggar. Sure enough, the police stopped, roused the homeless man and shoved him into the van.

Tresha arrived home and opened the door. "Fillip! Have you seen the paper today?" She couldn't wait to see his reaction. *He'll be so proud of me.*

"Oh, you're home. Look at this." He pointed to the television.

The voice of the Minister of Infrastructure blared from the T.V. "Stay the course, fellow Covonans. The Freedom Party will soon initiate work projects to beautify our cities."

She held her chin high and dropped the paper on Fillip's lap. "Did you see the paper today?"

He read the headline and tossed it aside. "Pure nonsense. Despicable Freedom Party." He switched off the television.

"But, Fillip, I wrote the article."

He picked up the paper again and read. "You wrote this? Do you really believe this?" His face was grim.

"Why not? I saw the police pick up a panhandler on my way home from work. He looked so cold. At least he'll have a warm place to sleep and free meals."

"He'd be happier on the street. They'll send him to labour camp," Fillip said.

"Work projects are a good idea." She sat on the arm of the couch beside him. "Make the bums pay their own way. Less dependence on the state."

"I don't believe I'm hearing this from you. They're using the unemployed as slave labour. Don't you think they deserve a decent wage? You bowed to pressure from your editor, didn't you?"

She hesitated. "I have to make a living. What am I supposed to do?"

"You're a reporter. You're snoopy. Someone is getting rich from this city beautification scheme. Follow the money trail."

"I'm not snoopy!" She punched him lightly on the shoulder. "I'm curious. And what you're suggesting is dangerous."

He dropped the paper in the trash. "Then just keep on spreading government propaganda."

"Fillip! You know I have no choice!"

He shrugged and left the room. Tresha closed her eyes, not wanting to consider the possibilities, but realized she must write the difficult news stories and face the consequences as they happened.

§

As the weeks passed, Tresha documented the demolition of decrepit buildings in Ackim. Gangs of labour camp workers dressed in orange outfits cleared the rubble in preparation for construction of new buildings. She watched them from the window of her office and was distressed to see so many men and women, their eyes empty and hopeless, lifting pieces of concrete with their bare hands.

Tresha investigated the prison situation in Covona, interviewed struggling families whose only breadwinner was in labour camp, and heard stories of the terrible condition inside the camps. The pieces never saw print. Raimond told her they were too negative.

She reported on a train that had jumped the tracks, spilling thousands of litres of oil. Raimond said the government-owned railway company would raise objections if this was made public and refused to print it. Instead of giving up, Tresha decided to contact some of her trusted sources and investigate corruption in big business.

"I could be arrested just for having the information," she told Fillip at supper one night.

"What have you discovered?" Fillip leaned forward.

"Their only concern is their investors. Here's just a few examples. Zarling Oil and Gas won't allow imports of foreign oil. They can then charge the consumers in Covona whatever they want. Because the price of oil and gas is so high, it's too expensive for transport companies to make a profit. They're forced to sell everything to Zarling Transport at rock-bottom prices. There are rumours Zarling Hotels put rats and bed bugs in the competition's hotels, forcing them to close. There are insider trading schemes."

"Go to the police."

She gripped her knife in a tight fist. "I can't betray my sources. They would lose their jobs, or worse. Other reporters won't touch these stories."

"Frustrating," Fillip said. "I'm proud of you for doing this."

"The poverty rate in this country is at an all-time high." She poked a carrot with her fork. "Many Covonans are fleeing to Solime to find a new life. Did you know we will soon all have to turn in our passports and the borders will be closed? There are rumours Zarling wants to build a wall to keep us in."

"Unbelievable. Now, at least, we know," Fillip said.

"What good does it do? No controversial reports are printed. Even if they were, people want so badly for Aura to be the messiah, they wouldn't believe me. The Freedom Party would find a way to shush me, maybe permanently. I'm being slowly strangled."

Tresha's father sat in his wheelchair and listened to the exchange. He spoke in his slow, halting speech. "You need to take the information to Solime."

"What good would that do, Dad?"

"Maybe they'll help. They used to be our allies. I'm a veteran, remember? I fought side by side with Solimese soldiers for freedoms that are being thrown away in this country."

"I agree, Dad, but the borders will soon be closed." Tresha felt discouraged. "At the paper, access to international news isn't what it used to be. So many restrictions. We can report on how things are improving, but nothing negative."

Fillip perked up. "You still have access to world news."

Tresha paused for a moment to consider. "Some."

"More than the average person. You can be the eyes and ears of HRFA."

"I'm afraid."

"I know, but to sit back and do nothing makes us complicit."

Tresha stirred the beans on her plate and said nothing more.

§

A month later, and without any consultation with the public, construction began on a wall to separate Covona from Solime.

Raimond approached Tresha one morning. "I have exciting news for you. I'm sending you to report on the progress of the wall with one of our photographers. The two of you will make a minidocumentary to be shown nationwide. Make it sound positive, but hint at the dire consequences if anyone tries to leave the country."

"Oh?"

"Why the sour face? I thought you'd be pleased. Think of what this could do for your career."

She whispered, "How do I make a wall sound positive?"

"It's your job to quell people's fears. Use comforting words. I shouldn't have to teach you how to write."

"I feel like a liar."

[71]

"You don't need to lie. Just don't elaborate on every detail." Raimond squeezed her shoulder. "Don't disappoint me."

§

Tresha sat behind the wheel of the Ackim City News van, but it took much longer to arrive at the destination than she had anticipated. The road to the western border was clogged with construction vehicles and traffic moved at a snail's pace. She and the cameraman were stuck amid a convoy of flatbed trucks bearing huge slabs of concrete and steel girders. There were cement mixers, earthmovers, backhoes, forklifts, graders and excavators.

Tresha and a photographer arrived at the western border between Covona and Solime after many hours of driving. She wore a light jacket to cut the wind and tied a kerchief over her hair. The cameraman carried the shoulder-mounted camera. Tresha carried the microphone.

"The Wall of Aura is under construction. Drilling machines pound the ground." She had to shout to the photographer over the clamour. "See if you can shoot the wall from different angles to try to capture the size." The cameraman panned the partly finished wall, slabs of concrete as far as the eye could see. Hundreds of construction workers were on site. It was easy to distinguish between paid and slave labour in bright orange jumpsuits.

A Solimese plane flew parallel to the wall. Tresha gazed at the strip of disputed land between the countries. Solime's fence and Covona's wall drew two parallel lines stretching into the distance.

"Look at this," the cameraman said, as he focused his lens on a man in an orange jumpsuit splayed on the ground. The prisoner was laid on a stretcher and taken away on the back of a pick-up truck.

Tresha later tried to interview the foreman of the construction site. "How many have died so far constructing this wall?"

The foreman turned on his heel and walked away.

§

Tresha and the photographer flew to the east coast to report on the construction of the fence along the eastern seawall. Its purpose was to prevent people from escaping the country by boat. She walked along the beach, keeping her distance from the eight-foot-high buzzing electric fence. The fence blocked access to beaches to all except fishermen. Fishing vessels were inspected before leaving port to prevent people escaping by sea. Hundreds of sea birds, dead from electric shock, littered the sandy beach. A group of men in orange jumpsuits walked along the beach, stuffing the decomposing birds into black garbage bags.

§

After visiting the wall and electric fence and carefully editing the video to ensure no people in orange jumpsuits or dead birds were in the shots, Tresha sat down to write the script of her documentary. Tresha rose from her desk, paced the room and sat down again, ran her fingers through her hair and then typed.

> *Let's not look at the Wall of Aura as something to keep us in, but to protect us from covetous invaders who want what we have. Our beloved president cares deeply about the people of this country. Aura Zarling is never wrong and rarely has doubts. Don't think too much, but trust her to lead us to a better time. For your safety it's important for citizens to remain in Covona, unless you are given special permission to leave.*
>
> *To the north, the Keque Mountains between Covona and Dule and Sura are almost impassable. No one should dare go south, into Asciary with their terrible human rights violations. Every exit out of the country is blocked. We Covonans are prisoners in our own country. Disobedience of the law will not be tolerated.*

She gave the copy to Raimond for his approval. He reviewed the half-hour video and nodded his head. "It needs some sanitizing. Remove the part about us being prisoners. Emphasize how much our president loves us. Add a paragraph that informs people it is their duty to watch the news and read the paper. The president wants the population to stay informed."

To stay propagandized, you mean.

CHAPTER THIRTEEN

The Mercy of Quietus

All citizens were encouraged to watch television news and read the newspaper daily. Piter leaned in to watch Tresha on television in a media scrum with General Bont, the Minister of Health and President Zarling. Yun slumbered, her head on his lap.

Aura Zarling stood in the background wearing a black suit and a self-satisfied expression while General Bont spoke:

"The Freedom Party will from this day be called AZEN, Aura Zarling's Enlightened Nationalists.

"Be aware. Police now have more discretion to use whatever force necessary to enforce the law. Loyal business owners will hang the symbol of Aura Zarling's Enlightened Nationalists in the windows of their businesses." He displayed the sign. It was an uppercase "A" with a vertical arrow intersecting the middle, which pointed to the words, "Aspire! Battle! Conquer!"

"Any questions?" he asked.

The crowd of reporters shouted at once.

"Tresha has a question," Aura said, pointing to the audience of reporters.

"Your slogan suggests a military fervour," Tresha said. "Who are you planning to battle and conquer? Are we going to war?"

General Bont said, "This country is committed to peaceful existence with our neighbours. We aim to control the radical faction within our borders who seek to undermine government and destroy the fabric of our society. Rest assured, AZEN cares about your safety."

"Ms. President," another reporter called out, "The Minister of Education, Burna Oret, announced that parents are no longer the primary educators of their children. That responsibility is now in the hands of the government. Many parents object. How will you answer them?"

Aura smiled and stepped up to the microphone. "We aspire to gain the hearts of the people. Simply trust AZEN to lead you towards a bold and prosperous future."

Several reporters shouted questions at the same time. Aura Zarling pointed to a different reporter.

"Ms. President, could parents be arrested for homeschooling their own children?"

The smile remained on Aura's face. "Covona is supreme in education. Our qualified teachers teach children to self-actualize, to become self-secure, selfless and self-optimizing. Tresha has another question."

"Where is Ex-President Jomb? He hasn't been seen in the House of Government for weeks."

"Ex-President Jomb has retired to a mountain retreat for health reasons. It's time for me to announce some good news. AZEN will take concrete measures to control our burgeoning population."

Piter woke Yun. "Sit up. Listen to this."

Yun wiped the sleep from her eyes and blinked at the television.

"I'll let the Minister of Health explain," Aura said.

Lydothy Dawen spoke into the microphone. "This program is aimed at women who have had two or more children." He pointed to a slick ad of a happy couple running hand in hand with a cute little girl and boy across a well-manicured lawn, with the slogan, "Control the Population."

"Starting immediately, low-income women, prostitutes and drug addicts will be paid to have tubal ligations."

Aura took the microphone back and, smiling her white-toothed smile, said, "AZEN cares about you. The amount of money we are offering is not insubstantial; as much as two months of wages for some."

Piter said, "I hope they understand state hospitals are chronically underfunded. I wonder how they'll keep up with demand."

"Don't know." Yun yawned. "I'm so tired all the time."

"You missed your last menstrual cycle. Any chance you're pregnant?"

Yun smiled. "Well, yes. I was going to wait to tell you when I knew for sure, but I think so."

Piter hugged her. "That's wonderful news. I'm so happy."

§

Piter's fears came true. Hospitals were besieged by desperate women seeking the procedure. Normal disinfection procedures were often neglected and many women developed infections. This could have been another public relations nightmare, except the public never heard about it. Health care workers were afraid to speak up, and news stations were afraid to report the truth. Tresha told Piter she and her co-workers were threatened with jail time if any of the abominations were made public.

Piter overheard bits of conversation between his patients:

"Good thing prostitutes and drug addicts won't be able to bring more children into the world."

"Maybe they'll all die off. Good riddance to them."

"They're blights on society."

"People like that shouldn't be allowed to reproduce."

Knowing the truth, his heart was heavy as he went about his duties at the clinic.

§

As usual, the evening news began with encouraging words from Aura Zarling. Today's "Words to Live By" began with Aura walking across a lawn in front of her mansion. A dog hobbled beside her, its head down, tail between its legs. A light dusting of snow covered the grass. Piter sat back to enjoy a glass of ten-year-old port. Yun objected to spending money on such an extravagance. He was willing give up many things in these hard times, but wine was not one of them.

The camera focused in on Aura's face. Her eyes were wide and her mouth pouty. "Good evening, fellow Covonans. This is my dog, Max. He's been my faithful companion for twelve years." She stroked the golden retriever's head. "This poor guy suffers from arthritis, so I don't want him out in the cold for too long." She took a tissue from her pocket and dabbed her eyes. "Excuse me. I'm a little emotional today. His vet says he's suffering from cancer and the humane thing to do is put him down." Her lips trembled. "I'm sorry." She sniffled. "I bet some of you have animal or even human friends and family who suffer needlessly, like Max." She knelt in the snow and gently hugged the dog. "Don't worry, Max. The nice vet is waiting inside to put you out of your misery.

"Before we go, I want to tell you some good news. Now, anyone over the age of sixty-five can request Quietus, no questions asked. No longer do two doctors need to agree if you wish to end your suffering or that of your loved ones. Maybe you're just tired of living. Don't worry. No one can stand in your way. Let's be glad our citizens as well as our pets can enjoy a quick and painless passing. This government cares about you. Come, Max." She walked away. The dog followed slowly behind.

Piter gulped his wine. He sat back, a little stunned, remembering the Freedom Party's promise to alleviate suffering. With Yun expecting a baby, he needed extra income to care for his growing family. He had been practicing medicine at the Free Clinic for two years and was not much further ahead. He lifted his wine glass to his lips, forgetting he'd already finished it. Piter refilled the glass, wondering how long it would take to learn the euthanasia method if the need arose.

§

The day after Aura's announcement, a man in his seventies came to the clinic complaining of severe stomach pain. Piter felt the thin man's abdomen with his fingers, suspecting cancer, but was unable to confirm the disease because of the cost of the test. Even if it was determined to be cancer, this patient would not be able to afford the costly treatments. Poor citizens received next to no health care and the rich were favoured in every respect.

Piter said, "You need surgery. Some surgeons take charity cases. I can put your name on a waiting list and wait for an opening. I'm sorry to give you such bad news."

The thin man frowned. "You gotta do something for me, Doc. I don't want to die, but I can't take the pain no more."

"Painkillers are an option, but costly."

The man threw up his hands, looking like he might cry. "What good am I? Can't earn a living, sponging off my kid. He has a wife and little ones to look after. The kids see me in pain. They get upset. I can't hardly eat, can't sleep."

Piter knew where this conversation was going, but he didn't suggest the Quietus option. He liked to wait for patients to ask before he gave them a requisition.

"The president said you doctors got to help. I don't need to go to two doctors no more."

"I'll give you a requisition which you can take to the QRR Centre."

"I don't want to go to one of them damn places. I want to die at home with my family around me. You do it."

"A home euthanasia is possible, but I'm not licensed for that. Few doctors are. You'll have to wait about six months. Don't worry, they'll take good care of you at the QRR Centre."

"Please, Doc. I'm scared to go there. I've heard bad things about them."

"Like what?"

"Like they use people in experiments. I just want to die in my own bed. Please. Couldn't you do it for me? I'm afraid I can't pay you, but you could overdose me with something."

He'd heard of a weekend training course, after which he could obtain a license. Piter thought about Yun and the baby. This could be part-time job. They'd need more money when she could no longer work. "Let me consider that."

§

Later in the week, Piter went to a one-day training seminar to learn the proper procedure to administer Quietus. He listened to a presentation and watched a video. The procedure appeared to be efficient, simple and painless. The presenter warned that sometimes, due to patients' differing ability to tolerate the toxins, the procedure sometimes did not go smoothly. Another video showed a patient struggling to breathe for over twenty minutes, attempt to sit up, fight the doctor, babble incoherently and drool before the medicine took effect and he died of a heart attack.

Some of the doctors squirmed in their chairs. One young woman got up and left the room. Piter sat stone-still and watched, distancing his emotions. He wrote the test the same day so as to obtain his licence.

Only a week later Piter's licence to practice Physician-Assisted Suicide and Euthanasia came in the mail. "Practitioner of PASE." He went to the pharmacy to pick up a supply of life-ending drugs and carried them home in a large box. He placed the box in the front hall closet.

Yun looked at the box, reading the label. "Why are you storing medicine at home?"

Piter hoped she wouldn't recognize the names of the drugs. "We've had break-ins at the clinic. Don't want anything to happen to these." The truth was, he wanted to get an early start in the morning, do the job before going to the clinic. Piter avoided eye contact with his wife.

"What's wrong, Piter?"

"Nothing. I'm just tired."

"Are you sure?"

"I said, I'm just tired!"

After Yun went to bed, he stepped outside to use his cell phone. He called his patient and set an appointment for the following morning.

§

The next morning, before Yun went to work, she put her hands on Piter's arms and looked him in the eyes. "Something is bothering you."

"It's just work. You know how it is. So much pressure."

"I feel like you're not being truthful." She stepped back, folded her hands in front of her, and said in a small voice, "Is there someone else?"

"Yun! No! How could you think that?"

"Sorry. It's just—"

"I'm not having an affair." He kissed her on the lips.

"Good. That's what I thought." She stepped out the door on her way to work.

Piter checked his appearance in the mirror. It was important to look professional. He did up the top button on his shirt, adjusted the knot on his tie, checked to see his trousers were neatly pressed and brushed the lint from his suit jacket. He decided to walk the ten blocks to the patient's home, rather than take the bus, to dissipate nervous energy.

The neighbourhood where his patient lived was referred to as the "vertical slums," a row of densely populated, decaying high apartment buildings, one after the other. Not a tree or blade of grass could be seen.

Men sitting on doorsteps eyed him as he walked by. A woman bent over her washtub, straightened, looked him up and down, and narrowed her eyes. Two more women stopped their conversation and took a step back, fearful. Thin-faced children peeked at him from sooty windows. He imagined men in suits who frequented this neighbourhood were either here to collect rent or question someone.

Piter climbed seven flights of stairs, bypassing the broken elevator. He found unit 731, took a deep breath in through his nose and out of his mouth before knocking on the door.

A woman in her thirties answered, a baby on her hip.

"I'm Dr. Dram. Here to see your father-in-law."

Her eyes opened wide. "Oh. Come in."

She opened the door and Piter stepped into a dark apartment. All the windows, except one, were boarded up. He assumed the family was too poor to replace broken panes of glass. Evidence of water seepage marred the walls under the windows.

"He's in here." She opened a closet door and switched on the light. There was just enough room for a narrow bed and one wooden chair in the room. The bed was a nailed-together contraption covered by a wooden plank, a thin mattress and blankets. Piter's patient was curled into a ball, his face contorted in pain. "Doctor's here." She adjusted the baby to the other hip and touched her father-in-law's arm.

CHAPTER FOURTEEN

Quietus on Wheels

The walls of the sick man's tiny room were covered with cut-out pictures from magazines, scenes of beaches, forests and mountains. His son, daughter-in-law and three wide-eyed grandchildren were clustered around the bed.

"I taped up the pictures, hoped they'd make him feel better," his daughter-in-law said. She lowered her gaze, looking embarrassed. The corners of her mouth trembled as she fingered her necklace. The baby leaned his head against his mother's chest and sucked his thumb.

The kitchen faucet dripped like a distant heartbeat.

Piter touched the old man's arm. "Are you ready?"

The patient opened his eyes and nodded.

The son cleared his throat. "Dad, you sure?" He took a deep breath through his nose and pressed his lips together.

"I'm sure, Son. You'll be better off without me."

Piter retreated to the kitchen table to prepare the lethal ingredients and came back with two bags and two syringes. He handed one IV bag to the patient's son and gave the other to the woman. "Hold them high."

The woman held the bag above her head after handing the baby to her eldest child, a girl of about ten years.

Piter found veins in the bends of the patient's arms and taped the needles to his skin. He showed the old man how to start the drip. "Whenever you're ready, flip this up." Piter sidestepped out of the crowded room so the family could say goodbye in private.

The family blocked Piter's view. He heard low, murmuring voices and quiet weeping. Ten minutes later they emerged, their eyes red and swollen.

Piter entered the room to retrieve his equipment. "I'll call Recycling to pick up the body."

The son thanked him, put his hand on Piter's shoulder. "It was for the best, right? We couldn't afford chemo. We didn't want him to suffer."

Piter nodded. He had expected to feel torn, sad and maybe remorseful after his first PAS. Instead, he felt a rush of adrenaline and suppressed a smile.

After his first PAS, Piter received an average of one request per day. He was given a truck to drive with the logo "Quietus on Wheels." At the end of two weeks, Piter had assisted in ten more suicides. Not only did it become easier each time, but Piter began to look forward to the procedures. He would never admit it to anyone, but the thrill of taking a life was almost sexual for him. He was preforming a magic trick. *Nothing up my sleeve. Presto! You're dead.*

§

A phone call came for a woman afflicted with Alzheimer's disease. Piter was not sure of the legality of the request because it had not come from the patient.

"If she's not of sound mind she can't make such a decision," Piter told the son on the phone.

"Listen, Doctor Dram. My mom nearly set the house on fire, twice. I can't afford to have someone stay home and look after her. She's constantly wandering off when I'm at work. She has heart disease, is incontinent and she fights when I try to care for her. What son wants to change his mother's diaper?"

"I'll come tonight and see you, but no promises. I'll make a judgement call when I get there."

§

That evening, a middle-aged man opened the door. "Mom's on the couch."

The old woman seemed to know his intent the minute Piter walked in the door. "Get the hell out of my home, you monster!"

[83]

Piter came and sat beside her on the couch and put on his hand on hers, about to ask her feelings on physician-assisted suicide. She pulled her hand away, got off the couch and made a slow, stiff-legged dash for the door.

Piter hesitated. "If she doesn't want to die, I can't go against her wishes."

"Doctor Dram," said the son. "She's completely demented. I can't take care of her. You gotta help me." He ran ahead and put his hand on the door, holding it shut as his mother pulled on the handle. "Mom, please sit down and let the doctor take care of you." He grabbed her upper arms.

"Just wait until I tell your father what you're up to." She tried to wiggle her skinny arms from her son's tight grasp. She pounded her small fists against his chest.

"Dad died five years ago, remember, Mom?"

"No! You're hiding him from me," the woman screamed.

Still, Piter did not rise from the couch. He sat watching the pathetic struggle between mother and son.

"You see what we have to deal with every day?"

The law required the request for Quietus be made in writing, signed and dated by the person, but if the person requesting death was unable to sign, another adult, who understood the request, could do so in their place. Piter made up his mind. "I will do it, but we'll say it was your mother's decision. Agreed?"

"Yes."

Piter made the man sign a statement saying he heard his mother request Quietus. "You're going to have to hold her still."

The two men lifted the old woman up, one under her arms and the other by the ankles, and carried her to the bedroom. She wiggled and squirmed. The son held her down on the bed while Piter prepared the intravenous.

She kicked her legs and screamed, "Help! Help! Murder!"

Piter's heart thumped. He had difficulty finding a vein on the squirming woman and he missed several times, poking her in the wrong spot.

[84]

She winced and started to cry, looking at Piter with pleading eyes. "Please stop."

Deep inside, Piter felt something was wrong with this scenario, but it was too late to stop. The papers had been signed. *It's only natural for her to fight. That's instinct.* "I'll give her a sedative." He prepared a syringe and poked it into the muscle of her arm.

"God help me," she screamed. A few minutes later her body relaxed. Her eyes moved back and forth, watching the men. A line of drool dribbled from the corner of her mouth.

Piter was then able to prepare the intravenous lethal injection.

Everything was ready. All that was needed was for someone to start the drip. He stepped back.

"What are you waiting for, Doctor? Let's get this over with."

Piter's heart raced. *Of course, she can't do it herself. I can't expect the...* Piter forced his feet forward and flipped the switch, allowing the poison to enter the woman's veins. Tears leaked from her eyes, but she made no sound. Her breathing slowed. Two minutes later, she took one final gasp of air and let it out with a groan.

"Quietus comes," Piter said.

Her son stepped away, placed his hands on his hips and looked up at the ceiling. He wiped spittle from his mouth and flopped onto the couch in the other room.

Piter's armpits felt wet. He stood over the deceased woman—her eyes wide and mouth open, as if screaming silently.

He wrote a death certificate, but his hand trembled at the signature. "I'll call Recycling to take the body away."

Piter started the engine of the Quietus on Wheels vehicle but didn't put it in gear right away. He recalled something Fillip used to say, *People fear suffering, so they try to avoid it. The more they try to avoid it, the more they fear it. The vicious cycle gets worse until they try to control suffering by destroying the sufferer.*

"When you're right, you're right, Fillip, you old bastard," Piter said out loud and then smiled, feeling a rush of energy that he couldn't quite explain. He laughed, and realizing he sounded maniacal, he laughed

[85]

all the harder. His hysterical laughter was interrupted by a call on his cell phone.

"Dr. Dram, your services are required at the Ackim labour camp. The camp doesn't have a refrigeration unit and all our recycling trucks are busy. We'd appreciate it you'd also transport the corpses to the recycling centre. You don't mind, do you?"

Piter knew "we'd appreciate" was an order. Whether he minded or not was inconsequential. "Of course. Not a problem."

§

The camp was located about one hour west of the city, on a railway line. A four-metre-high electrical fence surrounded the compound. Outside, a dump truck unloaded a pile of gravel onto the road. A group of ragged men set to work, shovelling the gravel from the pile onto the road. A roller followed slowly behind, flattening the gravel down. Armed guards watched from the roadside. The group of prisoners stepped aside and took a moment to lean on their shovels while Piter drove by.

He showed identification at the gate, proceeded in and looked for the main office building amid row upon row of identical one-storey dormitories. He drove towards the one building displaying the flag of AZEN.

A uniformed man seated at a desk gave Piter directions to the prison hospital. "The building furthest south."

"May I ask why I've been called here?" Piter looked at the man.

The uniformed man squinted his eyes at Piter. "We have three on death's door. Thought you'd be the one to hurry them along."

"Yes, of course."

"How many corpses can you fit?" The soldier pointed to the Quietus on Wheels truck.

"Four. More if we remove the pallets."

"We have two in storage. I'm afraid one's a bit ripe already."

"Not a problem," said Piter. "Pile them one on top of the other. I'll drop them at Recycling."

§

Piter euthanized the three men. Two were already unconscious and one was in so much pain he almost looked relieved to see the eradication doctor. *I'll have to get a new name tag. Beneficent Executioner. Yes, I like the sound of that.*

While he waited for the dead to be collected and loaded into the truck, Piter took a walk around the compound. Through open doors he saw beds made from planks of wood covered with blankets. Electrical wires were strung from one dormitory to the next with a single electric bulb hanging from the ceiling. Some indoor walls were covered in cardboard.

He passed by the mess hall, heavy with the smell of potatoes and onions. A shirtless man, his chest wet with sweat, stood over a huge steaming pot stirring with a giant ladle. The ceiling above the cook was black from smoke.

He returned to his vehicle and despite the temperature hovering around zero Celsius, he rolled down the windows. The smell of decomposing bodies was overpowering.

CHAPTER FIFTEEN

Who is Loyal to AZEN?

Dr. Poil's eyes glistened with excitement on his first day of work. The new physician stood in the reception area of the free clinic as patients poured in the door and lined up to take a number. He was jittery with excitement as he told Piter of his plans to improve the lives of the poor in the neighbourhood. "We could open community kitchens and teach people how to cook nourishing meals."

"Perhaps." Piter was loath to dissuade the idealistic young man but thought the idea unrealistic. He stepped around Dr. Poil.

"We could open a recreation centre for young people to keep them off the streets." Dr. Poil followed Dr. Dram from the reception area to an examination room. "It wouldn't cost much. There are lots of abandoned buildings. We could apply for permission to use them, ask for donations of balls and equipment. They could play basketball..."

"While I applaud your motives, I don't think—"

"Don't give up without even trying," Dr. Poil said.

The phone rang. "Dr. Dram, it's for you," said the student nurse.

Piter breathed a sigh of relief and held up one finger, interrupting Dr. Poil's ramblings. "Excuse me. Gotta take this."

The call was from the warden of the city prison. "We require an eradicator tomorrow at the prison. Are you available?"

"Not sure I'm comfortable with an execution."

"The pay is double, but you must swear to speak of this to no one."

"Who is the condemned?"

"That's none of your concern, Dr. Dram. The AZEN courts have decided this man is a traitor. What is your reason for asking?"

The threatening tone in the man's voice made Piter stumble over his words. "I was just...that is, I've never...um, no reason. I'll be there tomorrow." Piter hung up the phone, wiped his sweaty hands on his trousers and then opened the door to see his first patient.

Quietus

§

Piter arrived at the Ackim City Prison before sunrise and followed a guard to the prison hospital located in the basement. Down the hall from the infirmary, where the sick lay shackled to their beds, was a small operating theatre. He had expected the room to look like a death chamber. Instead it was a typical operating room. The protocol here was stricter than a home euthanasia. Dr. Dram was expected to scrub in, to wash his hands and forearms thoroughly. The sharp smell of disinfectant soap rose in the air as he brushed under his fingernails. Piter wondered why this was necessary. It wouldn't matter if the condemned man got an infection. He was destined to die. Piter then dressed in a hospital gown, surgical cap, mask and rubber gloves before entering a brightly lit room.

The operating room had a gloomy feel to it, despite the overhead lamps, as if too much tragedy had passed in and out of the swinging doors. A narrow bed with wrist and leg restraints occupied the centre of the room. Beside it stood an IV pole.

At the head of the bed was an electronic monitor to measure heart and respiratory rate. The pulse oximeter stood ready, as did automated blood pressure gages. Piter checked to see everything was in order: Two bags hung from the pole—one filled with saline and the other with a powerful barbiturate, pentobarbital. The necessary needles had been prepared for him and were arranged on a tray on a small stainless-steel table. One syringe was filled with a muscle relaxant, pancuronium bromide, and the other with potassium chloride, to stop the heart. Normally, Piter would have measured the doses himself. *I guess this is the way things are done here.* He rolled the table beside the bed. Piter found a spot by the table and waited.

From outside the room came the sound of rattling chains. The doors banged open. Two guards, wearing masks, entered, followed by a potbellied, balding man who shuffled into the room wearing ankle shackles and handcuffs.

Piter recognized him as one of President Jomb's former advisors. The advisor was an outspoken critic of AZEN's euthanasia policies and had often rallied on behalf of doctors' freedom of conscience. "Doctors should not become hired assassins," the advisor had said. The underarms of his prison uniform were wet with sweat. Behind him were two more armed guards who waited outside the swinging doors. Piter avoided eye contact with the scared, middle-aged man.

A guard unlocked the man's restraints. "Get on the table."

The man obeyed.

"Lie down," the guard said.

The guards bound the condemned man's ankles to the table. His arms were stretched out, like he was about to be crucified, and secured with straps. His heavy breathing was the loudest sound in the room. Another strap was placed across his forehead, preventing him from lifting his head. The former advisor didn't fight, yell or curse his executioners as Piter had expected. Instead, his chubby face was resigned. He looked at Piter with wide eyes—innocent and almost childlike.

The backs of the heads of the two guards who stood outside the operating room were visible through the round windows. Two more guards stood inside the operating theatre, arms crossed.

Piter checked again. Everything was ready. He tied a rubber tube around the man's upper arm. "Any last words?"

"I don't regret anything. I vowed to fight until my last breath for what is right. Why are you here?"

Piter said nothing as he felt for a vein in the man's inner elbow. The condemned man continued talking.

"One day the people in this country will rise up and AZEN will be a thing of the past. Nothing will be left but a stain on Covona's history."

"The world is changing, sir," Piter said. "We all must adapt, or die."

"The truth has a way of making itself known, Doctor. I regret nothing."

Piter wanted to explain this was not the life he had envisioned, and if he had a better choice…but instead, kept his mouth shut and inserted intravenous needles into each of the man's arms. He attached the plastic tubes to the bags that hung over the bed, and started the saline drip.

The man turned his pale blue eyes to the ceiling. "Forgive us our trespasses as we forgive those who trespass against us—"

Though it wasn't necessary, Piter put an oxygen mask over the man's face in hopes it would make the man be quiet. He failed. The prayers, now muffled, continued.

Next, he connected probes on the EKG machine to the condemned man's chest and attached the blood pressure cuff. It measured 180/120, which was not surprising. The frightened man's heart was racing. Piter reached for one of the tubes, took a deep breath and said, "This will make you sleep." Piter started the second drip and, within seconds, the man's eyes closed. The heart monitor showed the heart rate of someone asleep.

Piter picked up a syringe filled with pancuronium to paralyze the diaphragm. He injected it into the port of the plastic tubing that ran to the man's vein. The condemned man stopped breathing. His lips turned blue. Piter watched the oxygen saturation levels decrease on the monitor from 99% to 79%. Finally, he injected the lethal dose of potassium chloride. "Quietus comes," he said.

Without warning, the former advisor gasped, opened his eyes and looked directly at Piter. Piter was startled. This wasn't normal! He picked up the empty syringes and re-checked that the correct dosage of each drug was given.

A minute passed. The EKG should have shown a flat line! Instead, it indicated the condemned man was suffering an intense heart attack. He moaned. His chest heaved. He wheezed and strained against his straps.

"He's getting air," Piter said. "The diaphragm ought to be paralyzed! He should be unconscious."

The former advisor's face was red and his tongue hung from his mouth as if he was strangling. He arched his back.

The guards stepped forward and stood beside the bed, hands on their hips, and watched.

"Without anesthesia, KCl poisoning is excruciatingly painful, literally burns up the veins as it travels to the heart," Piter said.

"You want us to do something, Doc?" asked one of the guards.

The other guard averted his eyes from the man on the table.

"No." Piter felt woozy. He wiped his forehead on his sleeve, saw the oxygen saturation in the man's blood had risen to 88%. *No! Too high.* The blood pressure had shot up again. He watched the man struggle for another minute before dying.

Piter's hands shook as he slowly removed the intravenous and other medical equipment from the dead man. He felt light-headed. *I messed up.* He left the room, peeled off the gloves and mask and slammed them into a trash can. He removed the gown and dropped it in a laundry hamper. He paced the hall, reviewing in his mind all the approved steps of the procedure, trying to think of what he missed. *I didn't draw the drugs myself.*

Piter entered the room where the drugs were stored. The pancuronium was one year expired, the pentobarbital, six months. Piter stopped, leaned against a wall and took a deep breath. *It's not my fault.*

He entered the hallway again and watched the guards push the body of the former advisor down the hall. The guards nodded at Piter as they passed.

Piter proceeded down the hall to the washroom, leaned over the sink and splashed water on his face. The mirror showed an intense man with sweaty, messy hair. Water trickled down his bony cheeks. The whites of his eyes were red, as if he'd been crying. Piter pointed at his reflection. "You're a murderer. A paid assassin." He laughed like a madman until his stomach hurt.

§

In his report, Piter wrote: "The student-nurse who drew the dose was inexperienced. There were many expired drugs on the shelf. I recommend, in the interest of efficiency and accuracy, doctors be allowed to draw their own drugs."

Afterwards, because his suggestions improved productivity and effectiveness, he was promoted to chief eradicator.

Piter began working mornings at the clinic and spending his afternoons at the prison, or making home visits with his Quietus on Wheels vehicle.

He wondered how he would explain his sudden pay raise to Yun, but he couldn't worry about that now. First thing he wanted was to find an even better apartment for them to live. He made a mental list of what he and Yun would buy. *New furniture and appliances, a new car, a crib for the baby.*

§

As leaves fell from the trees, Piter and Yun settled into a two-bedroom apartment complete with electricity and hot and cold running water.

Yun stared around the room, her eyes wide. "How can we afford this place?"

"I've been working overtime, treating patients at the prison," Piter said.

Yun accepted Piter's explanation without question but was flabbergasted the day he came home in a new car. He explained to her their newfound prosperity was due to a raise in pay. The government had finally discovered his worth.

She tilted her head. Her brow furrowed. "Why only you? Other doctors aren't getting your kind of salary."

"Don't worry about it. Aren't you happy that I'm bringing home more money?"

"Of course, I was just wondering—"

He raised his voice. "I don't want to hear another word about it. Trust me."

Yun stepped back. "Okay. I trust you," she said in a soft voice and stroked her expanding belly.

"Why don't you go and have a warm bath. You're always complaining how you never get a warm bath anymore." Piter gritted his teeth and felt his face grow hot.

"I don't always complain—"

"I'm tired, Yun."

Later that evening, Piter picked up the daily newspaper. The headline of today's paper read: "Who is loyal to AZEN?"

From this day forward, to reap the rewards that this country offers, citizens must have loyalty cards. A loyalty card will allow you state-of-the-art medical care, the best in housing, superior schooling for your children, and many other benefits.

In the next few weeks, citizens will receive a card in the mail with their assigned level: Level 1 – Elite, Level 2 – Loyal, Level 3 – Dispossessed, or Level 4 – Dysfunctional.

When in public, you must wear and prominently display your tags.

If you feel your level has been incorrectly assigned, you can make an appeal at AZEN Headquarters.

Piter looked across the room at Yun. No doubt he would be assigned the position of loyal, if not elite, but he worried about his wife. "You should read this." He pointed to the article.

Yun crossed her arms and glared at him.

He reached for her hand. "Sorry about earlier. I was grumpy."

"Humph," she said and sat next to Piter. He placed a pillow behind her back.

She grunted a little. "Thanks. I'll be glad when this baby is born." Yun picked up the paper and read silently. "That bitch! How dare she? It isn't right. We'll be dispossessed for sure."

"Maybe you, because of HRFA, but it's okay. If I'm loyal we can still have the benefits."

"I don't want either of us to be called loyal. This goes against everything we stand for."

He turned towards her with a steady gaze.

"Okay, everything I stand for," she said. "What will it take for you to realize AZEN is evil?"

"This is reality. No sense fighting it. To survive we need to be loyal citizens."

"Never!"

§

Two weeks later, their cards arrived in the mail. To Piter's dismay, they were both dispossessed.

Piter cancelled his first eradication the next morning and proceeded to the district office to appeal the decision. On the walls of the otherwise barren room hung a number of photocopied signs:

"Have identification ready."

"You are under video surveillance."

"All decisions are final."

"Aura loves you. Have a great day."

A zigzag queue snaked towards a glassed-in desk. Piter joined the line and for twenty minutes he shuffled forward, awaiting his turn. Ahead of him, everyone's appeals were denied.

"Next," said the man behind the glass.

Piter leaned his elbows on the high counter and spoke through the little cut-out hole in the glass. "There must be a mistake." He showed his identification tag.

The official typed Piter's name into his computer. "No mistake. You are dispossessed."

Piter was speechless for a moment. "But why?"

"Let me see. Ah, it says here you are associated with Human Rights for All."

"I'm not."

"We have proof." The official turned his computer screen towards Piter.

Piter saw a photo of himself holding the Human Rights for All sign and looking down at his cell phone, followed by a video of him being attacked and running from the police.

The official scanned the page of the computer with his mouse. "Because of that, you are denied loyal citizen status."

"You don't understand. It was a mistake. I was just holding the sign for someone..."

"Irrelevant."

"I voted for Aura Zarling. I've been obedient to AZEN."

The official tapped away at his computer and did not make eye contact. "Irrelevant."

Sweat prickled under Piter's arms. He fantasized punching his fist through the glass and into the official's emotionless face. He struggled to control his quivering voice. "What do I have to do to prove my loyalty?"

The official leaned forward on his high stool. "Be our guest at one of our new re-education facilities. Our six-week study will help you to adjust your thinking."

"Adjust my...?" Piter's stomach churned. He had heard of Re-Ed and understood the facilities to be more prison-like than educational. "What about my wife, Yun Dram?"

"Let me check." The official clicked his mouse a few times. "Hmm, she's known to associate with members of HRFA. She would require a longer stay, likely nine to twelve weeks. We have room in one of our facilities if you and your wife would like to join us."

"No. Impossible. She's expecting a baby."

"The offer stands. No one is forcing dispossessed people to be re-educated, not yet, anyway. If you graduate from the Re-Ed, you will be allowed to re-integrate back into society."

"If?"

"It's a challenging six weeks. Goodbye, Dr. Dram. Next!"

Piter bowed his head and slumped out the door. He drove home from AZEN headquarters, the events of the day rolling over and over in his head. *Damn Fillip and damn that sign.* Piter kicked the seat in front of him, and the woman seated ahead turned and gave him an annoyed look. He spent the rest of the trip clenching and unclenching his fists.

§

"How did it go at AZEN headquarters? Did the almighty officials listen to your appeal?" asked Yun.

The sarcasm in her voice stoked his anger. "It's your fault!"

Yun stepped back. Her smile disappeared. "Piter?"

"They have pictures of me holding that damn sign at the election rally and being attacked." He pointed to the thin, white scar on his head. "I could have everything I wanted if not for you." He struggled for self-control as his heart pounded.

Yun frowned. Her lips thinned. "I can't believe you're mad at me. Put the blame where it belongs, on that bitch dictator and her gang of thugs."

He pointed his finger, centimetres in front of her face. "You live in a dream world, you and your idealistic friends. Face reality, Yun."

She slapped his hand away. "She's the alpha bitch and you're just another dog sniffing her ass and lying belly up for her."

Before Piter could stop himself, he pushed her, the palms of his hands against her shoulders. Ungainly in her pregnancy, she lost her balance and fell to the floor. For a moment, he felt relief for punishing her, then regret. He gasped, "Yun! I'm sorry." He bent down to help her up.

"Get away from me!" She got on all fours and used the wall for support to stand. She turned to him, her face red with anger. "Bastard." She walked slowly to the bedroom and locked the door behind her.

He watched her go, hung his head and ran his hand through his hair. "I'm such an ass. I didn't mean it. Please, Yun, I'm so sorry."

"Leave me alone!"

Piter heard her sobbing behind the closed door. *What the hell is wrong with me?* He had to find a way to make it up to her.

CHAPTER SIXTEEN

Freedom of Religion

Light snow fell. Jakon was getting excited for Christmas. Tresha smiled, knowing he would never lose his childlike innocence. She opened the paper on a Sunday morning. "Listen to this headline, Fillip. 'Throw away your chains!'"

"What's it about?" Fillip asked. He sipped the last of his tea, rose and cleared the breakfast dishes from the table and then filled the sink with water.

"I don't know. I didn't write it." She read the article aloud:

> *Our country has seen highs and lows in our fight for freedom. AZEN tries to find middle ground, but church leaders won't compromise. They tell their followers not to join the Light of Aura Church. They steal from church funds. Worst of all, they abuse innocent children and have the gall to lecture us on moral behaviour.*
>
> *They fill the minds of their congregations with lies. The 'shepherds,' as they call themselves, fool their congregations, their 'flock,' into handing over money. We are not against those who obediently and blindly follow. People of Covona, help to free the sheep from the tyrants who run the churches. For their own good, they must be set free. Join us. Help free the innocent lambs from the wolves. Scatter the sheep. Tear down the fences that hold them in. The outlawed churches stand in the way of progress.*

"Sounds ominous," Fillip said. "I wonder what they're planning." He shut off the water and began to wash.

"Why don't they leave us alone? We're not hurting anyone." She felt weak in the knees as she dried the dishes.

"Churches stand for freedom and oppose this regime, as does HRFA. AZEN won't stand for that." Fillip checked his watch. "Speaking of which, we better get going before we're late."

She bit her lower lip. "I'm afraid. Maybe we should stay home."

Fillip put his "Dispossessed" tag around his neck. "We can't let them bully us." He held out her tag to her.

Tresha slowly dried her hands. "Fillip—"

"Don't worry. It'll be fine."

Tresha took the tag from his hand but didn't put it on right away.

Fillip placed a "Dysfunctional" tag over Jakon's head. "Come on."

§

Tresha's heart thumped as they walked to St. Anthony's Church. A dull headache started in the top of her head. She held Fillip's hand in a tight grasp.

"Ouch," he laughed. "Watch those fingernails." He patted her hand. "Relax."

She opened her hand and moved her jaw to release the tension.

They turned the corner and saw an angry throng gathered in front of the church. Tresha stopped. "Would it really be so bad to miss one Sunday?"

"Ignore them," Fillip said. He put Jakon between them. "Hold your head high." They walked through a gauntlet of jeering neighbours and up the stairs to the church entrance.

The onlookers taunted, "Baa, baa, baa…"

"Why do they hate us? What have we done?" Tresha asked.

A metal detector had been set up at the front door. Churchgoers walked through, one by one. All the people were ordered to open their coats while the police searched for concealed weapons.

"Put your handbag on the table, ma'am," the policeman said. "It's for your own protection."

Tresha obeyed and watched the policeman rifle through her purse. He inspected her wallet and left her tissues and hairbrush scattered on the table.

During the service, police officers patrolled the aisles, videotaping everyone. In all the years Tresha had attended services, this had never happened before. She was furious at the violation of their sacred space. Fillip sat up straight, recited his prayers and sang loudly, while Tresha shrivelled in her seat and didn't make a sound.

Afterwards, the congregation exited the church to a chorus of boos. A large angry mob had gathered in the street with baseball bats, spray paint and sledgehammers.

"Oh, my God." Tresha's voice shook. She grabbed her husband's arm.

Fillip again put Jakon between himself and Tresha. "Don't let anyone touch him."

With the other frightened parishioners, they descended the stairs, slowly pushing their way through the threatening crowd. Tresha looked from one face to another—bared teeth, flaring nostrils, feet set wide. She recognized some as her neighbours. They looked back at her with hatred, as if they didn't know her.

"This is the power of the propaganda machine," Tresha said. "People forget common sense and—"

Then came a shout, "Now!" The crowd, like a swarm of bees, acted as one and pushed their way up the stairs, shoving the parishioners aside, hitting them with their fists, elbows and knees. Churchgoers lifted youngsters onto their hips, screamed and ran for their lives. Children cried. Men shouted. Women screamed. People scattered in all directions with their hands over their heads. A few formed a protective barrier around two elderly couples and took a beating from the flying fists and kicks on their way down the stairs. The steps were slippery with newly fallen snow and several people fell.

The police made a poor show of holding back the raging crowd. They targeted the parish priest, handcuffed him while he still wore his robes and shoved him into a police car. Tresha, Fillip and Jakon held hands and ran towards home. Tresha glanced back to see her neighbours descend on St. Anthony's in an orgy of mob violence.

Later, on the evening news, they learned this same scene was repeated all over the country on the same day.

Tresha and Fillip's inquiries about their pastor were met with silence.

§

The streets were deserted and the people of the neighbourhood were asleep, exhausted by their tantrum earlier in the day. Piter pulled the car to the side of the church at just past three a.m. Yun sat in the seat beside him, licking her lips nervously. Tresha and Fillip sat in the back seat. Fog hung over the city like a wet blanket. Tresha was grateful for the fog. It would help mask the criminal thing they were about to do.

They stepped out of the car and Piter opened the trunk. Fillip pulled out a crowbar and held it with both hands. "Let's see what can be salvaged."

If caught, they would certainly be sent to jail. Tresha wasn't sure if it was her nerves or if something sinister hovered around the church.

The plexiglass board on the church yard normally displayed mass times. Today, it was covered by a banner. Fog prevented them from seeing what was written until they were up close. "Closed for renovations. Future Quietus/Recycling/Research Centre."

Yun leaned into Piter's chest and began to cry.

"Don't cry, my darling," he said. He tore down the sign and ripped it to pieces. "I'm not a believer, but it's wrong, what they did to your church."

They sneaked around to a boarded-up basement window at the back of the church. Fillip pried off the board and, with the crowbar, tapped away the broken glass. He and Piter slipped into the basement. Minutes later, they appeared at the open window with boxes containing valuables from the church, sacred objects and books. Tresha and Yun loaded them in Piter's car.

Yun put her hand on Piter's arm. "I'm so happy you helped us. I love you."

He smiled back and patted her knee. A look of warm affection passed between them.

"We better get out of here before someone sees us," Fillip said.

Piter drove in silence for several blocks. "I got a text from Hadar yesterday. His seminary was attacked. He and the others escaped. That's the last I heard. I don't know what happened to him or where he will go."

"Lord have mercy," Fillip said.

§

From that day, church services were outlawed in Covona. A great sense of loss settled in Tresha's soul, as if she was grieving a loved one.

Tresha and Fillip removed a closet door in their home, built a false wall and hid the forbidden literature they had rescued from the church.

CHAPTER SEVENTEEN
The Legend of Aura

Tresha and a cameraman gathered their recording equipment and rushed from the newsroom to cover a story unfolding in Ackim's city centre. A group of radicals were protesting the closing of their church.

Although it was mid-winter, the weather forecaster promised a bright, sunny day with a high of five degrees Celsius. They arrived to find about two hundred people gathered in front of a boarded-up church listening attentively to a pastor speak about keeping the faith and having courage. Patches of snow blown by the wind swirled against the walls, while in the sunny sections snow melted on the pavement.

The cameraman snapped a few photos and yawned. Tresha jotted some notes. People gathered in small groups to listen to the pastor. Children chased each other across the soggy grass. A woman sat on a bench and put a small blanket over her shoulder to nurse her baby.

At the screeching of tires, Tresha turned to see a police car arrive with red and blue lights flashing. Another arrived, and then another, until ten cars lined the curb. The cameraman photographed policemen in full riot gear jump from their cars and surround the group of peaceful protestors. The pastor stopped talking. His face paled. Mothers grasped their children's hands and edged away from the police.

As if on cue, a small group among the protesters began to chant, "Down with Zarling! Down with Zarling!" A man banged two garbage can lids together to keep the beat. A few more people in the crowd took up the chant. A man with a black bandana over his face threw something at the door of the church. Glass shattered. Flames shot up the door of the church. Tresha felt the heat from her place in the crowd. People screamed and ran. Children cried. Sparks flew to the roof tiles and too quickly caught fire, as if they had been doused with accelerant.

Tresha could not write notes fast enough. The police closed in, pushed people to the ground, and dragged them to waiting cars. A firetruck arrived, put out the fire and then turned its hoses on the crowd.

[103]

§

Tresha shivered. Her clothes and hair were still soaking wet, but this story couldn't wait. Rather than going home to change, she hurried to the office to write her report, her eye-witness account of what had occurred, complete with photographs.

The paper, the next day, proclaimed: "Radical Faction Riot in Downtown Ackim. Five hundred protestors attack police who tried to keep the peace." Photographs showed the raging fire and police putting people in handcuffs. Attached to the article was Tresha's name.

Tresha stormed into Raimond's office. "This is not what I wrote. This started as a peaceful protest. Children were there." She slammed the newspaper on his desk. "You twisted everything!"

Raimond leaned back in his chair and stared at her with dead eyes. "Your report did not meet our standards."

"You lied." Tresha's heart raced. She wanted to jump over the desk and wrap her hands around Raimond's neck.

He remained calm. "I'm restricting you to desk duty from now on—proofreading. Internet access is hereby denied to all dispossessed persons."

Tresha felt her heart drop to her stomach. "What?"

"Don't like it? Quit."

Tresha was light-headed. "Everything is changing too fast. What is happening to our country?"

Raimond ignored her and entered the newsroom to assign duties to the other staff.

The most trusted staff became filters. They received stories from the field reporters and were given internet access. Only they could read foreign news stories and decide which stories were suitable to Covonans. The filters passed the censored stories to a manipulator who changed numbers, dates, names and so on, to make the stories fit into AZEN ideology as per specific standards, rules and guidelines. The manipulator passed the stories to the creative writer who made the stories more interesting and entertaining for the public. The creative writer passed the stories to the proofreader, who looked for spelling, grammar and punctuation.

§

Tresha thought she may go mad. Hours and days crawled by with little relief from the boredom. The typical stories she proofread were puppies getting lost and their joyful reunion with their owners, cute children, or the list of crimes committed by dissidents. Occasionally, a foreign story crossed her desk. The common theme running through those stories were: Abban, Sura, Dule and Asciary were bleak, hostile and lawless countries. "How lucky we are to live in Covona."

One morning, she noticed her co-worker, a "filter" had carelessly left her monitor on when she left the room. Tresha sneaked across the aisle, leaned on her co-worker's desk and read the screen: a newspaper article from Solime. She struggled to remember her high school Solimese and determined the article said:

> *Covona is cloaked in secrecy. The once democratic country has been taken over by a dictator. Little is known about what goes on beyond our border, though the people of this country are eager to find out. An electric fence now stretches along their seawall. A concrete wall between our countries is under construction. Our Prime Minister has made repeated attempts to barter peace between our countries, but Covona remains hostile and unresponsive.*

Tresha returned to her desk, trembling. Though it was refreshing to be reminded that life carried on as usual beyond the borders of Covona, she knew the rest of her countrymen would never hear of this.

Knowing she could be severely punished, she put her proofreading aside. With her fingers poised over her keyboard, she thought for a moment and then wrote about Covonans forced to give up their passports and the destruction of churches. She told of the arrests of "dissidents," and about the women who suffered because of sterilizations. She downloaded everything onto two memory cards and erased the incriminating evidence from the hard drive of her computer. What she would do with the information was another matter. Other nations may have been sympathetic, but she doubted they would do anything to help, even if she got the information to them. She pulled the flash drive from the computer and held it in her shaking hand. While pondering what to do, Raimond entered the office. She slipped the flash drives into her bra.

He approached her desk. "I need to talk to you."

Tresha knew by his tone of voice this couldn't be good. "About what?" She did not meet his eyes. "About how you betrayed me?"

"Don't be so melodramatic. You knew the president when she was young."

"Yes, we were friends in school."

"The people want to know more about her. Where did she come from? How did she come to be the adopted daughter of Teador Zarling? I'd like you to tell her story."

"To be honest, I don't really have too many positive things to say. We had a falling out."

"Shush!" He turned his head quickly to the left and right and then leaned forward, speaking in a whisper. "Are you nuts? You don't speak ill of the president."

She spoke softly, glanced back and forth, copying him. "No one else is here."

"You might not believe this, but I like you, Tresha. I don't want any harm to come to you. If you have anything to say about the president, you'd better make it positive."

"Let someone else write it."

"This order came from Aura Zarling herself. She asked for you specifically to write her story." He placed a letter on her desk. "This was just sent to me. She liked your article about the riot at the church."

"Pfft! My article? You changed every word."

"I'm counting on you. The whole newspaper is counting on you to write something encouraging. No, make it legendary."

Tresha read the letter. "I don't know what I could possibly say—
"

He leaned on her desk and put his face inches from hers. "Are you refusing? You realize, of course, no one refuses direct orders from the president."

Tresha said, "I just have a few things to finish up."

"This takes precedence." The editor went back to his office. "Teador and Bel Zarling have granted you an interview. A limo is waiting outside to take you to the mansion."

Tresha threw on her coat, stepped outside and was greeted by a driver in a long black coat and shiny shoes. He opened the door of the limo and she stepped in. On the ride to the mansion, Tresha thought about the gawky, skinny fourteen-year-old girl she once knew.

§

New to the school and seeming too shy even to raise her eyes to look at the other students, Aura had walked into biology class and took the empty chair in front of Tresha.

Tresha felt sorry for her and tapped Aura on the shoulder. "Will you be my partner for the science experiment?"

Aura smiled, showing a gap between her two front teeth. "Okay."

From that day, Aura stuck with Tresha and they became good friends, eating lunch together, helping each other with homework and gabbing on the phone. Aura often forgot to call Tresha back and was perpetually late for meet-ups at the mall, but these small faults were nothing to break up a friendship over.

Aura wanted to be popular. She spent her school days following Massy, the prettiest girl in the school, down the hall and trying to get a seat beside her in class. Massy tolerated Aura for a while but soon told her to go away and stop bothering her. Tresha would never forget the look of hatred on Aura's face.

St. Martha's was a parochial school, and for the first time, Aura had to take religious education. She had never attended church before, nor heard any scripture. One day, she had asked the teacher, "Does virgin birth mean Mary and Joseph didn't have sex?" The rest of the students hooted with laughter. The teacher, after regaining control of the classroom, told Aura to read her assignments and stop asking silly questions. Aura was highly insulted. It was the only class in which she scored less than a B.

Months later, the poor teacher died in a fall down the school steps. "Serves her right, the fat bitch," Aura had said.

A year later, Aura's mother, Bel, a thirty-three-year-old former swimsuit model, now too old to pursue her profession, married fifty-year-old Teador Zarling, the richest man in the country. That's when everything changed. Aura moved from a two-room apartment into a mansion, went on holidays to exotic locations and came to school in beautiful new clothes. In front of dozens of students, she pulled one hundred frozen bills from her designer purse and bought lunches, snacks and gifts for those she wanted to befriend. The others, she ignored.

As Aura's best friend, Tresha was the recipient of many gifts, clothes and meals in restaurants. She visited the Zarling's sprawling mansion many times, followed Aura into the wide foyer, watched her drop her coat in front of the butler, making him bend to pick it up. Aura stuck wads of gum to the underside of the dining table and then, hours later, laughed at the maid who was on her knees under the table, trying to scrape it off.

In time, Aura got braces to straighten her teeth. She grew taller, bustier, prettier, more popular and conceited. Tresha, in turn, became popular by association.

Aura's mother put her on a perpetual diet and Aura couldn't pass by any reflective surface without stopping to look at herself. "Do I look fat?"

"No. You're very slim." This became Tresha's refrain.

Aura gazed into the mirror and turned her head from side to side.

Tresha compared her chubby cheeks to Aura's high cheekbones, her spotty face next to Aura's clear skin and her small hazel eyes next to Aura's large brown eyes. "I wish I was as pretty as you."

"You'll never be as pretty as me."

She followed Aura to the washroom five or six times a day to brush their hair, apply lipstick or just stand and gaze at themselves. She followed Aura's strict diet and lost ten kilograms, afterwards enjoying the attention she received.

Aura was given a Porsche convertible for her sixteenth birthday. Tresha rode with her to the shopping mall and Aura took the only handicapped stall in the parking lot.

A man in a wheelchair rolled up to the car just as Aura stepped out. "This space is reserved for handicapped parking," he said.

Aura turned her back to the man and stuck her bum in his face. "Kiss my ass." She laughed, grabbed Tresha's arm and pulled her towards the mall. After the shopping trip, a parking ticket was on the windshield of the car. They returned to the mansion and Aura handed the ticket to her stepfather, leaving him to pay it.

Aura's diet—no sweets, carbs or fats, and frequent meal skipping, was difficult to follow and Tresha began to put on weight again. Aura got after Tresha every day, reminding her to keep to her diet. When that didn't work, Aura resorted to mocking Tresha.

One day, after a teacher stepped out of the classroom, one of the boys got up, put his hand in the teacher's fish tank, grabbed a fish and swallowed it. Half of the kids hooted with laughter and the rest groaned with disgust.

Aura said to the whole class, "Don't eat them all. Save one for fatty Tresha in case she gets hungry."

Tresha didn't defend herself but smiled instead, refusing to let her classmates see her cry.

Later, at lunchtime, Tresha approached Aura and some other girls, a tray of food in her hands. They occupied the most important table in the lunchroom, the one by the window.

"I hope you're not thinking of sitting with us," Aura said. "You're so fat, I'm ashamed to be seen with you."

She couldn't understand how Aura could be so oblivious to her pain. Tresha could no longer restrain herself. She set down her tray and shouted, "You are such a bitch! I don't want to be your friend."

The lunchroom went silent. Aura got up and slapped Tresha's face. A collective gasp rose from the students. "From now on, no one will speak to Tresha until I say so."

Tresha stood with her face burning from the slap, anger and shame.

As the days and weeks of her punishment dragged on, Tresha became lonelier and more unsure of herself. She walked around the school like a ghost, ignored by everyone, until she could take it no longer. She followed Aura into the washroom and stood behind her as Aura applied mascara. "I'm sorry," she said softly.

"Pardon me?" Aura smiled, but her eyes were hard.

"I'm sorry."

Three girls entered the washroom.

Aura turned to face her. "What exactly are you sorry about?" she asked in a loud voice.

All four girls stared. Tresha wanted to disappear. "I'm sorry I called you a bitch."

"Aw, now see how easy that was? You may call me after school." She placed her hand on Tresha's shoulder, giggled and walked out the door.

§

Tresha entered the mansion. She had forgotten just how luxurious it was. She perched on a chair in the drawing room and waited. Bel entered and held out a well-manicured hand for Tresha to shake.

"Well, you've certainly gotten fat. Would you like a glass of water?" Bel asked.

"Yes, please."

While they were speaking, Teador came into the room, shook Tresha's hand, showed no sign of recognition, sat for five minutes, said a few words and left.

Tresha arrived back at her office two hours later and shook out her hands. "Time to write a fairy tale."

Aura Zarling, our beloved president, had a humble beginning. An interview with Bel, her mother, reveals another side to Aura. Bel was a beautiful young woman, a model, who fell in love with a handsome sailor who set off to defend our country. A terrible battle raged day and night and the unfortunate young man was lost at sea. She never saw him again. All that remained of him was a letter promising his everlasting love to Bel and their unborn child.

"He gave me a book of poetry," Bel told this reporter.

She showed me the book and opened it to reveal a stain on one of the pages. "He gave me a rose when we kissed goodbye on the shore. I pressed it between these pages. It's long gone, of course, but this is where it was." She ran her fingertips over the page.

Poor Bel, left alone, gave birth to a perfect baby. She wrapped the tiny girl in a soft blanket and stepped outside into the fresh, cool air of morning. A lover of Greek mythology, she remembered the legend of the virgin huntress, Aura, the titan of the breezes. "I took this as a heavenly sign that my daughter was destined for greatness," Bel said. "And I named her Aura. I had no one to help me with my newborn infant except for a kindly couple who cared for Aura while I took a job waitressing. I caught the eye of a modelling agency and before long, everyone knew my name, Bel Charr. Even after having a baby, I got back my girlish figure." Bel winked at me and gave me a sly smile. "You wouldn't know to look at me now, but my beauty also caught the eye of Teador Zarling and we married in a lavish ceremony. Aura was fifteen years old. She was my bridesmaid."

Teador Zarling spoke up. "I knew Aura was special. I had a dream she would lead the country to glory."

This reporter knew Aura in high school. She was even more beautiful than her mother, but she was never vain or proud. Many young men were attracted to Aura, but she never had a serious suitor. She believed it was her destiny not to have a family, but to lead people.

"Aura said she would not marry or have children. The people of this land are her children," Bel said.

One day, she will make us a great nation again.

§

When they were teens, Aura had told Tresha about the elderly couple who took care of her, that she hated them, especially the woman. "The old lady scared me when I was little, screaming at me all the time. She was only nice when my mom was there. I got back at her. When she got Alzheimer's, I used to pinch her to make her yell and put crumbs in her bed. Old people are so creepy."

Tresha stood beside his desk while Raimond read her story. "What do you think?"

"It's pure drivel. You sure about this?"

She nodded, not feeling sure at all. She hated writing the piece but knew she, like everyone in the country, was under pressure to conform to the new reality. Tresha doubted Bel really knew the Greek origin of the name. In the legend, what Aura hunted was men, killing them by filling them with arrows, until Zeus turned her into a stream.

"If the president doesn't like it, you pay the price, not me." He emailed it to the office of President Aura Zarling.

CHAPTER EIGHTEEN
Transformation and Affluence

Tresha's heart pounded when she was called to the editor's office in the morning to discuss the president's reaction to her piece. She took a deep breath, opened his door and was relieved to see a smile on his face and him holding his arms out to her.

"She loved it. Come over here." He took her in a tight embrace.

Tresha held her arms limp at her sides as Raimond hugged her.

He led her out into the main room, where seventeen people sat in front of computer screens. "I would like everyone's attention," he shouted. He placed a hand on her shoulder. "This lady here has just made our paper the greatest in the country. As of today, our distribution is nationwide. A raise in pay and new laptops for everyone!" The entire staff stood up and gave Tresha a standing ovation. She smoothed her blouse and forced a smile.

§

For the first time in years, Tresha didn't have to worry about how to pay for groceries. In a giddy frenzy, she purchased new clothes, including a warm wool coat to get her through the rest of the cold winter. Tired of the sidewalks and roadways covered with dirty snow and the drab, washed-out clothes of people around her, Tresha picked the brightest colour she could find, purple. She felt like royalty walking down the streets.

She hired a man to fix the roof and replace a broken window on her home. Most important, she hired caregivers to look after her father and Jakon while she was at work.

Tresha couldn't escape the reason for her newfound wealth when Aura Zarling appeared on the evening news holding a pocket-sized book. "Citizens of Covona. I present to you, *Transformation and Affluence*. It's just a little book of my thoughts and feelings."

"What new horrors do you have for us today?" Tresha asked the television.

Aura said, "With the help of our brilliant scientists, we will speed up the process of natural selection. Objections will be raised by those who will to stand in the way of prosperity. They want to take food from your table. We have seen the light. It's only reasonable we do something to control the population. With your help, we will build a strong country made of intelligent and able-bodied people.

"A copy of *Transformation and Affluence* will be sent to every man, woman and child. Display your copy in a prominent place in your home and read it every day. Remember. I am the chosen one. I forsook marriage and family to lead you to glory."

Tresha put her hand over her mouth, snapped off the television and leaned back in disbelief. "Dear God, what have I done?"

§

The Farwell's books arrived in the mail a week later, wrapped in pink paper. Tresha and Fillip sat on the couch and opened their copies.

Tresha turned to page three:

AZEN promises to:

1. Support scientific research, relieve suffering and reduce health care costs.

2. Encourage patriotism by confirming loyalty and duty to country.

3. Be tough on crime, reduce the prison population, drug addiction and homelessness.

4. Improve access to Quietus to reduce stress on families caused by the burden of caring for the aged and dysfunctional.

5. Improve standard of living by increasing productivity and reducing dependence on the government.

Tresha shuddered. "Vague promises can be interpreted in so many ways."

Fillip's forehead was creased with worry. "Aura feeds people propaganda and then sits back and watches lies grow into doctrine." His fingers trembled as he flipped the pages of *Transformation and Affluence*. "She aims to become our demigod."

Tresha turned back to the table of contents. "Here's a laugh. There's a section on freedom." She found the page. "'Laws imposed by religious institutions hold us back and squash our liberty. I'm asking you to believe in me, because I stand for freedom.' This is so twisted." She skimmed through the book. "Oh, my God!"

"What's wrong?"

"I can't believe…" Her eyes teared up. She pointed to the section she wanted him to read, not trusting herself to read the words out loud:

> *We must be more compassionate and caring to families burdened by dysfunctional individuals. The poor and the dispossessed need our help to prosper in society rather than being weighed down and pulled further into the vortex of poverty. To address this problem:*

> *The dispossessed must apply for procreation tickets. The tickets may be used for normal procreation, adoption or surrogacy as the couple sees fit. However, if the parents give birth to a subnormal child, the woman will be sterilized and the child eradicated. If parents are not able to earn an adequate income, both must be sterilized to prevent dependence on the state.*

> *Those with birth defects, incurable diseases, and the sickly elderly, have little quality of life. We want our citizens to be happy and relieved of the affliction of caring for handicapped family members.*

They both turned their eyes to Jakon, who sat in the middle of the floor building a tower of blocks. He looked up at his parents and smiled.

CHAPTER NINETEEN

Eviction

Piter sat on the couch beside Yun to hear an announcement from the Minister for Spiritual Welfare, Kriston Boals.

Minister Boals' chubby face was lit up with a smile. His thick black hair was combed straight back, each hair plastered into place like Count Dracula. "The Light of Aura Church is contemporary, with modern ideas, and will take care of the spiritual needs of a shrewd and discerning people. We're not like the archaic institutions who invented moral laws to control you. Would a kind God want you to suffer?" The minister's double chin wiggled as he exclaimed with arms spread wide, "Join us for Sunday services. We welcome all people, regardless of your situation in life. Leave your differences behind. We can't have any derisiveness at the Light of Aura Church."

Yun said, "They've invented a church for people looking for moral permission to kill themselves."

Piter turned off the television. "Some lives aren't worth living."

"People have intrinsic value."

He raised his voice. "I don't like it when you preach to me, Yun."

"What were you just doing to me?" Yun asked.

"Forget it. I don't want to argue."

Piter got up to use the telephone. He tried Hadar's cell phone again, but the line was no longer in service. There was no use trying to call the seminary. The building had been burnt to the ground by a mob of hoodlums. He'd read about it in a trusted news source, the Ackim Times. Piter's heart ached with worry.

§

He had a pulling sensation in his gut the next morning as he watched Dr. Jeniver Bant pack the last of her belongings from the Free Clinic. She had been offered a job at the QRRC, Quietus/Recycling/Research Centre.

She lifted the box and headed for the door. "Join AZEN as I did, Piter. Society is changing. We must keep up. Go apply for your loyalty card. What are you waiting for?"

There was no way he could tell her why he wasn't allowed a loyalty card.

Jeniver said, "You should see the top-of-the-line equipment I'll get to work with. I'll have all the funds I need to do my research. The president supports the sciences."

"Well, good luck to you." Piter returned to his office, sat at his desk and opened his mail. His read the official announcement from AZEN:

> *Parents and guardians now have the right to*
> *request Quietus for any dependent who suffers from*
> *chronic illness or developmental disabilities.*

He scratched the back of his neck. Quietus Centres were about to get busy.

§

That evening, he sat down beside Yun on the couch and sighed. All he could think about was Jeniver's happy face as she packed her belongings to leave the Free Clinic.

Yun reached over and tousled his hair. "What's the matter, Mr. Grumpy?"

"The Free Clinic doesn't pay enough."

"But you just got a raise in pay. We have all we need."

He squeezed his eyes, frustrated that he couldn't share the truth. "Other doctors are doing better than me."

"You're envious."

"After all my hard work, I'm entitled."

"I'd rather starve than have you work at a QRRC, if that's what you're thinking."

He clutched the couch cushion in his fist. "I want something more out of life."

She raised her voice. "Those places are assembly lines of death. People with serious disabilities should be worried. Please don't apply there."

He turned his face from her. "Okay. For you, I won't." Piter removed the "Dispossessed" tag from around his neck and dropped it on the side table. He put his hand on her swollen belly and felt a slight movement. "I just want to take care of you two."

"I'll go back to work after the baby's born."

"You hate teaching."

"I love teaching. It's the new rules I hate; the things we must teach the students. Each morning we raise the AZEN flag, the children chant, 'Believe in AZEN and the Light of Aura Church.'"

"Put your beliefs aside while you're at work."

"Ridiculous. Impossible."

"Then just do as you're told."

"Did you know the children are told to snitch on each other and on their own parents?"

"About what?"

"Everything, like if they hear anyone insulting the president, or praying. We had a school assembly yesterday. The kids will all join a club called, 'The Children of AZEN.' The textbooks say people with handicaps aren't even human. Children are told to 'discipline' any moogies they see." She leaned into Piter's shoulder. "I hate Aura Zarling."

"Shush. Don't say that."

"I don't ever want to go back to teaching if I can't teach children kindness and integrity."

There was a knock on the door.

"Expecting someone?"

Yun shook her head.

The landlord's grim face needed a shave. His grey hair hung in his eyes. He handed Piter a piece of paper. "You have one day to pack your belongings and get out." His jaw shook.

Piter looked down at the notice of eviction. "What the hell? No. My wife's expecting... Why?"

[118]

"The dispossessed are no longer welcome in this building, even if you can afford the rent." He looked at Yun and his face softened a bit. "Look, if it was up to me…it's the rules." He turned, shuffled down the hall and knocked on another door.

§

Piter and Yun looked for other accommodations, but everywhere they went, they faced the same question, "Where's your loyalty card?" Doors were slammed in their faces. One apartment manager even called security to escort the couple out.

Piter reluctantly accepted the help of HRFA to find a place to live. They moved into a one-room suite in a building where the dispossessed were tolerated. Piter and Yun sold most of their furniture and, on a rainy afternoon, moved to the hovel.

Paint peeled from the walls. The refrigerator's motor buzzed angrily. Two out of four burners on the stove did not work. Mouse feces was evident along the baseboards and under the bed. Yun put everything edible, including salt and pepper, into the fridge.

Piter looked around the room—at the ancient appliances and worn, stained carpet. A musty smell hung in the air. "I've worked so hard only to end up where we started, living in a hell hole." He hugged Yun from behind, his hands rested on her swollen belly, his chin on her shoulder. Yun leaned her hands on the window sill, and they stared outside at the view. The apartment building next door was very much like their own. A woman stood at her window on the other side of the dirty back alley. Her hands were folded across her body as if she was cold. Their gazes met for a moment. The other woman drew the blinds, concealing herself from view.

In a monotone voice, Yun said, "We can't raise our child in this place."

Piter sat in the armchair. "We have no choice." Across the room, a cockroach scuttled down the wall. Piter took off his shoe and threw it. He missed the cockroach but made a large dent in the drywall. Heaviness filled his body.

From next door came the sounds of children crying and people arguing.

Yun said, "HRFA can help us escape. Maybe there's a way…"

"It's too dangerous, the condition you're in." He pointed to her pregnant belly.

"After the baby is born?"

"Impossible." Piter clenched his fists and brought them down on the arms of the chair. He decided he would have a solitary anti-celebration. He stood up and put his shoes and coat back on. "I'm going out."

"Where?"

"To find a bar."

She turned to him, her mouth tight. "Seriously? You're going to leave me alone to drown your sorrows at a bar with strangers?"

"Why not? Tomorrow is my day off. I'll do what I want."

She threw her hands in the air. "When you get home, sleep on the couch."

§

Piter stepped into the murky night. Steady rain fell on his bare head and dripped down his neck. A cab sat idling on the corner, its wipers swishing slowly.

Piter opened the door. "Take me somewhere I can get a drink."

The cab bumped and splashed through potholes while Piter stared out the window. Except for a few hunched figures walking on the sidewalk, the streets were all but deserted.

Ten minutes later, he ran from the cab to the door of the tavern, shook the rain from his coat and sat on a stool at the bar. A few other patrons occupied the dark, smelly room, clustered around round tables with dirty tablecloths. Music blared from an ancient jukebox in the corner.

He ordered a glass of white wine and took a sip, felt it flow across his tongue and down his throat with a pleasant and familiar sensation. The wine was sweeter than he normally liked, but he drank it anyway—anything to chase away his feelings of despair.

He downed a second glass and the buzz of the alcohol hit. Piter began to feel warm and cozy. The music sounded better than a half hour ago, and he bobbed his head to the beat.

A woman in a short skirt took the stool next to him. The sharpness of her perfume cut through the musty smell of the bar. "Buy me a drink?"

He signalled to the bartender. She ordered a beer and he another glass of wine.

"Thanks. You're looking a little down. Want to talk about it?" She coiled a strand of her long blond hair with her forefinger.

He turned his face from her. "I'm married."

"It's okay. I'm not looking to hook up. What's bothering you?"

He pulled his "Dispossessed" tag from under his shirt and showed it to her. "This."

She laughed. "You and everyone else in this dump. Want to dance?"

"Why not?" Piter threw back his glass of wine and plugged some coins in the jukebox. The two belted out the lyrics of the song while they shuffled and gyrated across the dance floor. He sat back down, sweaty from the exertion, his head a little dizzy, and ordered another round.

Over the next round of drinks, he began to tell her of his troubles. He was glad to be able to confide. She nodded with understanding, unlike Yun, who would have lectured him.

"I'd have no problem being married to a smart doctor like you. You care about people enough to end their suffering. You have nothing to feel remorseful about."

"Another round?" Piter asked, even though his head was spinning. "You're a gorgeous woman." The top buttons of her blouse were open, displaying a deep cleavage. He couldn't take his eyes off her breasts, tiny waist, tight butt and legs that went on and on. He salivated. "We should order some food."

They shared a plate of greasy, fried potatoes and battered fish, and more drinks.

He began to feel nauseated and unsteady. "I should get home."

"I'm a little short on cash. You don't mind paying, do you?" she said, pointing to the empty plates and glasses.

"Not at all."

"Great." She ran her hand up his thigh to his groin. "For three hundred frezens I'll do whatever you want. Let's go to the toilet." She pointed to the ladies' room at the other end of the bar.

He licked his lips and stood up. "No, I should go, my wife—"

She pulled down the shoulder of her dress, revealing one bare breast.

He stared for a moment, shook his head, turned and stumbled, banging his thigh on a table.

"Easy, big guy," the woman said. She laughed, took his arm and led him to the door.

He stepped outside. The rain had increased in intensity. Lightning bolts shot across the sky, followed by booming thunder. He ran unsteadily to a taxi waiting on the corner, but the driver wanted to be paid in advance. Piter felt for his wallet and found it was gone.

He walked home.

§

He awoke the next morning with a pounding headache. From the other side of the room came the low, murmuring voices of Yun and his parents. He sat up and held his swirling head with both hands.

"He's awake," Hyron said.

"You look terrible," Odilia said.

"Thanks, Mom." Piter wobbled to the bathroom, trying to control his nausea. He sat on the toilet to pee and afterwards climbed into the shower. He sat in the bathtub and let the lukewarm water pour on his head.

Feeling a little revived, he returned to lie on the couch. His mother reached into her purse and gave Piter an envelope containing five hundred frezens. "I know how upset you are having to live here. We've been saving up. Buy yourselves a few things for yourselves and the baby."

He gave the money back to his mother. "You need it more than us."

She raised her eyebrows. "No, really..."

"Yun, hand me my briefcase. It's in the closet."

Piter sat up and opened the case. Beneath his papers was an envelope. He tore the envelope, revealing a wad of one-hundred frezen bills.

Yun gasped. "Where did that come from?"

He counted the bills and handed half the stack to his mother.

Odilia's jaw dropped. "Five thousand frezens. Where did you get all this money?"

Piter decided he wasn't going to keep it a secret any longer. "I do a little extra on the side."

"Doing what?" Hyron asked. He came to stand beside his wife.

Yun's eyes opened wide. "You mean Quietus? Oh, no." She covered her mouth with her hand.

"It's legal," Piter said.

"Oh, my God. Legal or not, it's immoral," Hyron said.

"You were so distant, lately, so secretive. I thought you were having an affair," Yun said.

"It would be better if he was. I won't take your blood money." Odilia dropped the money on his lap as if it burned her hand. Her face turned red. "My own son. How could you?"

"That's why you're drinking so much. Your conscience is bothering you," Yun said.

He didn't see anger, only sadness and disappointment in the eyes of the people he loved. He'd have preferred it if they'd yelled at him. "You don't understand. I'm doing this for you, Yun, and our baby."

She rubbed her swollen belly and left the room without another word.

CHAPTER TWENTY

Baby Dram

Yun went into labour one week after moving into the new apartment. At three o'clock in the morning, knowing she wouldn't be admitted to a hospital, Piter helped her down three flights of stairs and brought her to his clinic where he had access to some medical equipment and painkillers. Many of his patients gave birth at the clinic.

She lay on a bed that had been used for expedited end-of-life care. Since the Quietus Centres opened, this section of the clinic had been reverted to its original use, caring for the dispossessed who weren't allowed in the hospital.

The usual surge of people poured through the doors of the clinic. Piter checked in on Yun when he could, about every half hour. As expected, her contractions came closer together and with more intensity.

When the clinic closed for the day, Piter saw Yun's labour was not progressing as it should. He didn't have training as an anesthesiologist and the clinic was not set up for surgery should she require a C-section. The hospital would sometimes take emergency cases if the dispossessed were willing to pay.

"I'm going to take you to the hospital, Yun."

"No. I'm scared."

"It'll be all right. They'll take care of you," he said, though he wasn't sure if he believed it. The day was muggy and hot. Piter drove to the hospital with the windows down while she breathed through heavy contractions.

He held Yun's arm, supporting her as she took small steps into the Emergency Room, helped her to a chair and then cut to the front of the line at the Admitting Desk.

"Back of the queue!" a young man said. "I've been waiting twenty minutes."

"Sorry, emergency," Piter said.

The young man stamped his foot. "So is mine!"

Piter leaned on the desk. "My wife has been in labour for fifteen hours." He pointed at Yun. "She's exhausted, likely needs a C-section."

"Your loyalty card?" the triage nurse held out her hand.

"We don't have cards."

"You're dispossessed?"

"Yes, but—"

"I'm sorry. We can't admit her." The nurse looked around Piter and called the next person in line.

Piter held out his hand to stop the young man from stepping forward. "I'm a doctor. The situation is critical. I can pay." He pulled out his wallet, displaying a wad of cash.

"Go to AZEN headquarters, obtain a loyalty card and when you return—"

Piter slammed his hand on the counter and shouted, "My wife needs to be admitted now!"

The triage nurse turned in her chair. "Security!"

A burly security man grasped Piter's arm.

"Please. I'm begging you."

A second nurse stepped from behind the counter and brought a wheelchair to Yun. Piter knew her from the Free Clinic. She had been the student nurse who had stitched Piter's head. He opened his mouth to speak to her, filled with relief, but she shot him a warning look.

"I'll ask the doctor to have a look at her, but you'll have to stay here," she said.

He paid the fee for the surgery, then flopped into a chair. He clenched and unclenched his hands. With elbows on his knees, he rested his forehead on the palms of his hands. An hour passed. He approached the admitting desk. "Any word on my wife?"

"Sit down."

"I was wondering if you could check—"

"The doctors are attending to her. Sit down."

The procedure was taking longer than it should have. Piter imagined his wife on the operating table. Any number of things could go wrong. Worry brought tears to his eyes.

He closed his eyes and distracted himself with happier memories of their honeymoon the shores of Covona in the city of Ducor—the chilly ocean water washing over their bare feet as they walked the rocky shoreline, Yun laughing at something he said, though he didn't remember what. They were full of hope then.

Piter felt a tap on his shoulder. "You can see your wife."

He was led to a ward containing twenty beds, lined side by side. Yun was curled up on her side on a cot. There was no infant in sight. He touched her hair, moving it from her face. She opened her eyes and blinked at him.

"How are you feeling?"

She shook her head but didn't say anything.

"Where's the baby?"

She looked at him and her lips trembled. "Dead."

He felt as if all the air had been sucked from his body and collapsed to his knees on the floor. "What happened?"

"They took his body away. I wanted to hold him. They wouldn't let me."

Piter felt pounding in his ears. His pulse raced. "I'll be back." He ran to the Labour and Delivery area.

"My wife, Yun Dram, just had a C-section. I want to see my baby," he said to a nurse behind the desk.

She raised her eyes to him and opened the file. "I'm afraid that's not possible." She snapped the file shut and walked away from the desk.

Piter reached over the counter and grabbed the file. He gasped. *My baby was a live birth.* It was determined the infant was "unlikely to thrive" and was euthanized. Reading further in the file, Piter saw Yun had been given a tubal ligation.

He slammed the file on the desk and went to search for the doctor responsible.

A nurse blocked his entry to the restricted area. She said, "The doctor's in surgery. You're not allowed in here."

Piter attempted to push past her. Two armed guards appeared, pinned his arms behind his back and escorted him to the waiting area.

"Get out, dispossessed scum." A security guard pointed to the door.

Piter held back his tears as he shouted, "This is your job? To bully people desperate for medical care? What happened to our country?"

Across the room, Yun sat slumped in a chair. "Oh, my God!" Piter said, and ran to her. The bandages on her abdomen were wet with blood. He lifted Yun in his arms and carried her out of the hospital. They arrived home and he carried her up the three flights of stairs and to bed. He pulled off the bloody bandages and looked with disgust at her stitched belly, at the large, jagged incision.

"What's wrong?" Yun asked.

"That will be a big scar," he said.

She flinched as he cleaned the wound with rubbing alcohol.

"Sorry." Piter covered Yun's incision with sterile dressing and gave her some painkillers he had taken from the clinic.

Later, he held a bowl of soup in his hands and urged her to eat. She shook her head and turned away.

"My baby. My baby," she said, over and over. Her face was pallid.

"You need to eat. Regain your strength." He fed her a few spoonfuls. She hardly had the strength to swallow her soup. His heart sank and he regretted every cross word he had ever said to her. She soon fell asleep.

For months, he had looked forward to holding their child in his arms and now he was left with nothing but the knowledge that they could never have another child. Hope was gone. He climbed under the blanket and cuddled her, careful not to touch her tender belly. He thought about what the future would be like. He decided when Yun recovered, he would endure the six weeks in Re-Ed, obtain a loyalty card, and move out of this decrepit building. He closed his eyes and imagined them back in a decent apartment. His car alarm went off. Piter jumped out of bed just in time to see someone driving away in his car.

§

The following morning, Piter climbed aboard a bus. The air inside was thick with the stench of sweat and the stale breath of fifty or so occupants. The sticky humidity was intensified by the sun that poured through the bus windows. With his long arms, he reached across some seated passengers to allow a breeze, only to find the window locked shut. He reached for the bar above his head and tried to maintain his balance on the jostling, bumping bus.

He stared out the bus' front window, thinking of the privileges he could gain with an AZEN membership—a better apartment, job, health care, and schooling...though that didn't matter. He would never have children. He and Yun would be allowed to shop in stores other than the Shop and Save. He smiled. As a loyal or elite, maybe Piter could offer his brother protection.

Outside the bus window, a line of men in orange jumpsuits passed chunks of debris one to the other to load onto a dump truck. Armed men stood watch. The destruction of damaged buildings continued around the city.

§

Piter left Dr. Poil's office with a slip of paper in hand. He was grateful to the young doctor for giving Yun a prescription without seeing her. It was the clinic's policy—doctors could not prescribe medicine or treat their own family, except in an emergency. Piter had explained to Dr. Poil that Yun's surgical site infection was getting worse. It was tender, red and oozing pus.

He arrived at the pharmacy as soon as they opened and before he saw any patients.

The pharmacist glanced at the prescription for Cefazolin. "We don't have any. Sorry, Dr. Dram." She looked at Piter over the top of her glasses and shrugged her thin shoulders.

"What antibiotics do you have in stock?"

"None. We have a few painkillers, some eczema ointment and some laxatives."

"What? Why? Can you call around?"

"No one has any meds. Dr. Poil's patients cleaned us out. We expect another shipment in about two weeks."

Piter stepped back, shocked. "That stupid bastard."

He stormed back to the clinic and found Dr. Poil in his office. Piter came around the desk, grabbed him by the collar with both hands and yelled into his face, "How much have you been prescribing?"

Dr. Poil put his hands on Piter's wrists, stood and pushed him away. "Let me go! What the hell is wrong with you?"

They stood face to face. "There's no medicine left for my wife! The pharmacy is empty. Did you think we had an endless supply? No shipment for two weeks."

Dr. Poil readjusted his glasses that had slipped down his nose and he raised his hands in a defensive pose. "I'm sorry. I didn't know."

Piter pounded his fist on the desk and scattered Dr. Poil's papers on the floor. "Idiot!" He left the office, slamming the door on the way out.

Yun was so much on his mind he had difficulty concentrating on his patients' problems. Each time a patient left his office with no prescription he fumed at Dr. Poil's irresponsible behaviour, giving away all the medicine and leaving none for Yun.

When his work day finally ended, he rushed home to find Yun lying in bed.

"I'm so tired," she said.

He felt her warm, flushed face. "You need to eat something," he said.

She shook her head. "Not hungry. It hurts." She held her hands over her stomach.

Upon examination, Piter saw the incision was fiery red. The thermometer showed she had a low-grade fever of thirty-eight degrees Celsius. He gave her some acetaminophen, angry he couldn't do more. A knock came at the door.

"Expecting someone?"

She shook her head.

Tresha, Fillip and Jakon stood at the door, their arms full of groceries. He invited them in.

"We brought some things for you. How's Yun?" Tresha asked.

"Not well. The pharmacy is out of antibiotics. She needs some yesterday. I feel helpless."

Fillip said, "I know a man who sneaks medicine out of the hospital to sell on the black market. It will cost a lot, at least eight hundred frezens for a ten-day dose."

Piter didn't hesitate. He opened his wallet and handed over the cash. "I'd be so grateful."

"Can we see her?" Tresha asked.

Piter led the way to the bedroom and they gathered around the bed.

"How are you, dear?" Tresha asked.

Yun answered in a croaky voice, "Better."

Piter bit his lower lip and averted his eyes from his wife's pale, sweaty face.

Tresha sat on the edge of the bed, held Yun's hand and spoke softly. "We're going to find you some medicine and when you recover we will carry on with the plan to help you and Piter to escape from the country. You remember the procedure to get to the first safe house, of course."

Yun nodded, put her hand on her belly and winced. She looked at Piter with a pleading expression and shook her head from side to side. He realized he was not the only one who kept secrets in this marriage. Piter was too surprised even to speak.

"When the time comes, we'll let you know which border guard has been bribed," Fillip said. He looked at Piter's stunned expression. "As Yun knows, we have a few on our payroll."

"Piter, I—"

Piter interrupted Yun. "We won't talk about it now. Wait until you've recovered." He covered her with a blanket. "Let's let her sleep." He pointed to the door. Wanting to sound casual, he asked, "So…how many are part of HRFA now?"

"Thousands," Fillip said. He laughed at Piter's expression. "I know. It's surprising. Of course, we only know a few by name and a few more by number. Yun has worked so hard, helping people across the border. It's time you two benefitted."

The organization was bigger and more complex than Piter had imagined. All this time, Yun was part of a well-organized underground that sneaked people out of the country and never said a word to him. Piter ran his hand through his greasy hair, trying to comprehend this revelation. While he was impressed by her bravery, he was peeved she kept this secret. "You want some tea or something?"

"Sit down, Piter. You look tired. Let me get it," Tresha said. "You don't mind if Jakon and I use your kitchen." Without waiting for an answer, she opened his cupboard, took out a pot, put it on the stove and opened a can of soup. Jakon heated hot water and poured it into a teapot.

Piter was tired, hadn't slept, eaten well, or even showered in days. He sat on a kitchen chair and wiped his sweaty hands on his pant legs. "It's so discouraging. The individual has little chance against the system," he said. "Look what they did to Yun. There is no way we can get out of the country."

"Keep the faith," Fillip said. "Concentrate on the successes we've had." He pulled a map from his pocket and laid it on the table. "Your first safe house is here." He pointed to a spot on the map. "As Yun explained to you, bring only the essentials, and as much money as you can. I know you two were going to wait until after the baby was born..."

Piter listened and nodded, pretending he knew of this plan. "It's such a risk."

"True, but many are willing to take the risk for freedom." Fillip smiled. "AZEN will fall one day. You'll see."

"We have people who will help you every step of the way, but only when you're ready," Tresha said. She handed Piter a bowl of soup.

Jakon came behind his mother, taking small steps, concentrating on carrying a cup of tea. He placed it on the table.

"Thank you, Jakon," Piter said.

"I didn't spill," Jakon said. "Drink it!"

Piter sipped. "It's very good. Did you make it?"

"Yep." The boy's face lit with pride.

Piter was surprised the young man was so happy, despite his handicap. AZEN taught that moogies were a great burden to their families and society. Tresha and Fillip didn't seem to think so.

CHAPTER TWENTY-ONE

Hadar

Tresha and Fillip awoke to persistent knocking on the door. They hurried down the stairs and Fillip opened the door to a scraggly-bearded man. The hood of his coat covered his eyes.

"What do you want?" Fillip asked, his voice harsh.

"It's me. I need help."

"Hadar?" Tresha whispered. "Come in." She stepped aside, letting him slip in, looked up and down the darkened street, saw no one and closed the door.

He pushed down his hood, revealing a frightened face. His cheeks were sunken and lips chapped.

"You must be hungry." Tresha took his coat and led him to a chair.

While Hadar ate a bowl of instant noodles, he explained they received a warning minutes before disaster struck. All the seminarians managed to escape and scatter, but their home was burned to the ground. "They're after me. All clergy and religious are being thrown in jail."

"We have a concealed closet where we've hidden books and other things. You can hide there," Fillip said. He led the way downstairs and pushed aside a bookshelf on wheels.

Hadar nodded his head when he saw the wall panels hiding the entrance to the room. He ran his fingers over the edges. "Hardly noticeable. Very clever."

Fillip said, "You'll be able to get out on your own if you want, since the shelf is on wheels."

Tresha slid the panel open. "Sorry there's not much room in here. I can take out some books."

Hadar looked at the stacks of religious articles and literature. "I'll be fine. I'll have time to read and pray. You're brave for opening your door to me."

Fillip arrived with a pillow, blankets and tea. The three sat on the basement floor.

Hadar said, "I spoke to my parents. How are Piter and Yun after the loss of their child?"

"Piter is not doing well emotionally and Yun is sick with an infection," Tresha said.

Hadar closed his eyes for a moment. "My mother told me Piter is an eradicator." Tears welled in his eyes.

Tresha gasped and gave Fillip a worried look. "Dear God! He's not on our side. We talked about our safe houses in front of him. How does your mother know, Hadar?"

"He told her. Please don't tell him I'm here."

Fillip said, "We won't tell. Tresha, it's my fault. I should have suspected. He didn't come to the meetings anymore. Yun always said it was because he was too busy. How many people did I endanger by showing him the map, the locations of our supporters?"

Tresha said, "Maybe it's okay. Yun knows him better than anyone and she obviously trusts him."

Jakon came down the stairs and regarded the bearded stranger.

"Come, Jakon. Say hello to our friend." Tresha held out her hand and Jakon sat on the floor with them.

Fillip said, "We'll have to be cautious no one finds out you're here, Hadar. People get food coupons for snitching on their neighbours. We'll have to fire the caregiver for Jakon and Tresha's dad. We can't risk anyone finding out about you."

Hadar looked at the teenage boy. "People know about your son?"

Fillip nodded. "We're afraid for him."

"Can you get out of the country, or find someone to take him?" Hadar asked.

Tresha tightened her grip on Jakon's hand. "People don't have to send the disabled to Quietus. It's a choice. Besides, he'd be scared without us."

Hadar leaned forward. "Can you trust the government? They gave us false hope, promising safeguards to protect people who can't defend themselves, like the elderly. You need to be proactive."

Tresha thought she might burst into tears. Hadar spoke the truth. Her child's life was in danger. "How do we fight a force like AZEN? Look how many people are in prison or have simply disappeared. In the last six months, one member of the opposition apparently committed suicide. His wife said he wasn't depressed. Another died of a drug overdose and she was part of the war against drugs when the previous administration was in power. Two were killed in car accidents. Three more are in jail under charges of terrorism just as they were bringing forth patient abuse complaints in Quietus Centres. Too much coincidence."

Fillip said, "We can't fight them. For now, all we can do is undermine them by helping people get out of the country."

§

On the front page of the newspaper the next day was a picture of Aura Zarling in a pink dress. Behind her was an apple tree, full of white blossoms that surrounded her head like a halo. Beneath her picture was a quote:

> *Let's urge our old relatives to show their love for the country by not being burdens. Help them to choose Quietus. They should not be forced to endure more years on this planet when they can no longer work and contribute. This is a quality of life issue. Elderly people aren't happy with their loss of independence and poor health. What about their emotional well-being? Have pity on your old relatives. We, in Covona, are proud of the accomplishments in the field of medicine and pain-free Quietus.*

The story that followed had the headline: "Citizens Urged to Curb Offensive Speech."

> *AZEN is introducing a linguistic cleansing program. Criticism of our government, the president, or AZEN's decisions are hereby banned. The media, employees of all educational institutions, medical facilities, and government and private individuals are*

[135]

expected to comply. Citizens guilty of linguistic offences, spoken or written, will be punished. Dissenting speech will not be tolerated.

Practice mental hygiene. Control your thoughts to control your speech.

§

A few days later, Fillip came home from work gloomy. He kissed Jakon on the top of his head and flopped onto a kitchen chair. "They fired me. Thirty years of tenure, and they fired me."

Tresha gasped. "Why?" She placed his supper on the table in front of him.

"The new rules. A student accused me of being offensive. I said in class last week that elderly people were dying at an alarming rate in this country; an undisputed fact. Apparently, her feelings were hurt because her grandparents died recently."

"That was last week, before the new linguistic offences law."

"Doesn't seem to matter to the university."

"Did you speak in your own defense?"

"I wasn't given an opportunity. They brought us both in front of a panel. I opened my mouth to speak and she broke down and cried. I was fired on the spot for causing her distress."

Tresha got up from the table and stood in front of the window as her family ate. Spring was almost at an end. Light rain fell. Drops traced little paths down the pane. Her meal sat uneaten on the table. "What are we going to do, Fillip?" She turned and stroked Jakon's hair. "What if they come for him, or Dad, or they find out about Hadar? I couldn't bear to live without my loved ones."

Tresha's father sat in his wheelchair at the table doing a sloppy job of eating porridge. It was smeared on his face and his bib. He insisted on feeding himself but did permit Tresha to wipe his face.

"Tresha, sit down and eat," her father said.

"I have no appetite. Maybe we should just take re-education, join AZEN and—"

"Never," Fillip said.

"I'm grateful Raimond is letting me work from home. He's an elite. They get all the privileges." She wiped a wet cloth over the already clean countertop.

"I won't sell my soul to the devil," Fillip said. "Please eat."

She ate a forkful of stew. "I'm still searching for antibiotics for Yun."

Someone pounded on the door. "Police! Open up!"

Before Tresha had a chance to open the door, it crashed open. Tresha screamed as wood splinters flew across the room. Four policemen in uniform charged into the room, weapons drawn. They wore battle armour: bullet-proof vests, helmets and pads covering their arms and legs. The AZEN crest showed on their chests, an uppercase "A" with a vertical line running down the centre. A man with a ponytail sauntered in after them, hands behind his back, with a smirk on his face.

Ponytail was about thirty. A sprig of blond hair hung over one eye. He barked at Tresha to sit down at the kitchen table and sat across from her. He pushed her plate aside, put his elbows on the table and folded his hands together.

Fillip winced as two policemen placed him in handcuffs and took him outside.

The other two policemen charged up the staircase. One was tall and lanky. The other was built like a brick. Tresha tried to stay calm by taking slow, deep breaths. Jakon sat on a chair beside his mother and hid his face with his hands.

"You appear nervous, Ms. Farwell." His calm voice was sticky sweet, like syrup. He smiled, but his eyes were cruel and intense, like a lion on the hunt.

Tresha flinched at the sound of smashing glass, knowing it was the china dishes her mother left her. "They're breaking our things."

"My men must be thorough in their search." He looked hard at Tresha with unblinking eyes and she dropped her gaze to her lap.

Heavy boots clomped on the floor above. Her father slumped in his wheelchair; his breathing was heavy and congested.

Ponytail pushed a photograph towards her, a photo of a clean-shaven man. "Do you know this man?"

"Yes. It's Hadar Dram."

"Where is he?"

"I don't know."

"I think you do."

Tresha started to shake. She was afraid her expression would give something away.

Ponytail smiled a thin, ugly smile. His tongue shot out of his mouth to lick his lips, like a snake closing in on its prey. "What about you, boy? Do you know where this man is?"

Jakon looked at the photo and shook his head. Tresha was glad Hadar now had a full beard.

"That boy is a moogie," Ponytail said. A look of disapproval spread across his face.

"That's a bad word," Jakon said. He stood beside his grandfather, who put his hand on Jakon's.

"What about you, old man?"

Tresha's father moaned, pretending he couldn't talk.

Ponytail snarled, "Relax, Ms. Farwell. Nothing will happen to your family if you tell the truth."

She felt sweat prickling under her arms. This was not the time to be truthful. "How would I know where he is?"

"Come on. Confession is good for the soul."

If his smile was an attempt to put her at ease, it had the opposite effect. She told him again she didn't know, pushed back her chair and attempted to stand. He caught her arm and made her sit down again. Holding her forearm in a tight grip, he rubbed his fingers across the back of her hand. "You can always tell someone's age just by looking at their hands. Loose skin, age spots. Don't you want to live your remaining days in peace and comfort? If you know where the fugitive is, tell us and you'll be rewarded."

She shivered, pulled her arm away and held her hands in her lap. Her face grew hot.

Two policemen, Lanky and Brick, stomped down the stairs again. Brick shook his head at the interrogator and then the policemen descended into the basement. Tresha bit her lip to keep from crying out. She prayed silently.

Ponytail said, "If you're lying I can't help you. Perhaps we need to take your husband to headquarters for a more thorough interview. We can be very persuasive when it comes to getting information from people. My men are outside talking to him right now. You don't want anything to happen to your husband, do you?"

She averted her eyes from his steady gaze and shook her head. She looked at her father and son. Her vision blurred with tears.

"How is your dad doing?" Ponytail asked, his voice suddenly soft.

Tresha's father sat in his wheelchair with a long line of drool hanging from his lower lip. He raised his eyes to the interrogator and moaned.

"Waste of space and resources." The interrogator looked from the old man to the teenager. "You should send them both to Recycling."

She hated the way that horrible man looked at her darling Jakon and dear father, as if they were piles of dung on the sidewalk. The stroke had destroyed her father's motor functioning, but didn't damage his hearing. She was startled again, this time by loud crashes coming from the basement. Her heart pounded.

Boots clomped up the stairs and the two policemen came into the kitchen. Their guns and clubs hung from their waists. She had seen police officers beating people with clubs. Her father looked at the policemen and grimaced.

Lanky said, "I didn't know vegetables could move."

Tresha wanted to slap the sneer off his face but dared not show any emotion.

Brick said, "No sign of the fugitive, but we found this." He dropped a prayer book on the table.

Ponytail clicked his tongue, looking at Tresha like she was a child who sneaked a cookie. "Now, Ms. Farwell, you know the law. This is unapproved literature. What are we going to do with you?"

"It was my mother's. I couldn't stand to part with it. It's nothing more than a keepsake."

Ponytail leant in close to her. "One more violation and you'll be sent to Re-Ed. Then, you'll have no one to look after the carrot." He pointed at her father.

The policemen laughed.

Ponytail put the book in a plastic bag, "as evidence," and wrote her a ticket for two hundred and fifty frezens for possession of contraband materials. He came around the table and grabbed a handful of her hair. He put his face so close to hers she thought, at first, he was going to kiss her. His breath smelled of whiskey. "I'd like to haul away these pieces of trash, right now." He pointed at Tresha's father and son. "But I won't. Not yet. I'll come back another day. Then you and I can have some quality time together."

She worked up a bit of courage which she didn't know she had. "Get out of my house!" She shook with rage.

Ponytail let go of her hair and placed his hand on her shoulder, squeezing hard. "There, there. You'll come around to see things our way. The day you decide to unburden this mess, I'll be here to cheer you on." He sauntered over to the broken front door and called outside, "Let Dr. Farwell go, men. The priest isn't here. Come on, you two," he waved at Brick and Lanky. "Let's leave Ms. Farwell to change her father's diaper." They all laughed and went outside.

Fillip came back in looking shaken and rubbing his wrists. He had a bruise forming on his face. "Everything okay?"

Tresha nodded and burst into tears. He held her for a moment. She removed her glasses and wiped her eyes with the back of her hand.

Fillip rubbed the blood from his wrists. "The cuffs were on so tight they bit into my wrists. We better go down and check."

Tresha put her finger to her lips and on a piece of paper wrote, *Bugs?*

Fillip squatted down and looked under the kitchen table. "I can't believe they thought we were hiding a fugitive. We're loyal citizens."

"It's for the good of us all, Fillip."

"Exactly, you can't fault people for doing their jobs."

[140]

"They found my mother's prayer book."

"Tresha, I thought you threw that away."

"Sorry." She pointed to him to go upstairs and indicated she would go down. "We have quite a mess to clean up. Better get busy."

Downstairs, she stepped over scattered debris. The furniture had been tipped over. The bookshelf lay face down on the floor. The wall panel was still in place.

Thank God. They didn't look too closely. She breathed a sigh of relief, opened the hatch and looked in at Hadar, crouching in the dark. His eyes were wide with fright. She put her finger to her lips and waved at him to come out. Tresha began searching for a listening device, but found none.

Hadar stepped out and stretched.

Together, they lifted the bookshelf, replaced the contents and wheeled it aside. She put her fingers to her mouth to show she was going to bring him food.

He wrote on a paper and handed it to her. *I'm putting you in danger by staying.*

She read his note, turned the paper over and wrote on the back. *You can't leave. Not yet. Hunters will be watching the house.*

CHAPTER TWENTY-TWO

Yun

Piter and Tresha walked along the banks of the North Omala River. The leaves were fluttering on the trees. A sliver of the moon hung in the sky, shedding a little light on the river to their left. The water churned with spring runoff. To their right, coniferous trees blocked their view of the street.

"Fillip is still trying to negotiate for some antibiotics on the black market. It's quite expensive, but I can give you antiseptic cream." Tresha handed him a tube.

"Thanks, but it won't help. I'm afraid she'll soon become septic. I'm a doctor and I can't heal my wife."

"It's all we can do for now. The guy I know asked for more money, says he's risking his life to steal it from the hospital."

Piter emptied his wallet and pulled off his wedding ring. "Is that enough?"

"It should be. We'll send someone to deliver the medicine to your home when we get it. Best of luck." She hugged him.

§

Rain tapped the window pane. Piter paced the room, waiting for a messenger to bring the antibiotic he had paid for. "I'm a failure. Where is the good life I promised you?" He rubbed his hands together.

Piter looked at his wife's fragile body stretched out on a smelly mattress. She lay shivering under the blanket and made no response. Yun had wet the bed and Piter was not able to clean it properly. He sat on the edge of the bed and took her hand. The room was cool, but her hand was hot.

A week ago, his baby died and now he feared for Yun's life. He thought about Tresha's offer to escape from Covona. It was a big risk, a death sentence if they were caught.

[142]

"Hold this under your tongue," Piter said, and placed a thermometer in her mouth. A minute later he read the thermometer: thirty-nine degrees Celsius. Her temperature was dangerously high. *Damn it!* "I can't live without you," he told her.

She opened her eyes. "Thirsty."

He lifted her head and gave her sips of water. Piter rubbed the back of his neck and paced the floor.

Yun moaned.

"God, if you're real, heal Yun." Piter dug through Yun's belongings until he found a prayer book, opened to a random page and began to read. He paced the room, prayer book in his hand. He wiped his unshaven face with the back of his hand.

Yun shivered and mumbled to herself.

"Wasting my time praying to a non-existent God." His choice became clear. Piter ripped the prayer book into pieces and threw it in the garbage. He put on his shoes and jacket. "I'll be back," he said and kissed her hot forehead.

He ran through the rain until he arrived at AZEN headquarters. It was early morning and they had just opened the doors. Falling to his knees he begged to join, said he would do anything. Rain water dripped from his hair and down his face. He told them about his sick wife. They took him by the hand, welcomed him, directed him to sit in a chair and put a warm, dry towel over his shoulders.

A paper was placed on the desk for his signature. He had to declare his faith in Aura Zarling's Enlightened Nationalists. Piter was still shivering as he signed the declaration.

A young woman entered and offered him a cup of hot coffee. He sipped. It tasted bitter.

"We've sent an ambulance for your wife" a bald, middle-aged man said. He sat across the desk and held a loyalty card out to him, but as Piter went to take it, the plastic card was snatched away. "Did you think it would be that easy? You must first prove your allegiance to AZEN."

Piter looked at the interrogator's dead eyes. A feeling of despair overwhelmed him and he couldn't control the tears.

The interrogator was unmoved. "We could just as easily destroy the card and have you executed. Your brother and some of your friends are involved in illegal activities. Tell us how to find them."

Piter's concern was for his wife. Other people came second. Still, he didn't want people to get hurt. "I don't know where they are."

"Don't insult my intelligence, Dr. Dram." Bald Man leaned back in his chair and twirled the card between his thumb and forefinger. "You will tell us what we want to know, either willingly or not."

Piter drooped his head, feeling helpless.

Bald Man cleaned his fingernails with the corner of the card. "I wonder how Yun is doing right now. Whether they provide treatment for her at the hospital depends on your answers to my questions."

He thought of his beloved Yun. It had been over an hour since he left her. He imagined her alone among uncaring strangers. Meanwhile, he would be taken to Re-Ed. The outcome would be the same. They would force him to tell everything he knew and Yun would be dead. He remembered the map Fillip had shown him. "Fourth Avenue and Tenth. There's a bunker in the basement."

"Excellent. What else?" Bald Man sat up straight and scribbled notes on a piece of paper.

"A cabin, six kilometres west of Lake Rania on Highway Three."

"Where is your brother, Hadar?"

"I honestly don't know. Please, my wife is so sick."

Bald Man handed Piter the card. "Your cooperation will be noted. If the information is correct, you'll be rewarded. If it is not, well, you'll find out."

Piter nodded.

"I'll call the hospital and tell them to begin treatment. Someone will give you a ride over."

§

At the hospital, Piter stood by Yun's bed and checked everything was in order. She was receiving intravenous antibiotic for the infection, vaso pressure medications to increase blood pressure, corticosteroids for the inflammation, and fluids to rehydrate her. An oxygen mask helped her breathing. Now it was a matter of waiting to see if the treatment would work.

He sat by her bed, dizzy with exhaustion.

At just past six o'clock the next morning, Piter awoke to the quiet. The oxygen tank continued to hiss, but gone was the raspy intake of Yun's breathing. He sprang from the chair. The plastic tube still ran to her nose, but her chest did not rise and fall. Her dark eyes were open, staring at the ceiling. Her mouth was open also, as if she was about to speak.

"Code blue!" Piter shouted. Placing both hands on her breastbone, he pumped rhythmically. Two nurses entered the room and pushed him aside to take over CPR, but Piter knew it was futile. He ran his fingers through her long, black hair, slumped back into the chair, put his head in his hands, and wept.

A nurse removed the oxygen tube from Yun's nose and the intravenous from her arm. He covered her body with a sheet and patted Piter on the shoulder, offering his condolences. "She's no longer suffering. Recycling will be here soon to collect the remains."

Piter blew his nose and focused on the sheet outline of his wife's body. He wiped his eyes and turned the three words, "Yun is dead," over and over in his mind, as if they couldn't possibly be true. He leaned his forehead on his hands. A beam of morning light streamed through a break in the curtains. Outside, birds began to chirp. He rubbed his cramped neck and thought of the people he betrayed. When he looked up, two AZEN police officers, wearing side arms and bullet-proof vests, entered the room.

"Come with us, Dr. Dram."

CHAPTER TWENTY-THREE

Confession

Piter sat in the back of the police car with his hands cuffed behind his back, too numb to care where he was being taken. Streams of sunlight penetrated the glass, causing sweat to roll down his forehead, but he was unable to wipe it away. His throat ached with thirst. Familiar sights rolled by outside the window—the same neglected buildings, struggling businesses and potholed streets. He was not surprised when they approached the barbed wire fence and guard towers of the Re-education Centre.

Piter sat in a small room, bare except for two metal chairs. A guard stood by the door, thumbs tucked into his belt.

Piter regarded his reflection in a large two-way mirror. Dismayed by his own bedraggled appearance and his resigned, scared eyes, he dropped his gaze to the floor. He opened and closed his hands to force circulation into his cold fingers, dropped his chin towards his chest and closed his tired, burning eyes.

A man with the tag "Interrogator" pinned to his shirt entered, pushing a cart. His pudgy, round face and quiet demeanor showed no signs of malice. The man could have passed for an accountant or a bank employee. On the cart were a laptop computer, wires and rubber tubes, a blood pressure cuff, finger pulse oximeters, and small electronic boxes.

"Remove the handcuffs," the interrogator said softly. He took some time setting up his equipment and then attached rubber tubes around Piter's chest and abdomen, along with a blood pressure cuff on his arm. "These will measure your respiratory rate and blood pressure."

Piter spoke with a dry, hoarse voice, "What is this?"

"A polygraph machine. Place your hands on the arms of the chair please." He put small metal plates on two fingers of Piter's right hand with strips of Velcro. "These will measure your heart rate and electro-dermal activity, the sweatiness of your fingers." On the index finger of Piter's left hand he placed the pulse oximeter.

"Why?" Piter concentrated on taking slow, deep breaths. Bruises were forming on his wrists.

"We just need to confirm a few details. No need to be nervous," the interrogator said, as if speaking to a child. The kind tone of voice didn't match his blank expression.

"I just lost my wife. I'm so tired. Can't it wait?"

The interrogator did not make eye contact. "No. Let's begin. Answer yes or no. Do you know where your brother, Hadar Dram is?"

"No." Piter struggled to control his trembling lower lip.

The interrogator typed on his laptop and continued. "Are you a member of Human Rights for All?"

"No."

"Did you disrupt the post-election rally of our president?"

"Uh, not on purpose."

"Yes or no, please." The interrogator's voice remained soft and detached.

"Yes, but…"

"Were you, at any time, involved in hiding forbidden items?"

"No." Piter spread his hands and looked at the instruments that measured his involuntary responses. The blood pressure cuff squeezed his arm. He wondered if his body would betray him and he struggled to stay calm.

"Do you know any members of HRFA?"

"Yes."

"Give me their names."

"Fillip and Tresha Farwell."

"Were they involved in illegal activities?"

"No."

The interrogator glanced at his computer screen and made a note in his book. He named several other people, some of them Piter's patients, asking if they were involved in HRFA.

"It's a drop-in clinic. I don't know the patients on a personal basis."

"Yes or no, please."

"No."

The interview continued for another hour. "That will be all for now. You will be taken to a cell to rest."

§

A cell door slammed shut behind Piter. A bunkbed occupied one wall of the tiny room. On the lower level a man lay snoring. There was a lidless metal toilet and sink. The walls were yellow concrete. Piter climbed to the top bunk and closed his eyes.

Before he'd slept long, they woke him up and took him to another room. No polygraph machine here, just a metal chair placed in front of a desk. Leather straps hung from the arms of the chair and the two front legs.

A stern-looking man with a large mustache sat behind the desk. He held a sheet of paper. "Sit," he said. "We're not satisfied with your responses on the polygraph, Dr. Dram. We'd like to ask you a few more questions. Promise you'll behave yourself and we won't need the straps."

A teenager stood beside Piter and smiled in a creepy way, like the kind of kid who delights in pulling legs off daddy-long-legs, burning insects under a magnifying glass or torturing cats. Piter leaned away from the acne-blemished teenager and placed his hands on his knees. He spoke softly. "The polygraph is wrong. I told the truth."

Mustache Man turned on a lamp and pointed it in Piter's direction. Piter remembered a movie where a prisoner was interrogated. He put his hand in front of his eyes, thinking the bright light was a cliché. "Will you turn the light away please?"

Mustache Man turned up the brightness and proceeded to ask the same questions asked earlier.

Despite his best efforts to stay alert and answer the endless stream of questions about exact locations where "rebels" could be found and where and when "illicit activities" took place, Piter felt his head bob. "I'm telling the truth." His eyes burned from sleepiness.

Sadness overtook him every time he thought of Yun. He cried like a child and wiped his nose with his sleeve. "Please, turn off the lamp. Leave me be."

"We were told you attended a meeting in a certain abandoned building."

"No, I never attended any—"

"What was discussed at the meeting?"

"I wasn't there."

"You're not being truthful."

The acne-faced boy slapped Piter hard.

Piter's face stung, but the slap made him more alert. "Listen. I only know they sneak people out of the country using safe houses."

"How are they getting people across the wall?"

"I told you as much as I know. I need to rest. Can we talk tomorrow?"

"I'm afraid not." The interrogator waved his hand at the teenage boy who punched Piter in the face.

Piter felt a "thunk" which disoriented him. He blinked his eyes and watched the teen's fist come towards his face again. He turned his head to the side, catching the punch in the jaw and feeling a "thunk-crack" as his teeth crashed together. Piter put his fingers to his cut lip.

"We need to know how dissidents are getting past the wall."

"I don't know. Honestly."

The boy grinned as he shook his hand out.

"These friends of yours are traitors. They are facing the death penalty, as are you, Dr. Dram, unless we get some answers. You joined HRFA, yes or no?"

"I was never part of the group. It was my wife. I proved my loyalty. I'm a doctor, an eradicator."

"Why didn't you stop her? Loyal citizens don't permit their partners to be a members of rebel groups."

Another hour passed and the interrogator's questions were unrelenting.

"Did Fillip Farwell invite you to join the rebel group, Human Rights for All?"

"Yes, but I didn't. May I have some water?"

The interrogator nodded to the acne-skinned young man who came back with a glass of water. As he reached for the glass, Acne-Skin threw the water in Piter's face and laughed.

Piter wiped his face, directing the drops towards his cracked lips and dry mouth. The questioning continued. The interrogator's monotone made Piter sleepy, but every time he closed his eyes, Acne-Skin slapped him awake.

The interrogator was quiet for a few minutes as he wrote on a pad of paper. He pushed it across the desk to Piter. "Sign the confession."

Piter took a deep breath and squinted at the paper with burning eyes, struggling to focus. "I can't sign this. I never said half of these things."

"In that case, we will go over it again." He snatched the paper away.

The interrogation continued for another interminable amount of time. Piter had difficulty keeping his thoughts straight.

"Were you a member of HRFA?" the interrogator asked for what seemed to be the hundredth time.

"Yes."

"There you go. See how easy that was?" The interrogator's voice softened and he turned down the brightness of the lamp a little bit. "Did you forget?"

"Yes. I forgot."

"Let me remind you of a few other things." The interrogator mentioned people that earlier Piter swore he'd never met.

"Yes. I remember him. He was at the meetings." Piter no longer cared what was true and what was false.

Again, the interrogator said, "Sign the confession," and pushed the paper towards Piter.

Piter's eyes were too tired to read the paper. He signed it.

He was shown to a cell with two sets of bunk beds. Piter took the empty bed and fell asleep.

§

The next day, Piter stood in a row with the other "students," at the Re-education Centre, all dressed in identical orange jumpsuits. They stood, hands behind their backs, feet hip-width apart, backs straight and eyes forward.

The commanding officer walked back and forth, holding a switch. He lashed out at a middle-aged man standing beside Piter, catching him across the cheek. "You may blink your eyelids. That is the only thing I should see moving. Understand?"

"Yes, sir!" The fear was palpable in the man's voice.

Piter stood as still as he could. From the corner of his eye he saw a drop of blood form on the middle-aged man's cheek.

"Dispossessed scum, you are here because you are in violation of AZEN principles. I am here to help you adjust your thinking." He stood with his face centimetres from a student. "Do you think you can adjust your thinking, scum?"

"Yes, sir!"

He continued to pace back and forth, slapping the switch on his free hand. "This centre is full, as are other centres around the country. Many criminals have been apprehended recently thanks to information we received." He stopped and stared into Piter's face. The commanding officer's breath smelled like bubble gum. "This will be the last blow against those who oppose AZEN. Do you support AZEN, scum?"

"Yes, sir!" Piter shouted.

The commanding officer pointed with his switch towards the television. "Private! Turn on the T.V. for these scumbags."

A young man in uniform pushed a button on a remote control.

The students watched recorded scenes of policemen breaking into basements, attics and abandoned houses. Men and women were thrown to the ground, handcuffed and taken away.

The commanding officer smiled. "This is the Final Purge. Those who haven't been caught yet soon will be. In the coming days and weeks, we will capture them all. The criminals will get what they deserve."

§

Back in his cell, Piter paced the floor and rubbed his hand through his hair. The frightened faces of people arrested and thrown into the police van appeared again and again in his mind. Some of them he recognized as his patients. Others were neighbours.

The next day he was sent to work shovelling snow from the roof of a three-storey building. It was an early snowfall, wet and heavy. Piter pushed the snow towards the edge, scooped up a shovelful and dumped it over the one-metre-high barrier to the ground. He was filled with loneliness for Yun and his baby. He thought about the lives he had taken and the people he betrayed, picked up another shovelful and dumped it. He stood at the edge of the roof and looked down, and then stepped back, shaking.

That night, Piter lay on his bunk and forced back the tears.

§

The meals at Re-Ed weren't large enough to feed a child, and every day it was the same—thin porridge in the morning, mid-day it was plain rice and for supper, beans and carrots.

Loud piercing bells rang at 06:00. Students stood at attention outside their cells to receive their daily chores. Piter often folded laundry from the time he got up until he went to bed, with two fifteen-minute breaks for meals. The mind-dulling monotony of performing robotic tasks put him into a trance-like state. He tried not to let his thoughts wander to food, or to Yun.

Once an hour, Aura's words were broadcast over the intercom system. On his first day at Re-Ed, he heard:

"All caretakers of elderlies and dysfunctionals are now required to report their charges to your local Quietus Centre. In due time, they will be dealt with. Anyone unlawfully harbouring a dysfunctional will face the consequences."

On the second day:

"Perhaps some of you have some lingering convictions passed on to you by your misguided parents or grandparents. Simply trust AZEN to guide you towards a bold and prosperous future."

After a week, he imagined himself taking a hammer to all the speakers. At night, even though the room was quiet, her voice still echoed in his head.

CHAPTER TWENTY-FOUR

Safe House

Rain dripped off the messenger's coat and onto the floor. He handed the package of medicine to Tresha. "They were loading Yun into an ambulance when I arrived. Piter was nowhere in sight."

Tresha's heart sank. She took back the antibiotic and dashed to the basement to show Hadar.

They had done a thorough sweep of the house and hadn't found any listening devices. They were free to speak.

Hadar's eyes opened wide. "Only the elite can travel by ambulance."

Tresha thumped her hand against her breastbone. "And no dispossessed person can become elite without first being re-educated. He's gone to Re-Ed. It's the only logical conclusion."

Hadar squeezed his eyes shut. "At least Yun will get proper medical care. I'm grateful, but how much does he know about HRFA?"

"Enough to do damage." Tresha felt her face grow slack. "How does a whole country get brainwashed? Ever since the war…"

"I'm leaving after dark tonight," Hadar said.

She grasped Hadar's arm. "Not yet. Let me arrange safe passage first."

"I won't put you in more danger."

"If they catch you—"

"My mind is made up," Hadar said. "Not only are you harbouring two dysfunctionals, you're hiding illegal literature and a criminal." He pointed to himself.

Tresha nodded and struggled for the right words, but nothing came to mind. She wrote on a piece of paper and handed it to him. "They can help you escape Covona."

§

The downpour continued into the evening. Hadar pulled the hood over his head. "Peace. God be with you," he said and disappeared into the storm.

Fillip arrived home less than an hour later. Tresha was just explaining to him the day's latest developments when she heard a commotion outside. She opened the curtains. Wind thrashed heavy rain onto the window, making it difficult to see outside, like opening her eyes under water. She opened the front door a crack for a better view.

A uniformed man pushed a wheelchair out of a house to a parked bus. Seated in the chair was an old woman, wrapped in a blanket. Tresha knew the elderly woman was over eighty years old and had supported her neighbour's decision to not send her mom to Quietus. The old woman's daughter walked, holding an umbrella over her mother. A man stood in the doorway; a child wrapped her arms around his waist. The policeman picked the old woman up, carried her inside the bus and plunked her on a seat.

Tresha closed the door and leaned against it. She shouted, "Fillip! Jakon! Dad! They're coming!"

Fillip locked the door. "They'll be here soon. Take Jakon. Go out the back door. I'll stay here with your father."

"Can we take him downstairs to the secret room?"

"We'd never get him down the stairs in time. Besides, they already know he's here."

Tresha turned to see her father on his bed. His sad eyes registered understanding. He waved his hand at Fillip and spoke in slow, slurred speech, "Go with your wife and child! I'm old. Doesn't matter about me."

"I won't leave you," Fillip said. He helped Jakon into his coat.

Tresha couldn't get enough air in her lungs and feared she might faint. She pulled on her coat and boots and grabbed their bags that had sat ready by the door since the day the interrogator came looking for Hadar. She touched her father's warm, weathered hand and looked with longing at her husband, pushing away the thought that this could be the last time she'd see them. "I love you both."

Fillip hugged her. "We love you, too. Your father and I will meet you and Jakon at the school as soon as we can. If we don't show up in the next few days, carry on without us."

"Only a few days?"

"No longer. Too dangerous." Fillip held her cheeks between his hands and kissed her softly. "Go! Hurry!"

She dared not speak in case the words came out as whimpers. Tresha took Jakon's hand and slipped out the back door.

Jakon stretched his hat over his ears. "Where are we going, Mom?"

"On an adventure." Tresha pulled her hood over her head. The rain froze on contact on roads and sidewalks. She hooked arms with Jakon but soon realized hurrying would be impossible. They took baby steps to avoid falling on the slippery surface. The icy shower stung her face. She squinted into the storm, cut across the parking lot of a local shopping mall and headed for a nearby abandoned school, the nearest safe house.

§

Tresha and Jakon sneaked to the back of the school and opened the door with a spare key given to her by a former teacher, one of many good people who had been arrested, sacrificed for the cause. Once inside, she switched on a flashlight and they walked down dark, quiet hallways to the gymnasium. The gym was the one room in the school with no windows, so they couldn't be seen from outside.

Their supply bags contained everything they'd need—flashlights, batteries, sleeping bags, food, water, toilet paper and extra clothes. She found a gymnastic mat for their bed and spread their sleeping bags. They had enough food and water to last about four days—more, if she was careful. A janitor's bucket placed at the far end of the room would serve their toilet needs.

§

Hours dragged by. Jakon became restless. She found a slightly flattened ball in the closet and they played catch until he dropped the ball and walked towards the door.

"Go home, Mom?"

She intercepted him. "No, Jakon. We have to stay here and wait for Daddy."

Later in the evening they ate their meal, sandwiches and water. There was no way to tell night from day inside the gym. She checked her watch often. Jakon paced the floor, muttering to himself. Many times, she had to prevent him from leaving the gymnasium.

"Time for bed, Jakon." They climbed into the sleeping bags. After extinguishing the flashlight, they were left in complete darkness.

"Leave the light on, Mom!"

Tresha wrapped her arm around her son as they lay side by side. "It's okay, Mom is here. Go to sleep."

§

Two days passed and then three. Little food remained. The flashlight batteries were almost dead. She alternated between moments of despair and hopefulness. Mostly, she felt helpless, like a rabbit in a hole, while wolves prowled outside. "Let's pray Daddy and Grandpa are safe. We'll stay one more night and see what tomorrow brings."

The gym was quiet except for Jakon's soft snoring. She stared into blackness and worried. The hours passed slowly while she waited for some sort of signal.

Tresha awoke to knocking on the gym door, three staccato taps followed by three hard knocks. "Fillip!" She turned on the flashlight, ran to the door and flung it open, but no one was there, only an envelope on the floor. Inside was a note: *A contagious illness has spread to members of your family*. It was code, meaning her husband and father had been taken away by the police. Her hopes dashed, she felt an ache in her throat and crumpled the paper. Also in the envelope was some money and directions to another safe house. She memorized and then tore the directions to shreds.

§

The sun had just risen over the horizon when Tresha and Jakon put on their backpacks and left the abandoned school. She warned Jakon to be quiet and she tried to look inconspicuous by avoiding eye contact with people they passed on the sidewalk. A city bus approached. They climbed aboard. She was happy the bus was mostly empty—less chance of being recognized. It occurred to her, as she glanced at people seated around her, how gloomy they all looked, as if all excitement for life had been sucked out of their bodies, leaving spiritless shells behind. *Or maybe it's just me.*

Her destination was the Hills of Wryt, close to the border of Solime where there was a cabin in the woods. Tresha was to make a phone call from a train station and say a package was to be delivered. The difficulty was how to get to the train station. Identification was required when boarding trains and she was a wanted woman for harbouring a dysfunctional.

They rode the bus to the end of the line, the western edge of the city. She and Jakon stepped off the bus and walked towards a gas station so he could use the toilet.

While she waited, Tresha approached a truck driver as he paid for his gasoline. "Are you heading west today?" she asked him.

He squinted. "Yeah." A bristly beard sprouted from his face and neck.

She whispered, "Do you have room for me and my son?"

"No, lady. No passengers in my cab." He counted his change, put it in his wallet and walked towards his truck.

Tresha followed him. "How about in the back?" she whispered.

He motioned with his head and they stepped outside. "Someone after you?" He kept his back to her and lit a cigarette.

"Yeah."

"I don't take risks for nothing." He shook the match and dropped it to the ground.

Tresha reached into her pocket, pulled out some bills and handed them over.

With the cigarette poking from the corner of his mouth, he quickly counted the money. "I can take you as far as Okenfreim. If you get caught I didn't know how you got into my truck. Understand?"

"Yes."

"I'll wait for you at the next exit sign, about a kilometre west." He stepped up into his truck and drove away.

She went back inside to fetch Jakon. "Come on, Jakon. We have to hurry." Together, they trotted down the road. Tresha had given the transport driver half her money. As far as she knew, he could just keep driving and she'd never see him again.

The rising sun shone on their backs as they jogged on the shoulder of the highway. She knew Jakon sensed the urgency even if he didn't understand the reason. She was grateful he neither complained nor acted up. They had to stop frequently to catch their breath. Tresha was sweating by the time she saw the truck around a bend in the road.

The hatch on the back of the truck hung open. Tresha and Jakon climbed in and squatted behind some boxes marked "Farm Supplies." A few minutes later, the door slammed shut and they were left in complete darkness, still unsure if this stranger would bring them to their destination or turn them in for a reward.

Jakon leaned his back against his mother's chest. She wrapped her arms around him. To pass the time, she sang softly in his ear and stroked his cheek. Their bodies swayed back and forth with the movement of the truck.

Hours later, the back of the truck opened. The late afternoon sun was blinding. Tresha struggled to stand on her cramped legs and hobbled to the edge of the truck, peeking left and right before lowering herself down. Jakon did the same. The driver was nowhere in sight. In the distance, she saw the Okenfreim train station. Tall fir trees stood like sentries in the distance. Without a goodbye or thank you, mother and son, wearing their backpacks, made their way to the train station.

The train station was just as she imagined it, an old-fashioned, raised wooden platform alongside the tracks. Inside was a ticket booth with one person in attendance. Tresha didn't enter but made a call from a phone booth outside to a number she had memorized. "Two packages arrived," she said, when the male voice answered. Tresha and Jakon found a bench, sat down and waited.

Tresha's eyes darted back and forth, searching the faces of the people on the platform. She didn't know who would come to meet them. Maybe it was a trap. A woman wearing sunglasses stopped and checked the train schedule on the wall behind Tresha's head. Tresha opened her mouth to speak, but the woman walked away. Next, a young man came to the station and sat on the bench beside her. He reached into his bag and put on a pair of sunglasses. That was the signal. "Do you know when the next train leaves for Covona City?" he asked.

Tresha said, clearing her throat, "It leaves at three." The train schedule on the wall said 2:45 p.m.

The man got up from the bench and walked away. Tresha and Jakon waited a couple of minutes, got up and followed the young man, remaining a good distance behind. The man cut onto a path into the woods. About fifteen minutes later, they met him again, face to face. He reached down to pick up a branch on the forest floor. The branch was attached to a hatch disguised by moss, turf and leaves. Beneath the hatch was a hole in the ground.

He pointed to a ladder. "Follow me." He backed down into the hole. "Close the hatch behind you."

Tresha followed Jakon down the ladder. She closed the hatch and they were in darkness.

The man turned on a flashlight and aimed the ray of light down a long corridor with wooden-beam-reinforced walls. "This way," he said. They walked through the tunnel for a few minutes and then the man opened another hatch on the other side. Tresha was surprised to find herself inside a cabin, face to face with a young pregnant woman.

She reached out her hand. "Hello, I'm—"

"No names!" the woman interrupted. "I'm Eighty-Nine and that's Eighty-Eight." She pointed to her husband.

"I'm Twenty-Six," Tresha said. She pointed to Jakon. "My son."

A brown and white collie came to greet them. "That's Panzer," said Eighty-Nine.

§

Later, Tresha and Jakon sat down to their first hot meal in days. "Lamb stew! This is wonderful."

"Things are getting serious," Eighty-Eight said. "So many arrests. They're calling it the Final Purge. They want to wipe out dysfunctionals and everyone who opposes AZEN."

"We decided it's too risky for us to operate this house anymore," Eighty-Nine said. "We got your message just as we were packing up."

"What if other people come here, looking for a way out?" Tresha asked.

"We can't take any more risks. My wife is six months pregnant. We must leave, for the sake of our unborn child. You two are welcome to come with us."

Tresha explained her husband was likely being held in Re-Ed and she wanted to wait in case he returned. She looked at Jakon, who gave her a happy grin. Her heart ached. In Solime, he was in no danger of being put to death because of his Down's syndrome. She sat in silence for a long time, gazing at her plate and then back at Jakon. "I want to stay and wait for my husband, but I'm worried about my son. If they find him…" She didn't finish her sentence. Tresha lifted her head and said to the couple, "Will you take him with you?" She choked on the words as they came out.

"We'll take good care of him until we meet again," Eighty-Eight said.

"How will we find each other, if we make it across the border? I don't even know your real names," Tresha said.

"The Solimese are bound to keep records of who crosses their border. Keep the faith," Eighty-Eight said.

"You don't mind keeping the dog?" Eighty-Nine asked. "She's good company."

Tresha put her hand on the dog's furry head. "I'll take care of her."

§

The next morning, Tresha packed Jakon's backpack and helped him on with his coat. She thought about the long and dangerous route ahead for her son. "Remember what I told you."

He pointed to himself. "I go to Solime with our new friends." He then pointed to his mother. "You stay and wait for Daddy."

"Yes. What else?"

"Be really good and brave. Mommy and Daddy will come get me."

"That's right." Tresha took a deep breath and held it.

"When, Mommy?"

"I don't know, but soon."

Jakon's lips trembled. "When, Mommy?"

"Soon. Don't worry."

Jakon struck himself on the forehead with his fist three times before Tresha reached out and hugged him.

"I need you to be brave." She kissed his forehead.

He pulled back and held her face between his hands. "Okay, Mommy." He kissed her forehead, put on his backpack and followed his new caregivers.

She followed the couple and her son through the tunnel and up through the secret hatch. They stood outside and waved goodbye.

They took him away. It took every bit of strength to ignore her maternal instincts and not chase after them. Tresha wrapped her arms around herself while watching them become smaller and smaller in the distance.

She returned, locked the hatch and walked the length of the tunnel to her new home. Her legs shook as if they were too weak to hold her upright. Tresha flopped onto a chair and stared into space.

CHAPTER TWENTY-FIVE

Re-Ed

After a six-week stay at Re-Ed, Piter and twenty-four other graduates stood in four rows of six facing the Senior officer.

"It is time for the Denunciation and Acceptance Ceremony," the Senior officer announced. Step forward when you hear your name. Before you can receive your loyalty card, you will first denounce the people who tried to stop you from joining AZEN."

One by one the graduates stepped forward.

"I denounce my parents," said a young woman. "They are dead to me."

The Senior officer took the "Dispossessed" card from the student's neck and replaced it with a loyalty card. "Welcome, good and faithful servant."

Another graduate said, "I denounce my brother, Wyn. He is dead to me."

"Welcome, good and faithful servant."

Another said, "I denounce my ex-friend, Horth. He is dead to me."

Piter heard his name called. He felt a lump rise in his throat but knew it was necessary to betray her name if he was to move forward and prosper in the new Covona. "I denounce my wife, Yun. She is dead to me." He wanted to denounce Fillip and Tresha, who had pulled Yun into HRFA, but was told by the Senior officer it was better to denounce his wife, thereby thoroughly breaking all ties with the past.

"Welcome, good and faithful servant."

The ceremony continued until all the new graduates received their cards.

"You are now members of AZEN," the Senior officer said. "You are now deserving of special treatment, unlike the swarming masses who refuse our generosity. Who is to blame for the troubles the dispossessed find themselves in?"

"The dispossessed bring their troubles on themselves," the line of new loyal members chanted.

§

The doctors at Re-Ed invited Piter to the staff lounge and placed in front of him a huge meal of steak, mashed potatoes with gravy and a crisp salad. The smells were intoxicating. Piter gorged, filling his stomach to the bursting point. Feeling nauseated, he got up, ran to the toilet and vomited. The other doctors sat at the table and laughed.

He returned to the table and wiped his face with a napkin. "You knew that would happen," Piter said. He sat back down in his chair and pushed the remainder of the meal away. "Why put such a large meal in front of me after I've been starved these past weeks?"

The head physician of Re-Ed said, "We're just having a little fun." He handed a few frezens to another doctor. "We place bets on who will finish the meal and who can hold it down. I had high hopes for you." He laughed. "Don't worry. You'll have your appetite back in no time." He leaned forward, elbows on the table, and crossed his arms. "Let's be serious. Dr. Dram, we've had a look at your university records. You were a top student."

Piter nodded and looked down at the scraps remaining on his plate—the piece of glistening fat, the chunk of beef, red and dripping, brown gravy swirling around in greasy puddles. He wondered if he'd have to run to the toilet again.

"We have an offer for you. Come work here at Re-Ed. The pay is better than in private practice, certainly better than the Free Clinic. The job benefits are great, free housing, medical and dental. What do you say?"

Piter knew this was a good opportunity for him, no way could he refuse.

§

He was given time to recuperate in an apartment equipped with every convenience. The first day, he walked around his new home, ran his fingers across the stainless-steel door of the refrigerator, peeked inside the oven and turned on the water faucet, letting it run cold and then hot. A picture window looked down onto the street. A police car sped by with its lights flashing and siren wailing. The trees were already dressed in red, yellow and brown leaves, a pretty sight ordinarily, but not to Piter. He saw the dying trees as a reminder of the dark, cold winter yet to come.

A life-sized portrait photo of Aura Zarling hung on the wall of his apartment. She was dressed in a dark suit with her hair pulled in a bun behind her head. Piter tried to take the photo down, but found it was secured to the wall.

He heated a kettle and made a cup of tea. Holding the steaming cup in his shaking hand, he wondered if he would ever be happy again. He placed the tea on the counter and clutched the edge of the sink until his fingers cramped. Piter had figured out, early on, the correct responses to the interrogators' questions at Re-Ed. It wasn't hard to parrot back what they wanted to hear. He would have said anything to get out. He sipped, but bitterness churned his stomach. He dumped the tea down the sink.

§

Skilled physicians were in high demand, so after a week of recuperating he began working at Re-Ed. Piter was glad he thought to wear a warm wool sweater under his lab coat. He sat on a stool, his back against a cold concrete wall, a stethoscope around his neck and clipboard on his lap. He eyed the various paddles, sticks and thin straps laid out on the table in the middle of the room. A severe interrogation was about to take place. The pen shook in his trembling hand.

A thin man in a suit and tie sat cross-legged on the far side of the table. The student sat shivering in a chair in front of the table dressed only in a pair of shorts. The young man's hands and feet were strapped to the metal chair. His eyes were wide with terror.

A guard stood with arms crossed behind the young man.

Piter blew on his fingers to warm them and wrote the date and time beneath the student's name and date of birth. He was only twenty-one.

The interrogator nodded to the guard. The guard pushed the young man's chair from behind, toppling it.

"Argh!" the young man yelled as his knees and head hit the floor.

Piter stopped himself from rising from his chair to help. The young man slumped his head to his chest and breathed through his mouth. His face was already beginning to swell.

The guard laughed and righted the chair. Blood dripped over the young man's lips and down his chest. Piter noticed two buckets of water next to the door, assuming it was for clean-up afterwards. The interrogator yawned.

"You okay, Doc? You've gone a little pale." The guard smiled at Piter. "You an interrogation virgin? I'll take it easy on him, for your sake."

Piter cleared his throat and asked, "Why am I here?"

"We can't have students dying before every bit of information can be extracted," the interrogator said. "It can take many sessions to gain the needed information—a risk, especially for older or fragile students. We want you to speak up and interrupt the session if you feel the student's life is in danger."

Piter stood and ran his finger along the bridge of the young man's nose. *Student suffered a broken nose*, he wrote on the clipboard.

The interrogator selected a thick strap and put a blindfold on the young man. "Who else was involved in spreading lies about our president?"

"No one. I'm innocent."

The guard struck the man across the cheek with a resounding *thwack*.

The man yelped. "No! I swear!"

The interrogator chuckled. "It's much more fun if they don't know what's coming." He pointed to a bucket, put his finger in front of his lips. "Shh." He picked up a bucket of cold water and poured it over the young man. The young man let out a high-pitched shriek.

Piter checked his medicine bag to make sure he had his thermometer. *Hypothermia a concern*, he wrote on the clipboard. *Temperature will be taken every half hour.*

For the next two and a half hours, Piter stared at the ceiling or the floor, anywhere but at the young man in the chair. He distracted himself by humming a lullaby his mother used to sing to him.

§

He attended many questioning sessions. At first, he left the questioning sessions shaken. Disturbing dreams filled his nights. Some mornings, Piter was reluctant to rise from bed, knowing what he would be a part of that day. Weeks passed. He realized how gentle his own interrogations had been in comparison. He wasn't convinced torture was the best method for gaining information. Students eventually said what they were told to say just to escape further punishment.

§

Day after day, he treated wounds left by the interrogators—broken bones, burns and soft-tissue injuries. He prescribed antibiotics and painkillers. Many students showed signs of malnourishment and, not surprisingly, depression.

He avoided eye contact and refused to converse with the students who became his patients. Emotions would only complicate his decision making. Piter marvelled at the equipment and medicine at his disposal. He imagined the good they could have done for Yun and the patients at the Free Clinic. He concluded the country was not short of medicine, as he had believed. It was simply denied to the lower classes.

In his free time, he was encouraged to continue research into the causes and treatments of amyotrophic lateral sclerosis, ALS. In his lab, he could forget, temporarily, the horrors of the things he experienced and witnessed.

§

One evening, Piter sank into his soft leather chair and watched the news anchor speak in an excited voice about the number of "rebels, agitators and criminals" who had been apprehended, thanks to tips from loyal members of the public. The news anchor's face was stern. "We no longer need to worry about destruction of property, bad influence on our children and on society. The criminals will get what they deserve." The camera followed a group of policemen into the basement of yet another house.

Piter couldn't bear to watch. He turned off the television and rubbed his hand through his hair. He got up to pace the floor, craving a drink. He imagined Yun's voice: "Your conscience bothers you. That's why you drink too much."

Tonight, I won't drink. Piter stepped into the shower and rubbed a soapy cloth over his entire body and scrubbed until his skin was red. Turning the hot water dial as hot as he could bear it, he repeated the process two more times. He turned off the shower and leaned both hands on either side of the faucet while water dripped onto the shower floor. He still felt dirty.

Later, he stood on his third-floor balcony and stared down at the sidewalk. He breathed deeply of the cool air, hoping to suppress the swelling ache in the back of his throat. *I should take the stairs to the roof and jump.* He stepped back into his apartment, weeping and shaking, sat on the sofa and struggled to catch his breath.

His phone rang. The caller ID showed it was his mother. He squeezed his eyes shut and ignored the call. The last time they spoke, his mother said he had become "hard-hearted" and he did not disagree.

Piter had appealed to the officials at AZEN that his parents, the only family Piter had left, would be given a place to live close to him. His father was sixty-four years old and his mother, sixty-three. He hoped they could live out the rest of their lives in a comfortable home instead of the sub-standard housing reserved for dispossessed citizens. Because of Piter's loyal status, the wish was granted. Perhaps she was phoning to thank him, but regardless, he was in no mood to speak to her.

Quietus

§

Piter opened a box filled with memorabilia. He had packed the box when he and Yun were evicted from their apartment. Piter pulled out a photo. In it, he and Hadar were wearing their caps and gowns, standing in front of a lilac bush, showing off their degrees. He remembered being so full of hope the day his mother took that photo. Piter could almost smell the lilacs. "Where are you, Hadar?" he asked the photo and placed it on the bookshelf.

He found another photo of his wedding day; a happy couple gazing into each other's eyes. His hand was on her hip, her hand on his arm. She had worn her hair tied back in a complex series of braids and ringlets that took the stylist two hours to create. Yun had never been one to wear makeup, but on their wedding day she did—eyeliner, lipstick, mascara—the works. He smiled, remembering she was afraid the makeup would rub off on her wedding gown. He held the photo a long time, looking at her eyes, the curve of her cheek, the happy smile. Piter tried to recall the feel of her small hip in the palm of his hand. He missed her until he felt his heart would break. "I should have taken better care of you, my love. I'm sorry." He kissed the photo and put it on the shelf.

Beneath the photos was Yun's favourite blouse. She had become too big for it in the later stages of her pregnancy. He brought the blouse to his nose and inhaled. Her scent was barely discernable.

He picked up a never-used baby blanket, blue, embroidered with yellow ducks, and wrapped it around his shoulders. Piter found a baby bottle he had purchased in anticipation of the birth of his child. He flung it across the room. It hit the wall and bounced onto the floor without shattering. Piter wiped the corners of his eyes with the blanket and stared out the window.

§

Piter was relaxing on the couch one evening when a seagull landed on his balcony and pecked its beak on the glass as if asking to come in.

Piter got up and opened the sliding glass door. "What do you want?"

The bird flapped off, leaving him feeling enormously lonely.

He stepped into the night air. Big, fat flakes fell from the sky and melted on contact with the pavement below, the first snowfall of the year. Below him on the street, a woman ran for the bus waving her arm. The bus kept going. He recognized her as a waitress at a restaurant he frequented on the ground floor of this building. She stopped running, checked her watch and crossed her arms.

Piter put on his coat and met her outside. He smiled. "I guess we just missed the bus." He remembered her name tag. "You're Tafflen, right?"

She blinked at him. Her dark eyes were rimmed with eyeliner and her lashes were thick with mascara. Her appearance, at first, was guarded, then she smiled and pointed at him. "Beef flank, medium-rare."

"That's right, but you can call me Piter." He laughed and held out his hand.

She shook his hand and then checked her watch again. "Next bus isn't coming for forty-five minutes."

"It's getting cold," Piter said.

"Where are you going so late at night?" she asked.

Piter hesitated, trying to think of a lie, but then thought better of it. "Nowhere. I saw you missed your bus and came out to talk to you. You want to come in for something to eat and a cup of tea? Or, I'll just call you a cab if you like."

"Sure. Beats going home to my empty fridge."

She followed him to his apartment. He was at a loss for words, regretting his impulsive act to invite her up. He stepped aside, motioning for her to enter.

She took off her coat and scanned the room. "Nice place."

He shrugged. "Tea or wine?"

"Wine would be great." She accepted the glass, sat on the couch and eyed the open box on the table. "Just move in?"

"No, just going through some old stuff a few days ago." He sliced some cheese, placed them with some crackers on a plate and sat beside her. Piter rubbed his hands on his thighs, uncertain about what to say. Before Yun, he'd only had one girlfriend.

Funny, he thought, how he was so confident in a professional capacity, but with a pretty woman beside him, he was at a loss for words. He was grateful she knew how to keep a conversation going by asking questions about his work and talking about herself.

Later, Tafflen checked her watch. "I should get going. Have to work in the morning."

"Me, too." Piter called a taxi and walked her outside to the sidewalk.

As the cab pulled up, Tafflen stood on her tiptoes and kissed him on the cheek.

"Can I see you again?" he asked.

"I'd like that." She pulled a pen from her pocket and wrote her phone number on the back of his hand.

He watched the cab until it disappeared around a corner. Later, he lay on his back on the bed. Piter felt better. Now he had something to look forward to.

CHAPTER TWENTY-SIX
The Human Psyche

Students in Re-Ed were usually released after they completed their time, but sometimes, they were sent to the main prison where they languished until they died of malnutrition and over-work. Some were given the mercy of Quietus. Much depended on the charges laid against them and the mood of the Commandant or the doctor in charge.

In time, Piter adjusted. He came to marvel at the skill of the interrogators, their persistence, patience and their knowledge of the human psyche. When students began re-education, it was typical to put them straight to work during the day, but at night to let them hear recorded screams and crying, supposedly coming from other rooms.

Students were interrogated without warning. Perhaps they were hauled from their beds in the night, or taken away from their breakfasts. They could be sweeping floors and guards would rush upon them, and push them to an interrogation room where they would be forced to stand unmoving for an hour or sit naked on a cold metal chair. Often, this was enough to get them to talk. The main method used was simply to wear students down with lack of sleep, lack of food and lack of kindness. Humiliation tactics were sometimes used, stripping students naked, making them drink their own urine, and so on. Piter considered these methods distasteful but knew they were effective. He rarely saw an interrogator lose his temper. He desired that level of self-control.

§

He and Tafflen had dated only a few weeks when he allowed her to move in with him. He offered to give her a monthly allowance. She seemed happy with the arrangement, provided she could bring Roary. Piter had never been a cat lover, but Tafflen said she'd be heartbroken without her "fluffy fur ball."

"Okay, but keep it off the furniture and clean up after it," he told her. Piter didn't dislike cats. He disliked the mess they made and the smell of litter boxes.

Tafflen greeted him at the door with a kiss, took his coat and hung it up. A white cat appeared from underneath the table and regarded him with suspicious blue eyes.

"Hello, cat," said Piter. She swished her tail at him and retreated under the table again. He sat at the table and extended his fingers to the white cat. She sniffed and rubbed against his black trousers, leaving behind tufts of fine fur. "Dammit, Tafflen. The animal is here one day and is already leaving fur on me. You're going to keep her brushed, right?"

"Sure." Tafflen placed a glass of wine in front of Piter. "Try this. It's a dry Chardonnay."

Piter sipped. "Nice." He read the label. "This is a Solimese wine. Where the hell did you get it?"

"Black market. Don't ask me how much I paid." She leaned in close to him so her breasts were in his face, put a bowl of snacks on the table and ran her fingers across his scalp. "You can thank me later." She winked at him.

He popped a grape into his mouth and crunched down. A burst of sweet juice exploded in his mouth. Not long ago, when Yun was still alive, grapes and foreign wine would have been an unthinkable luxury. Everything reminded him of Yun, he thought, as he drank his glass. The sadness usually came upon him suddenly and unexpectedly. Tafflen refilled his glass.

Piter remembered the first time he got drunk was at his parents' tenth anniversary party. He was nine-years-old and sneaked around taking sips from any unattended glasses. Later, his mother sat on the edge of the tub, her warm hand on his back while he vomited into the toilet. "That will teach you to avoid alcohol," his mother said.

§

After the evening meal, Piter sat back, as usual, to watch television. The cat put her front paws on the leather couch, stretched and clawed. "Stop it!" Piter yelled and slapped his hand on the cushion. Roary was unfazed. She blinked her blue eyes at him and leapt onto his lap. Needle-sharp claws dug into his legs. "Ouch." She rubbed her face on his chin. He extracted her claws from his pant legs and stroked her back. A sense of calm washed over him.

"She's a pretty cat," Piter said. He tickled the cat behind her ears.

"What about me?" Tafflen asked.

"You're a pretty lady," he said and petted Tafflen's hair.

She laughed. "Silly boy."

Piter hadn't realized how much he missed having someone around. Tafflen was lighthearted and affectionate. His worries melted away as she rested her head on his shoulder. She was always there for Piter, ready to attend to his every need. With her, he experienced tender care and, for a while, forgot the torture and unpleasantness of his job.

Tafflen sipped her glass of white wine while cuddling beside Piter. The newest edition of *AZEN Style,* a news and fashion magazine Tafflen enjoyed, was on the table. Aura Zarling's face was on the cover, with the headline, "Aura's Youthful Skin. Learn her Beauty Secrets. Also in this issue: Budgeting Tips for Tough Economic Times, and Report the Dysfunctional Next Door—Why it Helps Everyone."

"Why did you name the cat Roary? Does she roar?"

"No. I love the president so much. Aura, Roary, get it?"

"I see." Piter wanted to freeze this peaceful moment and hang onto it forever.

"How was work today?" she asked.

"Good. Our interrogators gained some good information."

She refilled their glasses. "Does it bother you, to watch the interviews? I heard it can get pretty, well, intense."

"Doesn't bother me anymore. I can slap a fly with a swatter or witness a brutal questioning with the same amount of blasé indifference." He took a large gulp of wine and smiled.

She stared at him, wide-eyed. "Really?"

"We have to protect ourselves from the radical forces that threaten our country. Isn't it better a few guilty people suffer than all of us?" Some days, Piter couldn't push from his mind the screams of tortured students, their pleading for mercy or begging for death.

"What if they're innocent?"

"Collateral damage."

"But, Piter…"

"Let's talk about something else."

§

The next morning at work, Piter leaned back in his chair and tapped the nib of the pen against his front teeth. He stared out his office window. Snow sparkled on the branches of the evergreen trees. A couple, bundled against the cold, hurried from their car to the building. Piter imagined he lived in a different time, a time in which he could treat patients with ailments such as sore throats and ingrown toenails, instead of burns and broken bones. He leaned over his desk to complete his notes of self-examination and self-condemnation expected by his commanding officer. This was necessary because a prisoner had died under Piter's watch while being questioned. The young man had passed out during his inquisition—not an unusual occurrence, but death followed so quickly Piter had been unable to revive him despite CPR and the assistance of a medical team. Piter replayed the scene over and over in his head.

Piter weighed his words before writing, *I failed to consider the physical strength of the student before interrogation and the number of previous questioning sessions he had undergone. I should have informed the interrogators that hanging the student by his ankles for four hours could put too much stress on his heart… Long live the president.*

Since the death of the student was his first failure, Piter was happy to learn at the inquiry, which took place the following day, he would only be docked a month's salary. *The lad was somebody's son…* He stopped his train of thought, vowed to keep his mind on the job and not let it affect him personally.

[175]

§

Piter had worked at Re-Ed for four months and was sitting alone in his office when he saw a familiar name on the list of newly arrived students. He leaned back in his chair with the document in his hand. "Fillip Farwell, you old bastard." Fillip had been held at the Okenfreim Re-Ed. To relieve overcrowding at the other facility, he was being transported to Ackim. Hatred burned in Piter's heart. If Fillip hadn't talked her into joining HRFA she could have gotten proper medical care and would be alive. *My beloved Yun died because of him.*

He wanted to see Fillip for himself and entered the students' sleeping quarters. A new poster hung on the wall—a giant foot hovered over a swarm of cockroaches. The poster read, "Purge Dysfunctionals for a Strong Society."

The guard woke the male students by flicking on the lights and blowing a loud whistle. The students jumped up and made their beds. They were allowed seven minutes to use the toilet and shave. They lined up side by side in front of mirrors. Piter remembered the military-style discipline forced on him in his days as a student at Re-Ed. He had nicked himself many times in his effort to shave quickly. Today, he stood straight and tall with his hands behind his back and watched the men hastily scrape razors across their faces.

Fillip spotted Piter's image in the mirror. His jaw fell open and he turned around. "Piter?"

A guard approached and shoved Fillip against a wall and held him by the neck. Fillip dropped his razor on the floor. His face turned red as his air supply was cut off. Piter smiled. He also felt like wrapping his hands around Fillip's neck.

"Students do not speak unless spoken to!" the guard said and released him.

Fillip fell to his knees, coughing.

Piter looked down at his former friend and teacher. "Nice to see you again, Fillip."

"Queue up for breakfast," the guard said.

The students shuffled in line to the mess hall. On the wall of the mess hall was a life-sized poster of Aura Zarling, smiling, with her arms outstretched, palms up, in a welcoming gesture. On the poster was written, "Follow the true path, my friends."

The students held out their bowls and received ladles of runny porridge, barely enough to feed a child. Piter's stomach heaved. To this day, he couldn't eat oatmeal.

He followed the students down another hall to the auditorium where they would receive the orders for their daily chores. Here was another poster. A crowd of happy people gathered under the "A" symbol. Under it were the words, "We're loyal to AZEN."

The students stood in straight lines, in complete silence. Guards walked up and down the lines. A man coughed and received a whack across the face with the switch. Further down the line, a man had a stream of mucus running from his nose to his mouth, but he didn't move. Piter smiled as he watched the man's nose twitch.

"Achoo!" A look of fear crossed the man's face.

Two guards descended on him and punched him repeatedly until he gasped for breath. The other students did not flinch.

A huge poster covered one wall of this room—a beautiful, flowery meadow with children running hand in hand. "We grow under the leadership of AZEN."

The students were called by number and given their jobs for the day. Fillip was sent to the stone yard. Piter knew this to be one of the most labour-intensive jobs. He watched Fillip leave the room with a small group of men.

Piter proceeded to the infirmary. On the wall of the sick-room was another poster. A priest in black was leading a group of sheep-eared people into the path of an oncoming train.

The intercom played the words of Aura Zarling over and over in a continual loop. She spoke softly, "AZEN cares about you. We relieve suffering. We care about your quality of life."

Piter used his lunch break to go to the gravel yard. He watched Fillip and other students shovel gravel from the north side of the yard to the south. Steam puffed from their mouths as they worked. A scarf was

[177]

tied around Fillip's head, but his hands were bare and red from the cold. When the last of the gravel lay in a huge pile, the students leaned on their shovels and were given a drink of water.

A guard shouted, "Students, pick up your shovels and move the pile of gravel to the other wall."

Fillip emitted a barely audible moan and for his complaint he received a punch in the face. A bruise formed on his left cheek. Fillip began to shovel. Blood dribbled from his nose and froze on his upper lip. He glanced at Piter but didn't speak.

Piter approached his former teacher. "It's for your own good," Piter whispered. "Keep your mouth shut, do as you're told, and maybe you can get out of here."

Fillip grunted as he picked up a shovelful of gravel. "Are you worried about me or yourself? I haven't told them everything."

Piter's heart began to thump hard. He remembered the books he had helped take from the church and regretted his foolish actions. Piter glanced at the guard, who seemed unconcerned the two of them were talking. "You still have them?"

Fillip gave him a thin smile. "Shh. I hope I'm not forced to tell."

Piter knew if Fillip implicated him in hiding forbidden religious literature they would both be punished, severely. He bit his lips. "What do you want?"

"I want to get out of here and go back to my family."

Piter growled his response, "I'll see what I can do."

"Is that a promise?"

"Yes." Piter turned on his heel and returned to his office trying to think of a way out of this. No one escaped from Re-Ed. The easiest method to silence Fillip was to kill him, before the interrogators learned anything about the books, but that would send up red flags. How could Piter explain Fillip's death? He could try to make sure he was present for all the questioning sessions, though that would be difficult if he happened to be off duty and one of the other doctors was present instead. Perhaps he could put Fillip into an induced coma, making it impossible for him to speak. But, how could he give him a near-fatal dose of drugs without the authorities figuring it out?

Piter stopped in his tracks when a thought occurred to him. Some students in the infirmary were sick from a highly contagious, still unidentified and deadly flu. They were held in isolation units. Dr. Marris from the QRR Centre came from time to time to treat them. *No one would question a student dying of the flu.* It was routine procedure before interrogations to assess the fitness of students. A twinge of conscience made him rethink his plan for a moment, but he buried his guilty feeling. His own life depended on it.

§

He dreamed about Yun again. She was crying and he went to comfort her. "My baby is dead." Yun cuddled a tiny body wrapped in a blanket. Piter pulled back the baby blanket and looked down at his own dead face.

CHAPTER TWENTY-SEVEN

A Bad Case of the Flu

Piter drew the razor down his neck and flinched as he nicked himself. He dabbed the blood with a bit of toilet paper. *The dead don't bleed.* After last night's dream, the thought was strangely comforting.

At the breakfast table, Tafflen chatted away, but Piter didn't pay attention to her words. He slurped a cup of tea, going over in his mind what he had to do that day.

He went outside, hailed a cab, plunked down on the torn seat and watched the scenery go by, hands resting in his lap. Outside an apartment building, two policemen dragged a struggling woman backwards, their hands around her wrists. Her heels made crooked tracks in the snow.

Upon arriving at work, Piter put on his white lab coat, clipped his identification badge to the left breast pocket and proceeded down the hall to the isolation unit. He was not responsible for flu patients, but no one questioned him when he donned a surgical gown, gloves, mask, and entered the ward. He approached the first bed and pushed aside the plastic tarp.

The patient's face was beaded with sweat. His breath was heavy and congested. "How am I doing, Doctor?" the man croaked.

"We're keeping a close eye on things." Piter patted his shoulder and then picked up a discarded tissue by the man's pillow, crumpling it in his fist.

Back in his lab, he opened the tissue and smiled. The tissue contained a good amount of bloody phlegm. Taking a syringe without a needle, he pulled on the plunger and drew the mucus into the barrel. Just then, he was called to go to interrogation room number one, for clinical observation. He put the syringe in a plastic bag and placed it in a cupboard.

§

The new student's eyes filled with hope when he walked in the door. "Piter?" She pulled against the straps on her arms and legs. She was the woman he had seen arrested on his way to work. He now recognized her as a friend of Yun's who had attended their wedding. With her arms and legs strapped to a chair, she shivered in a flimsy hospital gown. Her hair was a tangled mess and the sour odour of urine rose from her body.

Piter struggled to keep his expression neutral as he leaned against the wall.

The interrogator turned on a bright light and shone it in her eyes. She squeezed them shut.

"I see you know Dr. Dram. How do you know him?" The interrogator, who Piter nicknamed Slim, because of his large belly, leaned back in his chair and lit a cigarette. He blew the smoke out of his nose like a dragon.

"His wife was my friend." Her voice was hoarse and dry.

"Is that so, Dr. Dram?" asked Slim. He stared, unblinking.

Piter stood up straight. His heart raced. "It is, but she's no friend of mine." Though he knew it was foolish, Piter imagined the interrogator read his mind. He placed his shaking hands into his armpits and concentrated on making his expression blank.

Slim returned his snake-like gaze to the woman. "You're a spy. You're trying to sneak state secrets out of the country." He squashed his cigarette into an ashtray and lit another.

She lowered her voice to a whisper. "Please. I don't know any secrets." Her chin quivered.

Slim got up from his chair and stood behind her, placing a hand on her shoulder. He kept his voice even toned and calm. "It's all right. I just want to know a few little things and then you can go home. Okay? First, do you know Fillip Farwell?"

She nodded her head.

He spoke in a soft voice. "Did he direct you to spread illegal literature, the *Bible* and such, to our good citizens?"

Piter stiffened. *Bible?*

She shook her head. "No."

"I think he did." He blew smoke towards the ceiling. It hovered there, swirling in circles before dissipating. "Do you know Tresha Farwell?"

She squinted her eyes in the haze. "Please—"

He shouted, "Do you know Tresha Farwell?"

"Yes." She shivered. "I'm so cold."

He stepped close to her so he looked down at the top of her head. His hip touched her shoulder. "Tell me about HRFA."

"I don't know what you're talking about."

Slim squatted and pushed her hospital gown up to her thighs, displaying bare legs. He ran the tips of his fingers up and down one thigh and then tapped his ashes on it. The cherry of the cigarette was dangerously close to her skin. "You're a spy," he whispered.

She shook her head and then screamed when the lit end of the cigarette touched her leg.

"Oh, how clumsy of me," Slim said.

Piter remembered this young woman laughing and dancing at his wedding. He wanted to tell Slim to stop, to leave her alone, but remained motionless.

"There was an explosion at Deve Ski Resort. Do you know anything about that?"

"No, I…" The woman shrieked and acrid smoke rose into the air. "Ow, stop, please."

Piter clamped his jaws shut, not allowing himself to speak.

"Admit it," Slim said, bringing his cigarette near her skin again.

"Piter, help me," she turned her eyes towards him and screamed again when the cherry touched her leg.

Piter flinched and averted his eyes to the ceiling where the smoke thickened, churning around the ceiling lights, like a poisonous cloud.

Two hours and many cigarettes later, the woman admitted to planting a bomb at a ski resort. She signed a confession and was led out. Her thighs and calves were dotted with burns. The smell of smoke and burnt skin filled the air. Piter felt he might vomit.

"I think that went well, don't you?" Slim asked. He placed the signed confession in a folder.

Piter nodded. "Effective technique." He left the room and stepped into the hallway, feeling woozy. He opened the door to the courtyard where students marched outside in slow circles. The cold hit him like a slap in the face. He breathed deeply, filling his lungs with unpolluted air. Red-faced students trudged past Piter. Breath steamed from their open mouths and their noses dripped. Some had wrapped scarves around their heads. They buried their hands in their pockets or wrapped them in cloth, exposing freezing red fingertips.

He returned to his office but had difficulty concentrating. There was no time now to attend to the important task he had started this morning. That would have to wait until tomorrow. *I'll do it before the interviews.* Piter was grateful for the time and resources Re-Ed offered him. He had asked for money to hire an assistant and was surprised his request was granted without delay. Tomorrow he would interview several candidates for the job.

§

In the morning, he retrieved the syringe containing the deadly flu virus, put on his gloves, gown and mask, and went to see his first patient, Fillip Farwell.

"Have a seat," Piter said to Fillip and pointed to the exam table.

Throughout the physical exam, Fillip said nothing. He sat emotionless, allowed his blood pressure to be taken and sat still when the stethoscope was held to his chest and back. He opened his mouth, bent over and coughed when he was told.

"You seem to be fit." Piter wrote on his chart. "But before you go, I'd like to give you a flu vaccine. Rather than give you a needle, I'll administer this one nasally." He put the tip of the syringe in Fillip's nostril and pushed the cloudy liquid up his nose. "Breathe deeply."

Fillip obeyed.

§

Piter entered his lab to check the results on some research tests he was conducting—a drug therapy he hoped would slow cell death in people afflicted with ALS. He prepared some slides and placed them under the microscope, one after the other, all the while making careful notes. Two hours later, he got up from his stool and paced the room. *Nothing, no difference.* The drug was ineffective. There was no discernable difference between test subjects given the real drug therapy and the control group given the placebo.

To an outsider, his research would seem to be going nowhere. He had no promising leads but reassured himself he had ruled out another factor. In the scientific community, that was a step forward.

§

Of the five candidates, Piter was most pleased with the bright young woman who now sat across the desk from him. Cherrin Sayden was a graduate of Ackim College with a diploma in Laboratory Assistance and Procedures. Her background check revealed no affiliation with any radical group or religious organization.

"I looked you up and read your university paper on ALS, Dr. Dram. I can't say I understood most of it, but it was fascinating. Will I be helping you with that?"

"I believe so."

She giggled. "Wonderful! I'm sure everything you do here is amazing."

He made up his mind on the spot. Piter stood and held out his hand. "Congratulations, Ms. Sayden. Can you start tomorrow?"

She sprang from her chair and pumped his hand up and down. She spoke rapidly, "I sure can, Dr. Dram. I'm so excited to work with you. I've been dreaming of a job like this—"

"Fine, fine. Be here at nine a.m. tomorrow and I'll explain the procedures."

§

Three days later, Piter's duties were cancelled because of a special event. At nine o'clock in the morning all the students and staff were called to the auditorium and stood in rows in front of a large screen on the wall. Fillip Farwell seemed unsteady on his feet and his forehead was wet with sweat. Piter stifled a smirk.

Aura Zarling's smiling face appeared on the screen. "Behold, my people, the Wall of Aura." She stretched out her arm. The camera pulled back to reveal a massive wall. "It is my dream to keep my people safe within these walls. Solime may attack us again. Therefore, we must protect ourselves. Watch now, the test launch of a midrange ballistic missile. Following that, you will witness the launch test of our country's first hydrogen bomb. Be proud, fellow Covonans. We are a strong and flourishing country."

The screen shifted to show a rocket blasting off, lifting high into the blue sky.

"Cheer!" the Commandant shouted. He held his hands at chest level and applauded.

All those in the auditorium followed suit.

Next, the screen showed a massive nuclear explosion.

While the rest of the students clapped, Fillip's face lost colour and he collapsed onto the floor. Guards rushed in, hoisted him up and dragged him away.

§

The first thought that entered Piter's consciousness the next morning was it would have been Yun's birthday. He used to celebrate the day by giving her a bouquet of freshly cut spring flowers. Not a day went by when he didn't think of her, but today, more than ever, she was on his mind. He didn't believe she was "somewhere up there looking down on him," but he couldn't help but wonder what she might think if she knew what he was up to.

§

At work, he opened his office window to allow the cool morning breeze to drift into the room. The large maple tree outside was budding. A bird landed on a branch and whistled a merry tune. Piter turned to face the thin student sitting at the other side of his desk. The student's head was bowed and hands clenched on his lap. His head seemed too heavy for his thin neck. It hung with his chin almost touching his chest.

The average student at the centre lost ten to twenty-five kilograms. Many also shrank in other ways, losing their self-confidence and peace of mind. Their eyes shifted from side to side. They flinched at the sound of boot steps and some developed twitches.

Piter had the power to release some students, send them back for more education or recommend eradication. It was a substantial responsibility, but today the decision was not his. A note from his superiors stating he was to grant this man's release lay on Piter's desk. Still, he couldn't help playing with the man a little bit, like a cat with an injured bird.

"Have you repented of your crimes?" Piter tapped the pen on his desk, waiting for a response.

The student's head wobbled. He was a man in his twenties, though he looked older, having been through many interrogations. A badly healed gash on his cheek had formed into an ugly v-shaped scar. His eyes, sunken and bloodshot, looked out the window behind Piter's head. He mumbled something incomprehensible, raised a shaky hand, touched his lips and then let it fall again to his lap.

Piter wrote on the medical record, *Student has shown remorse. He is denied loyal status but is no longer a danger to society and will be released.*

He handed the release papers to the man.

The man looked confused. His dull eyes looked at the papers and then at Piter.

"You're free to go."

The corners of his mouth curled into a smile. "My wife and kids will be happy."

"The guard will show you the way out." Piter straightened the papers on his desk. The man had a spring in his step as he followed the guard.

§

Fillip was too sick with vomiting and diarrhea to be questioned. His fever spiked and he coughed blood. The interrogators didn't want to go near him for fear they might catch what he had. Death was imminent, but Piter wondered why the authorities were going through heroic measures to try to keep Fillip alive. Two weeks passed and Fillip was stable.

Piter considered asking the authorities if he could give Fillip a lethal injection. *It's the humane thing to do,* he imagined himself saying. That's when a call came in from the QRR Centre. They were looking for patients with cases of this strain of the flu to use as test subjects and would they please send them over. Piter had no choice but to sign the documents and allow for Fillip's transport. He did not hope for his recovery.

Piter received notice, the day after Fillip was moved to the QRR Centre, that he, too, would be transferred there, with a promotion. Piter would now be a doctor of Eradication and Research. With the title came the honour of being called "Loyal Elite." He agreed under the condition that he could bring his new lab assistant, Cherrin Sayden, with him.

CHAPTER TWENTY-EIGHT
Number Twenty-Six

Tresha and Jakon had sat cuddled in the black cargo section of the semitruck as it travelled westward from Ackim, Korgo, to the province of Sesal. The truck had driven across the plains of Covona, over hundreds of kilometres of prairie farmland. Her journey didn't end there but continued even further west to where thick forests of fir and spruce trees grew.

She had then sent her son to cross the border with virtual strangers.

Tresha took up residence in the cabin and managed a small flock of sheep. "Twenty-Six," as she was known, fed and sheltered her guests before directing them to the next safe house. She didn't know who operated the next house. He was known to her as "Forty-Eight." It was Forty-Eight's job to bribe border guards and instruct guests on where and how to gain access through the Wall of Aura.

She lived alone, except for occasional guests. Her son, she hoped, was already safe in Solime. She didn't know where Fillip was. At times, she despaired they both might be dead.

§

All through the autumn and the long winter, she operated her safe house in the forest. The weather warmed and life sprung up around her, but spring didn't make Tresha light and hopeful. Worry weighed her down.

Tresha lay in bed surrounded by darkness and missed her husband and child with an almost unbearable loneliness. She also thought of her father. *I never got to say goodbye. I hope he wasn't treated badly.* She closed her eyes and tried to remember each of their faces and the sounds of their voices. The only sounds she heard were the wind in the trees and the occasional hoot of an owl. She wondered if the world would ever be the same again; if AZEN could be defeated.

Panzer, the brown and white collie who came with the house, climbed onto the bed. Tresha wrapped her arms around the dog's warm body and wept into her fur.

Each morning after she woke up, she stretched and patted Panzer. "Time to attend to the sheep."

Panzer wagged her tail and scampered out the door. Tresha stood by the sheep pen and dumped some feed into the manger. "Breakfast time." She took the shovel from the wall and scooped manure from their pen into a wheelbarrow. "Thank you for the fertilizer, my darlings. I will use this in my garden." The morning sun felt good on her face. "Soon, I can let you out to graze," she said to the sheep. Over the winter, she had used up almost all the hay, but today, the snow was soft and melting. She knew it was silly to talk to the sheep, but Tresha had grown fond of them. Besides Panzer, the sheep were her only companions. They jostled and bumped each other, their woolly heads buried deep in the manger.

Tresha looked forward to summer. She didn't want to think about how she would get through next winter, or even how much longer she would live at the cabin. It was easier to think in the short term. She would grow a garden. The small flock of sheep would give her wool. She imagined spinning the raw wool on the wheel and knitting sweaters for herself and for the "guests" who stayed with her from time to time. "I'm glad Granny taught me how to knit." Tresha often talked to herself. The sound of any human voice, even her own, was better than none. Sometimes it was weeks between visitors.

The phone rang. She placed the shovel against the wall, went inside and picked up the phone. "Hello?"

"A package will be delivered at 12:45 p.m."

She hung up the phone and smiled. "Time to get ready for visitors, Panzer."

§

Tresha placed steaming bowls of soup in front of a couple in their twenties and their two children. They ate ravenously. Tresha was happy to

[189]

refill their bowls. Goodness knows they needed the nourishment. All four were painfully thin. The man said he had recently been released from Re-Ed. He stroked a v-shaped scar on his cheek.

In the next few days, five of the ewes gave birth. Tresha and the children were delighted by the playful lambs. She tried to resist the urge to pet and cuddle the baby sheep, though. Last winter she had to slaughter the old ewe and ram. She didn't like killing things but had to feed herself and the escaping dissidents—her guests, as she preferred to call them.

One of the children threw a stick and laughed as Panzer ran to retrieve it.

"Tresha?" the man with the scar said.

"Yes," she answered automatically and then tried to hide her surprise. Names were never exchanged between those escaping the country and those helping. Family members left behind in Covona were sent to jail if it was discovered relatives escaped the country. "How do you know my name?"

"Your husband told me you were operating a safe house. Fillip and I shared a cell. Heck of nice guy. Smart, too." His grin was lopsided due to the deep scar.

Tresha's heart leaped at the mention of his name. "How is he?" She wondered how her husband knew she was operating a safe house.

"I'm afraid he took sick before I was released. They took him to the infirmary about a month ago. Where's your son?" he asked.

"Gone to Solime. I sent him with some guests who came through here last winter. I'm surprised you know so much about me."

The woman's cheeks turned red and she dropped her gaze to her lap.

Tresha put her suspicions about her guests aside and was determined to be happy today, in this moment, when she had company and a distraction from her loneliness.

§

Soon it was time for the guests to leave. She packed food for their trip and led them through the underground tunnel to a forestry area west of her home and gave them directions to the next safe house.

"Come with us," the man said. "Wouldn't you like to be free?"

"No. I'll stay here." Each time she said goodbye to her guests, it was a temptation to escape to Solime with them, but she was determined to stay and wait for Fillip.

The man nudged his wife.

"Yes, come with us," she said. "Everything will be okay."

"No. I'll stay here. Good luck." She waved and watched the family walk away.

Now her cabin was deathly quiet again and she missed the noisy children. She sat at the table, staring out the window as night fell, warming her hands on a cup of tea. As Tresha readied herself for bed, she wondered if the man with the scar was being honest.

Hours later, Panzer stirred beside her. The dog growled, jumped off the bed and stood facing the front door with bared teeth.

Tresha rose from her bed and peeked out the window. Between the trees surrounding her home, beams of flashlights skimmed the snowy ground. She reached for her rifle.

The room was dark, but she didn't dare turn on a light. She knew where everything was in the one-room cabin. She reached for a few pieces of clothing that hung on hooks on the wall, a pair of trousers and her wool sweater, which she pulled over her sleeping clothes. Panzer began to bark.

"Shush!"

The more she hurried the slower she seemed to move. Panzer barked again with more urgency. Tresha pushed her arms through the sleeves of her winter coat and bent to tie the laces of her boots.

She held tight to her rifle and peeked out from behind her curtain again. There was only one way out. She lifted a hatch on the floor and climbed down the ladder.

Panzer whined. She put one paw over the edge of the tunnel and stepped back.

"Come, Panzer!"

The dog didn't move so Tresha climbed the ladder again, grabbed Panzer around the belly and carried her down the ladder. She closed the hatch behind her. In her haste, she realized she forgot to bring a flashlight into the pitch-black tunnel, but it didn't matter. Turning around, she felt her way to the back of the cool cellar. Tresha pushed aside a wall panel, stepped into the dirt tunnel and replaced the panel behind her. Panzer was close at her heel.

All was dark and quiet in the tunnel, like a tomb. Over the past months, she had led many guests along this route to freedom. The route led under the house and barn of the small farm, ending in a forested area. She held the loaded rifle and crouch-walked, her fingers skimming the wooden-beam-reinforced walls.

At the end of the tunnel she climbed another ladder and pushed the trapdoor aside, just a crack. Snow rained down on her head. The sun had not yet risen. Moonlight reflecting off snow was her only light. Hearing no sounds, she poked her head out and inhaled the cool breeze, a relief from the stagnant air of the tunnel. She straightened up in the middle of a wooded area. Her eyes were drawn back towards her cabin, to a line of bright vehicle lights and shadowy figures running towards the house.

"Tresha Farwell, the house is surrounded. Come out with your hands up!" called a voice over a loudspeaker.

The dog sat at the bottom of the ladder and looked up at her. "Come, Panzer. Come on, girl." Panzer climbed three rungs, but was frightened to climb higher. "You can do it. Come. Hurry!" Tresha lay on her stomach and reached her hand to the dog, grabbed her by the scruff of the neck and pulled her the rest of the way up. "Let's go."

They ran in a westerly direction, towards the Wall of Aura. Tresha ran until her breath was laboured. Her fifty-seven-year-old arthritic knees ached. At the sound of smashing wood, she stopped and leaned against a tree, holding her chest. She looked at the tracks in the snow and worried. Taking a deep breath, she carried on, running as fast as she could in the snow, zigzagging around trees.

She remembered the directions she had given to many desperate travellers. "Go three kilometres west in the Selp Forest until you come to the edge of the Kaye River. Proceed south along the banks of the river until you find a footbridge. Go across the bridge and continue west. There you will find a small trapper's cabin. The man there will give you shelter. If you're fast, you can get there in one hour. He will tell you which gate in the wall will be open."

Tresha tried to ignore the aching in her legs and the burning in her lungs but had to stop and catch her breath. Holding onto a tree for support, she looked behind her. No one pursued her. Under cover of darkness and happy to have a head start, she was hopeful of her escape, counting on number Forty-Eight to give her supplies and directions for the rest of the journey.

A snow drift provided a welcome source of hydration for her parched throat. She stood still, eating snow and listening. The only sound she heard was her own loud breathing. If her pursuers found the secret passage in the cellar, they would soon discover their footprints. The darkness was disorienting and she was unsure which direction to take. Panzer nudged her hand, ran a few steps and looked back at her. "Okay, I'll follow you."

Nearby, she heard rushing water "You did know the way, didn't you? Good girl."

At the riverbank, she trod on icy rocks. Ahead was the footbridge she had told her guests about but had never seen. She slipped but caught herself before falling into the rushing river. Once at the bridge, she looked behind her, to the left and right, and then sprinted across. She breathed a sigh of relief when she was back under the cover of trees on the other side. For the next half hour or so, Tresha walked a little, ran a little, hoping she was going the right direction and not walking in circles. Panzer followed behind her.

The sun started to rise. There, in the distance, was the cabin. Her legs shook with exhaustion. She emerged from the cover of trees and entered an open field. Close now to the cabin, she saw the snow around it had been trampled by many feet. Panzer growled. Tresha stopped short. *They're here. I've been betrayed.* She turned on her heel and ran back towards the cover of trees, racking her mind to think of another way.

A distant hum grew louder and louder. *A helicopter!*

[193]

She was so close to freedom, but there was no way through the wall. Every five hundred metres was a gate. Number Forty-Eight, who lived in the trapper's cabin, knew which guard to bribe. Without his help, she would not know which gate was accessible. She'd just have to take her chances.

Her compact single-shot rifle was cocked and ready. She was a decent shot, having taken down deer, coyotes and rabbits with the weapon. She hoped she wouldn't hesitate if she encountered a person.

From overhead came the whirring of helicopter blades. A spotlight from the helicopter skimmed the ground below. Tresha looked for deeper cover, further into the trees, but was startled by a sudden burst of light which followed her as she ran. Snow swirled around her like a blinding storm. Shouting came from all directions. She fired two shots, blindly, before being tackled to the ground. The weight of a large man fell on her, knocking the wind out of her. Something hard jabbed her at the small of her back, a knee maybe. A boot came towards her face.

CHAPTER TWENTY-NINE

Mindless Drones

Tresha awoke unable to move her arms and legs. The restraints were tight—straps around her ankles, wrists and across her chest. The noise was terrible. A throbbing pain shot through her head.

"She's awake," a man said. A thin light stabbed her eyes. Behind the flashlight was a man wearing a military uniform. "Significant swelling to the left cheek and eye."

"Let's get her to the hospital. We're screwed if she dies," someone else said.

Panzer lay her head on Tresha's chest as the helicopter rose into the air.

"That's a nice dog you got there. My kids always wanted a collie. Mind if I keep her?" a man asked.

Before she could answer, Tresha felt the poke of a needle in her arm and an oxygen mask on her face.

§

They lifted the gurney out of the helicopter and rolled it across a landing pad. The blinding sun shone on Tresha's face and she shut her eyes. The blades of the chopper slowed their dizzying rotation. She was at their mercy.

Inside, fluorescent ceiling lights flickered, one after the other, down the long halls of the hospital. Tresha could no longer open her left eye. They entered a room. A severe doctor with a day-old beard glared down at her. He opened her right eye with his thumb and forefinger and shone a pen-light. He held her chin tight and did the same to her left eye.

"Ah!" Tresha cried out when he touched her swollen eye.

He held his stethoscope to her inner elbow while the blood pressure cuff squeezed her arm. "Blood pressure is low. Get her on fluids. Possible concussion and cheekbone fracture. I want a head X-ray and an electrocardiogram. Get her weight."

A half hour later, the same doctor examined the results of the tests.

He took off his glasses, wiped them on his lab coat and spoke to a nurse standing by the bed. "She has a concussion. We'll keep her for the day for observation. Put a cold pack on her eye. By tomorrow she should be fit to be sent to Re-Ed. Make the arrangements." He dropped the file folder on Tresha's chest and walked away.

The nurse returned with a cold pack and placed it on Tresha's face.

"Thank you," Tresha said.

The nurse did not respond.

Forced to lay on her back, Tresha looked up at the ceiling. She closed her eyes and slept on and off. Later, the head of the bed was raised to a seated position. A bowl of oatmeal and a cup of tea was placed on a tray in front of her. Still, no one spoke to her.

It was challenging to eat the oatmeal. The leather restraints securing her arms to the bedrails gave her little leeway, but she managed. Despite her anxious, roiling stomach, Tresha forced herself to eat every bite. Anyone held at Re-Ed came out kilograms lighter than when they went in. Many never came out. She sipped the cold, weak tea and tried not to think about the future.

No one spoke to her the entire day, except two young policewomen who came to take her twice to the toilet. They removed her arm restraints and placed her in handcuffs. Her legs were chained together. Her body felt sore and bruised from the ordeal.

"Up." Tresha shuffled to the toilet with a policewoman on each side. "Sit." Tresha sat. The policewomen never took their eyes off her. They took her back to her bed. "Lie down." She lay back and again did nothing but stare at blank walls.

§

In the morning, Tresha opened her eyes to see a red-haired woman in a military-style uniform staring down at her. "Time to get up, princess."

The guard's cold eyes looked down on her with contempt. She removed the restraints and jerked Tresha up by one arm.

"Ouch!"

"Put these on." Red Hair dropped a baggy, bright orange t-shirt and a pair of elastic pants on the bed. She watched with a pinched mouth while Tresha removed the thin hospital gown.

Tresha glanced around. "I don't see my underwear."

The guard snorted. "Underwear? You really are a princess. I'm here to accompany you to your new home."

Tresha was grateful for the secretiveness of HRFA. She couldn't tell what she didn't know. Her only hope was that she not let AZEN know the things she did know—the whereabouts of some safe houses and some members of HRFA. She dreaded the interrogators and wished she could make her mind go blank.

Sitting in the back of the van, Tresha closed her eyes and tried to control her fear with slow breaths. *Aura proselytizes her demented views and, like mindless drones, people devour the poisonous words.*

After a half hour, bumpy ride through the city, Tresha saw through the tiny window slit in the back of the van, the tall razor-wire fence of the Re-education Centre.

CHAPTER THIRTY

Ackim Quietus/Recycling/Research Centre

A rusted iron railing and twelve cracked concrete stairs led to the front doors of Piter's place of employment. Scraggly bushes partially obscured a plexiglass sign outside the building. On it was written, "Ackim Quietus/Recycling/Research Centre: Offering Compassionate Quietus and Human Remains Reclamation."

The sign used to read, "St. Anthony's Church," before Aura Zarling became president. The cross was long ago removed from the peaked roof, along with everything else that served as a reminder this was once a place of worship. Over the arched door hung the uppercase "A" with an intersecting vertical line and the words: "Aspire, Battle and Conquer."

Piter ran up the stairs, irritated at being half an hour late for work. A taxi had broken down on the highway, tying up traffic for many kilometres.

He pulled open the heavy wooden door and stepped into a bright reception area. Summer sunlight streamed in through long windows on the eastern wall. When the church was remodelled to become a QRR Centre, the Minister of Culture determined the colourful patterns of stained glass were not overtly religious in nature and could remain as they added "cheery colour" to the room.

Plush chairs were arranged in two circles on either side of the reception room. A sign above the door read, "Quietus: A time of happiness, to be discharged, released from the stresses and pains of existence."

A man and a woman sat side by side and avoided eye contact with an elderly man who occupied a chair opposite them. The old man's cheeks were wet with tears. He wiped his nose with a tissue and watched two small children chase each other, ducking around chairs, laughing and shrieking.

Cherrin Sayden looked up from her desk and greeted him in her usual chirpy manner. "Good morning, Dr. Dram."

The children's high-pitched squeals sent surges of pain through his head and he regretted finishing the two bottles of wine he and Tafflen opened yesterday.

A small boy ran into his legs and looked up at Piter with a grin. "You know what, mister? You have a very sharp nose."

Cherrin snorted and covered her mouth with her hand.

He gave Cherrin what he hoped was his most serious frown and put on his white lab coat, clipping on his badge, "Dr. Piter Dram, Eradication and Research." He picked up a single file folder from Cherrin's desk. "Where's the file for my first appointment?"

"Dr. Gorge said he didn't mind filling in for you, since you couldn't be here on time."

He huffed and rolled his eyes, not surprised by Gorge's offer.

"It shouldn't have to be like this!" shouted the old man from the waiting room.

"Dad, please sit down," said the woman. She stood in front of her father with her hands on his shoulders, pushing him back into his seat.

Cherrin leaned forward and pointed to the old man. "Your patient," she said in soft voice. "His name is Imas Larium."

"Send a warning to security in case this one is a screamer."

She smiled. "Of course." Cherrin didn't seem to notice his sour mood. She never did. Day after day, her smile never wavered and her face was always jolly, welcoming clients to the QRR Centre as she might welcome friends to her home.

He glanced at Imas' file and saw he was only sixty but was suffering from ALS, amyotrophic lateral sclerosis. "Give me a few minutes before you bring them in."

His office resembled a posh hotel room. There was a bed, a nightstand, plush leather furniture and a refrigerator stocked with soda, juice, wine and beer. On the counter was a cake with candles, fresh fruit, pretzels and potato chips. The joyful time of Quietus was celebrated with family and friends who toasted the almost-departed, sharing stories and memories, until an eradicator, like Piter, arrived and administered the fatal dose.

Near the bed was a heart monitor, blood pressure cuff and a stand for holding intravenous bags. Hidden beneath the blanket were wrist and ankle restraints for the screamers.

His desk was concealed behind a screen divider at the far side of the room, beside a locked medicine cabinet. Piter sat at his desk to study Imas' file, happy Imas could be useful for his research.

From behind the screen, he heard the door open.

"Have a seat. Make yourselves comfortable," Cherrin said.

"How can I be comfortable? I'm about to die. God have mercy on my soul."

Imas sounded panicked, but Piter trusted Cherrin to handle the situation. Piter reached for the chemicals he needed from his medicine cabinet and measured the doses into syringes.

"Now, Dad, don't talk like that," the woman said.

Cherrin asked, "Would anybody like a glass of wine or beer? Would you children like soda or juice while you wait for Grandpa to change into his hospital gown? You kids step back now, so I can pull the curtain."

"I could use a drink," the man said.

The fridge opened and closed followed by the familiar sound of a popping beer can.

"I can't undo the buttons on my shirt," Imas said.

"Let me help you, Dad."

Cherrin said, "I'll take a video if you like. It will make a great remembrance for the grandkids. Would you like that?"

"Okay," the woman said.

The two children ran behind the room divider where Piter stood measuring doses for the syringes. They were both grinning, their cheeks pink with excitement. "We're going to have cake," the little girl said. "It's chocolate."

"Shoo. Go back to your mother," Piter said.

The children giggled and ran away.

"Let's cut the cake," Cherrin said. "I bet you kids would like some."

"Yes! Yes!" they said at the same time.

"Look at the beautiful cake, Dad. Would you like a slice?"

"No! Let's get this horrid business over with."

The sound of the woman's weeping filled the room.

Piter didn't like the emotional cases. He usually gave the families time to visit and reminisce before he attended to his duties but decided he'd better get to it before he had to call security on the daughter. He arranged the syringes on a tray, put a smile on his face and stepped out from behind the screen. "Happy Quietus, Imas."

Imas looked up and frowned. "Oh, look. It's the Grim Reaper himself. Stop smiling, you gangly ghoul. Do what you're paid to do."

Piter wasn't insulted by the comment. He'd heard worse.

"Aura have mercy," the young man said. He drank the rest of his beer in one gulp, belched and helped himself to another.

"Give us a few minutes. The children need to say goodbye to their grandfather. Wish Grandpa Happy Quietus." Her voice was cheerful, but the corners of her mouth trembled. She pulled the children to their feet and pushed them towards the bed where her father was seated.

The children stood awkwardly, looking at their grandfather. The little girl, her face smeared with chocolate icing, said, "Are you going to open presents?"

Grandpa put his freckly arms around the boy and girl. "Be good for your mom and dad." He stood, hugged his son-in-law and daughter, and then lay down. His hands rested on his chest.

Cherrin stood in the background with the camera, recording everything.

Piter pulled on some rubber gloves. "Let's pull down the gown a little way." He untied the gown at the neck and attached the heart monitors to Imas' bare chest. "Your heart rate is fast, but that's normal under the circumstances. Now, extend your arm for me." He tied a tourniquet above Imas' elbow and palpated for a vein. "You will feel no pain except for a sharp scratch. Are you ready?"

Imas closed his eyes. "Mind if I pray?"

Although praying aloud was forbidden in Covona, Piter didn't feel the need to enforce the law on Quietus. "Do what you need to do."

He inserted the intravenous needle, attached the needle to a tube and then hung a bag over the bed. "I'll start an IV on the other arm." He started the drip. "This solution will make you sleepy."

Imas muttered his prayers while liquid from the IV entered his bloodstream. Within seconds he stopped praying and fell asleep.

Piter turned to the family. "Do you want to be present for the second stage? You may leave the room now, if you want."

The couple looked at each other with uncertainty and then the daughter nodded. "We'll stay."

Piter inserted a needle containing a muscle relaxant into the IV tube on the other arm and watched the monitors until they detected no heartbeat. "Quietus comes. It's over." He turned off the monitor and stopped the drip.

The woman stood over her father. She started to breathe faster. "I'm not supposed to cry. This is a happy day." She began to sob.

The man burped. "It's the right thing, you know. With a terminal illness, he was past his usefulness…"

"Shut up!" she yelled.

The boy took his mother's hand while the father looked on.

"Is Grandpa tired?" asked the little girl. She leaned over the bed and stared at his face.

"I'll take the deceased away," Piter said.

"Where's Grandpa going?" asked the little girl.

Piter nudged the child aside and wheeled the bed out to the hallway and to another room, the holding area for the recently eradicated. If a researcher had no use for a body, the useful parts were removed for recycling and the remaining body parts were ground up to become crop fertilizer.

Two other bodies already occupied the room, left there from his colleague, and he couldn't help but notice, with some bitterness, that both had red toe-tags, indicating the bodies were for the exclusive use of Dr. Gorge Bigon. Piter covered Imas with a sheet, strapped him to the bed and hung a blue toe-tag on the big toe of his right foot with the words, "Imas Larium, for the exclusive use of Dr. Piter Dram."

He returned to his office, relieved to see the family was gone. Piter preferred it when people controlled their emotions; a much tidier way to deal with the whole procedure. He opened the refrigerator, poured himself a glass of wine and sipped it. He glanced, caught his reflection in the mirror, stopped, took out a comb and ran it through his hair.

CHAPTER THIRTY-ONE

Research

Piter completed his notes at his desk. "Imas Larium received two doses of respiratory depressant nine-thirty-five a.m. I will assess suitability for research purposes." He would need to proceed to the next stage before the body became too cold.

Piter stepped to the gurney, shone a pin-light into Imas' eyes and took his temperature with an ear thermometer: 35.5 degrees Celsius. He inserted a needle into the IV tube and pushed in the medicine.

Imas took a sudden breath and his eyelids fluttered open.

"How are you feeling?" Piter asked.

Imas blinked, smacked his lips and looked around the room, confused.

"Maybe these will help." Piter took a pair of glasses from a bag containing Imas' personal effects and placed them on the man's face. "You've been spared. Are you hungry?" Piter kept his voice flat and his face devoid of emotion.

"Spared? You're not going to kill me?"

"I'm going to undo the straps, but don't try to move too fast." Imas tried to sit up, but Piter pushed him down again. "Just lie still."

"I'm so cold."

Piter removed the sheet and placed two heated blankets over Imas' thin, bare chest.

Imas shivered, turned his head to the side and looked at two bodies on either side of him covered with sheets. His eyes grew wide. "Those people dead?"

"My assistant will soon give you a series of memory and physical tests."

"Why? Where's my daughter?"

Piter reattached the straps. Ten minutes later, after giving him time to warm up, Piter helped Imas sit up.

Imas grasped the edge of the bed. "I'm so dizzy."

"It will take a few hours for the medication to wear off. Put these on." Piter placed a pair of elasticized trousers and a loose t-shirt next to Imas.

Imas put his arms through the holes in the top. Piter helped him into the outfit, seeing the ALS was starting to affect the fine motor control of the subject's fingers. Imas sat in a wheelchair and Piter transported him down the elevator.

In the basement were barred cages in four rows of five. Each small cage contained a cot, toilet and sink, and a person. The cages didn't allow the subjects any privacy. The strong smell of disinfectant filled the air. Most of the test subjects lay listlessly on their beds, but Fillip Farwell was standing and leaning against the bars. "Hello again, Piter."

Piter ignored him. In this room, Fillip and the others were living research specimens, not people. He felt odd not exchanging any words with his former friend, but unnecessary conversation was discouraged between subjects and researchers. Besides, Fillip was not one of his test subjects.

Piter, Gorge, Jeniver and Pim were each allowed five test subjects at a time. In addition, each researcher was allowed two isolation chambers which were used for subjects with communicable diseases. Gorge liked to use his rooms for psychological experiments, such as sensory deprivation or the effects of solitude on the human psyche.

Piter unlocked an empty cage across the aisle from Fillip and rolled Imas' wheelchair into the room.

"No! Don't put me in here. I want to talk to my daughter."

"I'm afraid that's impossible. I'll check on you later." Piter locked the door behind him and proceeded back down the hall, pushing the empty wheelchair. He focused his eyes straight ahead.

Imas yelled, "What's going to happen to me?"

Piter ignored him and walked by the cage of one of Gorge Bigon's test subjects. He was struck by her odd appearance. Half of her face exhibited the typical signs of aging for a person of sixty-five years, but on the other side she looked like a thirty-five-year-old woman. He stopped to stare, realizing how brilliant a scientist Gorge was. "Was it painful?" he asked her.

She raised her eyes to meet his. "Like acid. I should be in a freak show. Dr. Bigon said he won't do the other side, wants a side-by-side comparison. When he's done with me he'll kill me, right?"

"Probably."

"What did I ever do to deserve this?"

He shrugged. "You're contributing to science. You should be proud."

She frowned at him. Her left eye showed the creases of crow's feet. The right did not. "Do you really believe that?"

"I look out for myself."

"I see. You're pragmatic. Well, that's one way to survive."

He was about to respond but stopped himself. He returned to his office, opened the refrigerator, poured himself another glass of wine and sat on the couch. He swirled the wine in his glass and sipped. *Not bad, a crisp Chardonnay.*

Holding the wine glass by the stem, he drained it, set the glass down, rinsed with mouthwash to mask the smell of alcohol and got back to work.

He stepped into the wide corridor, once the centre aisle of the church where he and Yun had married. Piter could picture the huge crucifix that once hung above the altar. All day, Piter was plagued by thoughts of Yun. She had walked up the aisle towards him, her hand on her father's arm. The church was full of family and friends. She was so beautiful; her long black hair was tucked behind her white veil.

Yun had told Piter her dress was "mermaid style," tight around the hips and flared at the bottom. He smiled, remembering the way the dress showed her gorgeous figure. He couldn't tear his eyes off her as he said his vows.

Yun looked up at him with her dark almond eyes. "I love you, Piter. I want to grow old with you."

"Me, too," he had said.

§

The pews had been removed years ago and walls were built on either side of the aisle, forming a hallway, which now led to the various rooms of the facility. Continuing down the hall, he opened the door to the laboratory.

It was a large square room. A long table stood in each corner of the room, one for each of the eradicator/researchers—Dr. Gorge Bigon, Dr. Jeniver Bant, Dr. Pim Marris and Dr. Piter Dram. Each station was equipped with the usual items: beakers, burners, funnels, gloves, graduated cylinders and microscopes. Clear cabinets and drawers lined the walls and contained everything needed to complete the experiments, such as tweezers, droppers, thermometers and test tubes. Piter had recently put in a request for a new centrifuge and CT scanner. He looked forward to their arrival within the week.

Two of his associates were at work at their stations. They looked up when Piter entered. Gorge Bigon, who had taken Piter's first eradication that morning, worked on the cream that reversed wrinkling of the skin. He loved to gloat about his success but was docked a month's salary one day for saying, "If I was in the private sector, I could get rich by selling this cream."

Piter knew better than to open his mouth and reveal personal feelings.

Gorge smiled in a friendly manner. He was a squat man with a large, round belly and a full beard that he loved to stroke, caressing it as if it were a kitten. He was five years younger than Piter but was fond of pointing out his higher position in the facility. He was the first to jump up and greet the Area Supervisor when she made her weekly visits. He showed her his organized files and announced loudly, "I have the highest rates of eradication in the city."

Cherrin called him an "ass-kisser" once, which elicited a rare smile from Piter.

Jeniver Bant, who once worked with Piter at the Free Clinic, was developing a drug she hoped would quickly tone muscles. "Surely, the sports industry would be interested in my product," she had said.

Piter went to his work station at the far end of the room, opened a locked cabinet and retrieved a bottle containing a formula he had worked on for months. Cherrin kept Piter's work station clean and orderly. His colleagues' assistants weren't as proficient or knowledgeable about laboratory procedures as Cherrin. He had asked her once if she had any medical training other than a lab assistant certificate she received from the community college.

She had giggled and said, "Me? Oh, no."

§

"Thanks, Gorge, for filling in for me this morning," Piter said.

Gorge missed the sarcastic tone in Piter's voice. He pulled off his rubber gloves. "No problem. Always glad to help. Did you hear the president sent me a note, telling me how pleased she is with my anti-wrinkle cream?" He stroked his beard.

"No, I didn't."

"She said, 'I have the skin of a thirty-year-old.'" He smirked. "I used it on my own hands." He held the back of his hands for Piter's inspection. "Want to feel them?"

"No."

Jeniver's hair was under a surgical cap and her face covered by a mask. She held a scalpel in her hand and examined the muscles of the upper section of a human body, evidently male, judging by the size. The head, internal organs and skin had been removed. Only the bones and muscles of the arms, shoulders and chest lay on a surgical table in front of her. The blood had been drained, but her surgical gown was stained red like a butcher's apron.

Piter put on rubber gloves and a face mask. He stepped over to her table and watched Jeniver's skillful hands as she cut thin slices of muscles to examine under her microscope. He glanced at the file. The torso belonged to a forty-four-year-old man with ALS.

"I treated this man for several months before eradicating him, to see if I could slow down the atrophy and increase muscle growth," Jeniver said.

"Results?"

She lifted her head from the microscope. "Disappointing. My experimental drug seemed to have sped up the process. Want to have a look?"

He took her stool and peered into the microscope. "I'd be interested in reading your report, if I may."

"Sure. I could use a second opinion."

"May I examine the brain and spinal column?"

"Okay. The brain's in storage. Why do you want it?"

"I'm looking for anomalies in the primary motor cortex." He put on a pair of gloves and helped her turn the torso over and cut away the spine. Piter put it in a plastic bag, labelled it and descended to the basement to put the backbone in the refrigerator.

As well as cages for the test subjects, the basement contained sterile surgical areas and refrigerator units for body parts. Neatly labelled containers held hearts, lungs, livers, kidneys, ovaries, gonads, eyes and brains. AZEN ensured no loyal person ever had to wait long for a healthy organ. Piter opened one of the refrigerators and found the container with the man's brain. He labelled it and the spine, "For the exclusive use of Dr. Piter Dram."

§

A new law had recently been passed. All people over the age of sixty-five were to be eradicated. No choice, no exceptions. The elderly population was decreasing at a tremendous rate. Quietus was usually celebrated close to the sixty-fifth birthday, but in the case of someone suffering from a terminal illness, it could occur sooner.

He sat across the table from his parents in their apartment. He spoke in a soft voice. "You must comply. It's your duty."

Odilia dabbed her eyes with a tissue and leaned her head on her husband's shoulder.

Piter sighed. "We'll put it off for a little longer, but why make it worse for yourself?"

Hyron stared up at the ceiling. His jaw quivered. "It's sinful. We won't go without a fight. That you can't understand our feelings shows me what kind of man you've become, Piter."

CHAPTER THIRTY-TWO

Baby X

Cherrin stepped into Piter's office, pushing a trolley loaded with food. "I brought lunch." She poured a cup of coffee for Piter and placed it in front of him. "Would you like ham and cheese, egg or turkey?"

"Turkey."

She handed him the sandwich and gave him a toothy smile.

"Thank you," he said, after realizing some sort of response was expected. He tore the plastic from the sandwich, crinkled it into a ball and tossed it in the trash.

"It's such a gorgeous day. Have you been outside?" She pulled up a chair to the front of Piter's desk and unwrapped a sandwich. "It would do you good to get out and get some sun on your skin." Cherrin took a bite. "I mean…not that you're too pale or anything…it's just vitamin D is important…"

"Don't you have work to do?" Piter asked. He was hoping to have a little time to catch up on his paperwork. He bit into his sandwich; the creamy mayonnaise overpowered the taste of the turkey. He washed it down with a slurp of coffee.

"Oh, gosh, silly me, giving a doctor medical advice. Personally, I love the hot weather—"

"Cherrin. I'm a little busy."

"Right. Sorry, Dr. Dram. Are you okay? You look a little down in the dumps."

"It's been a trying day."

She leaned in close to him. Her warm, brown eyes beheld his. "How come?"

"My parents…never mind." He drew back, pulled some paperwork towards him, pretending to study it. "I'd rather not discuss it."

Cherrin pouted. Little crinkles showed between her brows. "Oh, I understand. You can always confide in me, Dr. Dram. I'm a really good listener."

"Your eagerness has been noted." Piter gobbled up the rest of his sandwich and washed it down with more sips of coffee.

She finished her lunch, stood and began tidying the room, restocking the fridge and replacing the cake as she did after every Quietus celebration. When Cherrin finished tidying she returned to Piter's desk and stood smiling at him.

"Has my next appointment arrived yet?" he asked.

"Not yet. I'll bring her in when she gets here." Cherrin continued to stand in one spot, smiling.

"What do you want?" he asked.

"Dr. Dram, you never mentioned my hair." Cherrin turned her head from side to side and twirled. Lines of corn rows covered her head.

"Nice." Truthfully, he hadn't noticed the change until now.

"Do you really think so? It took three hours to get it done." She smiled and her bleached white teeth contrasted with her dark complexion.

He ignored her, thinking her impossibly vain and trivial.

§

An hour later, he sat reading Cherrin's comprehensive notes on Imas Larium. Piter measured a dose of his experimental ALS drug. As usual, the sharp smell of bleach assaulted his nose as he entered the basement.

Piter entered Imas' cage and shook him awake. "Time for your medicine."

"What is this?" Imas asked and then flinched at the poke of a needle in his shoulder.

"Something to make you feel better."

"Nothing will make me feel better, except to go home." His lower lip trembled.

Piter was reminded of a whiny child. "I'm working on a cure for ALS." He was usually careful to maintain distance from test subjects and regretted the words as soon as he said them.

"So, the guy across from me is right. You're using us like lab rats."

"What guy?" He tried to appear disinterested.

[212]

"Says his name is Fillip."

Piter turned to see Fillip standing at the bars of his cage, leaning his forearms on the horizontal rungs. "Hello, Piter."

"Fillip," he said, with a slight nod of the head.

"You finally acknowledged my presence. What kind of man have you become? You lock people in cages and experiment on them."

Piter turned back to Imas and puffed out his chest. "It's for the greater good. My colleagues and I are working on treatments for all kinds of maladies and cures for diseases. You test subjects contribute to society. We ensure you are treated in an ethical manner."

Fillip snorted. "You're full of it."

Cherrin came down the hall. "Your next client is here, a baby moogie."

"I'll be back later, Imas. Cherrin will bring you something to eat."

"What about me?" asked Fillip.

"Whether you get anything to eat or not is not my concern." He adjusted the sleeves of his lab coat, pulled on his shirt collar and marched away.

Glancing back, he saw Cherrin enter Imas' cage. She pulled the blanket over his chest and gave him a friendly pat on the shoulder. Piter decided he would have to speak to her about her inappropriate interactions with test subjects.

Piter picked up his pace and re-entered his office. Cherrin came in soon after carrying a cradle. From it came the cries of an infant. It was strange Baby X's congenital condition wasn't detected before birth and the fetus aborted, but sometimes pre-natal testing missed these things. Quietus on Wheels had brought the infant in live to keep the organs fresh. The parents of the baby chose not to accompany the infant. Of course, the mother would be undergoing a sterilization procedure about now. In any case, he was glad none of the baby's relatives were present. Piter could complete his work without all the crying and carrying on that often accompanied the eradication of a child.

Baby X whimpered a bit as Cherrin lifted her from the cradle and placed her on the white cloth. The infant's eyes were shut against the bright lights and her hands were clenched fists. She shivered and drew her knees to her chest.

Cherrin said, "It's a shame. She's cute."

The baby's arm veins were too small for his needles so he would need to insert the drugs through the baby's jugular.

Cherrin interrupted in a small, shaky voice, "What if, just this once, you didn't?"

He hesitated. "Ridiculous. Who would take care of her? You? Even an Elite would have difficulty getting permission to keep such a child."

"I just feel sad sometimes. She's so small and helpless."

Piter felt a twinge of sadness for the tiny girl but promptly buried the feeling. "She's not recognized as a person."

Cherrin stared at him with wide eyes. The baby put her fingers in her mouth to suck on them.

He pressed gloved fingers against the side of her neck, feeling for the jugular vein. "This won't hurt a bit." The baby's skin was warm and soft. Her small hand reached up and grasped his pinky. Her tiny, perfectly formed fingers were as delicate as flower petals. "Hold the baby still, Cherrin."

Cherrin held the infant's arms down.

"Quietus comes," Piter said and he injected the baby with the sedative. She squeaked when the needle poked her and then she closed her eyes. He finished the job with the other injections. Baby X took one small breath and was still. He deposited the needle in the sharps container.

Cherrin had her back to him and seemed to be examining a spot on the floor. "Take the body to Recycling." She turned towards him and he saw her eyes were wet. "Are you crying? There's no room for sentimentality." His anger rose. "And what were you doing in Imas' cage? Do not get personally involved with test subjects or our clients!"

"No, I'm not. I'm just bushed." She blinked and dabbed at her eyes with her fingertips and tried to control her sniffles.

"And don't forget to feed the test subjects! I don't want to have to report your actions today. Learn to control yourself."

She nodded, wrapped the infant's tiny body in a cloth, picked her up and ran out of the room.

Piter watched her carry the tiny bundle away. He hadn't been able to see or hold his infant son, who, if he had lived, would be over a year old. He stared blankly, confused for a moment about what he was supposed to do next.

CHAPTER THIRTY-THREE
A Progressive Age

Tresha walked with shackles around her ankles and wrists between two heavily armed men. She didn't know why they needed to take such precautions to escort a middle-aged woman to a cell. Her body ached and her left eye was swollen shut. Hunger clawed at her stomach, but a more pressing need was for water.

"Attention, staff and students. It is the top of the hour. Stand at attention for an announcement from our president."

The armed men stopped in mid-stride and stood straight and tall.

Aura said, "We live in a progressive age. You are not forced to take care of a child with cystic fibrosis, diabetes, autism or muscular dystrophy. We care about the people of Covona. We know the difficulties, expenses and heartache associated with raising a damaged child. Don't feel guilty about bringing them to Quietus. Rest assured, AZEN will guide you towards a bold and prosperous future. May you find spiritual comfort in the Light of Aura Church."

Tresha thought about Jakon, victimized for the crime of being dependent on others. She had been photographed, fingerprinted and now stood shackled in a hallway. It continued to amaze her how quickly her world had changed.

The guards brought her to a bare concrete cell and bound her to a chair.

Her throat was parched. "May I have a drink of water?"

The guards ignored her and left her alone in the room.

An hour passed, maybe two. A woman cried in another room. Tresha heard her beg. "Please, please." There were minutes of intense screaming and then silence.

Tears streamed down Tresha's face, but she couldn't wipe them away because of her shackles. She began to shiver, longing to be outside where the warm summer sun was shining. Her back and bottom ached from being forced to sit on a hard chair for hours.

Tresha couldn't believe Aura was in her life again and she was more under Aura's control now than when they were teenagers. *Then, I was ostracized. Now, it's a death sentence.* She ran her tongue over her dry, cracked lips.

Tresha continued to wait. All she could think about was water, and there it was, half a metre away, dripping from a leaky tap. She strained towards it but couldn't reach.

A thin-lipped man with a large mustache entered the room pushing a trolley. Cheekbones jutted from his face, giving him a skeletal appearance. On the trolley was some sort of electrical device. He plugged it into a wall socket.

"May I have a drink of water?" Her throat ached as she croaked out the words.

He said nothing but proceeded to place a series of sticky probes on her left arm. He turned the dial to level one and she felt a small electrical charge. The dial on the box went up to ten.

Tresha's lower jaw trembled.

"Now then," he said. "This is a simple machine. Level one will send a painless tingling sensation to your muscles. Level five will be quite uncomfortable. Level seven is painful. Level ten is excruciating. I will ask you a series of questions. If I am not satisfied with your response, I will turn the dial. The more dissatisfied I am, the greater the shock. So, you see the number and intensity of the shocks is entirely up to you. Let's begin. Who are your accomplices?"

She said nothing and then jumped at the jolt that made the muscles in her arm spasm. The interrogator's eyes showed no understanding, no mercy, like gazing into the eyes of a fish.

"Who are your accomplices?" His voice remained calm.

Again, she said nothing and a jolt ran through her and she let out a yelp. Her heart was racing. She closed her eyes to pray. *Lord, give me strength.* Minutes passed. More questions came and she pressed her lips together, refusing to speak. She received several more jolts. Her strength waned. She watched him fiddle with the dial, turning it up and down. His face was not angry; neither did he seem to be enjoying himself. Tresha's stomach roiled. He was too calm, turning the dial on the machine as if he was looking for a radio signal.

"Where are your safe houses located?" he asked in a tone like a friend might use when asking, "How are you today?"

She turned her face from him, readying herself for the shock.

A voice came over the loudspeaker. "Stop the interrogation."

The mustached man lifted one eyebrow, looked mildly surprised, shrugged, packed up his equipment and left the room.

Two women entered. One of them wrenched Tresha's head back while another forced a teaspoon of salt down her throat. She was left alone again, coughing and gasping for air. Thirst overcame her. Her throat hurt so badly she couldn't even moan. Even her eyes were dry and stinging. Water continued to drip from the sink. She turned her head away, forcing herself not to look at the water trickling down the drain, though she heard it, "drip, drip, drip…" Her head ached, a sharp, stabbing pain behind her eyes. She felt light-headed.

A female guard shook Tresha. "Thirsty?"

Tresha made a husky, croaking sound.

"Drink this," the woman said.

Tresha drank from the glass held to her mouth. The water had a slightly acidic flavour, but to her, it was the best thing she'd ever tasted. The guard filled up the cup from the sink and Tresha drained it, too. Her cuffs were removed and Tresha was permitted to lay down. Feelings of relief and gratitude were quickly replaced when she realized she had been drugged. Blurred outlines of people came in and out of the room, spoke to her, asked questions and she mumbled responses.

Later, she awoke face up on the narrow bed. The bright ceiling light speared her eyes. She turned away from the light, trying to remember what happened, but recalled events only in bits and pieces— running through the forest, the helicopter, firing her rifle, the blurry interrogation and this cold cell. She pulled herself up so her legs dangled over the edge of the bed. A sudden dizzy spell caused the room to shift position. The walls and ceiling merged into one another, bending and shifting shape, as if the walls were made of paper instead of concrete. The floor bent to meet the ceiling and the contents of her stomach roiled. She stumbled towards the toilet and vomited. The floor was so cool. Tresha laid her head on it, her arms no longer strong enough to lift her upper body. She awoke, shivering, crawled to bed, climbed in and nestled under the blanket. In what seemed like minutes a pair of strong arms hoisted her from the bed and to the floor.

"Time for your shower, princess," said a familiar voice.

Tresha inhaled sharply as a bucket of cold water was thrown over her head. Her back arched and chills coursed through her body.

Cruel laughter filled the room. "Get up. Put on some dry clothes. Time for breakfast."

She pushed the hair out of her eyes, pulled off her soaked garment and struggled into the dry prison uniform. With difficulty, she found the leg and arm holes. She'd lost track of time, didn't know how long it had been since she was taken prisoner, but if her stomach was any indication, it must have been a long time.

"What day is it?" Tresha asked Red Hair.

"Don't ask questions. Eat." She plunked a tray on the metal table that jutted out of the wall. "Put the tray through the slot in the door when you're done. There's no maid service here."

"What's going to become of me?" Tresha didn't expect a reply.

"Who knows? Maybe a labour camp, but I doubt it; probably eradication."

§

No one opened the door of Tresha's cell in hours. The flickering overhead light made it difficult to sleep. Her stomach complained of hunger, so she got up and knocked on the door. "Please. I'm hungry," she called. There was no response, so she sat back down.

The light was always on. She covered her eyes with her hands for a bit of relief. Tresha slept and woke, slept and woke, sometimes to the sound of someone screaming. Blocking out the sound was impossible. The silence was also frightening when all she could hear was her ghostly and hollow breath. Sometimes she believed she could hear her blood coursing through her body.

With no window and the same constant, glaring light, time lost meaning. Bored and on edge at the same time, expecting the worst, knowing she could be dragged down the hall at any time for interrogation, or perhaps to her death, she distracted herself by counting the tiles on the floor. Nineteen by twelve; each tile about fifteen centimetres square. She struggled to do the math, to find the exact size of her cell, but her mind wouldn't focus. Yet, it seemed imperative she find the answer.

She began counting the number of meals brought to her room, the only means of keeping track of time. Tresha slept for hours at a time, or was it minutes? Meals came at irregular times, or did they? Soon, she had no way of knowing how long had she been in the cell. Was it weeks or months? It was disconcerting to be unsure. Tresha ate every bit of the meals brought to her and then licked the bowls clean. Still, her stomach ached with hunger.

At times, Tresha panicked, gasping for breath in the confined space. She paced back and forth. Three sentences ran around and around in her brain: *The room is small. The room is bright. The room is concrete.* She lay down, got up, sat down and then paced some more.

One morning, they began playing music. A man in a falsetto voice sang: "Skidamarink a dink a dink. Skidamarink a doo. I love you. I love you in the morning and in the afternoon. I love you in the evening and underneath the moon…" Tresha smiled. She used to sing that song to Jakon. That was immediately followed by, "If you're happy and you know it clap your hands." It was a relief to hear music, even if they were inane children's melodies sung badly. The high-pitched man then sang, "Head and shoulders, knees and toes…" Tresha sang along. That completed, the trio of songs repeated, this time at a higher volume. The three songs were played again, this time at a faster tempo.

Hours later, Tresha was on her bed with a pillow over her head to try to block the sound. Evening came and the horrible tunes still blasted. "Shut up! Shut up!" She tore bits of cloth from her blanket and stuffed them in her ears. The sound was muffled, but still echoed through her skull. She longed for a bat to swing at the intercom.

The music stopped, a blessed relief. She lay down to sleep, but not long after her slumber was disturbed. "If you're happy and you know it and you really want to show it…"

"You evil devils! You sons of bitches! Shut off the music!" Tresha squeezed her hands over her ears and burst into tears. *They're trying to drive me crazy.*

By morning, the music had finally stopped. Tresha rose from bed on shaky legs. She put her mouth to the faucet and took a long, satisfying drink. The reflection in the mirror showed sallow skin and swollen, bloodshot eyes. Shivering in the cold, overly bright room, she took the blanket from the bed and paced back and forth. She began to sing in a high-pitched voice, "Skidamarink a dink a dink…" She clapped her hand over her mouth. "Oh, my God. What am I doing?" She was heartbroken that the cute little songs she used to sing with Jakon had become instruments of torture. Tresha wiped the tears from her cheeks and tried to remember the feeling of Jakon's arms around her neck. She realized how hard it was to love one's enemies.

Do what you want, you foul spawns of the devil. For the sake of Jakon I will stay strong.

CHAPTER THIRTY-FOUR

Following Protocol

Piter bought his parents a condominium in the best part of the city, new furniture, and provided them with a monthly allowance, and he couldn't understand why they were still critical of him.

"Do they ever consider how their actions affect me?" he asked Tafflen.

"We should have them over and explain things," she said.

§

A plate of cookies sat untouched on the coffee table. Heavy silence fell in the room after Piter explained his proposal. Odilia's tea cup rattled on its saucer. Her eyes teared up. Hyron frowned. His face flushed from his neck up to his forehead.

Their intense stares made Piter squirm in his chair. "Do you have anything to say?"

Odilia plunked her tea cup on the table. "You used to save lives. This is not the way we raised you."

"Not surprising, considering what he does for a living," Hyron said.

Piter said, "I'm helping to make this country great again. Aura says it is to be a celebration."

Tafflen cleared her throat. "Can I pour anyone more tea?" She stepped forward, offering the pot, but was ignored. She set the pot on the table, sat beside Piter on the loveseat and lowered her eyes to her folded hands.

"It's that bitch dictator," Hyron said. "She's got everyone brainwashed, including our son. I thought you'd be too intelligent to fall for her lies, Piter."

Tafflen gasped and covered her mouth.

"You used to support her, Dad. Remember?"

"Before I knew better. Her parents are both over sixty-five, yet they are still alive. I see the rules don't apply to everyone," Hyron said.

"I could report your unpatriotic comments, but I won't." Piter stared hard at them.

"Well, that's big of you," Odilia said.

Tafflen's face was ashen. "It was great having you. Come and see us again…" She sprang to her feet, took the tea cups, hustled to the kitchen, and didn't emerge.

Piter said, "I am loyal elite and my own parents dare to criticize our government. Do you know what would happen to me if anyone found out?"

"How did you become so utterly self-centered?" Odilia asked.

"I obey the law. That's how I survive. I advise the two of you to watch it."

"Your mother and I are nearly sixty-five. Obeying the law means we die soon," Hyron said.

"Glad you understand. Goodbye, Mom and Dad." He stood, clenching and unclenching his hands. When his parents didn't rise, he walked to the door and opened it for them.

§

Piter decided his parents' Quietus should take place on the same day even though his mother was six months younger than his father. He didn't want her to grieve for six months. He made appointments ahead of time and without telling them. When the day came, he had to get the help of the police to bring his parents to the QRR Centre.

"Piter, how can you do this to your own parents?" Odilia asked. She fought the policemen who restrained her arms. "Sweet Jesus, help me!" She wept with hiccupping sobs. Her eyes pleaded with Piter. Tears flowed down her face.

"It's the law!" he yelled. "There's no choice."

"Hyron, say something to your son. Make him understand."

Hyron stared straight ahead, his jaw tight. "Take care of my violin. Your mother has some jewelry to remember her by. I know you don't need the money." He did not look at Piter.

His parents were put in the back of a police car. Piter followed behind all the way to the QRR Centre in a cab, rather than sit in the same vehicle.

§

His father went first. He was stoic, didn't say a word and wouldn't look at his son. Piter struggled not to cry and felt ashamed for doing so. He gulped two glasses of wine.

His mother was a screamer when her turn came. Tears filled her eyes. "Please, Piter, change your ways before it's too late. Your soul is in danger."

"Mother, be quiet. Such foolishness." He was embarrassed by her behaviour, especially with Gorge in charge of the ceremony. Security had to be called, as was required whenever trouble ensued. Piter gripped the wine glass so hard, he was surprised it didn't shatter in his hand. "Why can't you accept things the way they are? Please, Gorge, let's just get this over with." Piter turned his back so his colleague wouldn't see how upset he was.

Odilia said, "I can't accept this evil. Hadar understands. I don't know what happened to you."

Piter turned around quickly. "How do you know? Hadar's missing."

"The reason you haven't found him is because he doesn't want to be found."

Gorge started the drip.

"You've spoken to him? Where is he?" Piter reached over to stop the drip, but it was too late. His mom lost consciousness. "Don't give her the second dose yet. I have to talk to her."

"You know I have to follow protocol," Gorge said.

"No!" Piter's wine glass smashed to the floor. He made a lunge for the IV tube.

Gorge nodded to the security guards who stepped forward and held Piter back.

"No, Gorge! You don't understand. I have to talk to her."

Gorge administered the second dose and then the third. Odilia stopped breathing.

Piter gazed down on his parents' dead bodies, into their sightless eyes. He realized he would never hear their voices again, never feel their touch, and for a moment he was breathless. He was a good citizen of Covona, always obeyed the law. Yet, a hole appeared inside his chest, vacant and black.

Gorge turned on the radio while he worked, putting away his equipment.

The radio played a sad violin piece Piter remembered his father playing: "Largo." He could almost hear his father's voice. "Did you ever hear a piece so full of despair and hopelessness?"

Piter felt dizzy and had to sit on the couch. "Please turn off the music, Gorge."

Gorge shrugged, switched off the radio and leaned against the wall. He stroked his beard. "Feeling a little emotional, Piter? Can I offer a sedative?"

§

Piter waited until he was alone in his office before weeping. He didn't blame Gorge, who was only following rules. Piter felt ashamed of his outburst, but Gorge was good enough not to report him.

Piter went home and drank glass after glass, until he passed out.

§

In the morning, the telephone woke Piter from a wine-induced slumber. He unwrapped his arm from around Tafflen's warm body and reached for the phone. He cleared his throat. "Dr. Dram."

"Good morning. Please hold for President Aura Zarling."

Piter bolted upright in bed and ran his fingers through his hair. Like all loyal citizens, he was expected to love, respect and fear the president. School children sang songs of tribute to her, praising her wisdom and strength, humbleness and mercy. The media looked to her for direction. The country's business leaders, experts in education, health and law all bowed to her commands. Piter's heart pounded. Aura Zarling was calling him at home!

"Is this Dr. Piter Dram?"

Her voice was so familiar, but she had never spoken to him directly. His head spun, imagining the implications. "Yes, Ms. President. It's a pleasure…"

"I have a matter to discuss with you."

Beside him, Tafflen also sat up in bed. Her eyes were wide and her hand covered her mouth.

"Yes, of course. What…?"

"Be at my home at four-thirty this afternoon. My assistant will make the arrangements with you."

Tafflen whispered, "What is it, Piter?" Her face was full of concern.

He shushed her and signalled her to give him something to write with. His hands shook as he held the pen.

§

When he arrived at work later in the morning, he approached Cherrin's desk and said, "I'll have to leave at three-thirty today. I've a meeting with President Aura Zarling."

Cherrin's eyes widened. "It must be very important. I can't wait to hear…"

He glared at her, cutting her off. "I've no time for idle conversation."

This morning's phone call kept replaying through his head, making it hard to concentrate. After four routine Quietus celebrations, two elderlies and two moogies, he proceeded to the lab and spent the afternoon looking through his microscope at slides of brain matter. Every so often he felt a stab of fear, imagining why the president wanted to see him.

AZEN was aware of his past association with that despicable human rights organization. He never spoke of his past life with anyone, except Tafflen. Piter wondered if someone in HRFA implicated him in one of their illegal operations. *Maybe they found Hadar.* Piter shook his head to try to stop the imaginings and carry on with his work.

Cherrin entered the lab, put her hands on the table and leaned towards him. "What do you think the president will say to you?" Her eyes sparkled.

He leaned back on his stool. "I don't know."

"What's this about the president?" Jeniver asked. She rose from her stool.

"Dr. Dram has an appointment to see Aura Zarling this afternoon," Cherrin said.

"What for?" asked Jeniver.

"Why you?" asked Gorge. His tone was envious. Gorge stood with crossed arms and glared at Piter. The three formed a semicircle around him.

"I don't know," Piter said. He didn't care if they believed him or not. He leaned towards his microscope again. "Now if you don't mind, I have work to do."

After work, Piter stepped outside. He raised his face to feel the warmth of the sun on this spring day and descended the stairs. Melted snow trickled through the eaves, gurgled down the sides of the building and flowed into the gutter. The trees seemed to have broken out in buds since this morning. The tops of tulips poked up through the muddy earth.

He hoped he would be around to see tomorrow.

CHAPTER THIRTY-FIVE

Meeting the President

Piter rubbed his clammy hands on his pant legs. At four-twenty, his taxi climbed the curved driveway to the top of a hill and then rolled through the gates of Aura Zarling's grand mansion. The sprawling house was as large as an entire city block. He stepped out of the taxi and was greeted by guards armed with automatic weapons.

"Remove your coat, sir. Raise your arms." One guard pushed the coat through an X-ray machine while the other used a hand-held metal detector to scan Piter's body.

Once past security, Piter stood in the foyer, which alone was larger than his whole apartment. A curving bannister led up a stairway. To the left was a dining room with ten chairs lined up on either side of a long antique table. Marble floors, plush furniture and a grand piano graced a large room to the right of the stairway. On one wall was a life-sized portrait of the president. A large window overlooked an extensive garden. The trees were trading green leaves for red, yellow and brown. In the distance was the Keque Mountain range.

The butler took Piter's coat to hang it up and guided him to a large office where a single desk occupied the centre of the room. He made the introduction, "Piter Dram, ER doctor," turned and left. Two more armed guards followed Piter into the room and never took their eyes off him.

A tall woman stood silhouetted against a window. She gazed out at the view of the city. Her long brown hair hung loosely down her back. She didn't turn around or acknowledge Piter's presence. He stood like a soldier, his hands at his sides, locking his shaking knees so he wouldn't crumple onto the floor.

Four huge television screens covered one wall of the room, muted, and simultaneously displaying different news stories from around the world. He gaped, not having seen an international news story in years. The people of Covona were no longer exposed to foreign television or internet, and as the president had said, "All the deceptions contained there." Printed words glided across the screens. There were scenes of civil unrest in Asciary, a federal election in Sura, a new treatment for lung cancer coming out of Solime, and a terrorist group had blown up a building in Dule. He was mesmerized.

Aura Zarling turned to face him. At fifty-seven-years-old, she seemed to not be subject to the same natural laws as the collective. He remembered a newspaper headline: "Her glorious self remains un-aged and uncorrupted. She truly lives as an example to us all." Piter knew plastic surgery and Gorge's formula were the reasons she appeared much younger.

"You knew Tresha Farwell," she said. Her voice was hard.

Piter gulped. "Yes, years ago, but I haven't seen her..."

"She was arrested. She's being held at Re-Ed. Did you know that?" She walked several steps towards him. Her tight grey slacks showed her lovely figure, but he dared not stare.

"No, Ms. President. I didn't." He clenched his teeth.

"You were friends, part of Human Rights for All." Aura grimaced, as if saying the name of the organization caused her physical pain.

"No, my deceased wife, not me."

"Her husband, Fillip, is at the QRR Centre. How's his health?"

"He is recovering from Solime Flu. We're so proud at the Centre. One of my colleagues is working on a vaccination—"

"Starting today, Tresha Farwell will be under your care."

"Yes, Ms. President."

"That despicable couple dared to oppose me, but the threat is all but eliminated." She smiled, showing perfect teeth.

Piter smiled also. "Thanks to your wise leadership."

She stood straight, thrusting out her chest. "My interrogators are skilled at finding information, wouldn't you say? You worked at Re-Ed."

"They are skilled, indeed."

"Tresha is feeble. I told them not to be too enthusiastic. Did you know she used to be my friend?"

"Yes. She told me."

"You will visit her. Tell her about how much better your life is now that you are an elite member of AZEN. Rub it in. Let her know how foolish she is to not follow me."

"Of course, Ms. President."

"Call me Aura. Can I call you Piter?" She stepped closer and looked up into his eyes. "You're tall. I like tall men." She rubbed the tips of her fingers up and down his arm.

He shivered. She was not what he expected. Aura was slim, almost delicate, with high cheekbones and big hazel eyes. Her hair was silky and shiny, her face unlined and her figure showed no sign of middle-age spread. She put her face closer to his. He resisted the urge to take a step back.

"Do I have beautiful skin?"

"Yes, Ms. Pres...uh...Aura."

"It's the latest in fetal transferal technology. I literally have baby-soft skin. Touch it."

He ran his fingers across her cheek and marvelled at the miracles of modern science. "Amazing."

"You've seen lots of people die, Piter. Does it hurt?"

"Depends how you go." Piter took a step backwards and put his hands behind his back.

"How's the study on ALS coming?"

"I'm testing a new drug therapy."

"I had high hopes for you. Apparently, you wrote an award-winning doctoral thesis on the subject and it turned out to be a complete flop." Her expression was stony.

He cleared his throat. "I'm testing a new combination. The results are promising."

She took a step forward. "I want you to speed up your investigations." Her perfume smelled of flowers.

"Years more of research are necessary..."

Her face turned red. "That's not what I want to hear!"

Piter stepped back in fear.

"Do you ever wonder why your experience at Re-Ed was more pleasant than others?"

He nodded. Piter was not beaten, starved or tortured excessively.

"Two reasons. Before you, we thought HRFA was relatively harmless, all those annoying letters and complaints. We didn't know they were the ones responsible for sneaking people across the border. We're grateful you told us. Also, medical researchers of your calibre are rare. I'm most interested in you continuing to research ALS." She smiled and her face softened. "You're a brilliant scientist. You got top marks at university. You've proven your loyalty to me."

"I understand."

"One more thing. I want you to be my physician. My last doctor suffered an unfortunate accident."

Piter could only imagine what kind of accident the former doctor had. "I am honoured."

"Yes. Of course." She walked to her desk and picked up a file folder. "These are my medical records." She gave him a leather satchel. "Study it and come back to see me in two days. I hope I don't have to explain to you it's confidential." She walked away from him and watched a news report of an uprising in Asciary.

"Strictest confidence." He wasn't sure if he should leave the room.

She spoke with her back to him, her eyes trained on the television. "You know, people say they want to be free, but what they really want is someone to tell them what to do."

He wasn't sure how to respond and opened his mouth to speak when she interrupted him again.

"Overall, people are not very intelligent. Not like you and me. They so easily forget things. That's what makes propaganda so easy. The trick is to create slogans and then repeat them over and over until the stupid masses have them memorized. Soon, you have everyone doing exactly what you say and thinking the way you want them to think."

"Like, 'AZEN guides you boldly towards the future.'"

She turned to him, her face lit up with a smile. "Exactly."

"Most wars are caused by religions," he said.

"I knew you'd understand, Piter. The fate of AZEN depends on me as long as I live." She waved her hand at him, shooing him away. "You may go now."

§

It was too dark in the taxi to read, so Piter held Aura's satchel in his arms, gripping it so tightly his fingers began to ache. He felt a stress headache coming on.

Tafflen met him at the door when he arrived home. "How did it go? What did the president say?"

"I can't discuss it with you. Get me something to eat," Piter said. He put the satchel on the table and sat, resting his head in his hands.

Tafflen rushed to the kitchen and put a plate in the microwave. She placed it on the table in front of him. "You okay, baby?"

"Yeah. Some time alone, please."

She scurried to the bedroom and closed the door.

Piter opened the satchel. He spun a mouthful of spaghetti on his fork and began reading Aura's personal medical records. He stopped chewing. "What the hell?"

It all made sense. Aura Zarling's previous physician had given her a diagnosis of amyotrophic lateral sclerosis and an estimation she had about three years to live. He gathered up the file, put it back in the satchel and locked it in his file cabinet. He paced the floor.

Tafflen peeked out of the bedroom door. "Anything I can do?"

"Not now. I need to think."

She pulled the door shut, making little sound.

Piter ran his fingers through his hair. *There is no cure for ALS. She expects me to be a miracle worker.* Three hours of worrying and four glasses of wine brought him no closer to coming up with any kind of solution to his dilemma. He went to bed, tossed and turned for another hour and then got up to take two sleeping pills, washing them down with another glass of wine.

§

He was running through Aura's mansion, hallway after hallway, trying to find his way out. He opened a door, entered the room, left by another door. Dark, winding hallways, never-ending flights of stairs…

"Piter, wake up." Tafflen shook him.

"What?"

"I've been trying to wake you for the last twenty minutes. What's wrong? Are you sick?"

"No." He blinked his eyes, still groggy. His throat was parched.

"Hurry. You'll be late for work."

Piter checked the clock. "Crap!" He jumped out of bed and staggered to the shower. A quick wash and then finished off with a blast of cold water. He threw on a suit, combed his hair, grabbed a cup of coffee and a bagel from Tafflen's hands, and rushed out the door to catch his cab.

At work, he received copies of Tresha's arrest papers. He scanned the pages and found a list of known accomplices. Beside each name was written a single word. By some, the word, "Deceased," and by others, "Incarcerated." Beside his own name was the word, "Rehabilitated." Beside Hadar's name, "Unknown." He sighed with relief.

Name: Tresha Farwell

Age: 57

Last Known Address: Range Road 4, Sesal, Covona

Physical description: Caucasian. Hair: grey. Eyes: green. Weight: 48 kg. Height: 164 cm.

Tresha Farwell's residence in the Selp Forest in western Sesal was forcibly entered. A tunnel was discovered through the pantry that led into the forest. Some officers pursued on foot while a helicopter pursued by air. She discharged a firearm at officers but no officers were injured. She was arrested and transferred to a hospital with head injuries.

With her group, Human Rights for All, Ms. Farwell taught dangerous ideas to the citizens. With no regard for the laws of Covona, she directed her group to

*cause havoc, vandalism and destruction to businesses
and honest citizens. Tresha Farwell and her cohorts at
HRFA are responsible for the explosion at the Deve
ski resort in the Keque Mountains. She is charged with
treason and will be confined to a prison cell and
questioned.*

The rest of the file contained information about HRFA's
underground activities—the sneaking of classified information and people
out of the country and the group's attempts to infiltrate government
agencies. The file also told of the many raids done on homes and listed
the many contraband items taken—Bibles, crosses and prayer books.

On the back page was a photo of Tresha on the day of her arrest,
her face swollen and bruised. He decided he must work hard to control
his emotions when he saw his old friend. AZEN made examples of
traitors. It wouldn't surprise Piter if Tresha was eradicated without trial
with all the evidence that was stacked against her.

If Tresha Farwell was a good citizen she would have deserved a
pain-free Quietus celebration at age sixty-five. He sighed. The Tresha that
Piter used to know was gentle and unassuming, hardly the dangerous
psychopath AZEN made her out to be. He had overheard discussions
between Tresha, Fillip, Yun, and the other members of HRFA. They
hated the changes Aura had brought on the country. He was glad he
usually remained silent during the conversations.

He laid the report on the kitchen table and took a deep breath.
He reminded himself of all the suffering in Covona before Aura. The
homeless—diseased, dirty and neglected, who had slept in cardboard
boxes on the street in all kinds of weather, while the handicapped,
terminally ill, and elderly occupied care centres, using up space and
valuable resources. That was not the case anymore. Covona relied on the
compliance of her citizens, whose worth was determined by what each
could contribute. AZEN was indeed creating a better world.

CHAPTER THIRTY-SIX

Conversation with an Old Friend

"Happy Birthday, Dr. Dram!" Cherrin said. She entered Piter's office at lunchtime carrying a slice of chocolate cake with a single burning candle and placed it on his desk.

He was touched by the gesture. Even Tafflen had forgotten. "Thanks." He blew out the candle and put a forkful in his mouth. His mother had always made him chocolate cake for his birthday. For an instant, he was a child back in his parents' kitchen with his mom smiling down on him. He swallowed the piece of cake and pushed the plate away. "I'm late. Thanks again for the cake."

Piter made his way to Re-Ed as per Aura's orders. He took the arrest report with him. He wondered if this assignment was a test of his loyalty or a punishment for past mistakes. In either case, he'd have to be careful what he said.

A warm wind blew on the first day of winter and quickly melted the snow. He sat in the back seat of the taxi, grasping the leather satchel. He was tired from a poor sleep and it promised to be a long, stress-filled day. The taxi slipped on the slick road and bumped over a pothole. The faint taste of blood reminded him not to chew his lips.

"They never sand the roads anymore and why they don't fix those holes?" the driver asked.

He took a deep breath and exhaled slowly. Until his meeting with Aura Zarling, he didn't even know Tresha was still alive, having heard nothing about her in the news.

"I don't like to whine, but before our current president, the roads were taken care of," the taxi driver said.

Piter was not interested in conversing with this woman and preferred she would just be quiet and let him concentrate. Lamp posts blurred past the window. First Fillip, and now Tresha; the past was coming to meet him again and he was not pleased.

"So, you were attending a Quietus celebration at the QRR Centre?" she asked, interrupting his thoughts again.

"Hmm? No. I work there."

"Oh. What do you do?"

"Eradication and research."

In the rearview mirror, he saw the look of fear in her eyes. "Please, I'm sorry about what I said, really sorry."

He could have her arrested but didn't want to be bothered.

"Please don't misinterpret what I said. I love the president…"

"I won't report you, but be more careful in the future."

"Thank you, Doctor."

He looked out the side window as they passed through the poorest section of Ackim, home to about five thousand underprivileged people. Smoke stains blackened the bricks of a burnt-out, three-storey building with boarded-up windows. An abandoned gas station and row upon row of tin-roofed shanty houses dotted the drab, flat terrain. Each hovel had a thin coil of greasy smoke emanating from an iron-pipe chimney. Laundry flapped from lines strung between houses.

He caught a glimpse, now and then, of children playing. The soft snow had been trampled between the shanty houses, creating muddy paths. Children's skinny limbs appeared from drab, tattered clothing; their feet and legs coated in muck. A row of women walked along the side of the road; each carried a large bundle of sticks on her head, fuel for their fires.

Melted snow created puddles of oily goo on the road that coated vehicles. Mud sprayed from the tires of a slow-moving truck and hit the front windshield of the taxi, obscuring the view. The driver turned on the wipers and then leaned back with one hand on the steering wheel. She rubbed the back of her neck with the other hand and whistled a tune which sounded vaguely like the national anthem. Her eyes flicked frequently to the rearview mirror.

They were now caught in the middle of a traffic jam. He had hoped to arrive at the Re-education Centre before one in the afternoon, but at this rate, he would be late. "I'll pay you double if you can get me there in ten minutes."

The driver swerved into the shoulder lane and hit the gas pedal.

Piter exited the taxi at Re-Ed on time and gained admittance through the gate of the barbed wire fence after going through the usual identification check, metal detector and a full body scan.

"Good afternoon, Dr. Dram," said a guard. "Ms. Farwell is in Block D."

Piter nodded, not recognizing the guard. There was a time he dreaded going to work here, to witness the stream of misery and the fearful, sometimes scornful gazes of the students, some of whom still held out hope they would find mercy. Piter now understood he needed the experience of working at Re-Ed to become the man he was today.

He proceeded down the main hallway. Through a barred window, he observed twenty or so students in the outdoor exercise yard pacing in a circle, heads down, one behind the other. He then continued down another long hallway, which contained the male students' barred cells. Two sets of bunk beds occupied each room with only a body's width between the beds. The female sleeping quarters were identical, but Tresha wasn't held there. He proceeded to Block D, the highest security area, saved for the worst criminals.

A guard unlocked the door and Piter stepped into a dank hallway containing four metal doors. He was allowed into a small, cold, windowless room. A fluorescent light flickered on the ceiling. Tresha sat on her cot, small and shrunken. Though she had been locked up for about seven months, she seemed resigned and almost peaceful. Her hair, now completely grey, hung around her shoulders, limp and tangled.

"Hello, Tresha."

She looked up. Her eyes grew wide. "Piter?"

Piter told himself on the way over to remain calm and focused, but the sight of his old friend, so weak and vulnerable, unsettled him. *The last time I saw her, she hugged me.* He perched on the edge of the metal chair that was bolted to the floor at the side of the room, leaned back and rubbed his chin.

He looked at the intercom box hanging in the corner of the room, used to both broadcast and listen. Piter cleared his throat and recited the words he had practiced in his head on the way over. "I've been asked to come and talk to you and I won't have you wasting my time. Who have you been working with?" He sat up straight and tall and put his hands on his knees.

Tresha kept her hands folded on her lap. She hung her head.

He continued, "If you cooperate, I'm able to request death by lethal injection for you."

"Why would I want that?"

"The answer is obvious. It's the honourable and painless route."

"Honourable? The last time I saw you, you were asking for my help." She pointed to her chest with her forefinger. The red imprint of handcuffs showed on her wrists.

He hesitated, remembering his pleas to Tresha to find medicine for Yun. It seemed like a lifetime ago. "You have no choice but to tell us everything."

"I loved you like a son," she said the words with tenderness.

He was not prepared to hear words of endearment, and for a moment, they distracted him from his purpose. "I told you, don't waste my…"

"Why does AZEN fear us?" she asked.

Piter was taken aback by her boldness and was speechless, amazed Tresha had the audacity to suggest such a thing. "Fear you? A middle-aged woman and her little band of zealots? Covona repelled the world's superpower, Solime. We are self-sustaining, strong." He stood and put his fists on his hips. "We built The Wall of Aura."

She raised her eyebrows, almost smirked. "The cult of personality."

"What?"

"You worship Aura with unquestioning faith, divinizing her. I can't believe you fell for the propaganda."

"Traitor!"

"Me? You betrayed your friends."

He frowned at her. "If you want me to feel guilty, I don't." He stamped his foot but then felt foolish for doing so. He paused to consider passages from Aura Zarling's book, *Transformation and Affluence*, for the right words to say. Any argument between citizens could be settled with an appropriate quotation from the book. The saying was, "Why look elsewhere when we have *Transformation and Affluence*?"

The perfect words came to mind. "The wheat has been separated from the chaff."

Tresha gave him a thin smile. "Which one are you?"

He took a deep breath. If he didn't get some information from her soon, he would be in trouble. "Did the interrogators speak to you?"

She hung her head. "Many times."

He was surprised so many months had passed and they still hadn't broken Tresha. Even the toughest people caved after a few sessions, weeks at most.

"At first it was rough, electric shocks, dousing, but now, for the most part, they let me be. They gave me something to drink one time and afterwards, the walls were singing. People came to talk to me. They were huge, giants. I could see the words come out of their mouths, like streams of colour."

Piter didn't believe in the use of hallucinogens. They produced unreliable results. "Tell me about HRFA. Who was involved? You're dead either way. What do you have to gain by not talking?"

"I vowed to stay true, until this country comes to realize how far we've fallen."

"Fallen? No. We are an advanced civilization."

Their conversation was interrupted by an announcement over the intercom. "All students and staff will now stand to hear the words of our beloved president." It was the top of the hour.

Piter snapped to attention—legs together, chest thrust forward, arms at his sides. Tresha remained seated.

"People of Covona," Aura's voice began. "All leaders of houses of worship, other than pastors of The Light of Aura Church, are enemies of the state. Kill the shepherd and the sheep will scatter. We will finally purge the country of the sickness they continue to spread. AZEN will rid the country of all those troublesome maniacs and their dangerous, outdated ideas. Religion is the main cause of war. Would you give a madman a laser gun? Would you give a pyromaniac a can of gasoline and matches? Their books are their weapons and must be destroyed."

"Oh, Aura." Tresha shook her head.

"We need to eliminate the scourge that continues to plague our country. Moral laws are made to enslave you. Pay no attention to excessive sentimentalizing. These people must be prevented from spreading their terrible lies. Thank you and have a good day."

Piter's shoulders drooped. Hadar was in even more danger. He stood and knocked on the door to be released.

"You can't stay a little longer and visit?"

"I have someplace to be." He left the room.

CHAPTER THIRTY-SEVEN

Loneliness

Tresha was alone after another despicable announcement from Aura. The visit from Piter was such a surprise. How wonderful to have company, but Piter said he had to be somewhere. She was disturbed by his appearance. Gone was the friendly, eager face she had known when they were friends. The man's frosty expression chilled her. She wondered if there was a shred of conscience left beneath his tough exterior.

Tresha suspected it was winter because of the drop in the temperature of her cell. Her frail body shivered. She wrapped a thin blanket around herself and curled into a ball in the corner of the bed.

How she missed the sounds of nature and her cabin in the woods! Birds tweeting, sheep bleating, wind blowing through the trees, Panzer barking. She was overcome with sadness and started to weep. The sound of her sobs echoed off the walls. For a moment, it sounded as if someone beside her was crying and she glanced to the side. *No, I'm alone, so alone.*

The tears and mucus dripped down her face. There was no toilet paper. She had used the last of it and didn't know when she would get a new roll. She wiped her eyes and nose on her sleeve. Today she heard a faint buzz. Where was it coming from? She walked the length of her cell and back, listened, and then looked up at the fluorescent ceiling light. Tresha laughed out loud, feeling a sense of triumph. The room was not silent after all. Closing her eyes, she amused herself with pleasant memories.

She slept, dreaming of walking through an open field with the sun shining down on her. Upon opening her eyes, she saw she was in the same dull, cold cell. She paced like an animal in a zoo. Three steps. Turn around. Three steps. Turn around. When she was a child, she watched lions and bears trace the same patterns in their cages, back and forth, back and forth. Now she knew why. A body needs to move. It screams for release.

§

Piter opened the door again and interrupted her pacing. "Good morning," he said in a monotone.

Tresha was confused. "Morning? Weren't you just here?"

Piter ignored her question, sat down on the chair and hung his head. His hair was neatly combed and his face shaven. He wore a pressed, expensive-looking suit and polished shoes. A small potbelly hung over the top of his pants.

On his last visits to her cell, it was his steady gaze that disturbed her the most—hard and emotionless, like a shark. Today, he sat rubbing his chin as he always did when something concerned him.

"Something on your mind?" she asked.

He stood again and leaned against the wall, his hands behind his back, and didn't make eye contact. "No. Nothing." He stared into space.

Tresha forced herself to stop thinking about her own problems. "You've had a difficult time of it, losing Yun and your baby, I mean."

His jaw shook. He cleared his throat. He whispered, "I wish I could have saved them. If I had joined AZEN sooner..."

"We were all sad when Yun died. And then you left us. We were all heartbroken, especially Hadar."

Piter stepped away from the wall. He whispered, "How do you know? You've seen him?"

She was silent for a moment. "Yes."

With his eyes, he pointed to a thin wire running the length of the ceiling.

Tresha decided she didn't care if they were being recorded. "He came to us. We hid him in our basement. They came to look for him and he was right there." She smiled at the memory and loved rubbing AZEN's failure in their faces. "Hadar left but didn't say where he was going." She didn't tell him she had already helped Hadar escape Covona. He had come to her cabin in the woods on a cold winter day and she sent him on his way.

"Tell me where Hadar is. He will be given mercy if you hand him over willingly." Piter shook his head and mouthed the words, "Don't tell."

"Hadar wouldn't endanger our safety by telling us where he was going."

Piter pounded his fist into the palm of his other hand. "He must be brought to justice."

"Aura Zarling is not interested in justice."

Piter gaped at her. He shook his head as a warning. "She loves us like her little children."

"Mothers are not supposed to murder their own children."

He looked at Tresha and blinked his eyes. "What exactly did HRFA hope to achieve?"

She looked at the floor, at Piter's feet, and in a quiet voice said, "The freedom to live, and die, with dignity, like before."

Piter stood over her. "Dignity? Old people wasted away for years before they died of natural causes. I remember how it was. My grandfather suffered needlessly. It's a time better forgotten."

"Quietus is a great evil. Lord have mercy." Tresha feel a sudden chill. She pulled the blanket off the bed and wrapped it around her shoulders.

"It's forbidden to talk about God outside the walls of Light of Aura Church."

She laughed. "What are they going to do? Sentence me to death?" Tresha realized she had nothing to fear, not even death. A feeling of relief flooded her body. She looked hard at Piter and wondered again what happened to him to turn him into an unfeeling drone, one of Aura's possessions. She felt sorry for him.

Piter said, "Chapter two, verse one of *Transformation and Affluence*, 'Eliminate suffering for a happy life.' Don't you see? Aura saved us."

She arched her lower back, working at the sore muscles with her thumbs. "Quietus, the default way to die. You eliminate suffering by eliminating the sufferer. You should be ashamed."

Piter's eyes became distant and hard. "This is just another ploy you zealots use, to make us feel guilty. I work for the common good."

"Your parents wouldn't think so."

Piter growled his response. "You know nothing of my parents. I was good to them. I gave them comfort until their Quietus Day."

Tresha knew she touched a sore spot. "They're dead? I'm sorry to hear that."

"Their time had come."

"I haven't known comfort in a long time."

"Chapter five, verse three, 'You who are dispossessed, don't be concerned about the clothes you wear. Consider the birds and the flowers,'" Piter said.

She laughed at him.

His jaw dropped. "You laugh at Aura's wise words?"

Tresha couldn't believe her ears. "Those words are twisted from the *Bible*. I'm surprised you don't remember. Didn't your parents send you to Sunday school? Aura outlawed our faith, replaced it with a Church named after herself. Turned herself into a deity."

Piter's eyes grew wide. "You don't criticize the president." He trembled.

"It's the truth."

Piter got up, knocked on the door and was released.

Tresha watched him go, thinking his prison was worse by far than hers.

She remembered a conversation she had with her husband when they learned Piter was sent to Re-Ed:

"No one goes into the Re-Ed and emerges unchanged," Fillip had said. "They know how to break the human spirit."

"Piter won't betray us. He's a good man," Tresha had said.

"We'll have to be more careful. Send warnings to everyone. Who knows what he will reveal? Things are going to get even harder, more dangerous for us in the coming months."

§

Tresha reclined and covered her eyes with her arm to block the harsh light and hoped she could sleep a little.

"Ms. Farwell, time to wake up," said a shrill female voice.

Tresha was pulled by her arms out of bed and dragged to the floor. A bucket of cold water was poured over her head. She screamed at the shock of cold, choked, and looked up just as another bucket was dumped on her head. The water dripped off her hair, soaked her clothing, and leaked onto the floor where it flowed into the drain near the toilet. Tresha shivered. She curled her body, her arms wrapped around her legs, and lifted the balls of her bare feet off the cold concrete floor, balancing on her heels.

"Speak, traitor. Who are your comrades? Where are they?"

She set her lips together and resisted the urge to smile. Tresha couldn't have been happier to hear the guard speak those words. It meant not everyone had been caught.

Two women took turns with the buckets while a third, a thin woman in a white lab coat stood watching by the door. Tresha's teeth chattered and she lost control of her bladder.

"Are you getting cold? Would you like us to stop?"

She nodded her head, unable to stop shivering.

"Tell us where your comrades are hiding."

She said nothing and more water was poured on her head. Gasping and barely able to catch her breath, she prayed for strength to resist her tormentors. She forced herself to remain silent. Tresha moaned and held her hands to her chest as a sharp pain gripped her.

The women stared down at her.

"Could be a heart attack. Get her to the infirmary," the doctor said.

Tresha then stared at the floor as she was dragged down a long corridor. Her shoulders felt like they were being wrenched out of her sockets. Their hard hands bit into her arms. She wanted to use her frozen feet to walk but couldn't get them to obey her. They took her into a doctor's office. Someone stripped off her clothes and lifted her onto an exam table. She had lost feeling in her hands and could barely grasp the blanket folded at the foot of the bed. Shivering uncontrollably, she covered herself. Tresha couldn't keep her teeth from chattering. Someone came in, drew blood and left.

[245]

About a half hour later, a tired-looking, thin doctor entered the room. "I'm Doctor Pim Marris," she said. "Are you experiencing chest pain?" Her voice was flat.

"Not now."

"Tightness in your chest? Nauseated? Short of breath?"

"Yes, some."

"Your skin is pale, probably anemia."

Dr. Marris held the stethoscope against Tresha's chest. Her other hand was on Tresha's back.

"I'll send you for an electrocardiogram, but I suspect you just had a panic attack, Ms. Farwell. You don't appear to be in the best of health. I'll recommend less strenuous questioning, so as not to overly stress your heart."

Tresha felt the doctor's warm hand on her back, revelling in the touch of another human being, even if that human cared nothing for her.

"I'll give you a shot of vitamin B to perk you up." Dr. Marris injected the needle, turned and left the room. The guards returned and walked Tresha back to her cell. On the way, she saw other cells with bars instead of an iron door like hers. Each held two sets of bunkbeds with neatly made beds. They were all empty of occupants. She wished she had someone to share her cell.

She stepped into her cell and the door slammed behind her. Still shivering, she stepped across the wet floor and wrapped herself in a blanket. A tray was shoved through the door slot, a bowl of cold rice. Tresha picked up the bowl, sat back down on her cot and ate with her fingers.

CHAPTER THIRTY-EIGHT

It's My Life

A memory, as vivid and frightening as the day it had happened, resurfaced in Piter's dreams. He was body surfing with Hadar in the Cisco Ocean. A hard wave hit Piter, rolling him over and over in the surf. He was out of control, his body a mere plaything for the ocean, tossing him forward and pulling him back, scraping his skin on the rocky bottom until his lungs burned for air. Hadar's strong arms grasped him around the chest, pulling him to the surface. Piter woke up, sweating and gasping for air. He flopped back onto the pillow, unable to get back to sleep.

§

Piter climbed the stairs of the QRR Centre. He inhaled deeply through his nose and blew out through his mouth. Yesterday, his hope was to get something off his chest—his guilt at not being able to save Yun. Instead, Tresha filled his head with all sorts of nonsense.

His jittery thoughts went back and forth. *I should be grateful, but Tresha and Fillip broke the law by hiding Hadar in their house, but they kept my brother safe, but the law does not discriminate...* His mind swirled.

Cherrin greeted him as usual. "Good morning, Dr. Dram." Her face was lit up with a smile.

"What's so good about it?" He glared at his assistant.

Cherrin misinterpreted his grumpy mood as a joke and laughed. "Oh, Dr. Dram. You crack me up. Come on, it's spring. The birds are singing—"

Piter motioned with his head. "She mine?"

A teenage girl sat by herself in the waiting room, slumped in a soft chair, her hands clasped between her knees. Her dark hair hung loosely, partially concealing her face. She raised her head when Cherrin laughed. Her wide green eyes shone, contrasting with her brown skin. There was no joy in her eyes.

Cherrin's face became serious. She whispered, "Yes. Sixteen years old. Her name is Abree. Suffers from depression."

"She said she wants Quietus?"

"Yes. I asked if anyone would be accompanying her today. She said no. She came without telling her parents."

"Where is everyone?"

"Down in research. It's a slow day."

Piter had a heavy feeling in his chest. He didn't like eradicating healthy people, but his duty was to obey the law and the law said mature youth could request Quietus without parental consent. Besides, it was bad for the bottom line to turn anyone away. Eradications were what paid the bills, what made them profitable. Doctors were given a bonus for every eradication. The research department drained the coffers. "Send her in. Get her ready." He went to his office, put on his lab coat, reviewed her chart and prepared the lethal dose.

§

When he entered the Quietus room, the girl was sitting on the edge of the bed, her thin, bare legs swung back and forth. She was dressed in a hospital gown. "Why do I have to wear this?" She pulled up the gown, indicating the diaper.

"Saves on cleanup time after."

She whispered, "I'm going to poop myself?"

"Are you sure you want to go through with this?"

She shrugged. "Yeah. Whatever. I'm tired of being sad all the time."

"What's troubling you?" He forgot himself for a moment; not the sort of question a Quietus doctor should ask.

Cherrin stood beside the refrigerator. She raised her eyebrows at Piter. "Something to drink, Abree?"

"Just water."

He tied a rubber tourniquet around the girl's upper arm. "You've been cutting yourself." He indicated the crisscrossed lines of scars on her inner arms. Her nails were bitten to the quick.

"Yeah."

Cherrin handed the girl a glass of water. "Why didn't you tell your parents you were coming here today?"

"I know the law. It's my life. I can choose to end it!" The girl's face turned red and her lips trembled. Tears formed in the corners of her eyes. She wiped them away with the palms of her hands.

Cherrin brushed the girl's hair away from her face and looked her in the eye. "It's not too late to change your mind."

"Medications can control your moods," Piter said. "Depression can be a transitory condition for many teens." Again, he caught himself before he said more. "Lie on your back please."

"I bet the medicine costs a lot." The girl took a sip of water and reclined. "My parents have no money." She shivered. Cherrin placed a blanket over her body, leaving the arms free.

He prepared the intravenous in both arms and began the saline drip. Her innocent face looked up at him.

"Am I going to die now?"

"This is just water with a bit of salt, to open your veins."

"Does it hurt to die?" she asked. Her large eyes were fixed on the intravenous bags.

To ease her fears, he indicated the other bag hanging over her head, filled with the barbiturate. "This will make you sleepy, so you don't feel the pain."

"What pain?"

"Of the heart attack. This syringe"—he held it up to show her—"is a muscle relaxant to stop your heart. Once it takes effect, you'll be unable to move. This syringe"—he pointed—"is potassium chloride. It's lethal."

The girl's face turned pale. "I'm scared."

Piter spoke softly, "That's a natural reaction. There's nothing to be afraid of." He rested his hand on her forearm.

From behind the door came the sounds of a woman screaming, "Where's my daughter?"

"Mommy?" the girl whispered. She raised herself up on her elbows.

[249]

"Should we let her in?" Piter asked.

"No," said the girl.

"You don't have to go to Quietus today. You can change your mind."

Cherrin added, "The doctor is right. You don't have to…"

"Abree? Are you in there?"

The girl's eyes were wide. "Just do it," the girl said.

"Abree? Baby? Please. It's Mom."

"Should I call security?" Cherrin asked.

"No. Let her be." He started the first drip and, moments later, the girl's eyes fluttered closed. "She's asleep. She looks so peaceful, doesn't she?"

Cherrin turned to Piter. Her eyes were sad. She took a deep breath. "Dr. Dram. Maybe we should let her wake up and talk to her mom."

"Who are we to say whether she should live or die? She was clear. The law is clear."

Cherrin whispered, "Maybe the law is wrong."

"If the law is wrong, then everything we do here…"

The woman continued to scream from behind the door. "I know she's in there. Let me talk to my little girl." She pounded on the door.

"Dr. Dram. Let her mom talk to her." Cherrin spoke softly. Tears flowed freely now. "What if she was your child?"

"The girl has the right to do what she wants with her own body."

"I just want to take my baby home," the woman shouted.

"She's made her decision." Piter picked up the needle containing the muscle relaxant. His hand shook. He looked at his trembling hand, this appendage he couldn't control, as if it belonged to someone else. The woman's pleading tore at his heart. He put the needle down. "Okay, let the mother in. Abree won't know the difference."

Cherrin ran to the door and opened it. She led the distraught woman to the girl's bedside. The woman laid her head on the girl's chest and hugged her. "Doctor, don't kill my baby, please."

Piter remembered the day he laid his head on his wife's chest just after she died.

Cherrin pulled Piter by the sleeve until they were out of earshot. She sniffed and blew her nose into a tissue. "I've made a decision. I can't be a part of it, all the death and body parts. Every day I go home feeling like trash. I try to justify it, but I can't." She looked at the woman standing beside her daughter, stroking the girl's cheek and speaking gently to her sleeping form. "I'll give you my resignation at the end of the day."

"Don't be hasty. I'll get someone to cover our afternoon appointments. You and I just need a break. Let me talk to the mother." He tore off his rubber gloves and dropped them in the trash. *I've euthanized hundreds. Why is this girl different?*

He put his hand on the woman's shoulder. "We'll let your daughter wake up. If you want me to treat her, I will. I'll start by leaving a prescription for an antidepressant at the front desk."

"We can't afford..."

"I'll pay for it. My assistant will take your name and refer your daughter to counselling."

"Oh, Dr. Dram, thank you."

He removed the IV needles from the girl's arms. He wondered, as he left the room, if he couldn't do it anymore, either. He could simply pass all his Quietus cases to Gorge, who would, no doubt, be happy with the extra praise he'd get from management. Win, win. He stopped Gorge in the hall and asked him if he wanted to take over his afternoon appointments, told him he needed the time to do his research. Gorge readily agreed.

Piter looked forward to his glass of wine tonight, or maybe three or four.

§

After work, Piter returned to President Zarling's mansion, a task he had come to dislike. She sat at her desk while he stood in front, hands behind his back.

"How is my old friend, Tresha?" Aura asked. She smiled—teeth bared, eyes narrowed.

He drew back, cautious. "She's tired but seems to be enduring Re-Ed better than most women her age."

"That's because I won't let anything bad happen to her—well, nothing really bad." She leaned forward, elbows on her desk, hands folded. "I have another reason for calling you here."

"Oh?"

Her smile disappeared. "Why are you no closer to finding a cure? You know how important this is to me."

Piter's throat went dry. "It's difficult. We need more test subjects, people afflicted with ALS."

"I'll have my people search them out. I'll send you as many as I can. Make some room at the QRR Centre. This takes priority." She turned to her guards and waved her fingers, dismissing them. They turned and marched out the door. "Sit down, Piter."

Piter took the chair in front of her desk. She came around her desk and stood in front of him so her breasts were at his eye level. He looked up at her face.

She put her hands on his shoulders. "We'd be great together, you and I." Aura looked deeply into his eyes.

"Great together?"

"I want your professional opinion on something," she said.

"Of course."

Aura began to unbutton her blouse. Her fingers were clumsy and it took a long time. She tossed the blouse aside and then removed her brassiere. "What do you think of these?"

He was speechless.

"Oh, come on, Piter. Don't sit there opening and closing your mouth like a fish. You're a doctor. I had them done six months ago. Give me your opinion."

"Well, they're full, round and symmetrical. No visible scarring. Your surgeon did an excellent job."

"I'm so happy to hear that. Touch them. Tell me if they feel real to you."

His jaw dropped. "No, I don't think..."

"Oh, come on, touch them."

He raised the flat of his hand and pressed her left breast and hoped she wouldn't notice how sweaty his hands had become. "Yes, very real, just the right amount of firmness."

She laughed so hard she almost lost her balance. Aura leaned against her desk holding her stomach and laughed until tears streamed down her face. She stopped abruptly and put her clothes back on.

He cleared his throat and raised his eyes to the ceiling.

She turned to him. "What I revealed to you must be kept in strictest confidence."

He was confused for a moment, leaning forward. "Oh, you mean the ALS? Yes, of course."

"If you tell anyone, I'll have you killed."

He had no doubt of that. "You have my word."

"I was told I have only about three years to live. That's why it is so important the research be sped up. I want you to dedicate more time to the project. You will have your test subjects, whatever you need. Find the answer before my symptoms become obvious."

"I'll try, Aura."

Aura turned her attention to the television sets. He stood and made his way to the door.

She indicated with a sweep of her hand the screens on the wall, the news stories from around the world. "If only the world knew what I am capable of."

He stopped, mid-step and bowed his head, not knowing what to say.

"You're still hard at work developing vaccines? How's your research coming?"

"Not my research. I'm not privy to that side of—"

She touched her fingers to her forehead. "Oh, right, that's Doctor...?"

"Pim Marris."

"Yes, Marris. One day we will soon show the world our superiority." She was quiet for a moment, engrossed in a news story, and then turned to him, as if surprised he was still standing there. "We'll talk again tomorrow. You may leave."

[253]

Piter backed out of the room, resisting the urge to run.

CHAPTER THIRTY-NINE
Covona Research Centre

Piter's eyes felt heavy after a long, stressful day. Emptiness, like an aching hunger, clawed at his spirit. He struggled to put his finger on what troubled him. Perhaps it was that moment of weakness when he didn't euthanize the girl and paid for her medicine. At the time, he was comfortable with his decision to not involve himself with Quietus anymore, but now he second-guessed himself. His paycheque would be reduced. *No, financial benefits be damned.* His superiors may question his motives. *I'll just explain my research is more important.*

He sat in the back seat of a taxi. His eyes were drawn towards a little clothing shop. The door was open, likely to allow cool night air to enter the shop. Inside, seamstresses bent over their sewing machines, piecing together clothing. Next door was a vegetable market. Nothing foreign sold there, only what could be grown in Covona. Through the taxi's open window Piter smelled the damp, moldy aroma of potatoes and carrots kept too long in storage.

A young boy approached the car window, his filthy hands full of limp carrots. "Sir, lovely carrots for your soup. Real cheap." The boy's eyes were red and encrusted. Mucus ran from his nose. Piter averted his face, afraid to catch whatever virus the child was carrying, and rolled up the window.

Piter saw the way the common people lived, their poverty and daily struggles. He was one of them once but had managed to pull himself out of the ashes to a new, invigorating life, and figured if they just applied themselves they could do the same.

Perhaps his discontentment came from not knowing what happened to Hadar. He had everything he wanted, except his brother. They were different in so many ways, but maybe he could give Hadar a copy of *Transformation and Affluence,* then Hadar would understand. He imagined them together enjoying glasses of fine wine. Maybe he could even find a good woman for Hadar, if he would ever give up the ridiculous notion of celibacy.

Summer was coming. He was sure things would start to look up.

§

The next morning, as Piter was brushing his teeth, he received an urgent message to go to the QRR Centre. He arrived at work an hour early, at 08:00, and witnessed a chaotic scene. AZEN police were everywhere. Two buses, a line of police cars and about ten ambulances were parked in front of the building. One person after another was wheeled up the ramp or walked up the stairs to file in the front door. He sidestepped his way through the crowd that filled the lobby. The noise was deafening. Many of the people were crying and looking terrified.

Cherrin also looked as though she might cry. She ran towards him. She had to shout over the clamour. "I don't know what to do. All these people. They just keep coming."

Doctors Gorge, Jeniver, Pim and their assistants were setting up chairs for the people to sit. Many of the people looked disabled.

"Dr. Piter Dram?" A policeman walked towards him. "Sign this."

He handed Piter some sheets of paper, lists of names; nine pages in all.

"What is this?" Piter asked.

Another policeman came forward, pushing a dolly piled with boxes of file folders and left them at Cherrin's desk.

"A receipt for shipment."

"Shipment?"

"The president said to deliver these people here," the policeman said.

"How many?"

"Eighty-four. These are just from Ackim and local area. More busloads will arrive throughout the day from other parts of the country."

Piter's mouth hung open. "What am I supposed to do with all these people?"

The policeman shrugged. "Our job was to round them up and deliver them. We'll stick around to keep the peace until you can figure it out."

He looked around and suspected every one of these people was afflicted with ALS and were probably wrenched from their beds in the middle of the night. They had only twenty-four cells in the basement. He had no idea how he was going to deal with the situation.

§

The focus of the Ackim QRR Centre was changed from eradication of people to the eradication of ALS and the Solime Flu. Piter's colleagues were not informed of Aura's condition and the reason for the urgency involved in finding a cure for ALS. It would be up to Piter to motivate the team. He was to oversee the entire project.

"I am working under Piter, now?" Gorge asked. His face fell.

Piter chuckled. He looked forward to lording over the little toad. He wanted to put Gorge in his place. Best of all, Piter would be receiving a raise in pay, making him the highest paid doctor in Covona. He thought of all the things he could buy with the money.

Jeniver was beaming. "What a great opportunity. I always liked the research side of this job better."

The assistants were kept busy processing the many patients. Piter instructed Jeniver and Gorge to hire more staff. Dr. Pim Marris wouldn't be involved in ALS research. She was interested in another project— finding a cure for the highly dangerous and contagious Solime Flu.

§

The government appropriated a nearby elementary school to house and treat the new test subjects. Workmen were in and out of the school all day, removing children's desks and bringing in beds and medical equipment. Piter strutted about the new facility, ordering the workmen around, watching them jump at his every command. He was hopeful. With the large number of test subjects, maybe he really would find a cure for ALS. He would go down in history.

After spending the morning setting up the new facility, he sat in the back of the taxi on his way to another meeting with Aura.

The taxi pulled up in front of Aura's mansion. Piter stepped out and strutted up the stairs, already feeling at home.

Aura Zarling was seated behind her desk. All the television screens were black and silent. "Sit down, Piter," she said and indicated an armless wooden chair, set about two metres in front of her desk. Something in her tone sent alarm bells to his brain. Her long hair was pinned into a bun at the back of her head. The lines on her forehead and between her nose and mouth were pink and slightly swollen—the result of Botox, he assumed. The effect was to make her face expressionless and frightening.

"I'm disappointed in you, Piter," she said and glared at him from behind her desk.

He sat stiffly with his hands on his knees and felt a sudden urge to empty his bladder.

"We're no closer to finding any of HRFA's remaining followers."

"I'm sorry, Aura. What do you want me to do?"

"Are you an idiot?" she yelled.

Her security guards came forward, stood on either side of Piter's chair and glared down at him. His throat was so dry he could barely swallow.

"The two of you chitchat about morality while you should be grilling her on where her cohorts are. Very interesting tidbit about your brother, by the way. I sent in my interrogators to talk to Tresha."

He trembled, not daring to ask what happened to Tresha or what would happen to him.

"Tresha is feeble. Seems she had a panic attack. Good thing Dr. Marris was there."

He nodded, not daring to raise his eyes.

"Shall I order my interrogators to speak to you? They would teach you to not disobey my orders."

He dropped from the chair and prostrated himself on the floor. "Have mercy, President. I'm so stupid."

"Get up!" she yelled.

The guards' firm hands pulled him to his feet.

"Go back and speak to Tresha. Get some useful information, or you will pay."

The guards hauled him out the door and out of the building.

He made a quick phone call to Cherrin, to inform her he would not be back to the office today. Still shaken by the earlier incident, he struggled to control his voice. "I'm going to the Re-education Centre to speak to a woman being held there."

"Is it Tresha Farwell?" Cherrin asked.

"How did you know?" He was often surprised at Cherrin's intuition, at her ability to grasp a situation, and wondered again if her ditzy behaviour at work was just a facade.

There was a slight hesitation. "She's been all over the news and you used to know her."

"Yes, of course." He hung up the phone, too troubled now to think about Cherrin. He raised his hand at a taxi, climbed in and shrunk into the seat, feeling emasculated.

Nothing matters. Everyone dies, is replaced. Generation after generation of people born, live out their miserable lives, die, only to be forgotten. Meanwhile, the universe looks on indifferently. No better than the ants crawling on the ground. His hands curled into fists until his fingernails dug into his palms. *And Aura is the queen ant.*

§

Tresha appeared wan and tired. She wouldn't rise from her bed.

"The interrogators were enthusiastic last night?" Piter asked.

She grunted and winced as she rolled over on her side. "That's what you call enthusiasm?"

"Lucky for you I'll continue to question you instead of the interrogators. I won't use violence. They won't give up until you tell them what they want to know."

She looked up at him from her reclined position. "Do you ever regret joining AZEN?"

"I am asking the questions, not you." He hoped she won't notice how upset he felt. "Let me put things in order. I took the logical course and accepted AZEN as the new reality, the answer to our country's problems." He stood with a straight back, rocking a bit on his toes.

"They sucked you in."

"I made my decision." He tried to concentrate on the task at hand, but his mind kept drifting back to his brother. Piter feared for him. Hadar was too good and kind.

§

When they were children, the soft-hearted government thought drug addicts could be saved. Valuable resources were used to try to rehabilitate them. He and Hadar used to pass by the drug treatment centre on their way to school each morning. Addicts gathered outside the door for their daily doses of methadone. Their empty, haunted eyes watched the two boys. Piter kept his hands in his pockets, clutching his bus money and giving the addicts a wide berth.

Hadar had stopped, looking at a man with chapped lips. "Are you thirsty?"

The man nodded.

Hadar had reached into his lunch bag and gave the man his apple juice.

§

Tresha's voice snapped him back to reality. "You know what they did to me last night? They half drowned me with icy cold water. How is that an answer to anyone's problems?"

"It is acceptable to inflict pain on an individual if it is for the good of the country. It says so in *Transformation and Affluence*."

She sighed, as if it took every bit of strength to have a conversation.

"Do you ever think about Fillip?" he asked.

"He's constantly on my mind. I haven't seen him in so long. I feel better knowing he's somewhere in this building, but I wish I could see him."

"He's not here. Been transferred to the QRR Centre."

She sat up straight. "Will they kill him?"

"He's alive, for now. That could change. Have fun imagining the possibilities."

Tresha's already pale face drained of colour. "What is that supposed to mean? You were his friend."

"I'm not responsible for the choices he made."

"Oh, my God." She lay down and covered her eyes with the back of her hand. "Fillip predicted this, but people only hear what Aura wants them to hear. I am partly to blame, the articles I wrote."

"You did your job. You used to be a law-abiding citizen, but you became too involved with that group and their poisonous lies."

"What happened to you?"

He spoke robotically. "The worthless members of society need to be purged."

"That doesn't answer my question."

"I would rather live in a strong, rich nation. You and Fillip could have been living in freedom, like me, if you were law abiding."

"This is a dictatorship. Where is the freedom?"

He hated how Tresha had the ability to get under his skin. He shouted, "People can choose to live among us in peace, or apart from us, as the dispossessed."

"Just think, not long ago this country legalized euthanasia and now you kill people for a living."

"I provide a necessary service." He dug his nails into the palms of his hands, urging himself to keep his emotions under control. "Tresha, I'm here to question you about—"

"We are at the bottom of that slippery slope, the one they said didn't exist."

"You're ridiculous. Quietus lessens suffering—"

"It's not even voluntary anymore."

"Don't lecture me!" He clenched his teeth together. "Society needs change."

Her eyes flashed with anger. "People suffer now more than ever before. The guidelines meant nothing."

"Enough! Know this, Tresha. Fillip is under my care. Tell us what we want to know or he will suffer." He was satisfied by the look of shock on her face. "I need to get back to work. I have important research."

CHAPTER FORTY

Good Interrogations

The QRR Centre, including the former school across the road, was now home to one hundred and thirty-seven patients afflicted with ALS. A new batch of lab technicians were hired along with other required hospital staff—nurses, nurse's aides and cleaning staff. Together with the other doctors, Piter spent days reading the files of the new test subjects. All subjects received thorough examinations, including family histories. The doctors categorized them into levels of severity and conditions. Piter trained the doctors, nurses and lab techs in the development and implementation of the drug he was developing to combat this progressive, fatal disease. They gathered in the hall of the centre to listen to him speak.

"This disease attacks the nervous system, destroying motor neurons," he reminded them. "The first symptoms are subtle and can easily be overlooked; clumsiness, slurring of speech. The life expectancy is three to four years after the appearance of these symptoms. Fewer than ten percent live longer than ten years. There is no cure.

"A genetic component exists in five to ten percent of patients. The gene C9orf72 is linked to ALS and is known to be present in about forty percent of familial cases of ALS. In other researchers' experiments, mice bred to lack this gene did not develop ALS, but rather immune system dysfunction. This confirms the strong relationship between ALS and the immune system.

"The drug I had developed to reduce levels of the mutated C9orf72 was shown to be ineffective. However, most cases of ALS occur spontaneously, probably a combination of genetic and environmental factors. Our research will concentrate on identifying those factors and how they influence the development of the disease.

"We have a unique opportunity here to develop a treatment and ultimately a cure for this mysterious disease. President Aura Zarling assured us this project will be given top priority. Your jobs have been assigned. I will oversee the project. I expect the highest quality work from all of you."

The seminar ended with the scraping of chairs and murmuring conversation. Everyone departed the room except for Cherrin, who sat in the front row. Piter stood at the podium and shuffled his papers together into a file folder. Cherrin came and took the folder from his hand.

"I'll file that for you," she said.

He turned and walked away from her.

She scurried after him. "Dr. Dram. I was wondering, since I'm your assistant, and I know your research better than anyone, and the way you like things done…"

"What do you want, Cherrin?" He turned towards her, feeling impatient.

"Could I have a key to the patient cells, so I don't have to bother you every time someone needs to be taken for tests or whatever. I think it would save time…"

"Yes, fine." He reached into his pocket. "Go and have one cut. Return the original to me."

§

He returned home exhausted after another long, stressful day. He barked at Tafflen to bring him some food and a glass of wine. He closed the curtains to block the hot summer sun and sat on the couch. He noted the claw marks on the curtains and made a mental note to talk to Tafflen about her damn cat.

An interrogator was scheduled to speak to Fillip tomorrow. *Not much longer. They'll both be executed and I'll be done with them forever.*

Tafflen brought him a plate of food and he pushed it away. "You burnt it. Make me something else." He gulped his glass of cool white wine and refilled it.

She had a hurt expression on her face but did as she was told.

Roary jumped onto the couch and curled up on his lap. Piter petted the cat. He felt a moment of regret for yelling at his girlfriend but could not bring himself to apologize. He kept the bottle of wine beside him.

§

Piter went to see Aura first thing after work to relay his misgivings about interviewing Tresha. He shifted nervously in the wooden chair. "I'm a doctor, not an interrogator. Besides, the interviews are taking valuable time away from my ALS research." He told Aura he was sending an interrogator to the QRR Centre to interview Fillip in the afternoon. "Tresha will feel so bad about making her husband suffer she will surely talk," he said. He was sweating profusely by the time he finished.

Aura came around her desk and stood in front of him. He was too intimidated to meet her eyes and stared instead at her dainty ankles.

She smiled. "Tresha is a stubborn woman. I'll give her time alone in her cell. Your idea is good. We'll play her the recordings of Fillip's interviews and vice-versa. They will both be more cooperative."

Piter was surprised at Aura's concern. She had a beautiful smile—dimples, straight white teeth and full lips.

She put her hands on his shoulders. "I admire you and I don't question your commitment to AZEN. I would like you to continue questioning her, but since you seem to have a soft spot for her, I'm instructing Dr. Marris to take over the difficult questioning."

Piter nodded. He knew there was no sense trying to argue. "Thank you, Aura." He stood up to leave, but she pushed him back down to his seat.

"You came to me and told me what was on your mind. Few men have the balls to do that." She leaned closer to him and moved her hands from his shoulders to the back of his neck.

"Sorry, I…"

"We make a good team, you and I, don't you think?"

"Yes." He wondered why she stood so close to him.

She hiked up her skirt and straddled him. She kissed him and bit his earlobe. He was getting excited and put his hands on her waist.

"Come on," she said and took his hand, opened the door to another room where there was a queen-sized bed. "You look surprised to see a bed beside my office."

"I am."

"I never know when I might need a nap, if you know what I mean."

§

She was an enthusiastic lovemaker and kept saying things like, "What a great team we'd make. Wouldn't you like to live in this big house?"

He told her yes, he would love to have what she has.

She dispensed with him as soon as they were done; patted his bottom and said, "I'm pleased with your performance. Men in their thirties are so peppy."

Piter put his clothes back on while Aura lounged in the bed. "Go and say hello to our friend before you go home. See if you can get anything out of her; if not, I'll ask Dr. Marris."

He felt a little bad about breaking his promise to Tafflen and sleeping with Aura, but it's not like he had a choice. In fact, he was exhilarated he got to make love to the president.

§

Piter dropped in at Re-Ed. He expected to find Tresha cowering in a corner of the cell, begging for release, ready to do and say anything.

When the guard opened the door of the cell, Tresha was smiling.

Piter was surprised. "What are you so happy about?"

She sat up and wrapped the blanket around her shoulders. "I was dreaming about Jakon. I miss him so much, but even to see him in my dreams is a comfort. I feel like the dream was a gift from God."

"Pfft. How can you believe in a God that would give you a damaged son like Jakon?" He sat on the chair and crossed his legs.

An angry look took over Tresha's face. "The horrible mass slaughter of innocents that goes on in this country; it's beyond evil."

[266]

"The old system didn't work."

"The elite sit in fancy houses with everything they could possibly want, while people in this country die of malnutrition and curable diseases every day. Then they outlawed religion."

He recited words from *Transformation and Affluence*, "Covona requires fidelity to the country. We can't have the population mindlessly following some unseen God."

"I mindfully follow my unseen God."

Piter stood up and pointed a finger at her. "How dare you! Our noble leader has done great things, truly marvelous things. You people can't think for yourselves. Religion had to be removed."

"Almighty Aura can't stand that some people see God as greater than her."

"You're so self-righteous. Religious people think anyone who doesn't follow their holy book is going to be damned to hell."

She sat calmly and looked up at his face. "For a smart person, you're really very stupid."

He slapped Tresha across the face, leaving an angry, red palm print on her cheek. He trembled, clenched and unclenched his fists. He yelled, "The old gods couldn't save us from war and conflict, hunger and disease, from people wasting away in old age. We cleanse and purge the society of its worthless members. At least we're doing something about overpopulation. You will be punished!"

"I'm not afraid to die and I won't beg for my life."

"Will you beg for Fillip's life?"

The colour drained from Tresha's face.

Piter hammered on the door until the guard opened it. Feeling ashamed of his lack of self-control he hurried to the main door, stepped outside and breathed in the cool night air. He wished he could go somewhere far away and be free of Re-Ed forever. Looking up at the starry sky, he thought, *Maybe a distant planet will do.*

He took two sleeping pills before bed and washed them down with three glasses of wine, hoping not to dream.

CHAPTER FORTY-ONE

The Price of Power

Tresha's cheek stung from Piter's slap. Worse, a sickening sense of dread settled in her stomach after Piter said, "Will you beg for Fillip's life?"

Her cough worsened as the days passed. She felt icy cold, but at the same time, her forehead was damp with sweat. She shivered on the examination table while Dr. Marris held a stethoscope to her chest.

"You appear to have come down with a cold," Dr. Marris said. "Doesn't seem serious."

Tresha said nothing.

"Are you chilly?" Dr. Marris asked but didn't wait for an answer. "Let me turn up the heat for you." She left the room.

The room warmed and Tresha relaxed, but then it grew hotter. She began to feel sweaty and thirsty.

An interrogator entered the room. Tresha was made to sit in a chair and was asked a series of questions. "Who are your accomplices? Where is the criminal named Hadar Dram? Where are your safe houses? Who did you sneak across the border?"

Tresha remained silent throughout the questioning. She struggled just to sit upright on the chair.

The interrogator waved her hand in front of her face. "Hot in here, isn't it? Let me cool things down for you." She picked up a bucket and drenched Tresha with water. Tresha screamed. The interrogator turned on a fan. Minutes later, Tresha's teeth chattered.

An hour later, the interrogator entered again and repeated the same questions.

Tresha hugged herself to stay warm.

"Cold in here, isn't it? I better crank up the heat," she said.

"No, please."

The fan was shut off and the heat came on again. The cycle repeated for several hours until finally the guard returned and half-carried Tresha back to her cell. Tresha dropped to the floor and didn't have the strength to crawl to her bed.

The room spun in circles. Tresha struggled to stand but made her way to the sink. Her legs felt wobbly. She took a long drink, pulled off her damp clothes and then lay naked on her cot, alternating between sweating and shivering. Her body and mind were so confused she couldn't remember what answers, if any, she gave the interrogator. The lights in the cell were as bright as ever.

Just when she thought she might be left alone for a while, the door of the cell banged open and she was pulled to her feet. Tresha stood naked between two guards, trying to keep her balance. They supported her and without a word dressed her in clean prison clothes and a pair of slippers. In the warmth of the dry clothing she could stop shivering.

"What now?"

The women didn't answer. They cuffed her hands in front of her body and chained her ankles. The chain was short and she was only able to take small steps, difficult to do when the guards coaxed her to walk quickly, each with a hand around her upper arm.

She was in a state of constant apprehension, not knowing if she would endure more torture or be killed. The combination of hunger and her recent ordeal made her dizzy and she stumbled. A guard jabbed Tresha in the back with her baton and pushed her into another cell. Tresha tripped over the chains on her ankles and fell in a heap to the floor. The only things in this cell were two metal chairs. She pulled her tired body onto a chair.

"The prisoner will stand in the presence of the president!" the guard shouted.

Tresha recognized a familiar face at the door. It was Aura.

§

Aura looked Tresha up and down and wrinkled her nose. "This place stinks. We'll go to the cafeteria. This place is too disgusting to have a conversation." She turned and walked out of the cell.

"Yes, Ms. President!" the guard said. She pointed her baton at Tresha. "Move!"

Tresha shuffled out of the room and, with the guards, followed Aura down the hall. All down the hallway and into the cafeteria, people snapped to attention or flattened themselves out against walls, shrinking in the presence of the president.

They entered a sunlit room. The sight of daylight streaming through the large windows and the lush garden was more than Tresha could bear. She had been so long deprived of natural light, with all concept of time taken from her. She stopped and stared, stunned by the beauty of nature outside the window.

The guard pulled a chair for Aura and wiped the seat with a cloth. Aura sat and crossed her legs gracefully. Tresha stood beside the table.

"Take those chains off her," Aura ordered.

The guards hurried to obey.

"Sit," she said to Tresha. "It's been such a long time. I thought you'd be happy to see your old friend again."

Tresha pulled out a chair and sat down, both curious and guarded about why she was there.

"Leave us," Aura said and waved at her guard, dismissing him. "Tell the kitchen staff we want coffee and doughnuts."

The guard bowed and marched out of the room.

Aura smiled. "So, it's wonderful to see you again. How've you been?"

Tresha knew Aura could see her bruises and dishevelled appearance. She didn't know how to answer, so she didn't.

"Do you remember the fun we used to have? The parties?"

Tresha coughed, wondering if this was to be her final torture.

Aura tossed her hair over her shoulder, placed her hand on Tresha's knee and leaned over. "I've been dying to talk to you."

"What about?"

"Not even hello? How are you? Is that any way to greet an old friend?"

Tresha remained silent.

"Loosen up, Tresha. Why am I the only one who knows how to have fun? You were always so serious."

[270]

Tresha knew anything she said could be misconstrued, yet she had a hard time keeping her thoughts straight.

"You're nice and slim now," Aura said.

"That comes from not having enough to eat."

Aura threw her head back and laughed. "Same old sense of humour. I hear Dr. Piter Dram has been in to talk to you. Isn't he a doll?"

"He's not the man I once knew."

"You look so old. Ever think about colouring your hair?" Aura reached over and ran her hand over Tresha's untidy hair. She grimaced, looked at her hand and wiped it on a napkin.

"Not a priority right now."

Aura gave her a wide smile. "No, I guess not. Didn't we go to some great parties though? Everyone was looking at me. You were always so plain. Oh, come on, Tresha. Don't look at me with that sour expression on your face. I was good to you."

A nervous man appeared with coffee and snacks on a tray. He set them out on the table and scurried away.

It had been a long time since Tresha had coffee. She took a few sips. Her stomach felt queasy.

Aura seemed to have trouble grasping the spoon to stir her coffee. Finally, she pushed the spoon with one hand to the edge of the table to grasp it with the thumb and fingers of the other hand. Tresha wondered what was wrong.

Aura turned on her with sudden anger. "Are you laughing at me?"

"No."

Aura loved to mock people. She used to point to people in wheelchairs and call them gimps, or point to old people leaning on walkers and mimic how they walked and talked.

"Why did you come today, Aura?" Without asking, Tresha reached for a chocolate donut and bit into its gooey softness. The intense sweetness was overwhelming.

Aura appeared to give up on trying to drink her coffee and sat with crossed arms. "I haven't let my interrogators be too hard on you. You have no burns, no broken bones. You should be grateful to me."

Tresha swallowed the bite and took another. Its chocolaty goodness filled her mouth.

"I want to talk some sense into you. Do you realize I am the only one who can save your life?"

"You can allow me to live, but you can't save me."

"I don't want to listen to any of your religious crap!" Aura leaned forward in her chair, placing her elbows on the table. "You're the only girl who ever had the guts to stand up to me. I admire that about you. I'm offering you my friendship."

"Friendship?" *Aura is slurring her speech. I wonder if she's been drinking.*

"I'm willing to forgive you."

"That's kind of you."

"I know, especially after my people found this in your cabin in the woods." Aura tossed a memory card on the table. She also placed a piece of paper on the table. "You wrote some stuff about me. Now you know why you have to be kept in solitary."

Tresha took the paper and reread what she had written. It seemed like a lifetime ago and written by a different person:

> *Competing political groups in Covona are suppressed, as are any social groups and institutions who dare to oppose Aura Zarling's monopoly of power. The power lies not with the people but with groups of ruling elites, first in the military and police, then in the energy sector, media, transportation and education. With her group of leaders, she autocratically manipulates power to develop and maintain a monopoly. Our constitutional state is eliminated.*
>
> *Aura Zarling controls the nation by removing or restricting civil liberties. The citizens' obligation is to comply. Her decision making is aggressive and impulsive. Despite this, people flock to her. By trespassing on human rights, she gives herself more authority. She keeps control of people's opinions*

through manipulation of the media. The masses are forced to admire the personality of the leader.

She maintains control through intimidation—Aura's deep pockets are used to bribe or bankrupt. Her control of the police force and new stringent laws put a strangle-hold on businesses and individuals. Her ownership of major media allows her to use propaganda, twisting news stories to her own advantage.

Her councillors, advisory committees and organizations each compete for power within her web. She controls the strings, setting one against the other, disposing of anyone who demonstrates opposition. She buys favour from the elites, the ruling class, by giving them access to better housing, food and medicine.

This dictator's rise to power was the result of a democratic election, but since that time she has changed the political system to ensure she can't be removed. She prohibits opposing organizations and parties and has cancelled free elections. She calls herself President, to try to maintain the appearance of a democratically constituted government. It is not democratic. Anyone who doesn't act in accordance with the government's rules is considered a traitor and is sentenced to labour camp or executed.

"It's all true, Aura," Tresha said.

"Oh, I know it's true. That's what I like about you, Tresha. You get me. Just what were you planning on doing with the information?"

Tresha decided to tell the truth. "I was planning on smuggling it into Solime."

"I'm glad my soldiers found this before it could do me any damage."

What Tresha didn't tell her was that she had already sent a copy with one of her guests who had crossed the border.

Aura pushed the hair away from her face and leaned in to speak. "I'd like your opinion on something. It's something I came up with recently. I'm going to include it in my next speech: 'The abolition of religion as the illusory happiness of the people is the demand for their real happiness.'"

Tresha knew the quote. "Interesting. Karl Marx, right?"

"Right. You're so clever. We'd make a good team. If I could give you something, what would it be?"

"I want my husband to be released unharmed."

"That's it? I'm offering you so much more. Look how happy I am. I can do whatever I want, when I want. I am the most powerful person in the country. Watch this." She called the nervous man who served the snack to come forward. "Lick my shoe."

The man got down on his hands and knees and licked her shoe.

Aura laughed and pushed his face with the bottom of her shoe. "Go away, now."

Tresha had trouble not gagging on her doughnut.

"Don't you wish you had that kind of power? I can give it to you. I can give you everything you've always wanted. We could be great friends again." She took Tresha's hand. "Just tell me everything. Let me crush everyone who has ever opposed me." She opened her greedy eyes wide and tightened her grip. A drop of saliva rolled out of the corner of Aura's mouth.

"Why do you want to be my friend?"

"It's hard not having anyone to confide in."

Tresha had to remind herself she was talking to a human being, not the face of evil. Aura, despite having everything, was lonely.

The moment passed, though, and Aura's face became hard again. "I will give you everything you've always wanted."

"I don't want what you could give me. Your words are lies."

Aura's complexion grew red. She let go of Tresha's hand. A vein in her neck began to throb. "Not even my parents speak to me the way you do. I could have you torn limb from limb. I can have justice."

Tresha raised her voice. "You're talking about revenge. Your government is a death cult and an insult to justice." She decided to add another comment, even if it meant instant death. "People in this country hate you more than you can imagine."

Instead of being angry, Aura's face crumpled and she struggled not to cry. "I don't even know what you're talking about. My people love me. I am like a beloved queen."

"Who reigns through violence and fear."

"I thought we could be friends again, but you blew your chance." Aura picked up a doughnut from the plate. She took a big bite and shouted to the guards to take Tresha back to her cell. "No food for her, until I say she's allowed."

§

Hours later, Tresha heard the key in the lock. The cell door banged open and she cringed as a guard placed a tray beside her.

"Your supper, traitor. We'll talk later." She smiled and walked away.

Tresha thought it very odd considering what Aura said earlier. The food was delivered by a guard instead of through the slot in the door. She sat up and began to cough, wrapped the blanket around her shoulders, struggled to her feet and spat phlegm into the toilet.

She returned to her bed and lifted the lid. The tray was empty.

CHAPTER FORTY-TWO

How to Be a Friend

The temperature in Ackim, Covona, on that Autumn day was twenty-six degrees Celsius. In the evening, the room lit up intermittently with flashes of lightning, followed by rumbling thunder. Hail beat Piter's balcony window. Roary cowered under the couch.

Tafflen was standing at the stove cooking when the room went black. "Just in time," she said and lifted the pot off the stove. "Come for supper."

Piter lit some candles and placed them on the table. He sat, staring into the flames, wondering how he was going to tell her.

She placed a plate in front of him and kissed his cheek. "I'm the luckiest girl in the country. You should come and meet my parents soon."

Roary jumped onto his lap and kneaded her claws on his legs. "Ouch." Piter extracted the claws.

Tafflen picked up the cat. "Bad Roary. Are you making bread on Daddy's legs?"

Piter didn't smile.

"What's wrong, Panda Monster?" She sat across the table.

After several mouthfuls of chicken soup, he told her the truth, how Aura seduced him.

Tafflen's eyes grew wide. "Will she want to see you again?" Her voice cracked as she suppressed a sob.

His voice became deep and threatening. "Can I say no to the president?"

She lowered her eyes and swirled the soup in her bowl.

"Stop pouting," he said.

"It isn't right. You're my boyfriend."

He slammed his fist on the table. "I didn't ask for this!" The cat ran to the other room.

Tafflen flinched. "This is a bad thing."

He forced himself to relax. "You're just going to have to share me."

"What if she doesn't want to share? I'm afraid."

"Don't be stupid."

"I'm going to bed." She slumped to the bedroom and shut the door.

Piter ate alone and then stretched out on the couch to sleep. He heard Tafflen crying but didn't go to her.

She didn't get out of bed to make breakfast for him the next morning. "Tafflen?" He opened the door of the bedroom.

She opened her eyes. "Make your own breakfast," she said and turned her back to him.

§

The next morning, Piter lay on his back with one hand behind his head. The other was around Aura, her head nestled on his chest. She played with his chest hair with the long, manicured nail of her index finger.

"Tresha was the best friend I ever had. I went to see her, but she acted like she wasn't happy to see me. How can you make someone like you?" she asked.

"Try to fulfill some of their needs. Do something nice for them. What do you think she wants?"

"Her husband. Do you think we should stop interrogating Fillip?"

"If you want Tresha to be your friend."

"Okay. We're such a good team. You have the human touch. I can't wait for the day you develop a cure for ALS and I'll be free of this horrible disease. Tresha will be my friend again and you and I will rule the nation together. Won't that be wonderful?"

At the QRR Centre, they had begun the double-blind tests, where neither researcher nor patient knew who was getting the experimental drug and who was getting the placebo, but still hadn't found any reliable evidence the drug therapy was working.

"I better get to work," he said. He rose from bed, showered and opened a closet in Aura's bedroom filled with new designer suits, shirts and shoes she had bought for him. He chose an outfit and put it on.

When he turned around he saw Aura holding his cell phone. "What are you doing?" he asked in a gentle voice.

"Looking at the messages from your whore." She scrolled the phone with her finger. "She's wondering where you were last night."

"Please, Aura. Give me my phone." He held out his hand.

Aura laughed and rolled away from him. "Aw. This is so precious. 'I'm sorry I was mad at you, my little panda monster.' That's what she calls you?"

"It doesn't matter. I need to go to work."

"I don't like her," Aura said.

Piter's chest was tight, suddenly afraid for Tafflen. "She means nothing to me. You're my everything." He sat beside Aura on the bed and kissed her. He took the phone from her hand.

"You need to send her away. I don't like competition."

Piter forced a smile on his face. "She's as good as gone."

"Good, then you can move in with me."

"I can't be distracted from my work, Aura. It's very important."

She got out of bed and strutted around the room. "Okay, but only until you find a cure. If it wasn't for your work, I would lock you in my basement and never let you out. I'd have you all to myself."

Chills ran down his spine. He cleared his throat and brushed imaginary dust from his jacket. He picked up the house phone to tell the doorman to call a taxi for him.

She took the phone from his hand. "No more taking taxies to work, Piter. You have your own driver now. The limousine is outside waiting for you."

"Wow. Thank you." He stood straighter.

Piter stepped outside and, sure enough, there was a black stretch limousine. The driver hopped out and opened the door. Piter couldn't wait to see Gorge's face. He sent a text message to Tafflen: "You have a week to move out. And take your cat with you."

[278]

She messaged him back. "What? I thought we had something good. I can't believe you're breaking up with me by text."

"I'm tired of having you around."

"I thought you cared for me."

"Don't tell me you've fallen in love with me."

There was a long pause when Tafflen didn't respond. "No. I'm just here to take care of you."

"I can take care of myself. I don't want to see you again."

Tafflen didn't respond.

§

The day dragged by. He hated that he hurt Tafflen's feelings. She didn't answer her phone all day and he wanted to talk to her, to explain why he sent the text.

The sun was setting as the limo crept forward a few metres at a time in heavy traffic. It stopped at a red light in front of a brothel. A young woman stood in the front window displaying her wares. She caught Piter looking and lifted her bikini top, offering him a peek. She was young with a slim waist and large, probably surgically augmented breasts.

"Would you like to step out, sir? I can wait for you," Stann said.

"No. Take me home."

CHAPTER FORTY-THREE

Compliance Brings Happiness

The better and pricier condominiums, like Piter's, were situated on River Avenue. The limo dropped him in front of his building, but rather than going inside, he crossed the street and followed a short foot-path leading down to the river's edge. Here under the trees, it was peaceful. He needed to sort out what to say to Tafflen. A light wind swished intermittently through the treetops, accompanied by the rhythmic burbling of the river. During the day, traffic noises obscured the river's music, but at night it sang and danced. The blue-black surface of the water shimmered.

Piter craned his neck to the sky, hoping to see the constellations, but Ackim's bright city lights muted starlight. The air was crisp, the promise of colder weather on the way. He stepped with care from the river's edge onto a rock that poked from the surface of the water. Piter perched there, briefcase in one hand, the other extended outward for balance. From there he found another rock and another, following a weaving path, hoping to stay dry. It was a game he and his brother played when they were children. His black leather shoes slipped a bit on the glossy rocks and he almost lost his balance. He made his way back to dry land and sat on a fallen log. Dead leaves fell from the tree and landed on his head.

It had been a long, emotion-filled day. Piter and his colleagues had spent hours going over results of experiments. Gorge noted some of the patients seemed to show improvement at first but quickly regressed. In the end, Piter was as perplexed by the disease as when he started and wondered how he would explain this to Aura. To top it off, she had made him break up with Tafflen.

Casting his eyes down, he noticed a bottle caught in the reeds, its cap still intact. He smiled, remembering when he and Hadar had stuffed a piece of paper in a bottle when they were children. "If you find this message return it to Piter and Hadar Dram." Hadar had written a funny poem. Piter had drawn a picture of the two of them casting their rods into the clear, sparkling mountain streams that fed the North Omala

River. Hadar had tossed the bottle into the river and they watched it float away. It was a carefree and innocent time.

Piter picked up the bottle, wiped the mud onto the grass and undid the cap. The bottle was empty. On a whim, Piter took a pen from his pocket and a piece of paper from his briefcase and wrote: "Dear Hadar. I miss you. I promise to help you. Call me." He rolled up the paper, stuffed it in the bottle, tightened the cap and threw it as far as he could into the flowing river. He watched it float away. Suddenly self-conscious, he looked around, hoping no one saw.

§

Upon entering the condo, he saw Tafflen was gone, as were her clothes and a suitcase. He was relieved, for her sake, but the apartment was eerily quiet without her. From his north window, he had a clear view of the distant Keque Mountains. He stood a while, imagining his life without Tafflen.

He made a sandwich and sat in front of the television to watch a recording of a football game. An hour later, Piter took his normal dose of sleeping pills and climbed into bed.

He was surprised when he heard a familiar, "Meow." The cat jumped on the bed and settled herself on Piter's chest.

"Roary? What are you doing here? Why didn't Tafflen take you with her?" He stroked the cat's soft ears, happy for the company, but knew something was wrong. She may have left him, but she wouldn't have left her cat. He looked around his condo. Nothing was out of place. The smell of pine cleansers, sharp and sanitary, hung in the air. Books were still stacked beside the gas fireplace. The lamp shone down on the brown, leather reclining rocking chair. The seat was a little worn by the many hours he'd spent studying his medical journals and textbooks. Tafflen liked to sit on the arm of the chair and ask him questions about what he was reading, a habit he found irritating at the time. Now, he wished she was here to bother him.

In the morning, and several times throughout the day, Piter tried Tafflen's cell phone, but got no response.

Roary jumped onto his lap when he got home. She rubbed her head on Piter's chest.

"Where's Mommy?" he asked the cat. Throughout the evening, Roary followed him all over the condo, to the kitchen, the study, the bedroom. He bent and stroked the cat's back. "I know. I miss her, too."

A picture of his deceased wife and a picture of Tafflen stood side by side on the mantle. He touched the frames of each.

Out the west window was a view of the river framed by green pine, and deciduous trees dressed in red, yellow and brown. A line of cars creeped forward down the street.

Not a speck of dust was to be found, except in one corner—a ball of white fur swirled round near the warm air vent.

He picked up Roary, put her in a cat carrier and called a cab. She mewed all the way to Tafflen's parents' home. He knocked on the door, cat carrier in hand, and introduced himself to the woman who opened the door.

"Where is my daughter?" asked the woman. "She usually calls me every day."

"I was going to ask you the same question," he said.

Over tea they exchanged what they knew of the situation, which was not much.

"She left Roary behind. Very strange." The cat walked with confidence across the floor, jumped onto a couch and settled down to sleep.

He looked around the nicely furnished home, surprised by how well they lived. Tafflen had told him her parents were struggling financially. "How do you afford to live in a place like this?"

"Tafflen's been sending us money ever since she moved in with you," the mother said.

He sipped the last of his tea, stood and thanked the woman. "Let me know if she contacts you," he said.

§

Piter was in Aura's bed again that afternoon.

"Compliance brings happiness. Wouldn't you agree, Piter?" She was straddling his body, looking down at him. Her breasts looked even larger from this angle.

He watched her facial expressions as she ran her finger down his bare chest to his belly button. "Yes, I agree."

"I've always liked to be in charge, even back in grade school." Aura got off him and rolled onto her back. "But running this country is so much work. I'm afraid some of my ministers are traitors. I'm having them questioned at Re-Ed."

"We do have to be careful who we trust," Piter said.

"Exactly." Aura got out of bed and put on a negligee. "Sometimes I feel lonely."

"Like that saying, 'it is lonely at the top.'" He got up, reached for his underwear and put them on, and then reached for his shirt.

"I worked hard to get to where I am." Aura sat at her dressing table and pulled a brush through her long hair.

He pulled up his trousers. "I'm sure—"

"Staying at the top, though. That's the hard part, thinking my advisors might be plotting behind my back. Not you, though. You would never betray me."

Piter tightened his belt. He longed to find the right words to ask the question that was on his mind. "I got home last night and Tafflen was gone, which was good. I told her to leave, but nobody knows where she is."

Aura picked up a pillow and hit him over the head. "Don't mention that whore's name in my bedroom!"

"Sorry. I was just wondering—" He backed up, hands in defensive mode.

"You're wondering if I had something to do with it."

He backed up to the wall and slipped on his shoes. "No, Aura. It's just her cat—" He got down on one knee and struggled to quickly tie his laces, eager to leave.

With hands on her hips she stomped over and glowered down at him. "Do you care more about her than me?"

"No, of course not." Piter, on his knees, hugged Aura's legs. "She means nothing to me. You are my world. My one and only."

"Okay. I forgive you. Get up."

Piter breathed a sigh of relief and rose to his feet.

"When I defeat Solime, you will be by my side, Piter." She wrapped her arms around him, laid her head on his shoulder.

"How can you defeat Solime?"

"First, I will make them weak, and then I will attack. You know I've been building up my army. I'm thinking of conscripting all young men and women into the army, make them serve so they're ready when I need them. What do you think?"

"I would never question your decisions."

She tickled him under the chin. "You're so cute when you're submissive."

"Aura, how do you plan to make Solime weak?"

"My secret weapon." Aura pretended to cough and then she laughed.

CHAPTER FORTY-FOUR

Thanks for Caring

Piter opened his eyes and looked at the cheerless sky through his bedroom window. Cold fog hung in the air, the type of fog that seeped through outer layers of clothing, "chilling you to the bone," as the saying went. He pressed the snooze button and pulled the blanket to his chin, not wanting to rise from his bed.

Ten minutes later, he arose. Outside, a sparrow, feathers puffed, sat on a frost-covered twig. Cars billowed clouds of exhaust that dissipated in the breeze. He got ready for work.

The frigid air hit Piter's face the moment he stepped outside of his condominium and into his limousine. On a whim, he said to his driver, "Take me past the Free Clinic."

"Yes, sir," Stann said.

Nothing had changed. People were lined up down the block, hands shoved in pockets, heads wrapped with scarves, stamping in place to keep warm while they waited to be let into the clinic. The people turned their heads to watch the limo go by. A wave of sadness coursed through Piter's body. "Life isn't fair, is it, Stann?"

"No, sir. It sure isn't."

§

Normally, Piter would have taken careful, slow steps in his research, but time was a factor. He began injecting a new drug of his own creation directly into the spinal cord of his human test subjects instead of starting with animal testing. He decided to increase the dosage by twenty percent on some of the test subjects and began to track their progress, or regress.

Cherrin walked behind him with a clipboard, recording everything. She wore a sad expression today.

"What's wrong with you?" he asked. "Not your usual happy self?"

"Thanks for caring, Dr. Dram. Sometimes, I just feel bad for these people."

"Don't get personally involved. Try not to think of them as anything other than test subjects, like the animals we use."

"Not easy," said Cherrin.

"When you get attached it's so much harder to do the things we do. Don't you agree?"

"Yes, Dr. Dram."

Some of the test subjects received a new treatment which Piter had designed—modified stem cells, administered intravenously. These highly adaptive cells, he hoped, would stimulate the existing cells to operate at a higher level and boost the body's own repair mechanisms. Piter was disappointed his previous treatment had not yet helped any of his test subjects, including Imas Larium, who was Piter's first human ALS test subject. Like the others, he hadn't improved.

He and Cherrin stopped at a cage where a woman was not given the stem cell treatment but a drug called riluzole. Her speech seemed to have improved slightly, though she complained of stomachaches.

"Why don't you just give them all riluzole?" Cherrin asked. Her pen skimmed over the page as she walked, following Piter from cage to cage. "It seems to help some of our patients."

"Test subjects, not patients, Cherrin. Riluzole reduces the levels of glutamate, a chemical messenger in the brain. It has side effects—like gastrointestinal problems—and it doesn't work for everyone."

Piter continued his rounds, down the hallways of the school that had been converted into a research centre. He entered one room after another filled with barred cages containing human test subjects. The people called out to him, begging to be released or that loved ones be allowed to visit. He ignored them, as per protocol. The test subjects' emotional needs were not to be considered by the staff at this facility. The researchers' interest was getting results through methodological means. Today, Piter couldn't stop thinking about Tafflen and Hadar. He knew, deep down, all these people missed their families, too.

§

The last time Piter saw his brother was soon after he and Yun married. They went to visit him at his home in Ducor. Yun and Piter held hands and watched the sun come up over the Cisco Ocean. Piter couldn't imagine the beautiful view spoiled now with an electric fence.

Hadar had owned a small single-engine boat and took them out in the morning to fish. Hours later, they came to shore with three fish in the cooler. They built a small fire from driftwood and then filleted and fried one of the fish on the beach.

Hadar shook some salt and pepper on the fish. "Okay, dig in."

The three of them attacked the sizzling hot fish with forks, eating straight from the frying pan. They relaxed on blankets, throwing scraps of fish into the air and watching seagulls swoop, competing for the scraps. Hadar laughed at the birds' aerial athletics.

§

"Dr. Dram?"

Piter snapped back to grim reality—to this dreary former school, once filled with children, now knowing only despair, death and dying. The stink of body odour and human excrement hung in the air, badly masked by disinfectant.

"I'll type up a report for you. It will be on your desk this afternoon," Cherrin said.

Piter cleared his throat. "Fine. I'll leave you to it."

§

Hours later, Piter was about to go to lunch when he passed by one of the rooms holding test subjects. Through the open door, he spotted Cherrin sitting on Imas' bed. No longer able to walk, Imas didn't need to be kept in a cage. There was no danger of him escaping. Piter thought it strange they were talking, because Cherrin had already attended to Imas that morning. Cherrin was writing on a sheet of paper. She saw Piter, stood and placed the paper beneath a stack of others on a clipboard.

[287]

He entered the room. "What are you doing, Cherrin?" His voice was stern.

"Completing my notes on a test subject." She giggled. "Well, back to work."

He stopped her at the door, his arm blocking the way. "You've already seen him today. Let me see what you've written."

Cherrin tried to hand Piter the top piece of paper, but he grabbed the whole clipboard from her hand.

She let out a little gasp. "Dr. Dram…"

Piter removed the last page and held a crudely drawn map in his hand. He recognized the western border of the country, and the road names, but wondered what the x's and stars signified. "What is this?"

"It's nothing," she said. "Imas was just showing me some of the places he's been…fishing."

Piter witnessed enough interrogations to know when someone was lying. He said in a quiet voice, "What's going on?"

"Okay—" Cherrin said.

"Cherrin, do you really think you—" Imas said.

"Come with me." Cherrin led Piter back to his office and closed the door behind them. She stood in the centre of the room. Medical journals and textbooks filled a bookshelf. On his desk were neatly stacked piles of papers and folders.

He sat behind his desk. "What's this about?"

"Before I tell you, do you know what happened to Tafflen?"

"No. What?" He leaned back on the couch, preparing for bad news.

"Gorge delivered her to Quietus last night. The order came directly from the president."

He cleared his throat. "I knew it." Piter felt his jaw shake, but he refused to cry.

Cherrin spoke softly. "Do you want to see her body before they start recycling?"

Piter shook his head. His throat ached with the effort of trying to hold back the tears. "I never told Tafflen."

"Told her what?" Cherrin looked at him with concern.

"I broke up with her to try to save her life. She died without hearing me say I love her."

Cherrin sat beside him on the couch and put her hand on his arm. "I'm sorry."

"My wife, son, parents, and now Tafflen. I lost everyone." His voice cracked. He rubbed the tears from his eyes with the palm of his hand. The truth hit him hard. Hot anger flared in his chest.

She extracted the map from his hand. "You never saw this."

Piter rubbed both hands down his face. "The map is an escape route?"

"Yes. You're not the only one who's been hurt by this regime, Dr. Dram. So much death. What about Imas and the others held in cages, medical experiments forced on them?"

"But we're working on a cure for ALS. Those people are going die anyway."

Cherrin rolled her eyes. "I'm your assistant. I know the pressure you're under to find a cure quickly. Even if you can find a cure for ALS within the year, and I doubt it, it doesn't justify how badly they're treated."

In his heart, he agreed.

"The president will grow tired of waiting. Do you think she won't eliminate you as soon as you've served your purpose? You're just a pawn."

Piter felt dizzy for a moment. He turned his head and sighed. "What can I do about it? We're all helpless pawns. All your plans will fail."

"We will only fail when we stop trying. Will you help? Imas knows a way. I need to get out of Covona soon."

"Why? What did you do?"

"Gathered information."

"You're a spy?" The words cracked as they came out of his mouth.

"I have information about everyone's research, even Dr. Marris. We must stop the president before she kills tens of millions. The world needs to know."

"What are you talking about?" He was beginning to think Cherrin had lost her mind.

"Do you ever wonder what Dr. Marris is working on?"

"Yes, but…"

"Come with me." Without waiting for a reply, Cherrin quick-walked down a long hallway while Piter hurried to catch up. She stopped at the refrigerator units and used her key to open the door. Inside, she showed him many sets of lungs stored in clear plastic bags and labelled with names of the deceased and day of death. The lungs looked as though they'd been eaten up by disease.

"What happened to these people?" Piter asked. He had seen the effects of chronic obstructive pulmonary disease, cystic fibrosis and lung cancer on lungs, but these organs looked like those taken from autopsied bodies of people who'd died of the Solime Flu.

He remembered what Aura had said to him the night before. She would make Solime weak before she attacked them. He answered his own question, "Dr. Marris created the Solime Flu. She's been infecting people." His heart thumped, barely able to comprehend Aura's cruelty and ambition. He thought about Fillip, and how he had almost died of this flu.

"Yes. And Dr. Marris is the only one who has the vaccine. We need to find it and get it across the border."

"Do you know how hard that would be?" Piter shivered in the cold room.

"I'm friends with her assistant," Cherrin said.

"Do you work for HRFA?" Her expression told him she did. "How long have you been keeping this secret from me?"

"Since the beginning. It was hard keeping up the charade, pretending to enjoy the work."

Piter felt his world being torn to pieces and falling in splinters around him. He pulled at his tie as if he couldn't get enough air. "You can't defeat AZEN."

"Maybe not, but we can save millions of lives," Cherrin said. "Will you help?"

"The president is sick with ALS. She won't live more than a few years."

Cherrin's eyes widened. "Of course. Makes sense with all the effort poured into the research. When she dies, General Bont will step forward to keep the regime going. He'll be just as bad, or worse. Will you help us?" she asked again.

"Why do you trust me?"

"I see you may have had a change of heart. Besides, I need bribe money to get across the border."

Piter didn't hesitate long. He knew what he had to do. "I'll give you what you need, but can we help Fillip Farwell? Know anything about his situation?"

Cherrin said, "A shipment of prisoners is leaving for the labour camp within the week. I'll see if he's among them."

"It might be too late," Piter said. "I would need permission to have him released."

Cherrin paused, furrowed her brows. "You need permission from the president."

"How? She will never allow it."

"It's up to you to find a way, Dr. Dram."

CHAPTER FORTY-FIVE

Solitary Confinement

Tresha hadn't eaten in days, but worse than her hunger was the recording of her husband's screams she was forced to listen to last night. Her worry for him had kept her awake most of the night. She wrapped the blanket around her shoulders, coughed, leaned her head over the edge of her bed and spat on the floor.

It was hard to calculate time in solitary confinement, but judging by the number of times the food cart had passed by her cell without stopping, she estimated it had been four days since anyone opened the door. Tresha longed to hear birds twitter and feel sunshine on her face, or rain. She tried to imagine these things, but it was hard to distract herself from her aching stomach and head. She placed the blanket over her head to give her eyes some relief from the glare of the overhead lights.

Tresha knew at any moment she could be dragged out, interrogated again or killed. On the other hand, she might languish in this cell, slowly becoming weaker and thinner and never see another human being again. She listened to the buzzing of the fluorescent light. An ant traced a meandering pattern up the wall of her cell. "Are you looking for food, my friend? I wish I had something to share with you, then you'd keep me company."

The ant disappeared into a crack.

"Is anybody there? Oh, God, please, somebody help me." Nothing but silence. Tresha coughed hard, gasping to try to get enough air in her lungs. She rose from her bed and, holding onto the sink for support, took a drink of water. Light-headedness was a signal she'd better sit down. *Aura offered me her friendship. What a joke.* "I could sell my soul to the devil for medicine, food, clothing and human contact. Man does not live by bread alone, but by... I don't remember the words. What does it say in the *Bible*? I can't remember. What good does it do if I can't remember the words?" She turned her face into the mattress and cried until she thought her heart would break. Her crying brought on another coughing fit. She tried to comfort herself. *I led others to freedom; two hundred and forty-nine escapees.*

Her only company since being arrested had been cruel guards, interrogators, Piter and Aura. She kept going over their conversations, reliving them. With nothing to do but daydream, think about food, reminisce, pray, sleep, wake up and start the process again, she was afraid she'd lose her sanity.

She closed her eyes and thought about the country she used to love. She and Fillip had stayed in a hotel in Citron on their honeymoon, swam in the pool, did a little gambling in the casino and watched a stage show. They danced in the ballroom. She imagined his hand on her waist. In her mind she saw the hotel, but when she opened her eyes and saw only the concrete walls of her cell, she felt as if all joy had been tapped from her body, leaving her empty and longing for the old days.

"I miss you, Fillip. I miss you, Jakon." She closed her eyes again to imagine her husband. Fillip was not a physically attractive man, but to Tresha he was beautiful. His shoulders were slightly hunched, as if he was in a constant state of deep contemplation. "Stand up straight, you're short enough as it is," she used to tease him.

He was quick with a smile, intelligent, gentle and kind, but would not back down from a fight. "The guards here are a bunch of chest-pounding, hooting apes compared to you, Fillip."

Hours more passed. Her feet were cold inside her thin cloth slippers as she paced the concrete floor. Three steps. Turn around. Three steps. Turn around. She stopped to examine her bruised, puffy face in the mirror, turned on the tap, took a long drink of water, and splashed her face. She resumed pacing, head down, concentrating on the cracks on the tiled floor that wound like tiny rivers towards the drain in the centre. She found if she blurred her eyes, she could almost see patterns and shapes made by the cracks.

Her empty stomach reminded her of bread. "Give us this day our daily bread, and forgive us our trespasses. As we forgive those who trespass against us," she whispered. *I can't forgive them. As we forgive those...forgive them.* "Fillip, I miss you, wherever you are."

She heard the door open and Piter entered. She was relieved to have company at last, even if he was here to question her again.

He pulled a sandwich from his pocket and handed it to her. He put his finger to his lips.

Her hands shook as she took the food. The sandwich was delicious, probably the best thing she had ever eaten. Roast beef, lettuce, tomatoes, cucumber, butter and mustard on whole wheat bread. She finished it and licked her fingers. That's when she noticed his face. Piter looked as though he was struggling to maintain a neutral expression. Tresha had wondered, at their previous interviews, if she was sitting with a robot instead of a person. Now, there seemed to be a hint of humanity.

He took the plastic wrapper from her hand and put it in his pocket. Piter said, "You don't look well."

Tresha got up and leaned over the small sink and looked at the mirror. "I look ghastly." She took a drink and brushed the greasy grey hair away from her eyes. "I don't know why I'm worried about my appearance. As if it makes any difference." She felt the need to keep talking after being isolated for so long. "I look old. I'm not, but I feel old. Covonans hardly see elderly people anymore." Exhausted, she sat on her bed.

"*Transformation and Affluence* states the elderly contribute nothing to the economy." Piter's voice was flat.

"A country without old people. I never would have imagined it would happen here. What is the weather like outside? Describe it to me."

Piter didn't respond. He kept his head down, bit his lower lip and shifted in his seat.

"Something wrong, Piter?"

"Tafflen is...dead." His voice was barely audible.

"Who's she?"

"My girlfriend."

"I'm sorry." She coughed into some toilet paper, bringing up phlegm tinged with blood, a new symptom.

He shrugged. Piter put his hand to Tresha's forehead and said in a quiet voice, "You're quite ill?"

"Doesn't matter. If I don't die of this, they'll kill me."

He took a deep breath and turned towards her as if he wanted to say something, but he didn't.

She felt a fever coming on and was finding it harder to keep her thoughts straight. Tresha had to recline. She wanted nothing more than to just sleep now that her stomach was full.

"Did they play recordings of Fillip's interrogations for you?" Piter asked in a soft voice.

Tresha felt like crying again. "My poor Fillip. I miss him so much. If I knew he was okay, then I could die in peace."

Piter took her hand and held it, he mouthed the words to her, "He's alive."

Her eyes widened. She took a deep breath, sat up and was about to speak again when another coughing fit overtook her.

"Your phlegm is blood tinged. How long have you had that cough?" Piter asked.

"A while."

"Has a doctor been to see you?"

"I saw Dr. Marris, after an incident with my heart, before I got sick with this."

"Dr. Marris? Did she give you anything?"

"She gave me a shot of vitamin B."

Piter got up quickly and left the cell without another word.

CHAPTER FORTY-SIX

Finding a Cure

Piter dreaded Aura's reaction. Her condition was deteriorating. His new drug therapy was ineffective, yet he had to convince her to submit to treatment.

Aura turned her head from the computer screen as he entered her office. Her mouth turned in a snarl and her face turned a furious colour.

She stood, placed her fists on her desk, leaned forward and spoke to her guards. "All of you, get out." Piter took a step back and gripped his medical bag in both hands as she stormed towards him. She met him at the door and pounded her fists on his chest and arms. "The medicine isn't working! I'm getting worse!"

He dropped the bag and raised his hands in defense while her blows fell on him. "Please, stop." He grabbed her wrists and tried to calm her. "The medicine takes time, patience, to work."

Aura leaned her head on his chest and wept. "I talk like I'm drunk. How can I deliver my speeches? I'm twitching all the time now, and look at my hands."

Piter took her hands in his. The fingers were curled towards the palms. "Open your hands."

Aura did so with difficulty. "What's happening to me?"

Behind Aura, on a television screen, was a news story from Solime. Covonan refugees were being welcomed, given food and shelter. He tore his eyes from the television to concentrate on Aura. "The motor neurons in your brain are starting to degenerate. They stop sending messages to your muscles. That's the reason for the twitching and spasticity. A therapist can help you with range of motion exercises and massage."

"No! No one must know about this." She winced in pain. "It hurts, Piter."

"I can prescribe some anti-inflammatory drugs and morphine for the pain. Some Lorazepam will help to decrease anxiety." He rubbed her arms up and down to calm her.

"What about something so I'm not so twitchy?"

"Muscle relaxants can be dangerous for a person with ALS. It can affect your ability to breathe."

"The other doctor told me my muscles will waste away, that I'll need a ventilator one day." Tears flowed down her face. She wiped them away with the back of her hand.

"Yes, under normal circumstances and given time, the disease will affect your breathing muscles, throat and tongue."

"You know I couldn't stand that." Her eyes flashed with anger.

"It won't happen to you, I guarantee it."

"If I don't see improvement soon, I'm blaming you."

"Trust me."

She screamed, "It's not fair! Bad things aren't supposed to happen to me. Make it stop!"

Two of Aura's guards burst through the doors and pointed their weapons at Piter.

He stepped back, hands in the air.

"Should we take him down, Ms. President?" one of them said.

Piter had a sudden urge to use the toilet.

"No. Leave us alone," Aura said.

"Let's go to the bedroom so you can lie down," Piter said. "It's best to continue with the treatment."

Aura walked ahead of him, his hand on her shoulder. She dragged her feet; her confident step was gone.

"Lie on your side. Curl your knees to your chest." Piter spoke in a calm voice. He opened his medical bag and prepared the medicine. "Take a deep breath. Relax." He injected medicine into her spine. "The stem cells are working right now, as we speak. They are retraining your damaged motor neurons to do what they are supposed to do. A few more days and you will see a difference."

"Really? Are you telling me the truth?"

"Yes, Aura. I've seen it work. Let me show you a series of videos I took of one of my test subjects named Imas. Here's the first." He took out his cell phone and held it so Aura could see.

Nurses lifted Imas out of bed and placed him in a wheelchair. Unable to sit up on his own, they placed a strap across his chest.

"Will that happen to me?" Aura started to cry again.

"Wait, this is a week later." Imas leaned on a walker and walked across the room. In the next video, Imas was walking unaided, with a slight sway.

Aura wiped her eyes and blew her nose.

Piter skipped to the next video. Imas unable to pick up coins from a table. Finally, he showed her a video of Imas picking up coins with only a little difficulty.

Aura was smiling. "It does work! Piter, you are a genius."

What Piter didn't tell Aura was that he was showing the videos in reverse order, having made sure they showed no time stamp. All he had done today was buy himself a few weeks at most.

§

Today's mission was accomplished. Piter rushed back to the research centre. He made sure his co-workers were not in the lab before setting up his microscope to examine a sample of lung tissue from someone who had died from Solime Flu. He slipped the slide under the lens. The destruction of the lung tissue due to hemorrhage was horrific. *Pim is foolish. The vaccine may work for now, but what about next year?* He had to stop her.

§

Piter approached Cherrin at four in the afternoon as she was getting ready to go home. He said, "Since you found a way into Dr. Marris' refrigerator unit..."

"The vaccine?" Cherrin handed him a paper bag. "It looks like AZEN is preparing for a vast immunization program in this country. I stole fifty doses. They won't notice—not right away, anyway. I've already given myself and some of my friends a shot. Roll up your sleeve." She injected him in the shoulder.

"I'm no angel, but what the president is planning is beyond evil," Piter said.

"What can we do?"

He sat at a computer and typed out everything he knew about AZEN's plans to infect Solime, put the document on a memory card and deleted the file from his computer. He gave the memory card to Cherrin.

She raised her eyebrows. "What—"

"Information about Aura and her germ warfare plans. Give it to them when you get there."

"Getting across the border is dangerous. I know someone who knows which guard to bribe. I'm worried about how to get safely to the border." The fear was evident on her face.

"Tresha Farwell operated a safe house. Maybe she'll know how to go about it. We'll take my limo."

They climbed into the limo and Cherrin tapped the driver on his shoulder. "Hey, Stann."

"Cherrin."

"You two know each other?" Piter asked.

Stann's reflection showed in the rearview mirror. He smiled.

Piter felt foolish for being so oblivious. He felt certain nothing could surprise him anymore. "Good. I'll need your help later."

"I'm happy you're on our side now, Dr. Dram." Stann said. He drove the limo to Re-Ed, parking outside the front gate.

"Wait here," Piter told Stann. He and Cherrin walked through the dismal hallways to Cell Block D. He handed Cherrin a surgical mask and gloves. "Put these on."

The guard unlocked the cell. Tresha was asleep on her bed. Piter woke her. "I brought someone with me today. This is Cherrin."

Tresha struggled to sit up and immediately had a coughing fit and lay back down.

He bent over and lifted Tresha in his arms. "This is serious. Let's go." They stepped into the hall. "Emergency!" he shouted. "Get a gurney!

This woman must get to the hospital. Solime Flu. Very contagious. Call an ambulance!"

A guard ran ahead to unlock the doors. She covered her face with her hands as Tresha was carried past.

Piter laid Tresha on the gurney and wheeled her out the door. She opened her eyes, looked up and gasped. "The sky, so beautiful, so warm. Oh, look, a bird." A smile spread across her face.

Piter held his fingers to Tresha's wrist.

Minutes later, Piter hopped into the back of the ambulance with Tresha while Cherrin got back into the limo.

He took the stethoscope from the paramedic. "Elevated heart rate." He heard wheezing, crackling sounds in the chest. "Get her temp and BP."

Tresha was not a loyal citizen, but since she was now Piter's patient they allowed her into the hospital. "No doctor is to attend to her except me," he told the staff. "Test for Solime Flu. She needs fluids, Amoxicillin, 500mg., Acetaminophen 500mg. I want a CBC and chest X-ray. And get her something to eat. She's starving."

A nurse ran to fill Dr. Dram's orders.

His cell phone rang. He read the call display: *Aura.*

Her voice was hostile. "I hear you took Tresha to the hospital."

He stepped into the hallway so as not to be overheard. "Another day in that cold cell and she'd have died. She was starving and might have Solime Flu."

"Damn. I forgot I gave the order of no food." Aura laughed. "It's not Solime Flu. I would never have allowed it. I'll assign a guard at her door."

"Then it's probably pneumonia."

"Keep me updated."

"I will, Aura."

"When will you visit me?"

"Five more days. There's so much more I must do. I miss you so much, Aura."

"Me, too." She hung up.

Piter returned to the room. He and Cherrin stood on either side of Tresha's hospital bed.

Piter bent over and whispered, "Cherrin needs to get into Solime. I gave her a memory card. Information I collected about Aura and her plans to spread a deadly flu."

Tresha said, "I prayed you would come around, Piter. I also collected information when I was a reporter, which I sent with one of my guests. Don't know if it ever got there. Aura has the other copy. I still have all the information up here, though." She pointed to her head. "Cherrin, when you get to Solime, will you find my son, Jakon, and make sure he's okay?"

"I'll try."

"Jakon is in Solime?" Piter asked.

She nodded. "As far as I know. We want to be with him, Fillip and I." Her eyes had a far-away look.

Cherrin turned to Piter. "You should help Tresha and Fillip to escape."

"Impossible. She's sick. He's going to labour camp."

Cherrin looked him in the eye and spoke in a steady voice. "You should go to Solime."

"There's nothing there for me," he said.

"Hadar is there. I helped him escape," Tresha said. "You can be with your brother again."

Piter made up his mind.

Cherrin pulled out the map Imas had drawn and showed it to Tresha. "Is this accurate?"

"It is, but I don't know who to bribe to get you past the wall," Tresha said.

"Stann knows," Cherrin said. "He's going to give me instructions later."

"Contrary to what you might think, travel during the day is safer." Tresha pointed with her pen. "That's about where my cabin was. Here's the spot where I guided people through, but don't go that way. It will be well guarded. There's another route, near where the Merd River flows into Solime."

"Sounds dangerous," Piter said.

"More dangerous than staying here?" Tresha asked.

"You sure you want to do this, Cherrin?" Piter asked.

"I'm sure."

"You have what you need?"

Cherrin lifted a backpack. "Vaccine is in here."

"And the memory card?"

"Sewn into my bra."

Piter opened his wallet and gave Cherrin a roll of bills. "We'll say you're going on vacation. Go home. Pack your bags…"

"I got this." Cherrin took the money. She looked at him with hard eyes. "Maybe you're not as evil as I thought you were."

"You thought I was evil?"

"I hated you. I hated myself for what I did." Cherrin stuffed the money in her pocket. "Maybe I'll see you on the other side." She left the room.

Piter said, "Tresha, I'll come back for you. I have some things to do."

§

Three days later, Tresha was showing steady improvement. On the third day, she had colour in her cheeks and was sitting up in bed slurping a bowl of soup.

Piter listened to Tresha's chest and read her chart. "You're showing great improvement."

"Any word on Fillip?" Tresha asked.

Piter said, "He'll be moved to labour camp in the morning."

"Oh, dear." Tresha's face fell. "My poor husband."

"Let me see what I can do."

It was past six in the evening when Piter returned to his lab. He prepared his medical bag and phoned Aura, saying he was on his way. In the crack of the sidewalk a wild flower grew. It was Yun's birthday. He plucked the flower and put it in his pocket.

CHAPTER FORTY-SEVEN
Quietus Comes

Piter met Aura in her office, took her hand and kissed it. He held his medicine bag in the other hand. "How are you, my queen?"

"I'm feeling better than before. More energetic because of your treatments."

"We should go to your bed."

"Oh, I like it when you're horny."

"I've come to give you another dose—"

"You know what I want a dose of. Come on, Piter. I've been so tense lately. I could use a little fun." They stood by her bed. She put her hand inside his shirt and started nibbling on his ear. "I can't wait until I'm recovered. We'll screw all the time. Tell me I'm beautiful."

"You are beautiful, Aura. But before we have fun, I need to give you your second dose."

"I thought it was supposed to be every seven days."

"I believe every six days would be better in your case." He pulled her hand out from under his shirt and reached for his medical bag.

"Oh, all right." She smiled brightly at him. "I have exciting news. Dr. Marris has finally developed a vaccine for the Solime Flu. We'll start a nationwide program to protect all our citizens. I told her to make an announcement tomorrow."

He tried to remain calm. "That is exciting. Then you plan to infect Solime?"

Aura pulled her shirt off over her head. Her head was shaking slightly. "You're far too clever for your own good." She wagged her finger at him. "I'm going to get out my riding crop and teach you a lesson."

"You're the clever one, my queen."

"You don't know the half of it." She thrust her chin forward. "Solime will be brought to its knees by the Solime Flu. A delightful name, right? Seeing as how it will be the thing that destroys them. They'll have to come to me for the vaccine. I will give it to them for a price. I'll demand to become their president. Kiss me." Her hands skimmed his chest. "Then we'll take Sura and Dule and every other country who has ever opposed me."

"Hundreds of thousands, maybe millions could die." He reached down and clutched her bum.

"I know." She tried to unbuckle his belt, but her hands wouldn't cooperate. "Take off your shirt."

Piter obeyed.

"I've told General Bont to prepare for war within the year. They're awaiting my orders. We'll sneak some of our infected citizens across the border. Stupid Solimese always flaunt it in my face when someone escapes from Covona. Soon, they'll be faced with this virus. They'll have no idea what to do." She laughed. "Now, let's get busy." She pulled him by the hand to the bed, then pushed on his shoulders to make him lie down and flung herself beside him. "It's great to be elite, isn't it?"

He struggled to control his anger. "You're right. It was bad when I was dispossessed. My wife died after a botched C-section."

She leaned back. "You're still upset about that? Get over it."

"She died needlessly. My baby died also."

She yelled, "Stop talking about yourself all the time. Do you want a new baby? I'll arrange it."

"No. It's just—"

Aura pulled away from him and sat up on the bed. "Seriously, what is the matter with you?"

"I'm so sorry. I'm just tired, been working so hard, day and night, on the cure for ALS." He brushed a sprig of hair from her face. "Let me prepare your medicine. I need to give you your shot before we make love. Time is of the essence." He got up and placed his medical bag on the bed.

"My plan is brilliant isn't it, Piter?"

"Oh, yes."

"Anyone who crosses me pays the ultimate price."

He fell to his knees in front of her and put his arms around her calves, his head on her lap. "You are my queen. I will worship you forever."

She ran her fingers through his spiky hair. "That's what I like."

He stood up, slowly, as if approaching a dangerous animal. "Lie down, please." He pushed her gently on her shoulder.

Aura refused to lie down. She held up her hand. "Wait. Did Dr. Marris tell you what she was working on?"

"No, but—"

"I better make sure she hasn't spoken to anybody. I'm going to call her." She made a move to get off the bed. "I can't let anything get in the way of my plan."

"Certainly. Let me just give you your shot first." He looked at his watch. "It must be given soon, for maximum effectiveness."

"Fine. Hand me my phone when you're done." Aura lay on her side and curled into a fetal position.

Piter nodded, found a spot in her spine and injected a strong dose of muscle relaxant. Aura's eyes popped open. She opened her mouth, but the muscle relaxant made it impossible for her to speak. She took short, wheezing gasps. He rolled her on her back. Her eyes moved back and forth, wide with fear. He pulled a stethoscope from his pocket and held it to her chest and listened. *Full cardiac arrest.*

"Quietus comes, my queen."

CHAPTER FORTY-EIGHT

Reunion

Aura's wheezing stopped.

Piter put his stethoscope to her chest again. *No heartbeat. Five more minutes to ensure brain death.* He checked his watch. *Six-thirty-five p.m.* He put on his shirt and packed up his equipment. At six-forty he straightened her legs, pulled a blanket over her shoulders, closed her eyelids and smoothed her hair. He closed the bedroom door behind him and entered her office. Piter searched through Aura's desk drawers until he found her official signature stamp. From his medical bag, he removed a form allowing him to take Fillip from Re-Ed, and pressed the stamp to the form.

Piter told the guard who stood outside the office door, "The president is sleeping. She does not want to be disturbed."

"Yes, Dr. Dram."

He walked out of the mansion, trying to appear unhurried. *I have until morning, or several hours at least, before someone has the courage to try to wake Aura.*

He stepped back into the limo. "Take me to the Research Centre."

§

Piter often worked long hours at the QRR Centre. The night cleaning staff showed no surprise seeing him there. He proceeded to the Solime Flu Unit and placed the form on the desk in front the nurse in charge. "Fillip Farwell is to be released to me."

"I'll have to check with Dr. Marris," the nurse said. She picked up the phone.

He tapped the form impatiently. "Are you questioning the president's orders? I want that man handed over immediately!"

The nurse gasped with fear. "No, I would never question... Yes, Dr. Dram." She hung up the phone, ran down the hall and returned minutes later, dragging Fillip by the arm. "Would you like him handcuffed?"

"Not necessary." Piter took Fillip's arm and marched him down the hall and out of the building. They stepped into the sunshine. An hour had passed since Aura's death, but it was not yet dark, due to Covona's long summer days.

Fillip's face was white with fear. "Piter?"

"Silence, prisoner!" Piter opened the door of the limo and they both climbed into the back seat. "To the hospital."

"Why are you—?"

"Just a quick stop. There's a bag of food beside you, if you're hungry."

Fillip snatched the bag, tearing the paper as he thrust in his hand and pulled out a sandwich.

"How've you been, Fillip?" Stann asked.

"Stann?" Fillip looked back and forth between the driver and Piter.

"We're going to escape from the country. We're stopping at the hospital to pick up Tresha," Piter said. He handed Fillip a bag of clothes. "We can't have you trying to escape the country in a prison uniform."

Fillip stopped chewing. His eyes were wide. "I'd almost given up hope."

§

The limo pulled up to the front door of the hospital. "Both of you wait here," Piter said to the driver and Fillip.

Piter took a bag of Yun's clothing he had stored in the car and went into the hospital. He nodded at the guard at the door of Tresha's room and entered. He shook her awake, handed her the bag and turned his back. "Get dressed. Put on the wig. Hurry."

"I'm ready," she said. Tresha had lost so much weight, Yun's clothing fit her, except for the tiny shoes. "I guess I'll have to wear the hospital slippers."

Piter opened the door and called the guard. "I need you in here to restrain this woman." The man entered the room and Piter stepped behind him and plunged a needle in his neck. The guard's eyes rolled back in his head and he flopped to the floor with a clunk. Piter dragged him to the washroom and closed the door.

Piter glanced into the hallway and saw no one. He motioned for Tresha to follow. "Walk slowly. Keep your head down," he said.

"Did you kill that man?" she whispered.

"No, but he'll sleep for hours." He led her outside to the limo. "You will need to restrain yourself."

Stann opened the limo door. Tresha took a deep inhale when she saw Fillip. She rushed into the car and threw her arms around him. She ran her hand down his thin cheek, convincing herself he was beside her.

"Highway Five, west?" Stann asked.

"That's right," Tresha said. "You should come with us."

"I wish I could, but I have a wife and kids."

"Your association with us will put you in danger," Piter said.

"True, but I don't have enough money."

"I'll take care of that," Piter said. He reached into his pocket, pulled out some money and handed it to the driver.

Stann's eyes widened when he saw the amount of money in his hand. "Doctor, that's over a month's wages. I'll collect the wife and kids and we'll make our way out tomorrow."

"I appreciate the risk you're taking. I'd like to take the limo once we reach city limits."

"A limo is not exactly an inconspicuous vehicle."

"I realize that. I have another plan. Just tell us how to get past the wall."

Stann made him memorize a phone number. "Tell them 'Seventy-Two' requires access. They'll give you a place, a day and a time for a drop-off for the cash. They'll tell you which gate will be open and what time. Be prompt. If you don't make it on time, the gate will close."

§

A half hour later they reached city limits. Stann opened the door and walked away. "Maybe we'll see you on the other side. He waved and walked away with a grin on his face.

Piter shuffled over to the driver's side and opened the divider. He smiled when he saw the two of them snuggling in the back seat. "You ready?"

"We're more than ready, Piter," Tresha said. "Thank you."

Piter turned the car in a westerly direction and drove for an hour and a half. "Here's the Highway Five turn off." He drove onto a secondary highway and then into a grove of trees that hid the limo from sight. "Everybody out." He led them to an old car parked at the side of the road and they all got in. "We'll drive as far as Klay and take the train from there."

"You certainly had this well planned out, Piter," Fillip said. He and Tresha made themselves comfortable in the back seat.

Tresha noticed Piter checking the mirrors. "I know you're nervous, Piter, but you need to slow down. We don't need the police pulling us over."

"Right. It will be a while before they figure out what happened to Aura Zarling," Piter said.

"What happened to her?" Tresha asked.

He didn't answer.

She leaned forward and put her hand on the seat near Piter's head. "What did you do?"

He looked in the rearview mirror and gave them a small smile. "Your high school friend is no more."

It took Tresha a moment to understand what he meant. "Did you—really? I don't know whether to feel relieved or horrified."

"Piter? Did you really kill the president?" Fillip asked.

Piter said, "It's a six-hour drive to Klay. We'll arrive around two in the morning. I doubt the trains run all night, though. We can sleep in the car before continuing in the morning. You two sure you want to do this? It'll be dangerous."

"I was imprisoned, shackled, beaten, and had electric shock to my scrotum. I battled a deadly flu. I have no love for this country," Fillip said.

"Oh, my darling." Tresha rested her head on his shoulder. "We both endured so much in the past year." She couldn't stop staring at Fillip's face. "I never thought I would see you again. You're so thin."

His eyes had a haunted look. "I missed you. Once we find Jakon, we'll be a family again. Try to get some rest," Fillip said. He kissed her cheek.

She stretched out on the back seat. Her head rested on Fillip's bony legs. "Fillip, what happened to my dad?"

"The day you and Jakon left for the school gym, they took both of us away. I never saw him again."

Tresha closed her eyes and imagined her father's gentle face.

§

Tresha awoke to the sound of the radio: "Attention citizens of Covona. This is General Bont. Be on the lookout for President Zarling's personal physician Dr. Piter Dram. He is believed to be in the company of Dr. Fillip Farwell and Mrs. Tresha Farwell, a pair of dangerous subversives. A large reward is being offered for any information on their whereabouts."

"Damn," Piter said.

Tresha sat up. She read a road sign out loud. "City of Klay, next right. Don't drive into the city. Let's get rid of this car. Leave it by the lake. We'll walk to the train station from there."

Minutes later, Piter pulled off the main road and onto a side road. They rolled the car into the ditch and proceeded on foot, about two kilometres to the Klay train station. Walking in the gutter beside the highway, one behind the other, they crouched down whenever headlights approached, stumbling in the dark on uneven ground.

Tresha wheezed and coughed. The more she hurried, the worse it became. Fillip took her arm to support her. "We're a couple of walking skeletons. Ouch! These thin hospital slippers do little to protect my feet."

They arrived at the station just before three in the morning. So far, they had been lucky. There was no indication anyone was following or knew of their whereabouts. As they suspected, the train terminal was closed and wouldn't re-open until six in the morning.

"It's good no one is here, no one to recognize us. Let's see if we can find a railcar to ride in," Fillip said.

They walked the rail line, trying doors on the railcars, but all were locked tight, except one, an empty cattle car.

"Here's one." Fillip laughed at Piter's reaction. "Don't worry. There are no animals in here now, though it will smell like it. They arrive from the countryside full of cattle and go back empty, except for us." Fillip climbed in first. "Hop on." He held his hand out to Tresha.

Piter gave Tresha a boost up and then climbed up after her. The cattle car smelled as bad as Fillip said it would. Tresha soon gave up on trying to find a clean space to sit and just looked for a dry piece of dung. She turned her face to the air vents lining the walls of the cattle car. Piter closed the door and the passengers were left in darkness. Tresha prayed no one would open the door and discover them. Soon after, the train began to move.

Tresha slept uneasily, listening to the rumbling of the steel wheels and the snoring of her two companions. She worried. In her weakened condition, she might slow down Fillip and Piter.

Hours later, train brakes squealed and they came to a stop. Daylight peeked through the slats. Piter opened the door and looked out as the sun was starting to rise. "We're near the town of Cos. Let's go." They climbed down from the cattle car, emerging into an area thick with trees.

"Where to now?" Fillip asked.

"Head west," Tresha said. She looked to see in which part of the sky the sun was rising. "Cos is just south of Lake Allore. It's best we avoid people." They walked along a forest path until they came to a dilapidated house. The grass was waist high in the front yard.

"Anybody live here?" Piter asked. He peeked in a window.

"Doesn't look like it," Fillip said.

Piter tried the door. "It's locked." He kicked the door, breaking the lock, and they stepped inside. Morning light filtered through grimy windows. "Let's rest for a while before we continue." They sat on some wooden chairs and each ate an apple and dried beef jerky.

"Thanks for the food and water, Piter. It's been ages since I've actually felt full," Fillip said. "How much further to the border, Tresha?"

"About twenty kilometres. We'll camp out one night in the forest, go the rest of the way when we wake up. Good thing the weather is warm."

"Right," Piter said. "We need to arrive at the wall by eleven in the morning. That's when the guard will open the gate for us."

Tresha was so tired she could hardly place one bruised foot in front of the other. "I don't know if I can walk that far."

"Piter and I will take turns carrying you," Fillip said. "Wouldn't it be better to try to sneak through the border when it's dark? What if someone sees us?"

"Night-vision cameras are mounted on the wall. They don't work as well during the day," Tresha said. She saw the questioning look on Piter's face. "HRFA operations have never stopped, despite the purge."

CHAPTER FORTY-NINE

The Wall

Piter lay fully clothed on an old mattress, staring at the ceiling of the abandoned house. They had rested only a couple of hours when Piter heard men's voices. He got up and looked out the window. The sun was an orange orb in the western sky.

He shook his companions and whispered, "Get up. Men in uniform outside."

Piter continued to watch out the window as the others gathered their belongings. Policemen banged on the door of the house next door and then pushed their way in.

"Now!" Piter said, and they sneaked out the back door and dashed into the forest.

They ran, one behind the other, on a forest path, stumbling over tree roots and scratching their faces on branches. Piter stopped running when Tresha started to cough. She covered her face with her arm, trying to muffle the noise.

"Sorry. Leave me behind."

"Don't be stupid," Piter said. "Climb on my back."

"I'm too heavy for you," Tresha said.

Piter laughed. "You're as light as a feather."

They continued their hike through the Selp Forest, Tresha on Piter's back.

Fillip said. "I can help carry my wife."

"No," Piter said. "Save your strength."

§

They walked, rested, ate, and walked some more. All the while, Piter was alert, startling at every snapping twig. When complete darkness had descended on the forest and they could no longer see the path, they stopped.

"How close are we to the border?" Fillip asked.

"A couple of hours walk. Let's make camp, sleep if we can," Tresha said. "It would be nice to have a fire, but we better not."

They built a bed of twigs to keep them off the forest floor and cuddled close together for warmth with Tresha in the middle. Piter spooned Tresha, while she hugged Fillip. It felt awkward at first, but they kept each other warm. A single blanket covered their cold, tired bodies. Piter didn't think he'd be able to sleep, though his exhausted body ached. In his mind, he replayed all the difficulties they'd encountered since leaving Ackim. So far, they'd been lucky.

The stars shone brightly here, away from city lights, twinkling above the treetops. Except for the breathing of his companions, it was quiet. Piter closed his eyes.

He walked alone on a straight dirt path through a flat, grey field. Not a tree or a blade of grass in sight. Behind him was the Wall of Aura. A man walked towards him.

"Hadar!" he shouted.

His brother reached out his arms to embrace Piter. A circle of light rose from behind Hadar and climbed into the sky, so bright Piter had to squeeze his eyes shut.

"There's still time, Piter," Hadar said.

"Time for what?"

The faces of people he had sent to Quietus appeared in front of his eyes, one after the other, hundreds of them, filling the landscape.

§

Piter awoke with a start and bolted upright. The rising sun shone in his face.

"You okay?" Tresha asked.

Fillip was still asleep. His arm was draped over her.

Piter wrapped his arms around his knees. "Yeah, weird dream. My brother was in it."

"Want to tell me about it?"

Piter was silent for a while. "I never imagined when I was going through medical school..."—he cleared his throat and ran his hand

[314]

through his hair—"that I would end up… I just wanted to help people. Everything changed when…so much death."

Tresha opened her mouth to speak, but he didn't wait to hear what she had to say. Piter stood up.

"I need to be alone for a while." He walked into the forest.

Leaning his back against a tree, he watched the top branches of the trees sway in the morning breeze. Light clouds drifted across the sky. Piter struggled for control, but the tears came anyway.

§

The sun climbed higher in the sky. The three walked in silence, trudging through the forest, following the edge of the river. They came to the tree line. They crouched, hidden behind foliage. In front of them were about ten metres of short grass and then the Wall of Aura.

The wall loomed, the final barrier to freedom. Piter had never seen it up close and it was larger and more threatening than he could have imagined. It stretched from the north to the south as far as the eyes could see. *Those concrete slabs must be four metres high.*

Fillip pointed to a metal pipe on the top of the wall, stretching the entire length. "That must be to stop people from trying to scale the wall. It would be impossible to get a grip on such a smooth pipe." Above the pipe was barbed wire.

Piter relayed the directions he was given after he paid the bribe money. "Do you see where the Merd River pours through the tunnel in the wall?" He pointed. "Beside the river is a guard tower." Piter checked his watch. It was almost eleven o'clock. "The soldier will come down soon, unlock the gate and walk away. We have ten minutes before he comes back to lock it again."

"Too bad the river flows so fast or we could just swim out of here," Fillip said.

"We'd either drown or die from slamming against those rocks," Piter said. "Did you ever hear from anyone who succeeded in getting to Solime?"

Tresha said, "No, of course not. People have no way of telling us if they arrived safely or not, but our government likes to announce when they capture dissidents. If we don't hear anything, we assume they made it."

"If we're caught, we'll all be sent to labour camp," Fillip said.

"More likely executed," Piter said. The grass between the line of trees and the wall was less than a metre tall. "We'll have to crawl. Even once we get through the gate we're not safe. We still must make it across the disputed zone. This soldier was paid off, but not the others." Piter pointed to other guard towers, each half a kilometre away. "Don't let them see you."

Tresha said, "We could be spotted crawling in the grass, but there, by the river's edge, we can creep through the foliage. It will be slow slogging. We'll have to be careful not to splash."

"What if we're spotted?" Fillip asked.

"Run," Tresha said.

The group waited in the shadows of the trees. The warm morning sun beat down. It promised to be a blistering day.

"I wonder what life will be like in Solime," Fillip said.

"Impossible to know," Piter said. "But at least we'll be free."

"Shh, look," Fillip pointed in the direction of a lone soldier climbing down from his tower. The soldier rested a rifle on his shoulder, ambled towards the gate and then walked away. The soldier stopped at the river, bent and scooped water with one hand and splashed it on the back of his neck. He took a drink from his flask, crossed the stream over the bridge and continued his patrol.

Piter checked his watch. "We have ten minutes."

"First Tresha, then you, Fillip," Piter said. "I'll bring up the rear."

"We'll never make it," Tresha said.

Fillip said, "Go, my darling." He kissed her and nudged her along.

Tresha stepped into the mud at the edge of the river. She stooped so her head was below the reeds and cattails, out of sight.

They gave her two minutes and then Fillip stepped into the water.

[316]

Piter waited two minutes, then looked to the left and right. He stepped into the water. The mud squelched beneath his feet, sucking his shoes off. He left them behind and grabbed handfuls of the long, tough grass growing on the river's edge to pull himself along. Fillip's footprints had already disappeared, filled up with mud. Stooping, he plodded through the muck counting the seconds in his head, *ten, eleven, twelve... Do I hear footsteps?* He ducked and peered through the foliage. *Nothing.* He continued. *Thirteen, fourteen...thirty-nine, forty...* He rounded a bend. The wall loomed in front of him.

The gate was slightly ajar. *Tresha must be through.* Fillip emerged from behind the cattails, flat on his belly, creeping. He entered the disputed zone.

Piter got down on his belly, keeping low to the ground, he slithered towards and through the gate. A wave of relief washed over him. *I made it. I'm out of Covona.* He couldn't celebrate yet, though. He was now in no man's land.

Ahead was a chain-linked fence and guard towers belonging to Solime. He continued to crawl. Piter lifted his head in time to see Tresha walk through the Solime gate.

He heard a gunshot and a puff of dirt exploded near his face. Great dread filled Piter's gut. He stood and ran. Sharp stones stabbed his feet. He pumped his arms, urging his legs to run faster. The gate was in sight. Time seemed to slow, like a bad dream.

Fillip stepped through the gate and turned. Piter saw the look of alarm on his face.

A hot, piercing pain entered Piter's back and he fell forward. The smell of dry earth filled his nose. His lungs strained to draw breath. The pain was intense.

He remembered Abree's words, *"Does it hurt to die?"*

Piter coughed. Blood filled his mouth, coppery, slightly salty. He turned his head to the side and the blood spilled from his mouth onto the grass. *Why haven't I ever noticed how blue the sky is?* He tried to raise himself up but could not. *This is where I'll die.*

A shadow covered his face. In front of his eyes, a pair of black boots. Piter looked up. The soldier pointed a rifle at his head.

Piter waited for the bullet that would end his life. Instead, the soldier got down on one knee and removed some sterile dressing from his side bag.

"Just...kill...me." Piter's words were wet and gravelly. Every breath was like a knife slicing into his lung.

The soldier pressed on Piter's back. In his other hand, he held a phone. "I have Piter Dram... Wounded... Shot in the back... No. He's alone..."

Piter strained to get up, but his legs would not obey. He grasped tufts of grass and grimaced. Breathing was agonizing torment. *Pleuritic pain. I hope I bleed to death before they get me to the hospital.* He struggled to remain conscious.

The soldier held the phone against his chest. He looked down at Piter and smiled. "I won't kill you. There's a big reward for capturing you alive. I'm going to be a rich man."

A gunshot sounded. The soldier's head snapped back and he collapsed to the ground. Blood oozed from the man's forehead. The back of his head was gone. The cell phone lay in his open palm. "Private! Confirm your position! That's an order!"

Piter could not see what was happening but heard a vehicle approaching. He coughed, bringing more blood into his mouth and he moaned with pain.

The sound of a large armoured vehicle rumbled close to where he lay, then came the sound of pounding feet. A man in a Solimese uniform knelt between Piter and the dead Covonan soldier and put his fingers on Piter's neck. "He's alive! Bring a stretcher." The man bent over Piter and spoke close to his face. "Do you speak Solimese?"

"Yes." Piter concentrated on sucking air into his body, but it was like trying to breathe through a wet sponge.

"We're going to take you to the hospital. Don't move."

Piter found himself drifting away.

§

Piter awoke with his body and head strapped to a hard board, making it impossible to move. Intravenous bags hung over his head. Tubes ran from the bags to his arms.

A male voice spoke. "Gunshot wound to the back, suspected spinal injury. Might need a blood transfusion."

Piter tried to turn his head to see who was speaking but couldn't. He realized he was wearing a cervical collar and an oxygen mask.

He wanted to say, *Where am I?* It came out as a moan.

"He's awake."

"You're safe, Dr. Dram. We're on our way to the hospital," the bearded paramedic said. "I'll give you something for the pain." He held a syringe in his hand.

The bags above his head swung back and forth, back and forth. Piter's vision blurred.

Dr. Gorge Bigon stood over him, a needle in his hand, preparing to inject it. "Don't be afraid. This drug will make you sleepy. You won't feel any pain."

§

"No!" Piter said. "I don't want to die!"

"It's okay. We'll take good care of you." Piter opened his eyes to see a woman looking down at him. Other medical personnel surrounded him. "You're in the ER. We're going to insert a chest tube to drain the blood and air from inside your rib cage. It will give you some relief, and then we'll get the bullet out." They placed a mask on his face. "Breathe deeply."

§

"Wake up, Piter. Wake up. You're out of surgery."

He looked up at a middle-aged man. Piter swallowed painfully, as if a piece of glass was lodged in his throat. "Water?"

A nurse placed a straw in his mouth. He sucked.

"Can you feel this, Piter?"

"Feel what?" Piter looked down to see the doctor pinching his toe.

"How about here? Here?"

Piter shook his head. "What's the extent of my injuries?"

"The bullet punctured your left lung and lodged in thoracic T11. There's damage to the spinal column. You may recover some sensation, perhaps some bowel and bladder control—"

"Will I walk again?" Piter knew the answer before he asked the question.

The doctor put his hand on Piter's shoulder and spoke in a sympathetic voice. "It's not likely."

§

The day passed in a haze. At one point, there was a sponge bath, later, a meal. He awoke hearing a familiar voice.

"Piter!" Hadar ran across the room and held Piter in a gentle embrace.

Whether it was because of the pain, or the trauma of what he'd just gone through, or the joy of seeing his brother again, Piter could not control himself and burst into tears. Hadar gently squeezed Piter's face between his hands and smiled with tenderness.

CHAPTER FIFTY

Solime

Weeks passed and because he was left alone most of the time, Piter had nothing to do but contemplate his future and past. Both were bleak. Without work and without the doting presence of the women he had loved, he was lost. He longed for a glass of wine, to feel the familiar, sedating warmth. Without alcohol to dull his conscience, he was exposed to the naked truth of what he had done. The faces of innocent, trusting children and the confused eyes of the elderly, whom he had executed for the crime of being disabled or old, flashed through his mind. Hundreds died from a stab of his needle. Their last words still echoed in his mind.

He awoke mornings drenched in sweat. By day, Piter was faced with the reality that he would live the rest of his life as a paraplegic in a foreign country. His legs, limp and unfeeling, left him helpless and dependent on others.

§

He'd had one visit from Fillip, Tresha and Jakon. They had come to say goodbye, informing him they were moving inland, to Solime's wine country. Fillip had landed a position at a university there. They seemed happy and healthy. Piter was pleased for them. He wondered if they also suffered from post-traumatic stress but didn't ask.

Cherrin had also been to see him once. It was an uneasy visit. They talked briefly, though not about the past. She said it was something she'd rather forget. "I told them all about the QRR Centres."

"I know."

She said she was trying to get on with her life and was working towards a medical degree.

"That's great. You'll be a great doctor."

"Thanks. Listen, I'll come by again sometime to see you."

Piter nodded. He wasn't counting on it.

§

Weeks more passed. He rolled his wheelchair down the hallway to distract himself from the sameness of his room and parked in front of a window to watch people enter and leave the hospital. An ambulance, its siren shrieking, pulled into the parking lot. White-coated hospital staff ran out to meet it. Piter longed to be there with them, to feel once more the rush, the satisfaction of helping to save a life.

On the table beside him lay a newspaper. His Solimese had improved since he came to the hospital. Piter picked it up and gasped when he saw the headline: "Covona's 'Doctor Death' Recovering at Solime Hospital."

> *Piter Dram, the doctor suspected of assassinating the former president of Covona, Aura Zarling, is reported to be in a Solime hospital recovering from a gunshot wound.*
>
> *Some residents of Solime are campaigning to send Dr. Piter Dram back to Covona. "He's an evil man and must be deported," says Councilwoman Daeron. "At the very least, he should be jailed for crimes against humanity for his involvement in human experimentation."*
>
> *Other Solimese see Dr. Dram as a hero for disposing of the tyrant and helping to smuggle a life-saving vaccine to Solime. They want him freed unconditionally. The authorities are debating the issue.*
>
> *Dr. Fillip and Tresha Farwell, who escaped Covona with Dr. Dram, say he disposed of the dictator and conceivably saved many lives. Covona's human rights abuses under Aura Zarling are shocking to most Solimese. Also, per Ms. Cherrin Sayden, he and others held people against their will and conducted cruel experiments in centres of death...*

Hadar tapped him on the shoulder. "Glad to see you out of your room, getting around on your own."

"Oh! I didn't hear you coming."

Hadar pulled up a chair and sat. "Reading something interesting?"

Piter was afraid his facial expression would betray his emotions. He forced himself to smile. The highlight of his days were Hadar's visits. Piter felt calm in his presence. He still hadn't told Hadar the whole truth, but couldn't bear to have the last person on earth who cared about him turn his back. Piter set the newspaper on his lap. "I'm feeling stronger. They say they'll take the catheter out today and see how I do."

"So, they're sure you'll never walk? Any hope—"

"My spinal column was severed by the bullet." Piter paused, rubbing his hand over his chin. "It's strange to think...I guess reality hasn't sunk in." He pushed on the arms of his chair. "I'm as helpless as a kitten."

"You have a tough road ahead of you." Hadar stared into space for a moment. "Now that you're somewhat recovered, there's something I must talk to you about." His lips trembled.

"What is it?" Piter waited while Hadar found the words. He could guess what his brother was going to say.

"You had our parents killed." Hadar's eyes were like stone.

"It wasn't like that."

Hadar stood up and paced the floor. His hands were curled into fists. "What was it like? Hm? Did you have a joyful Quietus celebration? Did you enjoy a glass of wine while our parents were murdered?" His voice was bitter.

Piter remembered the day, the spell he was under. How he, how the whole country was deceived into thinking eliminating the elderly was right and proper. "It was the law, Hadar. You know that. It was hard for me. I wept—"

"Oh, you cried? I guess that's saying a lot for a cold, unfeeling robot."

"There's no need to be sarcastic. I won't try to justify it. I am sorry. I became a monster."

Hadar stood looking out the window, his back to Piter. "You and so many others. I can't forgive you. Not yet."

"I understand."

"I asked if you could be released into my care, but they say you're not ready."

"I'll probably be in here for a couple more months. Afterwards, who knows? They don't know what to do with me." He sat quietly for a moment and then thought he might as well get it over with. Hadar couldn't hate him any more than he did at this moment. "I haven't been truthful to you about all my work back home. Here, read it for yourself." He handed Hadar the newspaper. "Am I a criminal or a hero?"

Minutes passed as Hadar read the articles. Colour drained from his face. He sat on the bed as if his legs weren't strong enough to hold him up. "Is it true?"

Piter nodded. "I did what I was ordered to do." Hadar opened his mouth to speak. Piter interjected, "You're going to say that doesn't excuse my actions. I agree."

"How many?"

Piter looked at Hadar and with a straight face, answered, "I administered lethal injections to around nine hundred people."

Hadar made the sign of the cross and bowed his head. He rose from the bed and crossed the room to look out the window again and was quiet for a long time. When he spoke, his voice was deep and gravely. "And the experiments? You took people from their homes, held them in cages and injected them with drugs?"

"All true."

Hadar turned to face him, his face red and his mouth tight. "How could you?"

Piter felt an ache in his heart. "Zarling created an evil system. I got caught up. What could I do? I was trying to survive. I guess I'm not as holy as you, to be able to resist. You were always the good son—"

Hadar shouted, "Take responsibility for your own actions, Piter! Do you regret what you did?" He squeezed his eyes shut.

"It was another life."

Hadar took a deep breath and slammed his hand on the wall. He pressed his lips together and rubbed his fingers across his forehead. "Piter, are you sorry?"

"Yes, I'm sorry, dammit! I was miserable. I'm so tired of death. My past will haunt me forever. I can't undo what I did." They were silent for a while. Piter blinked away his tears. "Hadar, do you hate me?"

"You're my brother. It will take time to process all this." He left the room.

§

Piter sighed when he read the newspaper the next morning. The Solime Supreme Court was going to debate the law forbidding euthanasia. He remembered when Covona debated the same issue. It seemed so long ago. He skipped the article and read the headline of an editorial: "Covona's Future Uncertain Under General Bont."

> *Sections of the wall between our countries have been torn down. The once secretive Covona is coming under intense scrutiny by the international community. The question many are asking is: Since the death of Aura Zarling, will Covona remain a dictatorship under General Bont or return to democracy?*
>
> *Many wonder how a once democratic country came under totalitarian rule in such a short amount of time. When too much power is placed in the hands of a few corrupt individuals...*

Piter finished the article, flipped the page and read: "Solime Investigating Treaty Violations."

> *Solime officials are in discussions with General Bont, the new president of Covona, and members of AZEN.*
>
> *Prime Minister Veuil stated: "Covona's attempt to conduct germ warfare on our country constitutes international treaty violations. While no one wants another war..."*

Hadar entered Piter's room for his daily visit, holding a newspaper in his hand. "Have you seen this article about euthanasia?" He tapped his copy.

"Maybe they won't make the same mistakes Covona did," Piter said.

Hadar shook his head. "When people lose their moral compass, when others are considered burdens, well, you know what happened back home. Maybe I should start a chapter of Human Rights for All, here in Solime."

Piter felt his hopes rise as he heard the words. "Yun would have liked that."

They were interrupted by a man and a woman who entered the room without knocking and introduced themselves. She was a lawyer, squat and round, and dressed in a blue pants suit. He was a minister of government in charge of Health and Welfare. He wore an expensive three-piece suit and shiny shoes.

"Excuse us, Father, we'd like to speak to Dr. Dram alone," said the man.

"He's my brother. He can stay," Piter said.

The lawyer spoke first. "I'll get right to the point. Many in this country don't want you here, Dr. Dram. You conducted human experimentation and euthanized children and others against their will. You could face jail time here in Solime." Her upper lip barely moved as she spoke.

"It was legal in Covona," Piter said.

"That's irrelevant," the lawyer said. "You're in Solime now."

The minister held up his hands. "Now, don't panic. We have a proposal for you." He sat on the bed so he was eye level with Piter. "We could use a man like you on our ethics committee."

"Excuse me?"

"We're assembling a group of experts in social biology. Our goal is to improve the population of Solime. We want you to be part of the research team."

"Are you talking about eugenics?"

He waved his hand. "No, no, nothing as bold as that."

"What will this group of experts do?"

"First, we will attend to the social implications. We strive to develop a social consciousness regarding the production of children. The problem is how to get people to accept the ideas. Your experience in this area would benefit us."

"I don't have experience in that. Much of my research is in ALS and comes from forced human experimentation. I thought you people had a problem with that."

The lawyer said, "We're willing to overlook that if you will assist us."

The minister said, "You see, we have need to replace superstitious beliefs towards sex and reproduction with a scientific and socially responsible attitude. There are truths regarding environment and heredity. Wouldn't you agree?"

"Of course."

"Both factors ought to come under the control of the State, for the good of everyone, for the future of this country."

"What exactly do you want me to do?"

"Do I have to spell it out for you? We're talking manipulation of genes to develop the best characteristics and controlling the birthrate of the underprivileged."

Piter cleared his throat, uncertain of what to say.

Hadar said, "What you are suggesting is beyond repugnant."

The lawyer said, "With all due respect, Father, you are a priest with strong opinions of your own. You can't possibly offer anything meaningful to this conversation." A drop of saliva formed in the corner of her mouth. She looked at Hadar with narrowed eyes.

Piter raised his voice. "My brother's opinion is as important as any other. You can respect us or leave my room."

The lawyer said, "Let's not forget, you're both refugees in this country, supported by the taxes of our people." Her tight jaw and the ugly twist to her mouth showed her displeasure. She wagged her finger at Piter. "Why do you think our sniper took out the man who shot you? Why do you think we risked our soldiers' lives by sending them into the disputed zone? We wanted you alive."

"Don't forget, my friends and I prevented a potential epidemic in this country," Piter said. "Thousands, maybe millions could have died. I saw the effects of the devastating virus. Do you even realize the risks we took to bring you the vaccine? I could be living in luxury right now, and not here, as a damn paraplegic—"

The minister interrupted. He put his hands together in prayer position and pointed his fingers at Piter. "And because of your efforts, this country would like to reward you."

"But not without a few strings," Piter said. His was voice deep and tinged with bitterness.

"Call it a compromise. No jail time in exchange for coming to work for us."

"Piter! This is atrocious. Don't listen to them. Out of deference for the people who suffered…" Hadar's hand trembled as he ran it through his hair.

Piter looked down at his own hands, which were folded over the newspapers on his lap.

The minister grinned, showing a mouthful of white teeth. "Now, now, no one is going to suffer. We care about the people of Solime."

Piter's voice became deep. "This country is no different from Covona."

The lawyer said, "What happened in your country was tragic, but it can't happen here. We have a democracy and laws to prevent abuse."

"As we did," Hadar said.

The lawyer's face turned red. "If you don't cooperate, you could go to jail."

"Now, now, let's keep this on friendly terms." The minister spoke softly, "While your brother is entitled to his opinion, remember this is not a dictatorship like Covona. Here, we have air-tight guidelines to protect the vulnerable. The people of Solime have no reason to be afraid. In exchange for your knowledge and expertise you will be given freedom and a good job. What do you say, Dr. Dram?"

The thought of being sent to jail made Piter shiver. He scanned the faces of the people in the room. To his left, the emotionless lawyer stood with hands clasped in front of her body, tapping her thumbs

[328]

together. To his right, the smiling government man was offering him a way out. Piter could get back into research, a field he loved. He could again experience the beauty of new discovery. Hadar stood in front of him. His eyes pleaded.

Piter pushed on the arms of his chair to straighten his back and then lowered his gaze to his lap. He placed his hands on his legs, those heavy, useless appendages which would forever be his burden. "I thought this was a free country, but you're not offering me a real choice."

The smile faded from the minister's face. "Dr. Dram, we need an answer."

Piter looked the minister and lawyer in the eyes. "Day after day, people arrived at the Quietus Recycling and Research Centre. They left in pieces, their useful parts extracted and the leftovers discarded as refuse, the dignity of the person destroyed. I will no longer be the cause of others' suffering or death. I won't become that man again. Please leave."

Their faces fell and they left his room without speaking; first the lawyer, then the minister.

Hadar smiled and opened his mouth to speak.

Piter raised his hand. "Save your words."

Hadar nodded and left the room, closing the door behind him.

Piter took a deep breath and let it out through pursed lips. He smiled and spun his chair in circles. He was free. Quietus would never again be committed by Piter Dram.

ACKNOWLEDGEMENTS

I'd like to thank the many people who helped me on the difficult, exciting and sometimes distressing journey of writing Quietus:

My editor, Taija Morgan, for her keen insights and expertise.

My writing partners, Sherry Wong, Dusan Milutinovic and Rick Borger for their sharp eyes and thoughtful suggestions that helped me form my vision of Quietus.

Dr. Howie Bright, for sharing his medical expertise, and Joanne Bright, the first to read an entire early version of Quietus, for her intuition and attention to detail.

My friends in Calgary's writing community for their enormous help in reading portions of my early work.

Finally, my husband, James, and my children Karen, Michael, Emily and Thomas, who listened to my rantings and helped me clarify my thoughts as I created the world of Covona and all the troubled individuals who dwell there.